The Key Quest
A Kingdom of Lorr Novel

I0693044

M.J. Stewart

Other works by M.J. Stewart

Kingdom of Lorr series (Epic Fantasy)

WorldGate Crossing

The Return

Demon of Lorr

Key Quest

Displacement

Displacement: The Long Sleep

Heralds of the Culling series (Vampire action/horror)

Heir of Darkness

Blood of the Third

Previews and purchasing information at

https://majorstewart.com/

Copyright © 2014 by M.J. Stewart

ISBN: Paperback   978-0-9889158-4-8

Ebook   978-0-9889158-5-5

PROLOGUE

Middle East, Gulf of Oman – several days ago

Captain Saint-Germaine grew more worried with the passing of every nautical mile. His crew did not share his concern, but then again, his crew was not privy to the knowledge weighing on him and his first mate like one of the forty-foot containers of crude oil they ferried across the gulf.

The demeanor of the two other men on the bridge, the first mate and the radio operator, were a study in opposites. The first mate was as anxious as the captain, and the younger man did not do nearly as good a job of hiding it. The radio operator, on the other hand, was almost giddy. He went about his normally tedious job with enthusiasm because he knew, as did the rest of the thirteen-man crew, that this was the most lucrative contract they had ever been assigned. That was all they needed to know.

The captain and the first mate, which was also the captain's son, Jonas, knew their client had not hired them through normal channels. The logistics company that usually contracted them had been bypassed. P.T.&A. Logistics did not have an exclusive arrangement with the *Königin Saint-Germaine* inland oil tanker, but as a matter of courtesy the captain coordinated his schedule with them on the few outside contracts he accepted.

This time was different. The time between their client's offer and the date to set sail was so short that Saint-Germaine did not get a chance to contact P.T.&A. He barely had enough time to get his crew together and ready the *Königin Saint-Germaine*. The incredibly short time frame gave the captain pause.

In most cases, such short notice would have made him refuse the contract. But when the client offered them almost three times the normal price for a job like this and then wired two-thirds of the commission up front, how could the captain refuse? Yet he nearly refused anyway. Suspicion tempted him to return the money, so certain was he that this was too good to be true.

For the sake of prudence he decided to find out as much as he could about this mysterious client. After demanding full disclosure from his would-be benefactor and doing his own diligent research, he found out that the client, who was posing as a billionaire oil baron from the Middle East, was actually a front for the United States branch of an international clandestine intelligence organization.

That certainly explained the exorbitant price they were willing to pay. He was well aware of how wasteful the American government could be with its money. They also guaranteed the security of the small inland oil tanker as it hauled a full load of crude oil across the Gulf of Oman from Gwadar to Muscat. They would not tell him why the oil was being moved, of course, but the captain was smart enough to know that it had to be some kind of secret payoff for some kind of secret deal struck between the three countries.

The Americans were true to their word. The *Königin Saint-Germaine* was provided with an armed submarine escort for the first half of the journey and an armed helicopter escort for this second half.

With the exception of the ever-present beeping of various instruments and intermittent buzzing of the communication systems, which had long since faded into background noise to the veteran seafarer's ears, all was quiet. The waters were calm. On a winter night like this, this close to the equator, the weather was temperate and pleasant. From inside the bridge the captain marveled at the light of the half moon and countless stars bathing the night sky. Silvery light shimmered softly off the glassy surface of the gulf waters. Saint Germaine never grew tired of the sea's beauty.

All of this should have been more than enough to ease the hard-to-define unease of the captain and his son. The captain taught his son many of the things he had learned from his own father. One of the most important and useful lessons was that when something seemed too good to be true, it was usually because it was.

Both men were on edge, and they would be until they completed this voyage and collected the remainder of their generous commission.

The intercom buzzed. The radio operator answered, frowned and then placed the communication on the speaker.

"Captain Saint-Germaine," a panicked sailor began. "The escort helicopter has abandoned us and we have found timed charges hidden in several places around the hull!"

The captain's eyes went wide. "Timed charges, you say? *Explosive* charges?"

"Yes," the sailor confirmed. "No one here knows how to disarm them. We don't know how many there are. We've found two but there may be more!"

A dozen worried thoughts stormed through Saint-Germaine's mind. A thorough inspection was made before they set sail and nothing was found. This sabotage had been perpetrate by a member of the crew. Who would have done this? Was one of his men a terrorist? Had the Americans made them unwitting pawns in some secret war?

"First mate," the captain beckoned to his son. "Take the bridge. Ready the life rafts. I'm going to have a look."

The first mate took the controls as Captain Saint-Germaine rushed to the door of the bridge. The door handle would not turn and the door would not open. The captain tried again more forcefully but the door would not budge.

"Sir?" asked the first mate from the opposite side of the bridge. "Is something wrong?"

"Very," the captain answered. "This door seems to be locked. But it locks from the inside and swings inward."

Before his son could reply, both men were struck dumb by another strange occurrence. The ambient silver glow shining through the fore bridge windows from the full moon and stars blinked out as if a light switch had been flicked to the "off" position. They looked through the front of the vessel and gasped in unison at the phenomenon before them.

A massive disk of blackness emerged from the depths of the gulf less than a quarter of the ship's length ahead of them. It was half again as wide and tall as the inland tanker.

The bottom third of it was submerged beneath the calm waves. It greedily swallowed the water and even the glow of the night sky and the light reflecting off of the water's surface. The men could literally *see* the light being sucked into the two-dimensional vacuum.

Any order the captain wanted to yell was choked off by fear and awe. In any event, there was nothing he could do and no order he could give that would stop the vessel's momentum from carrying it into what he could only describe as a hole in the very fabric of existence. He was about to command a full stop and drop anchor anyway…

But then the screaming started.

Saint-Germaine had been involved in more than one battle and more than one accident on the high seas during his time in the German navy. He had heard men scream before. Screams of anger, pain and fear, the screams of the dying, none of these things were new to him. But the hellish sounds of terror that echoed from the deck and from the rear compartments of the *Königin Saint-Germaine* that night were like nothing he had ever heard.

What made the sounds even worse were the inhuman roars that accompanied the screams. It took only a few seconds for the captain to realize that the monstrous sounds were more than just roars. They were sounds of laughter; perverse, taunting, malevolent guffaws that erupted as the human screams were cut short one by one.

"Weapons!" The captain shouted.

It was too late to stop the ship from going into the void, but he would be damned if he would go down without a fight against whatever was attacking his crew.

The radio operator ran to a tall lockbox in the corner of the bridge and in short order retrieved a Heckler & Koch G.36 automatic rifle and clip, which he tossed to the captain. By the time Saint-Germaine slapped in the thirty-round magazine and looked up, his son and the radio operator were loading magazines into identical weapons.

"We'll not be sitting ducks in this bridge," Captain Saint-Germaine vowed.

He pointed the nose of his rifle at the door latch. Just as he was about to pull the trigger, the tanker floated into void.

The ship lurched violently, throwing all three men to the floor. Blessedly, none of the guns went off. Unfortunately the lights did go off, along with the radio and the LED illumination from all of the various communication and navigational equipment. The bridge was summarily plunged into total and complete silence and darkness.

Even if he had the chance, the captain would never have been able to accurately explain what he experienced next. There were vague comparisons he could make, but nothing he could say would truly capture the agony and dread. As a man who had lived half his life on the high seas, the captain was accustomed to physically tumultuous experiences, but he had ridden through tropical storms on the Atlantic and Pacific Oceans with far less turmoil than he felt in that fathomless blackness.

Once, he had been foolish enough to voluntarily take a turn, literally take a *turn*, in one of those giant centrifuge devices used in the training of astronauts. The operator was ridiculously overzealous in his control of the machine. As a result, the ride left the captain with a headache, sick to his stomach and disoriented for an hour after the ride ended.

What he felt in the void was exponentially worse.

The ship vanished. There was no deck under the captain's feet, no bulkheads, no other people around him. There was only the void. He tumbled and twirled through infinite space and time with such speed that the friction threatened to burn his flesh from his bones. His stomach felt as if it had turned inside out. He thought his brain would explode from the colossal pressures being placed upon it.

And then it was over.

The captain was back on the bridge, lying facedown on the cold floor and bleeding from his eyes, ears, nose, and mouth. Moonlight shone through the portals again. After a few moments of spitting and coughing he slowly pushed himself to his hands and knees, took a deep breath, and gave his arm a hard pinch to make sure he was alive and awake.

The next thing he did was struggle to his feet to search for his son. Upon standing, he saw the radio operator sprawled on his back at the foot of his bolted-down chair in a spreading pool of blood.

The radio operator's eyes bulged open in a terrified sightless stare and his mouth stretched agape in a silent scream. His torso was torn open from the top of his chest to his navel. The captain quickly looked away, not wanting to see any more details of the horrid butchery.

"*Ach mein Gott!*" he swore.

Filled with dread for the fate of his son and determination to find him, the captain quickly found the automatic rifle he dropped when the tanker was swallowed by the void. He looked frantically around the cabin in the starlight and moonlight. The navigation and communication LED's had become functional again and contributed their illumination.

The screaming had stopped. There was no wind whistling along the deck. The beeping and buzzing that had once been only background noise was now nearly deafening in the otherwise eerie silence.

His son was no longer on the bridge and the door was open. With his automatic rifle loaded and ready, the captain crept out onto the deck. He looked left and right and down to the main deck from his elevated position. Jonas was nowhere to be found.

The captain noticed that the night seemed brighter than it had before, which caused him to look up at the sky. The instant he did he was shaken to his core.

The constellations were completely different. Captain Saint-Germaine had seen the stars from the oceans and seas from both sides of the equator yet had never seen an alignment of stars anything like what he saw that night. His gaze followed the pale moonlight spilling out from where the moon was hidden behind the high peaks of mountains that were not there before the sudden appearance of the void.

The captain stood transfixed and wondered where on earth he was and how on earth he got there. The drifting tanker eventually carried him to a break in the towering peaks of the unfamiliar mountains, to a point where he could see the source of the unusually bright moonlight. The sight Saint-Germaine saw shocked him so severely that he swooned. He had to catch himself on the rail to keep from falling over to the lower deck.

Saint-Germaine did not see the half-moon he expected to see. Instead, he saw *three moons*.

Two of them were so close they overlapped a bit. The one in the rear was larger and higher than the one in front. The third moon was about half the largest moon's span and hung to the right. It was roughly the same size and floated at the same level as the smaller of the overlapping moons.

"*Mein Gott!*" he swore again. "Where *am* I?"

"Why do you all cry for God when He is surely nowhere to be found?" asked a mocking but familiar voice from somewhere behind the captain.

Saint-Germaine turned, leveling his rifle, but stopped short when he saw his son standing before him.

"Jonas!" He cried, lowering his weapon. Relief flooded through him so thoroughly that he did not immediately wonder at the strange words Jonas had just spoken or the alien timbre easily discernable in his son's voice. "Jonas, you're alive!"

The first mate chuckled darkly. "In a matter of speaking, I suppose I am. Tell, me *father,* do you really want to know where we are?"

The captain's smile faltered, his relief finally giving way to worried confusion. "Of course I do. But why are you speaking this way?"

"We sail south along the Straits of Issill," Jonas said, pointedly ignoring the captain's question. He continued to explain with condescending patience. "The Earth's Blood Ocean is behind us. The Ascendant's Heart Sea lies ahead.

"Those mountains you see to the west line the coast of the Kingdom of Issillorah. And though you cannot see it because of the darkness and the distance, the Kingdom of Hendragorn lies to the east.

"The *Königin Saint-Germaine* will enter the Ascendant's Heart, where it will sail south by southeast until it reaches the mouth of the Tyne River West in the Kingdom of Lorr. And then this vessel will sail east along the river to the Great Lake Onyx, where my servants wait to receive it."

Captain Saint-Germaine's perplexed frown grew deeper with every strange word the other uttered. There was one thing, however, about which he was no longer confused. He raised his automatic rifle and put his finger on the trigger.

"What have you done with my Jonas?"

The stranger with the familiar face rubbed his bloated stomach mockingly.

"The same thing I am about to do with you, decrepit little human."

The three moons swept behind the higher peaks once more, throwing the tanker under a blanket of inky shadow. The eyes of the thing that looked like Jonas began to shimmer with a sinister blood-red glow that grew terribly brighter as the moonlight dimmed, and then he took a long step forward.

"Stay back!" Saint-Germaine warned.

"Or what?" the other mocked, taking another step. "Will you shoot your own son?"

"You are no son of mine," the captain growled as he pulled the trigger and held it firm.

The demon's body shuddered with the rapid impacts of the bullets but it did not stop advancing. Instead, it roared with amusement and lunged forward.

The captain's last thought was:

Too good to be true, indeed.

Like that of every other ill-fated crewmember that dreadful night, Captain Saint-Germaine's agonized scream lasted for only a moment.

PART I

DISCOVERY

Chapter 1: Return to Ridgeland

1.1

Days after the massacre on *Königin Saint-Germaine* and several hundred miles southeast, Dayna Greenridge and Ethan Sureblade sat at the driver's bench mounted at the front of an horse-drawn wagon that happened to be airborne. Quick the changeling, in the form of an avicaw – a massive long-necked black bird that was, from breast to tail, half again larger than the wagon in which they rode – ferried the wagon using a harness fashioned from strong ropes and leather straps.

"I suppose the Old Ones *do* smile on us...sometimes," Dayna said as the town of Ridgeland appeared over the eastern horizon.

The changeling avicaw squawked his agreement.

The two suns were still making their ascent, pulling the shadows of the sprawling Runestone Mountain range slowly away from the town and chasing away the predawn chill. The cool wind of their flight pushed Dayna's long bushy hair away from her tired but pretty face. Despite the growing warmth of the new day, Dayna kept her cloak clutched tightly about her shoulders. More than just the fading bite of the autumn morning caused the lingering chill bumps on her honey brown skin. The all-too recent memories of her and her husband's imprisonment sent slivers of ice all the way to her bones.

She looked over her shoulder at her husband, Jon "The Firemaster" Greenridge, where he lay sleeping. Even though he was wrapped snugly in a warm woolen cloak, a shudder ran through him from time to time. Dayna guessed that he also shivered from more than just the cold.

Jon was a tall and slender man but captivity and torture left him almost skeletal. Dayna knew that beneath the cloak his dark brown skin was ashen and riddled with cuts and bruises. His head, which had once been covered with long twisted locks of coarse dark hair, had been shaved bald and was replaced by rough stubble and scabrous abrasions. Dayna did not want to imagine what had been done to him. There was no doubt in her mind that his was a fitful sleep full of nightmares.

During their captivity Dayna had been physically abused as well, but in unspeakable ways that left more psychological scars than physical ones. The few scars she did bear upon her skin were nicks and bruises from their fight to escape.

Dayna knew neither she nor her husband would ever be the same. She could only pray to the Lord Ascendant that they would eventually find some sense of what passed for normalcy in their lives.

Ethan Sureblade looked down at the town and breathed a deep sigh of relief. The sigh sent a jolt of pain through his back and shoulders but he stopped himself from wincing.

"Yes," the sixteen year old agreed. "The Old Ones certainly do smile upon us. I was expecting the scythe wings to be sent after us. Yet here we are."

While he spoke, Ethan absently reached over his right shoulder to tap his index finger against the silver staff strapped diagonally across his back. The staff – called a *gun,* pronounced "goo-en" – was an enchanted weapon made for him by the offworlder Child of the Old Ones called Raxe. When the weapon was bestowed upon Ethan, Raxe told him it was the only weapon Ethan would ever need.

The staff, long and slender and flawless, was made from titan's ore, an unbreakable metal used by the Old Ones in crafting their divine weaponry. Once forged, titan's ore yielded gleaming silver metal with the faintest hint of azure at its core. Both Ethan and Raxe made tremendous sacrifices in the crafting of the weapon.

Until recently, Ethan's most prized possessions had been the broadsword, bow, lasso, and javelin passed down to him from his deceased father, the legendary hero Meldrick Sureblade. All of those weapons had been committed to the magic-infused molten titan's ore used to forge the *gun*. Raxe painfully committed the very flesh and blood from his right hand, his strong hand, leaving it permanently deformed, to the same molten ore to empower the enchanted weapon.

Considering all they had to give up to create the *gun*, it was difficult for Ethan to believe that at one time he had actually decided not to use it. Without it, though, Ethan would not have survived the events that had taken place two nights earlier. Now he knew without question that it would indeed be the only weapon he would ever need.

THE KEY QUEST

Jon the Firemaster awoke where he lay in the back of the wagon. He stayed awake just long enough to pull himself to a sitting position and glance over the edge of the wagon. When he saw the Runestone Mountain range looming over the squat buildings and scattered houses of Ridgeland like protective giants, Jon smiled weakly and settled back to the floor of the wagon to resume his sleep.

Joel Harvey was also lying on the floor of the wagon, but not because he was sleeping. His body was not damaged as badly as Jon's, who had been imprisoned longer than Joel, but Joel suffered from his own collection of cuts and bruises. His arms and torso were peppered with small branding scars. The brands were shaped like miniature broken broadswords in honor of Dragon-fang, the broken greatsword wielded by the false baron who held Joel, Dayna and Jon prisoner. Some of the branding scars were covered with puffy scar tissue, some with blisters that threatened to rupture at any moment, and some with crusted scabs.

Even if the lingering pain of his cruel captivity had not haunted him, he would have still been unable to sleep. The flight in the airborne wagon was too terrifying. At the start of this flight, the wagon's rough movement was aggravated by the foul scent of the musty farm animals, stale hay, and manure that had undoubtedly been hauled in this wagon before they acquired it. All of this had Joel sticking his head over the side of the wagon several times to empty his stomach over the Kingdom of Lorr. The dizzying view only added to his nausea.

Joel thought sky sleighs were bad. Sky sleighs did not provide as smooth a flight as a decent sized airplane but at least they were towed by two or more avicaws. Multiple avicaws made for a much smoother ride than just one. The construction of a sky sleigh, with walls all around and a roof overhead, added a sense of security that simply did not exist in an uncovered wagon.

Worry tied his stomach in knots as much as the motion and view. To Joel, the tow harness that Quick and Ethan constructed from rope and common horse reins seemed woefully insufficient for this task. Joel could hear the leather straps straining and the wood of the wagon creaking for the entire trip, which took about a day and a half. How Dayna and Ethan could sit right up front in this biting cold without any kind of safety constraints was beyond Joel. Even under the thick woolen cloaks that Ethan and Quick were thoughtful enough to bring for the escapees, Joel found himself shivering from fear and the cold.

Joel patted the pockets of his tattered blue jeans, the last remnant he possessed from his home across the WorldGate, and located the pouch of medicinal herbs that he used to relieve his asthma. To his pleasant surprise, he did not need it. He had not needed it for nearly a week, which was the longest he had gone without having an asthmatic episode in years. The effects of the herbs were apparently cumulative, but as he did not know exactly how long the effects would last, he felt better having them within reach.

The young girl they called Arrowhead and the huge man they called Hammer got up earlier. From the time they woke up in the back of the wagon, they sat up straight and gazed down at the earth and up at the sky the entire way. And Joel was sure that if Jon had been able, he would be right there with them. These people were crazy.

So Joel lay in the back looking at the two-foot high sides of the wagon. Looking up was not an option. All he saw there was the underside of the avicaw. It was not particularly revolting but seeing the bird framed by sunlit azure sky and clouds only reminded him how high in the air they were.

Sunlit, he thought with a scoff. *Suns*-lit was a more accurate way to phrase it. Joel would never grow comfortable with the two suns and three moons of this alien world.

He tried to distract himself with thoughts of home, of running barefoot in the grasses of well-manicured lawns or the sands of one of the many Chicago beaches that lined Lake Michigan. But those particular attempts at distraction proved to be ineffective. When he thought of home, all he could think about was his wife and the increased danger in which he had placed her.

While being held prisoner with Dayna and Jon in the dungeons of "Baron" Tauran's pilfered castle back in the barony of Eastedge, Joel actually struck a deal with the demon Dierglyorr. The deal was that Joel would not assist the demon's enemies in any way in their attempt to thwart its plans. In return for Joel's neutrality, the demon would halt its pursuit of Joel's wife on the other side of the WorldGate.

But when the false baron and his lackeys attempted to rape Dayna in front of Joel, with her beaten and broken husband right there to bear helpless witness, Joel could not stop himself from acting. He found a way to manipulate his mostly uncontrollable power just enough to break free from his chains and incapacitate two of the guards before they could have their way with Dayna. Joel freed Dayna, refusing to let her remain a prisoner of the brutes that ran the castle. She immediately freed other prisoners in the dungeons, most of them supporters of the rightful baron.

The released prisoners revolted in the dungeons just as a force made up of more supporters of the rightful baron assaulted the castle from the outside. Joel, Dayna, and Jon used the chaos to make good their escape, with timely assistance from Quick and the surviving members of the Keeper's Hounds, Ethan, Hammer, and Arrowhead – who had also helped to spearhead a revolt outside the castle. Tauran's imprisonment of Joel, Dayna and Jon was done for the demon Dierglyorr, though Tauran had no idea that the demon was his employer.

This left Joel with no doubt that the demon would consider Joel's actions a deal-breaker. That meant the demon would soon resume its pursuit of Lisa if it had not already. And where the demon might have only killed her before, it promised to do much more to her if Joel violated their agreement.

"Wait!" Ethan called, snapping Joel out of his troublesome thoughts. "What is that?"

Dayna looked where Ethan pointed. "It's the infected," she gasped. "It's the so-called 'walkers.'"

"Now I *know* I'm not looking over the edge of this damn wagon," Joel mumbled.

Joel had heard of the walkers but he had not seen them. They were created by a foul spell unleashed at the command of the very same demon that had orchestrated Joel's imprisonment and torture. The spell caused a terrible change in those killed or injured by the tooth or claw of demons.

The first walkers were the injured and dead victims of the conflict that took place three years earlier and was dubbed the Cursed Opening. Those killed rose from their graves. The survivors of demon-inflicted wounds transformed into something less than human.

From their description as violent animated corpses in various states of decay, creatures that could infect the living with the same terrible affliction, Joel had no desire to see them. He kept himself pinned to floor of the wagon.

"Is that a large ditch they're trapped in?" Ethan asked.

"Yes," Dayna answered. "But not for long. Look at how they're tearing at the earthen walls, making them slope. I don't know how much longer it will hold them."

"I pray that those companies of infantry and cavalry down there can hold them," Ethan said.

"How close to those things are we going to land?" Joel asked worriedly.

"Don't worry," Ethan assured. "We'll land miles to the east of them. Besides, you and Quick won't be staying long. You'll soon be travelling southwest to the Demon's Spine to rejoin your fellow offworlder."

Joel said nothing to this. He would be more than happy to get away from the walkers. However, the prospect of meeting up with Ryan, or Raxe, as he was called in this world, not to mention Ryan's daughter and the off-putting Ranger Elf was not much more appealing.

When Quick finally – and blessedly, if one asked Joel – lowered the wagon to the ground, Joel sat up. He saw four people and four horses standing just beyond the wagon. One of them was a tall, rail-thin old man with piercing gray eyes, long, barely-kempt hair and bushy whiskers. He stood a few feet away from a saddled gray stallion that grazed freely without paying attention to the newcomers.

To Joel, the old man looked like a starved, poorly groomed Santa Claus, but instead of a red suit trimmed with white fur

6

this man wore a long gray robe very similar to Rionn Lorr's brown robe.

A wizard, Joel knew. He had the unique ability to scent magic. The ability was still largely new to him but he was finding that he could detect subtle variations among different people and different types of magic. The old man's scent was reminiscent of the scent that emanated from the Head Mage Rionn Lorr. There was enough of a difference to indicate to Joel that this man was not a Child of the Old Ones and not as powerful as Rionn Lorr, but there was something about his scent that hinted at a great deal of power.

The man standing next to him looked a few years younger than the wizard. He was a couple of inches shorter and almost twice as broad, with a muscular build and a slight paunch in the middle. In contrast to the wizard's unkempt look, this man had close-cut dark brown hair and a short, neatly trimmed mustache and beard. His long cloak was pulled back to reveal a narrow, dark green shoulder to hip sash pulled across a brown leather and mail hauberk.

The hauberk hung loosely over dark brown woolen breaches covered by thick leather cuisses at the thigh and steel-banded leather greaves at the shins. The breaches were tucked into high riding boots. He did not have the scent of magic about him but as a soldier he looked pretty powerful in his own right.

The third man was dressed in similar armor but he did not sport the sash, leading Joel to conclude that the sash was a sign of rank. He was not as tall as his commander and was considerably younger and slimmer of build, though he was muscular compared to the skinny wizard. He stood next to and held the reins of a lean cavalry horse.

The fourth person was a youngster barely in his teens standing several feet behind the three older men. The top of his head was covered with light brown hair that would have been called a mullet in Joel's world. He was dressed in a light gray tunic tucked into woolen breeches of a darker shade of gray. He stood between two horses, an immature mottled gelding on his left and a tall, healthy bay on his right. The gelding nibbled on the grass at the youngster's feet while the bay eyed the newcomers warily. The young squire tried to keep his head bowed respectfully but he glanced up and over at Ethan more than once.

Ethan was unable to contain the wince as he stepped gingerly down from the wagon. His knees were sore beyond belief, as were his thighs, buttocks, calves, arms, stomach, shoulders and chest. Raxe had warned him about the *gun's* magic, which imparted to Ethan the fighting skill and knowledge that Raxe had accumulated in over thirty years of training to become a martial arts master.

Raxe told him the magic would contort his body in ways it had never moved; that it would strain muscles he had likely never used. He taught Ethan exercises that would minimize the painful aftereffects of the magic's use. Ethan performed those exercises dutifully every day just as Raxe instructed yet still he was in agony. He wondered how much pain he would be in if he had not performed the exercises so diligently.

As he shook off the pain he noticed the young squire's attention. He wanted to say something about it but as a Keeper's Hound, which was an elite military unit, ceremony dictated that he greet his commanding officer first. He stood straight as a board, ignoring the back pain, and raised his right forearm horizontally out in front of him and placed his right fist to his heart in salute.

"General Ramos, sir," Ethan greeted.

Hammer and Arrowhead followed suit. The big decorated warrior returned the salute and then dropped his arm. The three Keeper's Hounds lowered their arms and then turned and bowed to the wizard.

"Master Mage Delthar," they said in unison.

The old man acknowledged them with a nod. The three of them then turned to the younger soldier and saluted. When he returned their salute, Ramos turned to Joel and spoke.

"You must be Joel Harvey," the general said. "It is quite an honor to meet another Child of the Old Ones."

"Yes," Delthar agreed, his cold gray eyes appraising the offworlder. Joel tried to get a read on him but too much of his face was hidden behind his unruly gray mustache, beard, and eyebrows. Joel thought he saw a slight twitch where the mouth should be just before the wizard continued. "Perhaps now we can change the tide of this conflict."

Ramos extended his right hand. Joel reached forward to shake it but the general instead gripped Joel's forearm forcefully. Joel had forgotten about the standard greeting and was not prepared for the contact. He grimaced with pain and reflexively snatched away.

Ramos's thick dark eyebrows bunched in burgeoning anger at the perceived insult. Joel, however, was too tired and still in too much pain to be intimidated. He simply met Ramos's gaze and gingerly lifted the sleeve of his tunic. Ramos's anger turned to surprise when he saw the raw branding burns, the purple bruises and scabrous cuts on Joel's forearm.

"My apologies," Ramos said quickly. "I did not know."

Joel nodded. "No problem, general."

Ramos chuckled. "Your fellow offworlder and I also got off to a less than desirable start," he said. "Although this time, I doubt it will lead to the Rites of Challenge."

"I don't know what that is," Joel said, "but from the way it sounds, I certainly hope not."

"This is Colonel Horn," Ramos said, indicating the other soldier.

"This is my squire while I'm in Ridgeland," the general said, gesturing to the boy. "His name is James Smithson but he's called 'Little Mole.' He's a local of Ridgeland aspiring to be a royal squire or groom. He overheard that we were coming to meet you all and asked to join us in greeting you. He wanted to meet the storied Keeper's Hounds in person, particularly you, Sureblade."

Ethan nodded. "I'm glad our reputation precedes us."

Little Mole was about to reply when his eyes widened and he gasped. Ethan noticed that the youngster was looking somewhere behind the Keeper's Hounds. He turned to see Quick, newly transformed to his human form, striding over to the rest of them. Little Mole apparently had never witnessed a changeling's transformation. Not many people had.

The changeling stopped in front of Delthar and greeted both him and the general with a bow. "Master Mage Delthar, General Ramos," he said respectfully.

Delthar and Ramos gave acknowledging nods. By the time Quick straightened Delthar had turned his attention to the wagon, where Dayna had climbed into the back and was rousing her husband.

"How is Jon?" Master Mage Delthar asked worriedly.

"He's recovering," Dayna answered. "He's been through so much."

"Indeed," Delthar returned. "You both have. We'll hurry to Ridgeland where he can receive the proper medical care. A carriage should be arriving for you all very soon. Quick must be exhausted after ferrying the lot of you across the kingdom. I'll not burden him further."

"How did you know we were coming?" Dayna asked. "We were not able to send anyone ahead."

"My farsight," Delthar told her. "I scan the region several times a day. One cannot be overly cautious in these perilous times."

"Then you know the infected are almost free of the pit," Dayna said. "Is there a way to keep them there? Perhaps the pit can be made deeper or wider."

"We've investigated that course of action," Delthar replied. "As you know, the Ocean Crystalline is just on the other side of the Runestones. There are sizable underground streams running through this area. If we go any deeper, we risk tapping such a stream and flooding Ridgeland. In any event, last night's rain has softened the soil. The pit wall would not be sustainable."

"Master Delthar," Quick said. "I wish that we could stay, but I must return Joel to the Demon's Spine straightaway to rejoin with Raxe."

"Nonsense," Delthar said with a dismissive wave. "He will be of no use to anyone without some attention from our healers, a good meal or two and some real rest. You'll leave in the morning."

Joel was eager to put some hot food in his stomach, as long as he could get out of the area before the walkers escaped the pit.

"Now that's what the hell I'm talking about," he blurted, ignoring the curious looks the comment brought his way. He scratched at the heavy stubble on his jaw as well as his scalp through his matted, filthy, coarse hair. "A bath, shave and a haircut would be really nice, too…"

1.2

The wizard and the soldiers rode a few yards ahead of the carriage and talked among themselves. Joel, Jon, Dayna and Hammer rode inside the covered carriage. Ethan and Arrowhead sat shoulder-to-shoulder outside on the bench behind the wagon driver's perch.

"I'm still disappointed in you," Arrowhead said to Ethan without looking at him, a stoic expression on her face.

"I know," Ethan said. "I understand your disappointment but I won't lie and say I'm sorry for what I did."

"You never answered my question, though," Arrowhead reminded him. "Did you slay the false baron Tauran, even as he ran away, to keep him from harming anyone else? Or were you avenging your father's death at the hands of the Finder by killing the man who happened to be wielding the same weapon that killed him?"

Ethan was silent for a time. He had asked himself the same question countless times during their flight from Eastedge to Ridgeland. He had killed men in self-defense but never had he killed someone as he ran away. His father taught him it was the height of dishonor to kill a defenseless or fleeing enemy. Meldrick Sureblade and the Lord Ascendant would not condone what he had done. Ethan would pray for forgiveness from both of them. While he did not know if they would forgive him, he had no doubt that they would understand.

"Both," he finally admitted. "I did feel some vindication for striking him down even though he was fleeing. That bastard had to pay for his crimes. He had to be kept from committing future atrocities."

Arrowhead still didn't turn to face him. Though when she spoke, her voice betrayed the emotion she so thoroughly kept from showing on her face.

"I understand all of that," she said. "But when you did it, I saw something in your eyes, Ethan. It frightened me, and it's something I don't ever want to see again, at least not under those circumstances."

Ethan frowned. "What did you see?"

"Joy," Arrowhead answered immediately. "You seemed to enjoy it."

"No," Ethan said, "I took no pleasure in killing Tauran. I only felt it had to be done. If he would kidnap an infant and slit her throat to gain control a barony as small as Eastedge, what would he have done to achieve an even higher station?"

"Promise me, Ethan," Arrowhead demanded. "Promise me that I'll never see that look in your eyes again."

Ethan was being honest with her when he said he took no pleasure in killing Tauran. What he did not admit to her, however, was that he felt a great deal of satisfaction and pride. And because the young Sureblade could not imagine ever loathing anyone else the way he loathed Tauran, he knew the promise Arrowhead was asking him to make would be an easy one to keep.

"I promise," he vowed. "Under similar circumstances, you'll never see that look in my eyes again."

Arrowhead seemed to be satisfied, if not entirely pleased, with his answer. She rested her head on Ethan's shoulder and slowly turned until she was looking into his blue eyes.

"You know, Ethan, this is the closest we've been to being alone since we reunited."

Ethan felt the warmth of her breath on his cheek. The warmth flowed through him and lessened the burning soreness in his muscles and joints.

"I know," he said. "Between the riding, fighting, and David sticking his big jealous chin between us at every opportunity, how could we ever be alone?"

Arrowhead shrugged. "It's not my fault if the leader of a revolt took a fancy to me while you and Quick wandered aimlessly through Hell's Mountains, but enough about him. Baseless jealousy does not become you." She favored him with a sensuous smile. "This is the first chance I've had to tell you how much I missed you."

"I missed *you*, Arrowhead," Ethan whispered.

Her arching eyebrows knitted in mock anger. "You can call me Nicolette, *Ethan*."

Ethan smiled. "With your hair is tied back like that, and wearing your fighting gear, you *are* Arrowhead. She's just as beautiful as Nicolette, of course, but she's fierce and dangerous, too."

"Do you prefer Arrowhead to Nicolette, then?" she challenged. "I don't mean the name. I mean the *woman*."

"In the field, yes," Ethan admitted. "What about this: I'll call you Nicolette when I see you in your night gown again."

Her eyes lingered on Ethan for several seconds before she spoke, and during that pause, those beautiful pools of hazel were Ethan's entire world.

"All the more reason to end this conflict as quickly as possible," she said softly.

"Do we have to wait that long?" Ethan lowered his head to kiss her.

"Master Ethan!" came a harsh whisper from the side of the carriage.

Ethan snapped up, leaned out over the side of the bench and saw the squire trotting up next to him.

"Please, James, just call me Ethan."

"I can't," the younger teen said. "How could I? You're Ethan Sureblade, youngest ever to be accepted into the Royal Academy, Eagle Eye of the Keeper's Hounds and eldest son of the great Meldrick Sureblade. You are a hero to all of the young squires and grooms who aspire to be soldiers."

Ethan felt his cheeks warm and hoped the others had not noticed. Out of the corner of his eye he saw Arrowhead cover her mouth to conceal a snicker.

"Then call me Eagle Eye," Ethan said. "I insist."

"Only if you call me Little Mole," James said with a nod.

"If you insist," Ethan said with a grin. "But that name sounds more like an insult than a moniker."

"It's not an insult, I assure you, Eagle Eye. They call me Little Mole because even though I'm thirteen, I know the labyrinths within and beneath the Northern Runestones better than anyone."

Ethan was hardly interested in mountain labyrinths. He had his fill of them after being held by dwarves with the rest of Raxe's search party under the Hells. He would not mention that to Little Mole, though. He changed the subject.

"So, Little Mole," Ethan began, "Besides all of the titles I didn't know I had, what have you actually heard about me?"

Little Mole smiled, eager to share his knowledge. "I've heard you are a great tracker; that you see things differently than others. They also say that you were the point man for the Hounds when it was time to kill a loosed demon."

Arrowhead did not try to conceal her amusement this time. She giggled out loud.

Ethan turned to Arrowhead and shrugged helplessly before turning back to Little Mole. It was true that he had been the primary tracker. His tracking skills, along with his sharp eyesight that allowed him to read the crimson shard of Sollustre's Eye – an enchanted artifact that revealed the location of demons – made him the logical choice as the team's tracker. That bit about being the point man when they actually attacked demons, though, could not have been further from the truth.

"That last part is not quite right," Ethan pointed out, "as my teammates can attest."

"Indeed," Arrowhead chuckled. "But the rest is true. And he is an excellent fighter."

"This is why I asked to accompany the soldiers to greet you," Little Mole explained. "My father is the stable master at the local barracks. I hear the soldiers talking all the time as they bring their horses to and fro.

"When I heard you were coming I knew I had to meet you and quickly. At first they would not let me act as squire for the general but my grandfather is a retired infantryman who served with the general. I was able to convince grandpa to ask General Ramos if I could –"

Ethan held up an open hand. "Little Mole, you still haven't told me the 'why' of things."

"Sorry about that, Eagle Eye," Little Mole said, a little embarrassed. "Everyone says my mouth rambles on like a runaway war wagon. I'm not sure why I go on and on this way, but –"

"You're doing it again," Ethan reminded.

"Of course! The 'why' of it is your tracking skills. It's your ability to see things, to notice things that others can't."

"What are you asking of me?" Ethan asked, suddenly intrigued. "Do you want to show me something?"

"If you'll let me."

Arrowhead leaned over to listen more closely. "Go on."

"I think I know what the walkers are after."

Ethan and Arrowhead shared an incredulous glance before turning their attention back to Little Mole.

"And what would that be?" Arrowhead asked with feigned interest.

"You don't believe me," Little Mole said. "No one does. I didn't expect the soldiers to believe me. Why would they? In their eyes I'm just a child. But you, Eagle Eye, are only a few years older than me. I thought you might be willing to at least consider…oh, never mind."

Ethan studied the boy closely. He had a hard time believing such a story but Little Mole looked sincere. Ethan knew a little bit about not being taken seriously. His first year as a Keeper's Hound was spent trying to convince everyone that his appointment to the elite demon-hunting unit by the Head Mage was based on his skills as a warrior and tracker, not out of entitlement by being the son of a deceased military hero. He decided that he would hear what Little Mole had to say…out of empathy if nothing else.

"I'll hear you out, Little Mole," Ethan said.

"Really?" Little Mole asked excitedly. "Well, like I said, I know the labyrinths within and under the Runestones better than anyone. I explore them often, sometimes by myself and sometimes with friends. But none of my friends are brave enough to venture as deeply as I have."

Ethan nodded patiently. Arrowhead sighed impatiently.

"Deep in the mountains, there is blood."

"Blood?" Ethan and Arrowhead asked in unison.

"Yes!" Little Mole insisted. "Blood, red and hot, flowing through narrow rivers in the bowels of the mountains. If you go deep enough you can see it through fissures in the floor of some of the tunnels. They're almost as deep below the mountain as the mountains are high but you can see them in some places because they glow so brightly. You can even feel the heat rising from them if you go deep enough."

"Blood," scoffed Arrowhead. "I think this one sneaks nips out of his father's flask."

Little Mole cast an exasperated glance at Arrowhead and then returned his gaze to Ethan. Ethan appraised the boy again, looking for any signs of deception or whimsy. His father had taught him some of the signs to tell when people were being insincere. His fighting instructors taught him to read body language. Ethan used everything he had been taught and found only sincerity coming from Little Mole. That did not mean the youngster was telling the truth, of course. There was the possibility that he had convinced himself of something that was simply not true.

Little Mole mistook Ethan's appraisal for disbelief. "I tried," the youngster sighed with slumped shoulders. He heeled his gelding to a trot. Ethan watched him ride away.

"You don't really believe he saw rivers of blood, do you?" Arrowhead asked in disbelief.

"Little Mole may not have actually seen what he says he saw," Ethan said thoughtfully. "But I believe he saw *something*. I want to see for myself what he says he saw."

"What?" Arrowhead asked with a grin. "I dare you to say that again, Ethan, only faster."

Ethan smiled. "I'm going to have him show me."

1.3

HELL'S MOUNTAINS – SOUTHERN RANGES

Near sundown, on the opposite side of the Kingdom of Lorr from where the walkers stalked Ridgeland, a tall man stood at the crest of a hill overlooking a small village. It was one of many foothills just to the east of Hell's Mountains, dwarfed by the imposing mounds of jagged earth and stone dotted with sparse shrubbery that stretched to the north and south for as far as the eye could see.

The man was close to seven feet tall, long of limb, lean and taut as if chiseled from pale, teak-colored marble. A chill autumn wind whistling down from the mountains pinned his cloak to his broad back and shoulders. The fabric of his sleeveless tunic strained against his muscular chest. The tunic was tucked into loose-fitting woolen breeches held up by a wide leather weapons belt that held a number of knives of varying sizes. It also held a dirk on his left hip that looked almost like dagger against his lengthy frame, and a broadsword on his right hip that looked only slightly larger than a straight sword hanging next to his long legs. His breeches were tucked neatly into soft-soled hide boots.

His only adornments were the ugly, roughly circular, blackened, fist-sized object hanging from a leather thong around his neck and the blue-furred headdress that sat atop his wide head.

His vantage point at the top of the hill allowed the tall man to see the entire village, from the goat farm on the southwest edge to the cow pastures on the northeast. The village itself was only slightly larger than the combined pasturelands. Just south of the cow pastures, farmers used whips and barked commands to oxen pulling plows. Just north of the of goat farm, a group of weatherworn men harvested crops of varying sorts.

He did not know the name of village, and as far as he was concerned, the village would remain nameless. All that mattered was that there were resources there to exploit.

He would do just that, for he was the High *Ken d'Zanir* Chieftain Rkam Lonos. Although the Kingdom of Lorr was not his native land, the village would belong to him this cool autumn morning.

Armed men surrounded the village. There were scores of them. Many of them rode coursers and some rode robust warhorses while others were on foot. There was a distinct difference between the mounted men and the others. The mounted men were better equipped and wore polished leather armor. They were undoubtedly dispatched from the land's baron or estate lords to provide more protection than the local authorities could muster. Word had apparently been sent about the *Ken*'s exploits at Port Lorrian. Most of the sentries' attention was turned to the north, where they were expecting their enemy to come from if they came at all.

That was why Lonos stood atop the hill just beyond the edge of the mountain range. They had traversed seldom-used mountain trails for days. It added time to their trip but made it more difficult for them to be tracked and allowed them to avoid being seen until they wanted to be seen. Food however, was sparse. His men and their mounts required more sustenance than the mountains could provide. It was time to make a foray out of the cover of the mountains in order to secure more provisions.

"Chief Lonos," came a deep but respectful voice from down the western slope of the hill upon which Lonos stood.

Lonos turned, not bothering to hide his irritation. "Why do you interrupt my contemplations, *Ken* L'Atir?"

"Is it not dangerous for you to stand where you are standing?" L'Atir asked. "Are you not concerned that the easterners will see you?"

"Not from this distance. Our skin complexion and clothing are the same coloring as the mountains behind us. They will not see me without spyglasses. In any event, they have been warned to look for us to approach from the north. They barely even glance this way, the fools, and when they do they are nearly blinded by the setting suns."

"Of course, sir," L'Atir capitulated. "My apologies for questioning your wisdom."

He also questioned Lonos's wisdom about dishonoring the *Ken d'Zanir* yet again by doing to this village what he did to the larger town of Port Lorrian. He would not dare to voice such concerns to his superior, though. A bloodlust had overcome the *Ken* Chieftain and L'Atir had no intention of drawing his ire. The last time L'Atir questioned Lonos, he proffered three fingers to his Chieftain in apology for the insult, knowing Lonos would refuse the offer. He dared not make the same offer this time.

The *Ken* chieftain ignored L'Atir and lifted a hand to shade his eyes as he glanced up at the suns. The bottom of the lower sun, the northern one, was a finger's width away from the peaks of the Hells. The smell of burning pitch was strong in his nostrils.

"L'Atir," he commanded. "Go and ready the men."

"As you command," L'Atir said. "Glory to the Grim God S'Zan."

"Glory to the Grim God S'Zan," Lonos returned with a distracted nod. "Now, go."

As L'Atir hurried back down the hill, Lonos turned his attention back to the village. *Men, women and children*, he thought, *all of them healthy and strong. Their livestock is hearty and plentiful. We shall dine well this night.* Knowing that L'Atir was in place by now, Lonos raised his fist high. He watched his shadow stretch out before him on the dusty hill for a moment more and then he dropped his fist.

The deep snap of two-dozen ballistae being triggered in perfect unison reverberated in his ears. He looked up to see the broad, black, sharpened wooden bolts soaring far overhead. When the bolts were a quarter of the way to their destination, another two-dozen followed and then two-dozen more followed them.

The last set was aflame with ignited pitch, giving the appearance of a wide flaming tail trailing behind the rows of cold, dense wood that preceded them.

The ballistae that launched the wickedly sharp blackwood projectiles like giant crossbow bolts had been aimed perfectly, as Lonos knew they would be. He lifted his fist again as his eyes followed their deadly path. In the span of another breath he dropped his fist again.

This time he heard the rapid footfalls of six-dozen of the *Ken d'Zanir* mounts. That was the only sound they made as they charged up over the hills to either side of the mound upon which Lonos stood. Their land dragon mounts were super predators even though they were semi-domesticated. The warriors that rode them were predators as well. The men and mounts were disciplined and determined, set upon their task of taking the town.

Not counting their long muscular tails, the giant lizards the *Ken* rode were as long as horses though not quite as tall. They had six legs, two pair of spindly, almost grasshopper-like forelegs and a pair of thick reptilian hind legs. Those legs propelled them down the hills toward the village twice as fast as the swiftest horse could run. Their chameleon heads stayed as steady as arrows in flight while their legs pumped furiously and their tails whipped to the left and right. Their chameleon eyes pivoted up while their heads tucked low, brandishing the cluster of short sharp horns and one long, dominant horn protruding from the center of the cluster.

The rough men riding the monsters, all of them close to the same height and musculature as Lonos, bent low in their saddles, the loose ends of their headscarves streaming behind them. All of them wore malicious grins in anticipation of the carnage to come.

Rkam Lonos wished there could be more of them. He had lost over sixty men in this campaign, more than any other company he had ever commanded. Four had fallen at Port Lorrian on their failed attempt to assassinate the Head Mage, Raxe, Quick and Ethan. That was only because of the unanticipated presence of that damned Ranger Elf.

They would be prepared for the formidable elf when they ran down their prey. And they *would* run them down.

Although they slew many more than they lost, a few *Ken* had fallen when they razed Port Lorrian. Even more of them died upon the Echelon One Mage's ice island at Lake Onyx. The water witch Sabrina took the most *Ken* by far when she ended that skirmish. Her giant wave swept scores of them into the middle of the Great Lake Onyx and drowned them.

Lonos sincerely wished he could be there when she reaped her reward for helping the easterners but they had business to attend to in the south. His warriors needed this victory. It would whet their appetite for the battles to come.

Someone in the doomed village finally saw the oncoming host of blackwood bolts and raised the alarm. Bells tolled and heavy horns sounded. By then it was far too late.

Lonos watched the villagers burst into panic. They ran this way and that, taking cover in homes and barns, behind trees and under carts. He heard their screams of fear and warning just as the blackwood bolts rained down upon them with all of the fury of the Grim God S'Zan Himself, the one true god of all of the fallen Old Ones.

S'Zan was the god of war and blood, of pain and death. While the other Old Ones died in Heaven's War, S'Zan lived on in the *S'Zan Rho* people. His awesome presence burned brightest in the *Ken d'Zanir*, the elite warriors of the *S'Zan Rho* nation. This village of heretics would make a fitting tribute to His honor. The people of this land worshipped the weak Old One for whom this kingdom was named. That made them less than human in Rkam Lonos's opinion, undeserving of mercy...including the children.

The villagers' screams of fear and warning quickly turned into cries of pain and hopelessness. The blackwood bolts tore through thatched roofs, wooden walls and sturdy carts, their sharpened points finding the flesh of the people hiding under and behind them.

The bolts drilled into the earth with explosive force, sending a thundering drumroll echoing off of the mountain range miles away. Trees were splintered, glass paned windows shattered. Cows and goats were skewered, pinned to the earth, lowing and screeching.

The last volley brought the fire. This region was cool and dry in autumn. The fire hungrily consumed the wood and dry grasses within the village. It did not take long for the flames to lick up the walls of the homes and barns and ignite the roofs.

THE KEY QUEST

The crackle of fire soon joined the terrible cacophony of destruction that was music to the *Ken* chieftain's ears.

A hush fell over the area after the last of the blackwood bolts struck. A few seconds after the last drumbeat echoed off of the mountains, there was no longer a need for stealth. The savage battle cries of the *Ken d'Zanir* shattered the brief silence. A paltry cry of defiance, full of false bravado and laced with fear, came back at them from the survivors of the mountain village guard. Surprisingly, there were quite a few of them. Their numbers were greater, in fact, than the *Ken*'s. Their numbers, however, meant little.

By the time the mounted guard navigated through the litter of blackwood bolts, the *Ken* riders were charging full speed across the village border. The line of well-equipped mounted fighters crumpled beneath the onslaught of the heavier scaled beasts and the men who rode them.

The land dragons went right for the necks and undersides of the horses. They growled and hissed and spit as they attacked. Had they been in the wild, a spray of corrosive acid would have accompanied their spit. Their masters took away their acid to domesticate them, but in most cases, as in this one, the fearsome beasts had no need of their acidic spray. Their rows of sharp teeth and horn clusters were more than enough against man and horse. The *Ken* warriors hacked at the men as they went down with their horses. More than a few of the men and horses were torn asunder by the land dragons after they fell.

Many of the land dragons leapt clear over the mounted guard while their riders swept down long-handled spears, axes, and an assortment of devastating polearms. They crushed skulls and severed heads and cleaved torsos and broke backs as they passed.

It took less than two minutes to push past them and then they were in the village. The land dragon mounts ran so swiftly that they could charge right through rows of fire without being burned. Some jumped over the fires, easily clearing the tongues of the flames by inches or feet. The beasts swarmed the pasturelands at the corners of the village to snatch up goats and carry calves away.

Some of the larger land dragons even culled fully-grown cows and bulls from the herd. They dragged them away with a bit of awkward effort yet even with such a burden, they still loped almost as fast as a horse could trot.

They darted into houses and came out again with people clamped in their jaws, some struggling desperately and others flopping around like limp ragdolls. Their riders rode into the houses with dry swords and rode out with bloody blades. Those that rode in with bloody weapons rode out with even bloodier ones. A few rode out with a screaming woman wrapped in their long powerful arms or held tight against the land dragon saddles. Lonos looked at them and smiled.

Prince T'Cheln undoubtedly would disapprove of this attack. He would call it dishonorable. Rkam Lonos did not care. These eastern infidels were beneath the dignity of the *S'Zan Roh*'s honor.

Whistling with two fingers in his mouth brought his own land dragon. It was time for the High *Ken* Chieftain to whet his blades.

All of his blades.

Chapter 2: Confrontations

2.1

HIGHWAY 80, NEBRASKA, USA

The darkness outside the bus was almost complete. There was a new moon in the small hours of the morning on a particularly desolate stretch of Interstate 80, making the Great Plains of Nebraska nothing more than an ocean of night beyond the dim lights of the speeding eastbound bus.

Dark figures, blacker shadows silhouetted against the black depths, swept past on both sides, all in the same direction. Some of the figures were larger than others and went by so swiftly that they were only a blur. Some were smaller than others and moved by slowly. Some of them had little squares or circles of light, like eyes that followed the bus until they faded from view.

Dan watched them all. He stretched out across two seats with a rough, dirty wool blanket covering him, imagining the shadowy shapes beyond the bus lights were golems of different sizes, observing the bus's passing and spying on Dan and his charge, all the while reporting their progress to their demon master.

Of course, he knew that was not the case. The figures could have been anything, from squat houses in the distance to closed gas stations to abandoned vehicles on the side of the road. But the cold dread that Dan felt growing ever stronger fueled his paranoia.

The demon's magic was closer now.

The bus was just east of Waverly, Nebraska, northeast of Lincoln. Lincoln was just about where, if Dan's senses were not mistaken, the evil magic was passing through that very moment. Dan had felt it moving toward him steadily and swiftly from the south, presumably State Highway 77. Within moments it would make its way to I-80 and be just a few hours behind them. Dan tried to suppress his worry and focus on what to do next.

Lisa sat at the front of the bus. Dan made sure they did not appear to be traveling together. People would be on the lookout for a young woman and an old man travelling together regardless of appearance. By now many of the news outlets had suggested that the kidnapper and the abducted – or the possible fugitives, as some reports started suggesting – often wore disguises.

Lisa and Dan had boarded separately and sat on opposite ends of the bus. Because of his effective disguise as an old, dirty, and possibly intoxicated old vagrant, Dan had the last few rows to himself. That worked fine for him because that meant no one was there to see the worry creasing his wrinkled brow and the deepening of the ancient frown lines around his mouth. There was no one to wonder why a seemingly inebriated old vagabond was reading a small atlas so intently.

He tapped his earlobe to activate the communication device disguised as a hearing aid in his ear. When Lisa tapped her earring/comm device in reply, Dan mumbled:

"Change of plans. We get off at the North Platte station."

"Why?" came Lisa's whispered voice.

"They're getting closer."

"So we're *getting off* the bus?" Lisa asked in disbelief.

"They've gotten bolder," Dan insisted. "They took out half a floor of a Las Vegas hotel to get at you. Now we're endangering everyone on this bus."

"What about *us*?" Lisa returned, her voice low but charged with worry.

"Do you trust me?" Dan asked.

Lisa frowned and broke the connection.

I'll take that as a yes, Dan thought with a grin.

2.2

UNDERGROUND BUNKER NEAR LEBANON, KS

Jorgé Barboza straightened up in his chair as he scrolled through the report on his nineteen-inch computer touch screen. It was a lot of nothing. Someone wrote a six-page PDF document just to say that an oil tanker disappeared without a trace in the Gulf of Oman. He was waiting for the satellite images, hoping for a visual of the fate of the *Königin Saint-Germaine.*

All he knew was that it was an unsanctioned oil transport. They could not find any record of the shipment in the shipping company's files. His sources had yet to find any evidence of the existence of the corporation that contracted the *Königin Saint-Germaine* or the origin point of the oil. The ship's charter was falsified, which was not an easy thing to do.

The only evidence he had at this point that the transport had even taken place had come from visual confirmation, both eyewitness and video, of the boat being loaded and leaving the dock. Everything checked out on the surface, but once Barboza's people dug deeper, they ran into to ghost corporations and poorly forged documents.

To pull off an illegal shipment of this magnitude while hiding the evidence of its origin this thoroughly took a frightening amount of pull. The ability to hide it this effectively from Jorgé Barboza, the director of the Global Organizational Defense branch – or *GOD* branch – of the organization was even more frightening. He had access to the most sensitive intelligence from every major government.

Only another branch of the organization would have the kind of resources and influence to do something like this, and Barboza had a good idea which branch that was. All he had to do now was prove it. But first, he had another project to check up on. He hit the speaker button on his phone and dialed a number. After a series of clicks, whirrs and beeps, and then twelve rings, a young man answered.

"Not a good time, boss."

"You always say that, Merge," Barboza returned.

"Because you always call at a bad time," Merge said.

"Where are you?"

"Still in Vegas. These termination branch bozos are chasing their tails. They know the girl stayed in the hotel, which was why they blew a chunk of it to hell, but she wasn't there when they did it."

"And they have no idea where she went?" Barboza asked.

"Not yet," Merge answered. "They've got people canvassing the plane, train, and bus stations and sifting through the video. It's weird, though. They can track them. I mean, it's like they can follow them from a distance but they can't figure out where they're going. I'm still having a hard time believing an old man and a veterinarian are giving them this much trouble."

Barboza shrugged as if Merge could see him. "We both know by now that there's a lot more to the old man than meets the eye. Hell, his grandson, too. There's been no sign of Ryan since the motel incident. How are the termination guys tracking Dan and Lisa?"

Merge chuckled. "You won't believe this, boss. The guys I'm trailing are using a freaking dog to track them, an *ugly* freaking dog."

"And you're sure they don't know you're following."

There was an unmistakable note of concern in Barboza's voice that irritated the hell out of Merge.

"Stop worrying about me boss. You know this is what I do. Nobody loses me and nobody knows I'm following until I want them to."

"Dan and Lisa lost you," Barboza reminded him.

"Yeah…" Merge replied, chagrined. "But not because they knew I was there. They just happened to give me the shake when they shook the assassins, and that was fluke. If I had known they were using teleportation tech I would've been better prepared."

Barboza paused for a moment and then continued. "Are you sure it was *tech*?"

"C'mon man," Merge admonished. You're not on that magic kick again, are you?"

"I'm not having this conversation with you again, Merge. How you can still doubt it after all you've seen with the G.O.D. branch is a mystery to me. As young as you are, you should have a more open mind."

"I've seen freaks of nature, paranormal phenomena and even alien crap," Merge allowed. "But I haven't seen magic…because there's no such thing."

"Just keep your eyes open, kid. You've probably already seen it and without recognizing it."

"Didn't you just say you weren't having this conversation with me again?"

"Just stay with the agents," Barboza instructed. "They'll lead you to Dan and Lisa eventually. Just be sure to get ahead of those bastards when you know where Dan and Lisa are. I don't want them harmed."

"If you let me get off the phone I will be able to stay with them," Merge complained. "Hey, did you record my girl in her workouts the way I asked."

"What are you talking about?"

"You know what I'm talking about, boss. I asked you to get some footage of that otherworldly booty either on the treadmill or doing squats, preferably squats."

Barboza scoffed. "Hell no. And she'd break in you in half if she heard you talking about her like that."

"Prude," Merge accused.

"Alright, kid. Get back to work. Check in again as soon as you can do so safely."

"Yeah, yeah, yeah. Stop babysitting. I'm out."

Barboza clicked off and leaned back in his chair. He could not help being concerned. Merge was the youngest operative he had, not quite out of his teens. But the young man was right. His abilities made him the perfect surveillance operative. No one ever knew he was watching and no one had ever eluded him before.

Dan and Lisa had eluded him, though, which was not a good sign. And if that ugly dog Merge mentioned was using some supernatural ability to track the unlikely pair, it might be able to use that same ability to detect Merge's presence. It had not detected him so far, which was good sign.

But Barboza had seen enough over the years to know that things usually went wrong just when people thought they had everything under control.

2.3

THE KINGDOM OF LORR – LORR PALACE

Just an hour past sunrise, Rionn Lorr stood behind an alchemist that was busy mixing powdered and liquefied chemicals in a small stone bowl. Several other accomplished alchemists sat at different places around the room. Each was fitted with a new high magnification scope, the design of which was inspired by the offworlder Raxe's description of a microscope from his world.

Each alchemist had a bowl or beaker in front of them along with a sliver of wriggling flesh that had been sliced from the still-animated severed head of the unfortunate Captain Johnican, one of the first victims wounded by a demon during the Cursed Opening to transform into the dreaded walking dead. Rionn was immensely thankful that Master Mage Delthar thought to preserve a sample for them to study instead of completely obliterating the warrior. He was just as thankful that the offworlder gave them the idea of the magnification scopes.

The scopes, to everyone's initial amazement, actually revealed to them the "bugs" that Raxe spoke of that might be responsible for carrying and spreading the plague of walking dead. As of yet, unfortunately, no one had been successful in finding anything that would repel the microscopic organisms attacking human flesh.

The Head Mage's days and nights had been spent working with healers, his half-elf wife included, as well as alchemists. When he was not working with them he pored over text after text for signs of any cure that would reverse the demonic infections without having to kill the hundreds of healthy, innocent people who had been tainted.

The vanguard of walkers was always much easier to dispatch. They were unnatural shells that soldiers were more than happy to send back to the grave. The second wave, however, included fellow soldiers, friends and in some cases even family members.

31

Rionn did not know how long the royal forces could defend Ridgeland under such circumstances. Something drastic would have to be done soon and Rionn dreaded what that meant. His constant worry led to a lack of sleep that left him exhausted both mentally and physically.

He turned at the sound of the door opening. The King, flanked by Ministers Artemis and Geoffrey, stepped into the room. The three Home Guards that always shadowed the King stood outside the door. The people working earnestly at their stations looked up in surprise to see the King himself and the two high ministers enter their midst, but after only a moment's pause they went back to their important work.

"Minister Geoffrey," Rionn greeted. "It is indeed good to see you safely returned."

Geoffrey nodded gravely. When he spoke it was clear that he had no time for pleasantries.

"The walking dead have worked themselves free of Delthar's improvised trap," he informed. "They kept digging and digging at the walls of the ditch until they were sloped enough for them to climb out. Delthar couldn't use his whitefyre to make the ditch deeper for fear of rupturing an underground stream and flooding the area. He wanted to expand the ditch but it rained the night before. The earth was too wet to maintain the integrity of the ditch walls. The walkers have resumed their march."

"Ridgeland's citizens have been completely evacuated," King William said. "The soldiers watching over the ditch attempted to drive them back."

"Attempted," the Head Mage noted. "How did they fare?" He feared the answer even as he asked the question.

"Not well," King William answered. "Ramos reported that morale is very low among the Ridgeland defenders, and understandably so. They want to heal the invaders, not hack them to pieces. Their hesitation caused many of them to die and many more to be wounded and transformed as well. Less than a third of the company escaped unharmed…physically, at least."

"Their numbers continue to grow while ours continue to dwindle," Geoffrey added. "With the city empty, I would rather let the things have the town for now…until a method to heal them has been found."

"But that is exactly what the Dierglyorr wants," Rionn Lorr insisted. "It must be. There is something of critical value in or near Ridgeland, otherwise the demon would not concentrate its forces there."

"You know that I have the utmost respect and trust for you and your opinion," the king assured. "But I cannot continue to risk lives on possibilities and suppositions. We have come to ask if you have found a solution through magic, alchemy, or medicine. If you have not, I will have to give the order that the Conjurers' Alliance use their whitefyre to eliminate this threat once and for all." The king paused and settled his heavy, copper-haired brow in a serious gaze at the Head Mage. "Have you found a cure?"

The tone of finality in the King's bass-heavy voice curbed any further argument. Rionn Lorr returned the king's stare with one just as sharp.

As Head Mage and a Child of the Old Ones Rionn Lorr had the authority to overrule the King in matters of magic concerning the Kingdom of Lorr. Every sitting king knew this. Both men, however, knew that exercising such authority was not something to be done lightly. Firstly, invoking the overruling authority in error carried grave consequences for the Head Mage. Secondly, to invoke the overruling authority would be to imply that the Head Mage believed king's decision, no matter how well meaning, was a threat to the well being of the Kingdom of Lorr.

An insecure king could construe such an implication as a lack of trust. It could cause a rift between the two highest powers in the Kingdom. A king with a fragile enough ego might consider such an action tantamount to treason.

Rionn and King William had not agreed on everything over the years. Rionn Lorr, however, had never invoked his overruling authority. He never had to. Their disagreements were usually over minor issues that Rionn had no problem deferring to the King. They were usually in agreement in matters of grave importance…until now.

They had not discerned any potential threat posed by the occupation of the town. Use of devastating whitefyre to wipe them all out when a cure could still be found was a pointless waste of life. Worse than that, a large number of the infected were not even soldiers. They were innocent civilians: peasants, farmers, housewives and *children* from all over the Kingdom of Lorr. Their loved ones held out hope for a cure. There were more than a few whispers from factions that blamed the Head Mage, and by extension the king, for allowing this plague to occur. Wiping out the walkers could potentially cause the kind of unrest that led to rebellion.

Rionn knew what he had to do. He hoped he would not regret his decision.

"I have not, my King," Rionn Lorr conceded. "But I cannot allow the death of so many innocents. I apologize for this, but I will have to invoke my overruling authority."

King William's tense posture relaxed, which unnerved Rionn even more than if the usually hot-tempered king had gone into a rage.

"Do you know what this means?" the king asked with an icy calm, placing a meaty hand on Rionn's lean shoulder.

"William," Rionn started. "You must know that it is not my intent to undermine you."

"Of course it's not," the king agreed. "That's not at all what I am saying. What I am saying is that by invoking your authority, you take full responsibility for the consequences.

"If you're wrong, by decree of our predecessors and Lorrian law, you will have to step down from the post of Head Mage. You will be banished from the Kingdom that Bears Your Name. Of course, all of this is assuming that the Kingdom of Lorr still exists when all of this is over."

The Head Mage nodded. "I do understand and I am willing to take that chance. But I have a question for you, old friend. If I am right, and we defeat the Dierglyorr, what will become of *us*?"

"You are asking me if this will tear a rift between us. If we will be able to coexist peacefully if you've overruled me to the benefit of the Kingdom." King William grinned. "Hell, man, if you are correct and we defeat the demon I might bloody well kiss you right on the mouth!"

Rionn laughed at the unexpected reply. "I don't think either of our wives would appreciate that, but I appreciate the sentiment."

They laughed for a moment longer. Artemis and Geoffrey joined them, the longtime friends and colleagues relishing a rare opportunity for mirth during such grim times. The moment was all too brief. The king's smile melted back into a frown before he spoke again.

"Our warriors will stand down but remain ready to act in any way necessary when you find a cure. In the meantime, we will quarantine the town."

"That is a wise decision," Rionn Lorr said, nodding in acknowledgement of the gratitude in the king's eyes. "And we *will* find a cure. I vow it."

"I pray that you do, Rionn," the king returned as he and his ministers left the room.

Rionn gnashed his teeth in frustration as the men filed out. In a matter of hours Ridgeland would be completely unprotected. Pulling back the warriors could be potentially catastrophic, he just did not know why or how. He did know that the whitefyre solution was unacceptable. Hundreds of people, warriors and civilians alike, men, women, and children, entire families in some cases, all with a chance to be saved, would be burned to ash so fine that a single grain would be smaller than the molecules they saw through the scopes that Raxe inspired them to craft.

The king never shied away from his duty, no matter how unsavory. When Rionn thought about it, though, he was certain that King William was actually *relieved* that his Head Mage had taken this responsibility out of his hands.

And he did not blame King William one bit.

2.4

The small kerosene lamp burned low in the darkness, providing just enough light to cover an area roughly six yards in diameter. Lisa and Dan sat at the center of the lamplight, bundled up against the cold in long hooded bubble-goose parkas Dan produced from his duffle. Lisa soon discovered that he had a few other interesting things in that bag.

She watched him retrieve a campfire tripod set consisting of three narrow rods, a couple of hooks and a chain, and a compact butane torch. He then produced a fist-sized brick of candle wax, a cast iron pot about six inches in diameter with a thin half-loop of steel for a handle, a smaller pot with a spout, five ramekins neatly stacked one in the other, and a length of string. He retrieved a hunting knife, a small waterproof bag of black powder, and most curiously, dried sprigs of rosemary. Finally, he pulled out a thumb-sized vial of clear liquid, a glass syringe with a squeezable bulb and a sixteen-ounce bottle of distilled water.

"What the hell are you making?" Lisa asked. "Scented candles?"

Dan grinned. "Yeah. Very special scented candles."

"Is this like Voodoo?" Lisa asked.

"Not really," Dan said with short shake of the head. "Now pay attention. You might learn something."

Lisa paid very close attention.

The first thing Dan did was use the small butane torch to heat the hunting knife blade until it was glowing hot.

"I'm glad there's no snow on the ground," he said as the jabbed the knife into the frozen soil. The heated blade tip bit easily into the cold hard earth and Dan began to work it in a near-perfect circle close to a foot in diameter. Dan continued to talk as lifted the blade, heated it, and stuck it into the ground again.

"I'm drawing a pentagon inside the circle, now," Dan explained. "The horizontal line at the top, one point at the bottom. Four of the five sides represent each natural element: earth, air, fire, and water. The fifth side represents spirit.

"Now I'm drawing this small circle with four lines radiating from it in the space between the top horizontal side and the curve of the circle. It's the symbol for the sun, which is also the symbol for life, or spirit.

"In the spaces between the two upper diagonals and the large circle, I'll draw something that looks like the Nike swoosh for air on one side and on the other a series of a pair of curved lines that'll join at the top to form points. They'll probably look like rough sketches of animal fangs to you but they'll represent fire.

"Between the two lower diagonals that form the bottom vertex and the circle I'll draw a few wavy lines for water on one side and on the other, an upside-down 'V' that's supposed to be a mountain, or earth, of course. Altogether this image forms one of the many symbols of magic."

Lisa watched as Dan drew the things he mentioned. He paused to heat the knife again and continued. This time he drew a line from the bottom vertex of the pentagon to each end of the top horizontal line of the pentagon, dividing it into three wedge-shaped sections. In the left wedge he carved out a small circle and then worked the blade back and forth within it, gouging out a tiny hollow. He went to the wedge on the right and meticulously carved out a smaller version of the circle-pentagon magic symbol. He looked up at Lisa.

"The little hole in the left wedge is supposed to be a filled-in circle," he explained. If I were using ink it would be a big dot. It represents darkness, also concealment. That's the spell I'm trying to invoke, a concealment or cloaking spell. In the right wedge, the smaller magic symbol inside the circle represents the target of the spell, or the entity the subject of the spell will be concealed from. If I had just drawn a circle without putting anything inside, I'd being saying I intended us to be concealed from everyone and everything, like we weren't even here. We'd be lost to sight, scent, hearing, even touch. We'd be like immaterial ghosts."

"So why not leave the circle empty?" Lisa asked. "Wouldn't that make it easier for us?"

Dan smirked. "It'd be like we didn't exist. We wouldn't be able to interact with anything in the physical world. With that kind of spell a third party would have to bring us back. I wouldn't be able to draw the spell form if I couldn't touch a drawing implement."

Lisa frowned. "Oh. Didn't think about that."

"Besides, a target of that magnitude would take more raw power than I can muster."

"What about drawing eyes?" Lisa asked. "To make us invisible."

"Sure," Dan confirmed. "I could've drawn an eye to make us invisible, or an ear to make us inaudible." He grinned wolfishly. "… or a tongue to…"

"That's enough, you old freak," Lisa chided. "So why not make us invisible?"

Dan chuckled. "Believe me, Lisa, that could have quite a few annoying, unexpected and disastrous repercussions."

"Like what?" Lisa asked.

Dan shrugged. "Well, people would be constantly bumping into you on the street and then freaking out because they couldn't see who or what they bumped into. Like a car running a stop sign and running over you because the driver thinks no one's there."

"Oh, yeah…" Lisa muttered.

"Not as simple as it seems, eh?" Dan noted. "But the magic symbol narrows the target to magic, any kind of magic. That narrows the scope of the target to a more manageable level. Whatever supernatural means the demon is using to track us won't work."

Dan's sly grin returned. Lisa had been around him long enough now to know he was still smiling at that tongue remark. She did not realize how reassuring that grin had become. She had not seen it since Kentucky. After Nathaniel's betrayal, an old friend and the son of an even older friend, Dan had grown more and more sullen, more preoccupied. He tried to hide it but Lisa could see his sadness and it made her even more worried than she had been.

But now that Dan was doing this…this…magic, he had his old spark back. He seemed to be back in his element. The oldest living Child of the Old Ones continued to explain as he worked.

"I wish this didn't have to take so long," He said. "If I was a wizard with internal magic to draw on I wouldn't need all these props. I could work this spell much quicker. A real witch or sorcerer wouldn't need all of these props, either. Even though they have no internal magic, their affinity and training would enable them to construct these symbols in their minds. They'd have the focus and mental dexterity to recite and direct the spell while holding the image in their head. All they'd need is the candles."

"You're having fun, now, aren't you?" Lisa asked.

"I haven't done anything like this in years," Dan admitted. "I wouldn't call it fun, exactly, not under the circumstances. It's damn sure interesting, though."

"OK," Lisa said. "So you've got the spell and the target. What goes in the middle wedge?"

"Us," Dan said. "We're the subjects. I'll need a sample."

Lisa looked at the old man suspiciously. "What *kind* of sample, Dan?"

"You're choice," Dan told her. "Blood makes the strongest bond. Technically, a strand of hair or sliver of skin will work. But blood makes the strongest bond."

Lisa tilted her head to the side. "Are you trying to tell me that blood makes the strongest bond?"

"Stop stalling."

Lisa sighed and took off her left mitten and sighed. "Will a finger do or do you have to cut a vein or something?"

"A finger will do."

"I hate needles, Dan."

"You're a vet, girl. How are you afraid of needles?"

"I'm not afraid of *giving* a shot, just getting one."

Dan rolled his eyes. "Hypocrite. I guess you're in luck, though. I'm not using a needle."

Lisa's eyes widened when Dan reached for the hunting knife. He wiped the blade down, put the torch to it yet again to sterilize it by fire, waited for it to cool down, and then pricked both his and Lisa's forefinger. Lisa winced but took pride in the fact that she did not snatch her hand away.

After squeezing a few drops of blood into the middle wedge of the divided pentagon, the small bag of black powder was next. Dan poked it with the hunting knife and poured a narrow stream of powder into the grooves he had just carved into the frozen earth, tracing the entire image with a thin layer. He even covered the stains where their tiny blood droplets were soaking into the earth. The powder had a stale and faintly sulfurous scent. She remembered the scent from one of her father's antique rifles. It was gunpowder.

Dan quickly assembled the tripod campfire set above the image. He hung the cast iron pot from the chain-and-hooks assembly, poured half of the bottle of water into it, and then placed the smaller spouted pot into the water. The rosemary went into the smaller pot, as did the liquid contents of the glass vial. Lisa smelled lavender when Dan popped the lid.

"Lavender oil?" Lisa asked.

Dan nodded. "It has magical properties. Now…I need you to be quiet, very quiet, for a minute."

Dan closed his eyes and breathed deeply. He began to murmur words that Lisa could barely hear and could not understand. She watched as a minute passed, and then two, all the while Dan breathed and mumbled. As if echoing from the woods surrounding in the clearing, his voice seemed to float into her ears from every direction.

Lisa started to worry. Dan sat right beside her in the lamplight yet he seemed miles away. He had entered some kind of trance. A peaceful expression softened his wrinkled brown face and that, under their less than desirable circumstances, made him seem even further away. That, in turn, made Lisa suddenly feel utterly alone. She started to wonder if and when he would come out of his trance.

And then she wondered what kind of wildlife roamed the Great Plains. Were there wolves out here? Bobcats?

As if in answer, or perhaps in response to the mystical energies that Dan was invoking, a chorus of coyote howls filled the night.

And then, with a flash, the gunpowder ignited. Lisa jumped and stifled a scream. She had been expecting Dan to use the torch to light the gun powder, but the torch was lying several feet away. Dan brought that fire to life with magic. And even stranger, it burned a pale blue, and its scent was nothing like the acrid sulfurous odor Lisa expected. Its scent was thick and cloying, but not overpowering.

The water in the larger pot came to a boil in less than fifteen seconds. In another fifteen seconds the combined scents of the burning powder, heated rosemary and lavender oil began to waft up in slow wisps of steam. The compound fragrance ignited warmth within Lisa that started at the crown of her skull and washed down her body in a slow, undulating wave.

It lasted less than three seconds but time seemed to slow. In that short time Lisa heard Dan's whispers again. Like before, the murmuring floated to her from every direction, rhythmic and soothing. When the whispers went silent and the warmth faded, the sensation lingered like a soft echo.

"I felt the magic," Lisa whispered with wonder.

Dan turned to her and smiled. "So did I."

He lifted the spouted pot from the hook over the fire, set it on the cold ground and then reached to his right to pick up the bulb syringe. With his left hand he retrieved the empty vial that had contained the lavender oil. In a couple of quick, smooth movements, Dan used the bulb syringe to refill half the vial with the rosemary and lavender infused water. He then stoppered the vial with his forefinger and tilted it to soak his fingertip.

"You're not going to…?" Lisa started.

Dan dabbed the oil behind each ear and held the vial out to Lisa.

"Your turn."

Lisa did as she was told with an incredulous frown. Dan dropped the cube of wax into the spouted melting pot and placed it back in the boiling water.

"This water is permeated with the concealing spell," Dan explained. "The heat, smoke, and steam acted as the medium

41

to transfer the spell into the water and wax. It doesn't take much. These dabs behind the ears will keep us hidden until we wash it away."

"But then we can be found," Lisa said worriedly.

"That's what the candles are for," Dan assured. "When we settle in for the evening we burn the candles to keep the spell airborne. The candles burn slow so they'll last a while. I'll make more a little later, but this will get us started. Wizards wouldn't even need the candles. They'd just will the spell around themselves and the other subjects."

Lisa stared at the old man for a long time. Her expression went completely blank, but her eyes never left him.

"What?" Dan asked, suddenly self-conscious.

"I believe you," Lisa said as if it was a revelation to her. "I'm surprised I'm admitting it, but there's no doubt this time. Does that mean I'm getting used to this?" she finally looked away. "I don't know, sometimes this all seems like a dream, and then –" she trailed off.

"Sometimes it's too, too real," Dan finished. "I know the feeling. I felt like that through two wars, when my only daughter died, when I watched Ryan take the wrong paths in his life. It's so bad that in the rare quiet times you just can't believe it's really happening."

Lisa nodded. "I keep falling asleep thinking, I mean really *believing* that I'll wake up in the morning in Joel's arms back in Chicago."

"And then the heartache comes," Dan said. "The fear comes back right along with the adrenaline. And then you're running and fighting for your life."

"How long do think it'll be before we're running and fighting again?" Lisa asked.

With a small, wistful smile Dan said, "I don't intend to run anymore."

"Wait, what?" Lisa stammered, shaking her head as if there was a strange buzzing in her ears. "What the hell does that mean?"

Dan's smile faded and his face turned serious again. "I mean, with this spell, we don't have to run. I can keep us out of the organization's sights indefinitely. I mean I can avoid their mundane resources. That was never a concern. I just had to find a way to shake the demon's magical resources."

"So what's next?" Lisa asked.

Dan scratched his head. "Let's see, we make these candles, walk back to our hotel across the highway and checkout. Then we steal a car, find another hotel, light the candles, and turn in for the night. In the morning we steal another car and go back to Chicago."

"Let's steal another helicopter," Lisa said mischievously. "That was scary but kinda fun."

Dan wagged a finger. "No more helicopter rides, young lady."

Lisa gave him a sidelong glance. "Remind me to ask you why you didn't use this spell sooner."

"Shut up and watch the wax, woman."

"Dan," Lisa continued, ignoring his command for silence. "I'm worried about the baby."

"The baby's fine," Dan assured.

Lisa looked doubtful. "How can you know?"

Dan smiled. "Magic. The energy I feel from the life growing inside you is stronger than it was when we met. If something was wrong, believe me, I'd know."

"All the same, Dan, I'd feel better if I could get a checkup. Maybe we can find a free clinic somewhere along the way."

"I don't know if that's a good idea, Lisa. It's a sure bet that the the organization knows you're pregnant. They'll be ready for that."

"So what am I supposed to do?" Lisa demanded, growing agitated. "With all the running we've been doing, all the stress, the fear…"

"How far along are you?" Dan asked.

"About three months."

"And how do you feel?"

"Physically, I feel fine," Lisa admitted. "But I'm scared, and I have been since all of this started. That can't be good for the baby."

Dan sighed. "I know a couple of places in Chicago, some off the books medical facilities with an exclusive and private patient list. Let's get back home and get settled in first. I can have someone come to us. Does that work for you?"

Lisa gingerly touched her stomach. "I guess it's going to have to."

Chapter 3: There Is a Way

3.1

"There *is* a way," Azhju'lestra said conspiratorially.

Both the offworlder Raxe and the Ranger Elf Rell Kallen looked up at her in surprise.

Raxe was finishing up a set of one hundred slow push-ups, using the exercise as a form of meditation. The push-ups tortured his damaged right hand. The sporadic bleeding had stopped but the tendons beneath the Titan's Ore that had fused with his flesh still screamed with pain.

There was also a residual ache in the parts of his fingers where the flesh had been completely seared away and replaced with a coating of Titan's Ore over the bones. That, and the fact that his fingers were all but paralyzed in a claw-like grasp, forced him to do his push ups using the heel of his right palm. He used the pain and exertion to clear his mind and help him focus on the problem at hand

He wished he could do some stretching, too, but his gear would not allow it. His enchanted armor, forged by the Old Ones known as the GateKeeper and his son, the original Raxe, allowed far more comfort and range of motion than any metal armor made by man. Even that, however, was not quite enough for the elaborate contortions of his flexibility exercises. He was not in the least bit tempted to remove his armor, either. After all they had been through to finally arrive at Mar-dah's mountain, all of the deadly surprises, he was not about to get caught without his armor. The only time he removed even a part of it was when he had to relieve himself.

The Ranger Elf had been stalking the perimeter of the spell-shielded mountain since sunrise. And now the early dusk of approaching winter had already lulled both suns behind the jagged peaks of the Demon's Spine Mountains. The lengthening shadows did not discourage Rell Kallen. Neither did the sights or smells of the multitude of decomposing carcasses spread around the mountain.

The elf simply stepped over or around the remains of animals of varying species, both large and small, most of them with portions of their heads neatly burned away. Some were sheared down to neck-stumps or even to their shoulders and forearms, depending on how quickly or forcefully they were moving when they came into contact with the deadly invisible field surrounding the mountain.

The view was grisly, to say the least. The stench was so heavy in some places that it seemed to be a living thing. None of this gave the determined Ranger Elf pause. Try as he might, he could not find a way through the formidable barrier, but he was too anxious to just sit and do nothing. He had stopped only to take a bite of hard bread and give his tired legs a brief respite when the young girl spoke.

His pointed left ear twitched forward to contradict his uninterested tone. "There is a way, you say, tiny one? And just what way would that be?"

"Water," Azh said. "Underground streams branch from the Ocean Crystalline and run deep beneath the mountains."

"Of Course," Raxe realized. "There would have to be springs within the mountains. Mar-dah would have had to get water from somewhere."

"And what makes you think the barrier does not intersect the streams beneath his mountain?" The Ranger Elf challenged. "What if the malevolent wizard thought about that when he cast his barrier spell?"

Azh slowly cocked her head, as if listening to something the other two could not hear. Rell Kallen's ears shifted ever so slightly this way and that in an unsuccessful attempt to detect whatever it was that attracted Azh's attention. Even Raxe, knowing his senses were nowhere near as sensitive as the elf or half-faerie, found himself listening in vain.

After a long silent moment, the child spoke again. "There are streams running directly beneath this mountain uninterrupted. The sea creatures within them pass safely."

"How can you know this?" Rell Kallen questioned.

"I am the daughter of the Mistress of the Sea of Spirits," Azh reminded the elf as if she were speaking to child even younger than her. "The water and the creatures within them speak to me, even over vast distances.

"This mountain contains many pools that are fed from the underground streams. Many sea creatures travel through the mountains through those deep arteries. If they can travel into the mountain, so can we."

"Perhaps the barrier spell does not affect sea creatures," Rell argued, "Perhaps it is only lethal to surface-dwellers." He turned to the older Child of the Old Ones. "What say you, offworlder?"

Raxe did not answer. He stared at the mountain in an apparent daze.

"Offworlder?" Rell said firmly to get Raxe's attention.

"Streams beneath the mountains..." Raxe said in a near whisper to some invisible listener on the mountainside. "...arteries..." He fell silent once again and resumed his blank staring.

"Yes," the Ranger Elf confirmed. "That is what the girl said. What say you?"

Again Raxe declined to answer. He was too occupied trying to remember why those words rang so familiar to him.

He tried to remember who had told him but all he could recall was the voice. It was a deeply resonating baritone. The sound was as distinctive as Raxe's, but Raxe's voice was as rough as sandpaper. The disembodied voice in his head was as smooth polished glass.

"There are streams beneath the mountains."

Raxe replayed the voice over and over until he could finally see the mouth that formed the words.

> *The thick lips were dry and cracked, framed by dust and soot-strewn whiskers that had grown so unkempt that they almost concealed the mouth. The whiskers sprouted beneath a knob of a nose that was crooked from more than one fracture over the years.*
>
> *Dark brown eyes, set far apart, were darkened by red and brown vessels that dimmed the corneas and begged for rest, yet the determined intensity of the gaze burned bright enough to startle any listener into rapt attention.*

The image of the speaker clarified as he took several unsteady steps backward until Raxe could see his entire body.

The speaker was a male dwarf. Even though Raxe knew he had never met the dwarf, he felt as if he had known him his entire life. He could recall memories of when he was only as tall as the dwarf's waist and when the dwarf used to hold his hand and walk with him through the forest.

For some reason that he could not decipher, Raxe felt a warmth for this stranger that he had only felt for his mother, father, and much later, for old Shanderah, and it broke his heart to see the dwarf in such a damaged state.

The dwarf was heavily armored, though the armor looked as if it had done him little good. The armor, like the dwarf's face and whiskers, was covered with layers of dust and soot. The metal was scorched black in several places. The dwarf's cuirass was riddled with dents and gouges.

Streaks of dried blood could be seen between segments of the pauldrons. The chain mail covering the dwarf's thick, muscular arms and legs was ripped in some spots and completely torn away in others. His leg harnesses with their articulated knees were scuffed and battered and creaked as the dwarf took each labored step.

Raxe had to re-evaluate his earlier assessment. The armor had done the dwarf a great deal of good. Had he not worn it during whatever events lead to its current state, he would have been nothing but a lifeless, scorched husk of broken bones and torn flesh.

"Himple," Raxe said fearfully, calling out the dwarf's name. He did not know how he knew the name, and even more curiously, the

voice that came from his mouth was clearly young and feminine. Despite his confusion, Raxe continued to listen to himself as the voice went on.

"'There are streams beneath the mountains?' What mountains? And where is father? You never leave his side in battle."

"Your father has fallen to the dragons, young one," Himple revealed. His resonating voice dropped to a near whisper.

"I wanted to die by his side in glorious combat," Himple swore. "But he ordered me to return to you. He gave the last of his fading life force to secure my escape."

Raxe could feel hot tears streaming down his face. When he lifted his trembling hands to wipe them away, he noticed that the hands were slender and smooth. The skin was a slightly darker shade of brown than his. The nails were neatly trimmed and manicured. They were the hands of a young woman.

"Damn this Dragon War..." he heard his voice – the woman's voice – whimper.

"Do not fret, young Shanderah," Himple consoled. "Your father has merely gone to join your mother in the House of the Lord Ascendant. I will join them soon...but not before I relay your father's message to you, for that is why he sent me here.

"Had not the message been of such great import, I would have stayed and died at your father's side."

"No," Shanderah protested. "Not now. We must get you to the healers' complex. They can save you."

"I am beyond saving," Himple told her. "There is nothing left for me but your father's charge to relay his message."

Raxe could feel Shanderah's heartbeat quicken and her stomach tighten into a knot as she fought to contain the wail that wanted so desperately to escape. She had lost her mother at the start of the Great Dragon War. The thought of losing her stern but loving father so soon afterward threatened to overwhelm her.

The sight of Himple, her life-long friend and mentor, hanging on to life by the thinnest of threads, only added to her grief.

Fluttering hands wiped away more tears. Her legs grew so weak that she had to lower herself to a sitting position on the side of the dusty road. She sniffed rapidly and repeatedly, hard enough to almost choke, but even through all of this she still found the composure to listen to the dwarf's message.

"What did father say?"

"That there are streams beneath the northern ranges of the Runestones," Himple said. "Not streams of water, but of magma."

Himple noticed the confused expression on the other's face. "I know not why this information is so urgent," the dwarf admitted. "Your father did not know, either. He was given this information from his father. His father received this information from your grandmother, the way I now pass it to you.

"He said that you are to tell no one, *not even your most trusted allies, unless there are dire circumstances that require you to do so."*

"What kind of dire circumstances?" Shanderah asked, her voice low and trembling with grief.

"He said you would know when the time came," the dwarf answered.

And then he was seized with a fit of coughing that caused him to shudder and topple to his knees.

THE KEY QUEST

Shanderah gave an anguished cry and rushed to gather him in her arms. "Himple!" she shouted. "Don't..."

"I must," Himple said weakly. "But there is one more thing. He said that if you go the rest of your life without circumstances forcing you to tell anyone what I have told you, you and the Kingdom of Lorr will have received a great blessing from the Lord Ascendant.

"But if you do receive that blessing, then you must, before you pass from this living plane, share this information with one and only one person.

"This person must be sworn to secrecy under the same terms that you must swear to me. And we can only pray that person never has to tell anyone before they pass from this mortal plane."

The intensity in the dwarf's tired eyes started to diminish as he was overcome by another fit of coughing. Blood began to trickle from his nose and the right corner of his mouth. His breathing faded to ragged wheezes and his body trembled in Shanderah's arms.

"Himple..." Shanderah pled. "Don't leave me. You're all the family I have left."

"Swear to me, child, and to your father, and to the Lord Ascendant, that you will adhere to the terms of this secret," the dwarf managed slowly between wheezes.

"I swear," Shanderah promised. She no longer tried to wipe away her streaming tears. "I swear, Himple. I love you."

"And I, you..." he rasped.

When the wheezing stopped and the dwarf closed his tired eyes, Shanderah finally let her anguish free in a piercing, agonized howl.

Rell Kallen tapped his booted foot impatiently. Several breaths later, as he prepared to grab the strange offworlder by the shoulders and shake him into coherence, Raxe turned to him, his eyes red and watery.

"A barrier spell doesn't work like that," Raxe continued, surprising the others as well as himself with the unexpected declaration.

The canted eyes of the elf narrowed to slits. "What do *you* know about barrier spells?"

Raxe was having yet another one of those distant, vague recollections. The memory, like the one of the dwarf Himple, had that familiar yet disembodied quality to it, as if he had listened to it through another's ears. This recollection was not accompanied by the crystal clear vision he had moments earlier, but he was just as certain of its origin.

Shanderah's pain of losing her family still clung to Raxe. He had to clear his throat before continuing.

"A barrier spell would do the same to the fish as to the animals on the surface," he said with certainty, casting an uneasy glance at the scattered carcasses. "Mar-dah's barrier spell would be good, but like Azh said, it doesn't form a complete bubble around the mountain. It can't, otherwise he'd cut off his own water supply. He'd cut off a significant portion his food supply, too, assuming he fed on the fish that travel the streams that run through his mountain."

"There are streams and fresh water pools in the mountain range," Rell Kallen contended. "There are animals to hunt. Perhaps he had his minions fetch these things for him."

"That would be too risky," Raxe countered. "The man was in hiding. Any intelligent person in his predicament would hole up somewhere as self-sustaining as possible, and Mar-dah was intelligent.

"I doubt he'd leave the mountain unless he absolutely had to, or only if he thought it was safe, like when he almost single handedly took out the Head Mage, the entire royal court, and me.

"He would've been selective about who entered his lair and how often they did. Regular errand runners or treks outside the mountain to forage would eventually be discovered." Raxe nodded in satisfaction at his conclusion. "A barrier spell of this type would stop everything but air. Creatures, flowing water and even hot lava would be stopped. It makes sense that he would terminate the barrier to allow the subterranean streams to enter the mountain."

"When did you become such an expert on Mar-dah and barrier spells?" Rell Kallen questioned. "And what has hot lava to do with anything?"

"I'm not an expert on Mar-dah. I just know about hiding. As far as barrier spells and lava, well...that's a long story." Raxe turned to his daughter. "Azh, can you lead us to a stream with enough air pockets to keep me from drowning? I can't speak for the elf, but I don't have gills like you, sweetheart."

Azh grinned at the flattering sobriquet. "I can, father."

"Good," Raxe said. "Azh, I can't tell you how much you've just helped me out." He squeezed his daughter's shoulders and kissed her on the forehead. A surprised smile beamed across her soft features. "But I have to do something before we go."

3.2

Rionn Lorr paced the rows of worktables, oblivious to the animated discussions of the scientists around him, wracking his brain for a solution to the many threats facing the Kingdom of Lorr. From the defense of Ridgeland on the eastern border to the search for the Hell Key in the south, from Rell Kallen's true intentions for the Key to the Dierrglyor's malevolent schemes to conquer both sides of the WorldGate, Rionn Lorr could not allow his mind to rest for an instant.

Even during sleep, the Head Mage dreamed about the texts he had read over the past few days. He recalled the many theories he had discussed with healers and alchemists, all in an attempt to find some obscure clue that he might have missed to combat this terrible plague of walking dead. He found himself in a depressing psychological maze. Every path of thought that was initially promising led to yet another dead end.

Ridgeland would be deserted by now, he knew, except for its defenders and its gruesome invaders. They were undoubtedly swarming the town, doing whatever it was their demon master wanted them to do. Rionn considered all manner of hypothetical defenses to any threat he could imagine. As pointless and distracting as the exercise was, he could not seem to banish it from the maelstrom of other worries that swirled around his consciousness.

His frustrated reverie was broken by a strange hum in the air around him. What almost any other mage or conjurer would mistake for a quick breeze was immediately recognized by the Head Mage for what it really was. It was the whisper of magic, a small ripple in the ethereal pool of energy that occupied every element in nature.

The source of the magical flutter was within his cloak. In the next instant his box of reflection sand was in his hand. After the necessary preparations, he opened the lid and watched the words form in the sand.

Hope you get this soon, cuz. One of Shanderah's memories was sparked by Azh's words.

THE KEY QUEST

I am here, Rionn Lorr wrote with the small stylus contained within the box. *Joel has been found. Ethan remains in Ridgeland while Quick brings Joel to rejoin you in the Demon's Spine. What memory has been sparked?*

The news about Joel caused Raxe to exhale with relief before he answered the Head Mage.

Years ago, an old dwarf told Shanderah that streams ran beneath the northern ranges of the Runestones, streams of molten rock. He made her vow never to repeat it.

Rionn Lorr knew who the dwarf must have been. He had often overheard Catherine telling their daughter, young Shandie, tales of the dwarf Himple. The old sorceress Shanderah, the person for whom their daughter was named, told Catherine those stories when Catherine was a girl.

Himple was the captain of the Elite Guard assigned to protect Shanderah's parents, the administrative clerics of the Temple of Afenrhena before the temple and the order of Afenrhena was decimated in the Great Dragon War. Himple was best friends with Shanderah's father and, because her father and mother were among the most powerful conjurers in the Known Lands and more than capable of protecting themselves, Himple spent a great deal of time serving as Shanderah's personal bodyguard, mentor, and close friend.

Rionn stroked his chin as he considered what he read. He stuck the tip of his stylus into the sand and wrote:

Why would molten rock need to be kept secret?

Raxe's response came almost before Rionn Lorr had wiped the sand completely clear, as if the offworlder was anticipating the question.

It's DANGEROUS knowledge. What if the flaming lifeblood mentioned in the story of Daniatiae's fall was the molten rock that Shanderah had been told about?

Rionn Lorr was intrigued but uncertain. *Explain.*

The change of tense in the story of Daniatiae's fall, Raxe reminded. *You said the Kingdom of Lorr was often called the Lady or the Great Lady in reverence to Daniatiae Lorr.*

What if the past tense in the story refers to Daniatiae Lorr but the present tense refers to the Kingdom of Lorr in a geological respect?

The past tense would be what happened to Daniatiae during the battle. The present tense could be a geological threat that would continue to exist even today.

A spark of realization ignited in Rionn Lorr's thoughts. *It would be a threat that only someone or something from Heaven's War would remember.*

Something like the Dierglyorr.

YES came Raxe's quick reply. And then more words appeared. *Think geologically. Something is down there that only the tainted and pure can pass. The tainted could be some kind of supernatural creature that isn't affected by extreme heat, like the plague victims.*

Maybe the Dierglyorr used forgotten magic to start the plague because it knew the infected couldn't feel pain. The magma streams in the underground tunnel would turn that place into a giant oven. The touch of lava might burn the flesh of the infected but the heat would not harm them.

They'd be able to go near a stream of magma when the intense heat would repel almost a living creature.

The use of the words "tainted" and "pure" in this context sparked Rionn Lorr's memory as well. He had been assuming the use of "tainted" and "pure" in the text referred simply to good and evil. It was an assumption that was easy to make because Daniatiae Lorr was legendary for her altruism and forgiving spirit. In many ancient texts, however, those very same terms were used to describe creatures touched by hell and the Old Ones respectively.

And the Old Ones, the pure, were the only other beings that could withstand such conditions, Rionn Lorr wrote.

The word *Exactly* appeared in Rionn Lorr's reflection sand. It was followed by:

The flaws and imperfections could be geological faults. They could be great fissures beneath the earth that, if ruptured, would tear the continent apart.

THE KEY QUEST

Rionn Lorr had made it a point to memorize the text in the story. When he mentally recited it with Raxe's explanation in mind, the pieces fit perfectly.

> The world wept when Daniatiae Lorr, the first Head Mage of the Kingdom of Lorr, fell to the Leaders at the Runestone Mountains. Beneath the bejeweled bosom of the Lady, where Her precious stones look defiantly to the realm of shadows, spans an artery through which Her flaming lifeblood flows.
>
> There, where only the pure or the tainted may pass, they would be welcomed into Her embrace. And it was there where those whom She accepted would rupture that artery to expose her flaws and exploit Her imperfections in order to hew a wedge from the heart of the Lady, so that the wedge could be devoured for all eternity by the shimmering giver and taker of life.
>
> Daniatiae Lorr battled the pure and the tainted alike to stay this horror, but in the end, Daniatiae Lorr did Herself fall to those whom She accepted.

Rionn Lorr finally put it all together as the offworlder obviously already had. "Beneath the bejeweled bosom of the Lady" likely referred to the depths of the Runestone Mountains, where precious stones had been found for centuries until the northern regions were mined clean. The "flaming lifeblood" had to have been a metaphor for the streams of magma running deep beneath the mountains in the same area as the geological faults.

There were also those underground streams fed by the Ocean Crystalline that kept Master Mage Delthar from deepening the pit that temporarily imprisoned the infected.

Daniatiae Lorr gave her life to keep Her Kingdom's enemies from destroying the continent. They wanted to cause an earthquake that would "hew a wedge from the heart of the Lady," or break apart a massive chunk of the continent to let it sink into the ocean.

After the battle, all written records of the incident would have been destroyed or hidden the way so much of their ancient knowledge was after Heaven's War. The Old Ones could have easily used their omnipotent power to strike the incident from the memories of all but the line of Afenrhena. The Head Mage guessed the only reason they left a few links to the knowledge was in case a threat from Heaven's War somehow returned…exactly as it had.

Now I know the significance of Ridgeland, Rionn Lorr wrote. *They trade mining equipment to the dwarves of the Runestones, including explosives. The Dierrglyor's legion could take those explosives deep enough below the Runestones to cause an explosion that would rupture the arteries carrying the magma under the mountains.*

There are ocean-fed subterranean streams in that area, as well. They are likely separated from those magma streams by walls made of only a few dozen yards of rock and dirt. If the infected rupture those walls, the cold water and superheated molten rock could mix with a cataclysmic release of explosive pressure.

Another response from Raxe came even while Rionn Lorr wiped his last written words away.

I'll send word to Ethan in Ridgeland. You should send word to your people. The tainted have to be stopped.

I have to go now. My daughter may have found a way into Mar-dah's mountain.

One thing more, Rionn returned. *The Ken still pursue you. We have soldiers pursuing the* Ken*, but they may reach you before your support overtakes them.*

Be wary. The Ken *have an obsessive religious hatred for anyone who does not worship the Old One S'Zan as the one true god. That obsession, along with their contract, of course, makes you their primary target. Use this to your advantage, if you can.*

Raxe nodded to himself. He doubted that information would make any difference, but any intel was good intel.

Thanks for the heads up. I'll keep that in mind. Good luck, cuz.

Rionn Lorr was excited and relieved by the new information. It was far from good news but it was at least one puzzle solved. He would have smiled had the rest of their circumstances not been so dire.

His cloak fluttered as he turned and rushed from the room, causing a start among the alchemists near him. As he rushed to contact the king and his advisors, a thought occurred to him:

How did Raxe plan to send word across the kingdom from the Hells' to Ridgeland?

3.3

Ethan stood at the hilltop looking down on the town of Ridgeland with disgust, oblivious to the noises of the camp coming from the valley behind him. He was glad to be out of his leather armor and chain mail but he kept his weapon close at hand. His enchanted fighting stave was lashed diagonally across his back.

From an hour after sunup until a couple of hours before dusk Ethan fought alongside the Lorrian military against the walkers. When the soldiers were given the order to drive the walking dead back toward Delthar's pit, their directive had been to concentrate their efforts on stopping the *true* walking dead: those who were clearly animated corpses with bodies impossibly mobile even though they were in various states of decay; as well as those with such grievous injuries that they would not possibly be upright if not for the plague.

The problem was that by now the infected were starting to outnumber the dead. There had been a clear separation of the two, with the dead leading the column and the infected following behind. But because the infected walkers tended to move faster due to less physical damage, they had caught up and intermingled with the dead.

It was nigh impossible to immobilize one of the dead without stumbling into one of the infected. The slightest bump or any other type of physical impediment to their progress immediately sent the calm creatures into a berserker rage. In many cases it was hard to tell the newly deceased from those who were infected by injuries suffered in recent combat against the hellish multitudes. As far as many of the royal warriors were concerned, the distinction was understandably of little importance. They were fighting for their lives, souls, and kingdom.

There was an undeniable feeling of shared relief when the Lorrian soldiers received the word to disengage, but there was just as much trepidation and anger. As horrible as it was to fight them, the soldiers realized that to let the walkers continue unmolested hastened the demon's fell designs.

THE KEY QUEST

The nightmarish battle pushed some of the soldiers nearly to the point of madness. A fanatic sense of duty to their beloved kingdom clashed with having to strike down women and children and former comrades, causing something to break within many of their psyches. The result was a grim determination to strike down as many of the enemy as they could, regardless of the order to disengage, lest the walking dead spread their infection to every human in the known Lands. Those individuals had to be physically restrained, which resulted in several altercations between soldiers fighting on the same side.

Others questioned why the conjurers among them were not permitted to simply purge this demonic blight with a flood of their awesome whytefire. Questions led to suspicions. A few believed this crisis was the result some kind of research being conducted by the Children of the Old Ones that had gone terribly wrong. Ethan had even heard whispers that the Head Mage had placed King William under some kind of spell that made his highness amenable to this vile experiment.

It took all of the discipline Ethan could muster to stop himself from confronting those fools to force them to reveal the source of those vile lies. Nicolette, once again in her Arrowhead personality with her Keeper's Hounds gear augmented by chain mail and her hair pulled back into that severe ponytail, had been there to hold Ethan back. She had to remind him several times that there was far too much infighting going on already.

Ethan wished Arrowhead could be by his side as he stood on that hilltop. Her presence would have calmed the frustration he felt, but she was at the infirmary tent receiving treatment for her wounds. She had suffered some minor cuts and bruises, but by the grace of the Lord Ascendant, she had not been infected during the fighting.

Hammer was likely somewhere eating, napping or chasing the pretty young serving women.

From his perch Ethan could see the swarm of plague-ridden men, women and children as they streamed into town from the west. They had been coming into the town for hours, disappearing among the buildings before emerging from the eastern border of the town and making their way toward the Runestone Mountains.

They carried large sacks or pushed and pulled carts stacked with barrels. From the hilltop, not even Ethan's sharp vision could make out exactly what they were transporting. He wondered if what Little Mole had shown him was really the focus of these unfortunate creatures. He thought back to the trek Little Mole led him on the previous evening, through the caves and tunnels under the Runestone Mountains. Ethan recalled every detail with crystal clarity in an attempt to find some clue that would justify his suspicion.

The younger boy had taken Ethan through a complex maze of descending tunnels. Along the way he pointed out intersecting tunnels that he told Ethan were passages to other entrances to the mountain, including the most obvious one that faced the town. Ethan committed it all to memory without consciously trying, as natural for him as breathing. They finally came to a small cavern in the depths of the mountain with a pit in the floor. The hole was as and irregular oval that was close to ten feet wide at its widest point. Little Mole had Ethan peer into the pit, and what he saw amazed him.

He saw several lower levels of caves, all with an identical hole perfectly lined up with the one he was peering through. It was as if some terrible energy blasted through the mountain some time in the ancient past. The lower levels were so numerous and so deep that they eventually fell away into shadow, but at the bottom of it all, snaking through the darkness, Ethan could see a yellow-orange glow. The light and shadows flittered in the depths in a way that reminded Ethan of a lazy river seen from an airborne sky-sleigh. The movement was slower in this case, almost sluggish.

"Molten rock?" Ethan asked.

"Yes," Little Mole answered. "The dwarves call it lava. We call it the earth's blood."

Ethan turned his attention from that memory to the present. He studied the walkers and wondered again about the likelihood of the molten rock having anything to do with them. Other soldiers and volunteer defenders watched from the hillside, all of them as distraught as Ethan. As much as it hurt them to have to battle fellow citizens of the Kingdom of Lorr, it hurt even more to surrender the town. They understood the reasoning behind the decision to pull out but understanding did not make it any easier. Ethan, accompanied by Arrowhead and Hammer during the fighting earlier in the day, had to watch valiant men fall and some turn into the dreadful walking dead right before their eyes. It gnawed at his gut to think that those lives were wasted.

The one thing that puzzled them all was the fact that the invaders did not sack or loot Ridgeland. They were very deliberate in their efforts and, as far as the defenders could tell, none strayed to do anything other than follow those in front of them to collect whatever it was they were transporting to the Runestones. While none of them could tell exactly what they were moving, they all knew it was something sinister.

Ethan was so preoccupied with the scene below that he almost missed the warmth on his back. When he finally noticed, and realized the source, he snatched the staff from his back and held it in a defensive posture. He looked around for the threat that he assumed had ignited the magic of his new weapon but there was none. While the tingling warmth flowing into his hands was not as intense as it was when he fought Tauran and his *Ken* bodyguard, there was a definite urgency in the sensation.

He took three deep breaths and relaxed in the way the offworlder advised, allowing the warm magic to flow up into his wrist and then his arms. In the next moment a whisper brushed past Ethan's ear.

A second whisper, slightly louder, rushed past him as if carried on a brisk wind. Another sound came to him, louder, more than whisper. The sound was more like someone crushing dried leaves in their hand than it was like a voice, and the words were at first incomprehensible. The next time the sound came it was much deeper, like stones being rubbed together. It was a hoarse, rasp of a voice.

It was a familiar rasp.

Sureblade! Raxe's voice floated from the staff.

Ethan looked at the enchanted *gun* with wonder. His surprise almost made him lose concentration. He managed to regain enough of his focus to keep from losing his connection to the magic.

"Raxe?" Ethan said to the staff.

Good, the staff conveyed. *It works.*

"I didn't know you could communicate through the *gun*," Ethan said.

I wasn't sure I'd be able to, Raxe confessed.

"Keeping tabs on me, then?" Ethan questioned.

I got the idea from Rionn Lorr's reflection sand, Raxe told him. *I thought it might be useful to be able to communicate with you.*

"Can I initiate the magic?" Ethan asked.

It doesn't work that way.

"Why?"

Because I didn't know how to make it work that way. I don't know much about magic. I'm just glad, and lucky, that I was able to get this much right.

"As am I," Ethan said. "You are not upset that I chose to stay here instead of returning with Joel and Quick?"

Not at all, Raxe answered. *I'm glad you did. It was a smart choice.*

Ethan beamed at the compliment. "It's good to hear from you. We're in a bad situation here. I could use some advice."

Sorry kid, but I don't have advice. I have instructions.

"Whatever you wish, Raxe."

Are you somewhere where you can you see the invaders?

"Yes, and the sight galls me."

What are they doing?

"Strangely enough, not much," Ethan informed. "They're going into town and coming out with barrels and sacks and carts. We're too far away to tell what it—"

At that moment, Little Mole came running up the hill. He was huffing and puffing but his short legs powered him on. It took Ethan a moment to realize what the boy was shouting, but when he did, Ethan's heartbeat quickened.

"Explosives?" Ethan said to the staff. By that time Little Mole had reached Ethan and noticed that he was talking to his weapon. Little Mole gave him a strange look.

Yeah, the staff returned. Little Mole yelped at the sound. The staff continued as the boy stared in awe. *There's magma, molten rock in the depths of those mountains."*

"I just discovered that," Ethan said. "Do they plan to bring down the mountains and deystroying the mountainside towns? What's the point of that?"

Bringing down the right mountains could cause a chain reaction that would bring down more than just the nearby towns. It could be catastrophic for the entire Kingdom, Ethan. They have to be stopped.

Ethan looked down at the town again. His heart beat even faster. He wanted to sprint down the hill and engage them but a thought occurred to him.

"I cannot give the order to attack. I don't even know where the field commander is."

Don't worry about that, Ethan. The order will be coming soon enough. I just want you to be ready when it does.

"I will be," Ethan assured. And then another alarming thought came to him. "Raxe! The head of their column has almost reached the Runestones. Many of them will be inside the caves before we can mobilize to stop them."

Shit! Ryan swore. *Then find the field commander now and convince him to move* before *the official word comes from the capital. We can't afford to wait. Hurry!*

Little Mole sprinted off to find the field commander as if the staff had been talking to him. Ethan ran the other way.

Ethan went to the field commander's tent first but the man was not there. As Ethan continued his search he found Nicolette at the infirmary tent. Her hair was down, her fighting gear had been removed and her beautifully fierce battle-scowl was absent. She was up and about, assisting the healers and their attendants. She moved her bandaged right arm gingerly but did not stop helping.

When Ethan found her she was setting water at the tray of a gurney-bound warrior. She looked up and saw Ethan approaching and favored him with a small but heartfelt smile.

"You should be resting," Ethan chided.

"If I can't fight, I'll find another way to make good use of my time," Nicolette promised.

"Well, if you simply refuse to rest the way the healers have advised," said Ethan. "Come with me to help find the commander. I have important information for him."

Nicolette stepped closer, clearing a path for the high traffic of the infirmary tent. "What news?"

"I'll tell you when we find the commander," Ethan promised.

They left together and came across Hammer at the dining tent. Four attractive young serving maidens surrounded the massive man as he regaled them with war stories.

"And here are the other remaining Keeper's Hounds," he said to the ladies. "This is Arrowhead and Eagle Eye."

Ethan winced at the "remaining Keeper's Hounds" statement. It was a stark reminder that the rest of their elite force was dead. A glance at Nicolette told him that she felt the same sting. All they could do was shrug at one another. Both of them knew that sensitivity and tact had never been counted among Hammer's better traits. A couple of the pretty girls gave Ethan and appraising stare. Nicolette moved closer and took his left hand in her right. The cold glare she aimed at the girls made them look away.

"No time for talking," Ethan said. "We must hurry."

The grave look in Ethan's eyes told Hammer how serious the younger Hound was.

"Sorry ladies," Hammer apologized. "Duty compels me. That is the only thing that *could* pry me from such nubile beauties as yourselves."

He reluctantly extracted himself from the giggling women and joined his fellow Hounds. Ethan explained the situation to them as they resumed their search. They stopped several times to ask soldiers and civilian attendants of the commander's whereabouts.

THE KEY QUEST

When they explained why they were looking for him, the soldiers that did not know Ethan gave him incredulous looks. The story of the talking staff made it even easier for them to dismiss him as an overexcited boy with an overactive imagination. Ethan wished he could initiate communication with Raxe in order to demonstrate the magic as proof of his words, but even if he could, there was no time, so the search continued. The few soldiers that did know him, as well as several of the more open-minded volunteers, took him very seriously. They offered to help after Ethan's explanation.

Included in this group was One-shot, their commander in the Hounds. Ethan was pleasantly shocked to see One-shot alive and well, albeit a bit disheveled like everyone else in the camp. Hammer and Nicolette were not surprised at all.

"Commander," Ethan said, saluting One-shot and then shaking his hand. "Nicolette and Hammer did not tell me you survived the sky sleigh attack."

"I wasn't on the sky sleigh," One-shot replied. "I got orders that very morning to come to Ridgeland. I was in line for a promotion to squad leader in the Royal Army. The previous squad leader was killed in an early skirmish with those creatures down there." One-shot nodded down at the plague victims with a disgusted frown. "Saber had taken my place as the commander of the GateKeeper's Hounds. May the Lord Ascendant and all of the Old Ones welcome him and the rest of the Hounds into their kingdom."

"With all that's happened," Hammer added, "it never occurred to us that you didn't know. I guess you wouldn't have known, though. You were already with Quick and the Children of the Old Ones when we found out."

Hammer did not say that last bit in an accusatory tone yet Ethan felt guilty nonetheless. The young Sureblade still felt that he had somehow abandoned and betrayed his team by choosing to ride in the sky-sleigh *Sundance* with Raxe and Quick instead of *Cloud Chaser* with the Keeper's Hounds.

"Enough lamenting the past," One-shot declared. "We'll make sure their sacrifice counts for something. Let's start by finding Colonel Horn."

With their ex-commander's help, it was not long before a small team spread through the hillside camp looking for the field commander. After long minutes of searching without success, Ethan began to worry. So much time had passed that he feared the invaders would get enough explosives into those mountains to do a great deal of damage. Ethan was starting to seriously consider taking the underground passageways beneath the mountains that Little Mole had shown him when he heard a young boy's voice call his name. He turned to see Little Mole waving to him.

"Colonel Horn is back at his tent, Eagle Eye! Hurry!"

Ethan, One-shot, Arrowhead, and Hammer, accompanied by Little Mole and several volunteers and soldiers, sprinted across the hillside back to the commander's tent.

Two guards standing at the entrance to the tent saw them coming and stepped forward to meet them. Ethan did not recognize the guards and hoped they would not be as quick to dismiss him as many of the other soldiers had.

"The commander is busy," one of the guards informed a little more curtly than was necessary.

Ethan understood and did not take offense. Everyone was on edge and annoyed at having to watch the invaders take the town without resistance.

"I know he must be," Ethan returned. "But what I have to tell him is of great import."

"Tell me," the guard instructed. "I'ill relay the message."

"I have received word from the Child Raxe that we must stop the invaders," Ethan explained. "Those are explosives they are taking into the mountains."

"We know," the guard shared. "We were with the commander only minutes ago when he moved nearer the town for a closer look. It is peculiar, but the commander thinks it is hardly an immediate threat to us."

"But it *is* a threat," Ethan told him. "It is a great threat not just to us, but to the entire kingdom."

"They will collapse a few caves in the Runestones," the other guard argued. "How does that endanger the kingdom?"

"There is magma in the underground caves of those mountains. Raxe says those explosives are meant to trigger an earthquake that could cause disastrous harm to the countryside and beyond."

"How did the Child Raxe communicate with *you?*" the guard asked incredulously.

"Yes," the other guard joined in. "Who are you, young one, that a Child of the Old Ones would even relay such an urgent message through you?"

"I am Ethan Sureblade," the teen said, raising his chin and squaring his shoulders. "I am a member of the Keeper's Hounds and the son of Meldrick Sureblade, High Captain of the Home Guard. The Child Raxe has spoken to me through this," Ethan removed the staff from its strap on his back and held it up for their inspection. "It is a weapon that he, the descendant of the GateKeeper, crafted especially for me."

The staff's color was aesthetic but other than that the weapon was unremarkable at best. The doubtful looks on the faces of the guards betrayed their disinterest.

"Do you expect us to believe that?" one of the guards asked with a wry smirk.

"He speaks the truth," came a voice from behind the guards. The field commander stepped out of the tent. "At least about being a Sureblade son. His father was a friend and I have seen this young one on occasion."

"Colonel Horn," Ethan implored, "you must—"

"I heard the story," Horn interrupted. "However, you should know that I cannot move on the invaders until I receive the command from my superiors."

"The command is on the way," Ethan assured. "Raxe got word to me sooner, but you will be receiving word shortly."

"Then that is when we shall move, young Sureblade."

"It could be too late by then, Colonel Horn, you must understand."

The colonel only stared at the teen. Ethan started to argue more but he realized he was wasting time. Every second he spent arguing brought the invaders another second closer to their destination.

"*I* shall not wait," Ethan said.

"Don't be foolish," Colonel Horn advised. "You will stay here and wait with the rest of us."

"We're not under your command," Ethan said stubbornly. "The Keeper's Hounds are under the direct command of Master Mage Delthar and General Ramos. I will find Mage Delthar and convince him of our circumstances."

"Then do as you wish, silly boy," the colonel conceded. "I'll even tell you where Delthar is. He went into the tunnels to confront the walking dead alone. Apparently he believes he is as powerful as the Old Ones themselves. He did not even bother to ask for accompaniment. The old fool simply went in after them."

"You did not try to stop him?" Ethan asked.

"He struck dead the last soldier that defied him."

Ethan's eyes went wide but he kept silent. He heard whispers that Delthar killed the leader of a rogue militia and dismissed them as rumor. Now was not the time to argue.

Colonel Horn continued. "You are not under my command, as you say. If you want to be as foolish as that mad wizard, do not expect my soldiers to babysit you."

"I have the magic of the Old Ones with me," Ethan told Colonel Horn, brandishing the *gun*. "That's all I need."

He turned and ran down the hill toward the town. The other Hounds and Little Mole were right on his heels and several civilian volunteers followed. One-Shot and the other soldiers watched them go. The colonel could tell from their expressions and posture that they wanted to follow as well.

"You will wait until we get word to move, soldiers," he commanded. "It's bad enough that the Head Mage leads our king and ministers around by the nose. We'll not allow the Children of the Old Ones and their pet wizards to do the same to us. Do you understand?"

One-Shot and the others nodded.

Colonel Horn nodded his satisfaction. "As you were, then, and stay sharp."

3.4

It did not take Rionn Lorr long to find the King and his advisors. They were in the royal conference room, their war room during military crisis. The guards opened the heavy double doors and stepped aside as Rionn approached. The three men looked up from their intense conversation to see the Head Mage stride purposefully into the room.

"We now know the significance of the northern Runestones," Rionn Lorr began.

All three men leaned forward and waited expectantly. Rionn Lorr met each gaze in turn and took a deep breath before continuing. He did not like what he was about to do, but he knew it had to be done.

"We have discovered that there are streams of molten rock flowing beneath the mountains in the northern ranges. There are fault lines, there, as well. All of this is in addition to the underground streams of water that connect to the Ocean Crystalline, of which were already aware.

"The demon is using the infected to go deep enough under the mountains to drop explosives into the underground magma streams. His aim is to rupture those streams to aggravate the fault lines and cause a catastrophic earthquake that could tear the Continent of Lorr to pieces."

"How did you come to know this?" King William asked.

"There are literally hundreds of texts, each with thousands of pages," Rionn Lorr answered. "It has taken some time to find the answers we needed."

The Head Mage hated having to mislead them, but he knew William Broadbow well. The king might dismiss this information if he knew it was based solely on the offworlder's vision and two men's possibly interpretation of an ambiguous passage in an ancient text. He took care, however, not to tell them an outright lie. It was true that he and several scholars researched his vast libraries. He simply made it a point to not say whether or not the information came specifically from those texts.

"And now the walkers have unchecked access to all of the explosives they need," the king said quietly.

Artemis and Geoffrey knew that Ridgeland had an immense store of explosives that they used for mining and for selling to the dwarves that mined the southern ranges.

"They must be stopped," Artemis said dejectedly.

"Yes," Geoffrey agreed. "Plague or not, they cannot be allowed to use those explosives."

None of them were excited about resuming the fighting. Rionn Lorr hated to be the one to tell them that it had to be done. The king exhaled heavily and it came out as a low growl of frustration. William was a warrior before he was thrust into the role of reluctant king. He knew how he would feel if he had to draw steel against fellow soldiers, friends, and family.

This was one of the hardest orders he ever had to give.

"Rionn, send word to the Alliance mages accompanying the royal soldiers. They are to resume the attack."

Rionn was careful not to tell an actual lie, but deceiving them intentionally was essentially the same thing. He had known these three men for over half of his life, so he knew that while they trusted him with their very lives, they might have a problem accepting the truth. In fact, Rionn Lorr did not know for certain that what he told them was even correct. He *believed* it was true, though, and that was enough for him.

The Head Mage turned and left the war room. As he continued to convince himself that he had been right in deceiving the three men, a flare of heat high on his chest brushed his thoughts aside. He stopped in mid stride and pulled the front of his robes forward in order to look down at the many the chains and thongs around his neck that held various pendants, charms, and talismans.

From six of the chains hung round, smooth, polished translucent stones tinted with green. Speaking stones. Each one was the twin to a stone carried by each of the half dozen Master Mages of the Conjurer's Alliance. The stones hung at different heights. The highest one was flaring.

That was the stone of the highest-ranking member of the Conjurer's Alliance. It was Master Mage Delthar's speaking stone. Rionn snatched it from his cloak. It flared an alert to an urgent message…a deadly urgent message. He closed the burning stone in his hand and focused on the energy radiating from it. Within seconds, he was seeing through Delthar's eyes and hearing through his ears.

He wanted to speak but he saw that the Master Mage was under a withering attack from the plague-ridden walking dead. They fought in a dark cave intermittently illuminated by the erratic white glow of Delthar's whitefyre. Rionn saw Delthar's profusely sweating hands held out before him as if they were his own. Every attacker at whom the Master Mage gestured with his left hand immediately burst into white-hot flames. Everyone he pointed at with the wand in his right hand was lifted by a powerful gust of telekinetic force and tossed back down the tunnel from which they were streaming. But the infected continued to pour out of the wide mouth of the tunnel into the larger cave.

A surge of fear rushed through Rionn at the sight of the flames. He immediately thought of the explosives and the danger in which the Master Mage was placing himself. But when he focused his vision more sharply through Delthar's eyes his fear somewhat diminished. No explosives were visible among the attackers. Rionn Lorr surmised that this attacking group was an advance team to clear the way of any resistance while the others transported the explosives.

The Head Mage was also reassured by the acute mastery Delthar displayed over the whitefyre he wielded. The bursts were deftly confined to the bodies that fueled them and the intensity of the flames reduced the bodies to ash in a matter of seconds. The fire then extinguished itself the instant its grisly task was complete.

Delthar tried to strike the walking dead as soon as they appeared. He incinerated or threw back most of them but some managed to get through the flames or around the gusts. As Delthar diverted his attack to strike them down or away, even more poured into the cave. The Master Mage found himself being pushed back further and further until he was only a few feet away from the only other opening at the rear of the cave.

Rionn Lorr was thankful the Master Mage stayed behind to keep the walking dead at bay. While Delthar had been as clueless as everyone else about the creatures' aims, he believed as Rionn did that the demons could not be allowed to do whatever it was they were trying to do. The Head Mage was impressed by Delthar's ability to conjure two different types of powerful magic simultaneously and with such precision without having to utter any spells verbally. Rionn was also fearful for the old wizard. He saw his mentor's liver-spotted hands shaking from exhaustion even as he conjured. He could hear Delthar's labored breathing.

"I am glad you found the time to answer my summons, Head Mage," Delthar said, somehow managing to inject sarcasm into his winded voice.

"The king is sending the soldiers back into the fray," Rionn said quickly. "If you can hold out…"

"I cannot," Delthar replied. "Too many of them…"

"Then get out of there," Rionn urged. "You've delayed them long enough. Reinforcements will be there shortly."

"The soldiers will only be able to attack from the rear. These creatures may very well have accomplished their goal by the time the soldiers fight their way to the front. I must stay here to buy the army a little more time."

"No, Delthar," Rionn said firmly. "I'm ordering you to leave now!"

Rionn heard the Master Mage chuckle sadly.

"I remember when *I* was the one who gave *you* orders, my student," Delthar said. "But I must defy you in this, and give you yet another lesson. Your affection for me compels you to give that order even though you know it's not the logical decision. You know better than to let your passions rule your actions."

"Master Mage Delthar –" Rionn began desperately, but the old wizard interrupted him.

"I'll give whatever I have to in order to keep the Kingdom of Lorr safe, including my life. And one last lesson: a beast's natural instinct may lead it to feed on other species, but with the proper training, that same beast can be made to feed on its own kind."

"What does that mean?"

"I must now devote my full concentration to the task at hand," Delthar said. "May the Old Ones guide your hands and mind, Head Mage."

With that, the Master Mage broke the connection. Rionn Lorr looked up from his now dim speaking stone. King William, Artemis, and Geoffrey stood outside the war room door looking at the Head Mage with more than a trace of sorrow in their eyes. In his intense discussion with Delthar, he failed to notice that they had entered the hallway. They had been listening to Rionn's side of the conversation.

"He gives *his* life for the Kingdom that bears *my* name," Rionn Lorr said angrily. "His sacrifice will not be in vain."

The Head Mage walked swiftly away, making his way back to the alchemists' laboratory. He replayed Delthar's last words in his mind over and over and wondered what they meant. The Master Mage was telling him something of significance concerning their plight but Rionn was not sure what that something was.

He entered the laboratory and sat in a corner of the long, narrow research room while activity continued all around him. The sounds of metal clinking on glass and stone, hushed conversations and hurried footsteps comprised a prolonged drone that he barely noticed. He was too busy running through scenarios that might make sense of Delthar's words.

A beast's natural instinct may lead it to feed on other species, but with the proper training, that same beast can be made to feed on its own kind.

What beast? Was he suggesting that they turn the walkers against one another? How would they do that? In their demented state, he feared the infected would not even respond to mind controlling magic. And even if they did, Rionn knew of no spell or magic that could affect such a large number of people at once. Attempting to turn them against one another did not strike him as the solution.

He decided to make a mental list of everything he knew about their predicament and apply Delthar's lesson to each one. The seconds ticked away as he thought of and then dismissed several items before finally pausing at one.

He recalled the time frame surrounding the emergence of the plague. Captain Johnican's wife had been interviewed thoroughly after she finally recovered from the horror of her husband going mad with the plague, transforming into the monster that they called the walking dead, or walkers, and subsequently being brought down by Delthar. She told her interviewers that Johnican did not start displaying any sign of sickness until three nights earlier.

Three nights earlier was the same night the walkers emerged from their graves. So what could Delthar's lesson have to do with the time frame? Other than the fact that some spells take time to unfold, he could not think of anything. The spell could have been cast that very night or it could have been cast years earlier and timed to go into affect when it did. He could not see how the timing of the spell related to the lesson.

According to Ethan Sureblade, however, that was also the night he and the rest of the Keeper's Hounds confronted Tauran and his mercenaries with their captured demon. At first they assumed it was a weird religious ritual practiced by one of the obscure cults that existed in relative secret in the shadows of the Known Lands. The Hounds had run into that sort of thing on several of their missions. On more than one occasion, they found people worshipping captured lower-level demons and even making sacrifices to them. Later, he and others had come to believe that what the Keeper's Hounds actually witnessed was the casting of the spell that started the plague.

This conclusion, as useful as the information might be, still did not explain what Delthar said about giving beasts the proper training to feed on one another.

During Delthar's report about the Captain Johnican tragedy, The Master Mage told him that he felt a slight residue of magical discharge just before Captain Johnican attacked him and Geoffrey. But what was the catalyst? If Rionn knew the particulars of the spell he could perhaps find a counter spell.

He thought more about the scene that was described to him by One-shot, the commander of the Keeper's Hounds. The mysterious cloaked wizard and Tauran held a demon in one cage and an infant on a makeshift stone altar. How could that have started the plague? Was Delthar saying that magic was used to train the infected to attack the non-infected? But they already knew that.

Or did they?

In truth, the infected only attacked when provoked. They did not deviate from their path. They moved east almost mindlessly until someone engaged them and completely ignored those who fled from them. In Ridgeland, they did not pursue the soldiers into the hills when the order to retreat was given. All of these facts led Rionn to believe that the walkers were not instructed to attack humans. They had been instructed to transport explosives into the Runestones and to lay low anyone that tried to impede their progress.

From what Rionn Lorr had been told, the infected reminded him of army ants that attacked anything in their path while on their march. But if Delthar was not referring to the infected being the trained beasts, to what was he referring?

And then it came to him. The thought of army ants reminded him of the miniscule organisms swarming the cells of Johnican's flesh. Raxe had called them "bugs."

"Bugs," Rionn said aloud.

He rose and walked over to the nearest alchemist employing a scope. With a tap and a nod from Rionn, the alchemist moved away to let the Head Mage look through the scope. Rionn looked again at the multi-legged bugs attached to the cells.

The legs twitched periodically but the tiny creatures never left their perch. Rionn could have easily destroyed them but he had not yet found a way to kill the organisms without destroying the flesh on which they resided. Destroying the flesh defeated the purpose of his efforts. He was searching for a way to eliminate the infection without killing the living hosts.

Instead, as he had done so many times before, Rionn dropped a spec of magic onto the cell to repel one of the organisms. And just as before, the tiny creature was not destroyed. It merely detached itself and backed away from the cell for the briefest moment before rushing back to it and reestablishing its hold. Rionn noticed how the organism moved quickly, almost hungrily, to reattach itself. It appeared to Rionn Lorr the bugs were literally *feeding* on the cell, the same way a pack or flock of scavengers fed on carrion.

"By the Gods," Rionn Lorr breathed.

Did the old Master Mage have it figured out? Rionn had been thinking that the tiny bugs were by-products of the spell or perhaps even helped it spread, but now he thought they were both the targets as well as the vehicles of the spell. He instructed the alchemist he had displaced to bring him a sample of flesh from the second level demon the Hounds had slain the night that foul spell was cast. While the man rushed to do as he was instructed, Rionn found a sterile scalpel and took a deep breath. By the time the alchemist returned, the Head Mage had a bandage on his thumb and he had replaced the sample of Johnican's flesh with a sample of his own.

Rionn instructed the alchemist to remove a sliver of the preserved demon flesh and place it on the small glass plate with his sample. Rionn immediately saw that the demon sample was covered with the tiny organisms. But unlike the infected human sample, the bugs were inert. He carefully moved the samples closer until they were touching. Rionn watched for several seconds before he realized that he was holding his breath. He exhaled and continued to watch. Minutes had passed and still nothing happened. Rionn's neck started to get sore from its bent position.

Just as he was about to lift his head, he felt a slight tremor in the air around him. All of his attention went back to the image in the scope and on the aura of magic in the environment around him. Even though the sensation of energy that rose from the base of the scope was softer and swifter than a single flap of a fly's wing, Rionn noticed it instantly. He stared even more intensely through the scope and finally saw movement in the demon sample.

Within seconds, the tiny legs of the bugs in direct contact with the demon sample were twitching. And then they swarmed Rionn's sample. Some of the little organisms began to attack his sample while others seemed to attack each other. But as the bugs came into contact with one another, other, smaller bugs emerged from the union. They were mating and reproducing in a matter of seconds!

Rionn watched in fascination as the color of his healthy cells began to turn dull and change shape. The bugs continued to multiply until they totally concealed every cell in the sample. Within another few seconds, smaller bugs were crowded completely off of the sample.

Rionn prepared a sprinkle of destructive magic in the event that the detached bugs started to move toward other potential hosts. The magic however, was not needed. The organisms folded their tiny legs and curled into themselves before disintegrating only moments after losing contact with the human sample.

Rionn noticed that while some of the bugs he thought were mating actually were mating, many of them were not mating at all. Some had begun to actually attack and tear one another apart while others mated and the rest fed on the cells. This continued until the number of bugs quickly and visibly decreased. This reduction continued until there were only a relative few of the bugs remaining on each cell. After their activity stabilized, the surviving organisms continued to feed. The feeding went on for a time peacefully and the bugs no longer approached one another to battle or reproduce.

There was another fly-wing flash of magic and then the cell twisted, shriveled, and went completely gray. It was now identical to Johnican's sample. Rionn jumped so quickly that the alchemist behind him let out a little yelp.

"The bugs were dormant," Rionn Lorr said to the startled alchemist standing behind him. "The spell causes them to awaken when in contact with human flesh. The bugs had to have been embedded into their victims' skin during their encounter with demons and were lying dormant within them until the spell was cast."

Other scientists and alchemists heard Rionn and started to spread the word around the research room. The alchemist standing behind him stepped closer as Rionn peered into the scope again.

"Look," Rionn instructed one of the alchemists. As the young woman looked through the scope, Rionn spoke to the other alchemists and scientists that had circled him.

"The organisms multiply and feed. When their numbers grow too large, they compete with one another for a spot on which to feed. That behavior is common among many living creatures. It must be their natural instinct as well. When their numbers are small enough so that there is no competition, they feed in relative peace until they are introduced to another host. When that happens, the cycle begins anew."

"So the spell does not compel them to attack the human flesh," realized the woman looking through the scope. "They would do that anyway. The spell merely awakened them from their dormancy."

"And it must have been a compound spell," Rionn added. "There was one spell to awaken the organisms. That would trigger the activation of a second spell to implant within their hosts the suggestion to move on Ridgeland."

"Is there a way you can reverse both of the spells?" the alchemist asked.

"No," Rionn Lorr admitted, "at least not that I know of. But the bugs may have shown me a way to combat them." He paused and turned to the young male alchemist beside him. "Niven," he said, "bring a cup of water."

The Head Mage reached into his loose-hanging sleeve and produced a small pouch. He tugged the drawstring to open it and stuck his right thumb and forefinger through the lip of the pouch. He pulled out a pinch of powder so small that the men and women around him could not see it.

He pushed his fingers into his left palm then closed his hand into a fist. The alchemists and healers looked on as the Head Mage closed his eyes and whispered words that they could barely hear and could not understand. A violet glow began to shimmer through his clenched fingers. The glow intensified as Rionn Lorr's foreign words quickened and rose in volume. The glow faded when Rionn's voice lowered and went silent.

When he opened his eyes, Rionn saw Niven standing before him holding a tin of water. "Thank you," Rionn said as he took the cup with his left hand. He released the pinch of powder into the tin and lightly shook the glass. The alchemists near enough to see inside the cup looked on as the clear water turned into a deep, nearly opaque violet.

"Scalpel," Rionn asked. Nevin instantly put one into his waiting hand. Rionn dipped the small blade into the purple water, shook off most of the liquid and then brought the scalpel over to the sample. The young woman stood so that the Head Mage could sit down at the sample again.

Rionn looked into the scope and held the blade over his sample so that the small amount of liquid could run down to the tip of the blade, where the liquid formed a droplet that eventually escaped the blade and dropped onto the sample.

Almost instantly, the remaining organisms detached from his sample to attack each other just as they had when the sample had become overcrowded. This time, though, they did not stop battling when their numbers decreased. They continued to battle and destroy each other until there was only one of the bugs remaining on the sample. That bug scrambled back to the demon sample, where it even attacked the dormant bugs.

Once all of the dormant bugs on the demon sample were destroyed, the organism went back to the human sample and resumed its feeding. It fed and fed until it eventually burst into a dark liquid that soon dissipated until it disappeared.

The Head Mage allowed himself a moment to smile in cautious relief before handing the cup back to Nevin.

"Put a drop, a small drop on the other samples and see what happens."

Nevin did as he was told and passed the cup to other alchemists who did the same. Each gasped in turn as they saw the same results Rionn Lorr had. Nevin returned to Rionn's side.

"If I may, Master Lorr," Nevin said in a tone approaching awe, "what manner of alchemy did you use? The potion you created is eliminating the 'bugs' on every sample."

"It wasn't alchemy," Rionn said. "It was merely a spell. The powder is hex dust. As you know, hex dust serves many purposes. I used it as a vehicle to transfer my spell to the water. It was a compound spell similar to the one that I suspect was used to create the infected victims.

"One part of my compound spell increases their hunger and competitive instincts so that they destroy each other whether the sample is crowded or not. They will then gorge themselves without pause until their bodies can no longer contain the fluids.

"The other part is a self-replication spell that causes the spell to multiply within liquid until the liquid is saturated."

"You couldn't reverse the spell," Niven said, "so you merely intensified its effects. Genius."

"Only in its simplicity," Rionn Lorr concurred. "And we have the Master Mage Delthar to thank for the concept." His tone turned urgent as continued. "Niven, gather as many barrels of water as you can. Have the barrels brought here and saturate each one, just a few drops from the tin will do. I must pay a visit to Glynhalla."

"The weather witch?" Niven asked. He knew better than to ask why.

"Yes. Now hurry."

As the young alchemist sprinted out of the laboratory, Rionn began to work out the next part of the plan he was quickly forming. He hoped he would not be too late.

Chapter 4: Finding Access

4.1

Azhju'lestra stood at the edge of the deep ravine and slowly raised her arms. Her hands were spread wide, and as they ascended, so did her long hair, as if a soft breeze wafted up from the ground. Raxe, standing a few feet away from Rell Kallen, could not help but think of her mother, Sabrina, the Mistress of Sea. Sabrina's hair moved like that all the time whether she was using magic or not. It looked natural underwater, where waves would make anyone's long, flowing hair float on the moving water. It was a bit disconcerting, however, when she was out of the water and it still undulated as if moved by an invisible current.

By the time Azh's hands were level with her shoulders, Raxe could hear the sound of rushing water growing louder. When her arms were finally perfectly vertical, a waterspout came rushing up into view. It stopped rising when it stretched about a foot over Raxe's head and then it moved to within inches of the lip of the two-mile deep chasm. This waterspout was much wider than the first one she had called up to ferry them from the bridge. It was almost seven feet wide by Raxe's estimation.

He and the Ranger Elf watched as a small dome of air formed in the side of the spout right in front of the trio. It grew steadily and rapidly. Within moments a giant, invisible dome with a flat bottom hovered in the column of water. It was easily wide enough to hold the three of them. The girl lowered her hands to her sides but the water – and her hair – remained elevated. She looked at the human and elf and said:

"Come."

She stepped out into the dome of air within the waterspout. The soles of her hiking boots sank less than half an inch into the water and held her firm. Raxe and Rell Kallen stayed on solid ground. Azh looked at the two males and cocked her head in confusion.

"Are you not coming?"

"Riding on top is one thing," Raxe said defensively. "But if you're gonna do what I think you're gonna do…" he winced and shook his head.

"Do you not trust me?" Azh asked.

"It's not that I don't trust you, sweetheart. It's just...well..."

Raxe looked at her wide eyes. They looked light brown from this distance and from the shadow cast by the hood of water hovering more than two feet above her head. But those eyes were also confused and a little sad.

Raxe sighed. "Of course I trust you, girl." He stepped out onto the water.

He thought about the words his daughter spoke before they escaped from the doomed sky-sleigh in their uniwings and projected that thought to her:

"It looks like fun."

Azh smiled.

Raxe turned to face Rell Kallen. "What about you, elf? I don't think we'll be able to let you into the mountain from the inside."

Rell Kallen looked over the edge of the ravine. His sharp vision could not pierce the shadows and see the water miles below. He looked back up at the Children of the Old Ones.

Did this girl expect him to let her ferry him through an underground stream? As an elf in general, and as a Ranger Elf in particular, Rell Kallen was not accustomed to putting his life in the hands of others. Especially children. As resourceful as he was, he had no skill or magic at his disposal to escape from such a predicament should something go wrong. His Phoenix stone would do him no good down there.

But there was his duty to consider. He vowed to his queen that he would do whatever it took to acquire the Hell Key. The order of Ranger Elves did not take their vows lightly. Estra'hil Vah, beautiful matriarch goddess of the Elf Nations, would surely frown on him for shirking his duty. She would, however, welcome him with open arms if he died in the line of duty.

"And, oh yeah," Raxe added. He pointed behind and to the right of the Ranger Elf. "There's that."

Rell Kallen turned and looked in the direction of the offworlder's pointing finger. A pack of nine wallowgrumps, man-sized, frog-like, shark-toothed creatures, were leaping nimbly down the face of an adjacent mountain. They were hundreds of yards away but moving quickly.

The elf sneered and stepped into the waterspout.

"Be quick about it, then," he ordered.

Azh smiled again. Water suddenly rushed up to cover them, turning the vertically oriented dome of water into a spherical air pocket. The light from the daytime sky penetrated the column just enough to illuminate the inside of the sphere, but all they could see beyond it was moving, frothing water. It was like standing behind a heavy waterfall, only the water was falling *up*.

A few seconds passed while they just stood there. Raxe could not feel them descending. They merely watched the upside-down waterfall. Rell Kallen folded his lean arms and tapped his foot rapidly, splashing water onto Raxe's boot.

Raxe finally turned to his daughter. "This is interesting and all, but when are we going to move?"

Azh smiled wider. An oval window, roughly a foot and a half long and half as wide, irised open in the wall of water before them. The opening showed them the sheer stony wall of the ravine rushing past them in a blur.

Rell Kallen twitched a blonde eyebrow but said nothing.

"Oh," Raxe said as water rushed back in to close the little window. "Smooth ride, Azh."

The soft illumination within the sphere began to dim. It grew darker until the interior was pitch-black. Raxe was not sure how fast they were moving but he knew they would eventually travel through an underground stream and he had no idea how far under the mountain they had to travel. What worried him the most was the possibility that the deadly border warding Mar-dah's mountain descended this low. If it did, they could run right into it.

Raxe's estimated that only several minutes had passed even though it felt much. The darkness was starting to make him claustrophobic. Though he could not see anything he remembered how wide Azh's sphere was, and in his mind's eye he was imagining it closing in around them. The sound of rushing water surrounding them seemed to grow louder and closer. He could hear the slow, deep breaths of the Ranger Elf begin to quicken as time wore on.

And then a dull blue-green illumination filtered into the sphere. Or perhaps Raxe's eyes were growing accustomed to the darkness. He could see the silhouettes of his daughter and the elf and he could just barely make out the water surrounding them. He could also see silhouettes of sea creatures swimming to and fro outside of their air bubble. Some of the shapes were familiar, simple fish of varying sizes or eels of different lengths. But a few of the shapes were not familiar at all and were more than a little sinister.

Raxe saw something that looked like the shadow of a giant spider with twice as many legs. Each leg ended in a webbed foot that paddled it smoothly and swiftly through the water. He saw something else that had the outline of a serpent with a pair oversized fins just behind what Raxe assumed was its head and another pair near its tail.

The weird shapes distracted and unnerved him so much that he nearly missed the fact that the surrounding water was no longer rushing upward. It was flowing in a gentle current from left to right. A minute later the flow changed direction again and started moving down.

No, Raxe realized. The current was not moving down. The sphere was rising. The water eventually fell away and they rose softly to the surface of a slow moving stream, its color stained a sickly blue-green as it flowed through a huge cave. Behind them was a high wall that soared straight up over fifty feet, where it met a stalagmite-riddled ceiling. In front of them, less than a foot away and a foot above the surface of the stream was the cave floor.

The three of them stepped up onto the cave floor and cast cautious looks at the environment. The space was humid and musty and dim. What little light there was came from the thick blanket of weird glowing lichen growing on the cavern walls. The cave was roughly rectangular and about the size of half of a football field. The stream cut across the short side of the rectangle. Stalagmites sprouted from the floor here and there, but other than that and the stream behind them, the cave was empty.

THE KEY QUEST

Now that he was inside the mountain and the lethal barrier surrounding it, Raxe could feel the aura of the Hell Key. It was a cold, pervasive feeling of foreboding that radiated in stifling waves. He experienced the sensation of standing at the shore of a vast ocean, watching a storm roll in from a darkened horizon. He could feel rather than see sharp flashes of twisted, branching bolts of power arcing from one cloud of energy to another. The sensation reminded Raxe of the bright shock of pain he felt from across the WorldGate when Mar-dah first touched the Hell Key three years earlier.

"The Hell Key is here," Azh said. "It's somewhere far above us."

"Yeah," Raxe concurred, looking at the high ceiling as if he could see the enchanted greatsword through the stone.

Raxe looked at the four walls around them for some way to progress deeper into the mountain. Mountains and caves were starting to fray his nerves. From his trek into the cave of the dragon king WorldHopper during his first visit to Lorr to the time spent with the dwarves just days earlier, Raxe had had his fill of mountain caves.

"Now we have to get out of here and find the Hell Key," he said. "But I don't see a way out."

"We need to hurry," Azh warned. "The life in the underground stream is alarmed. Something is coming." Azh fell silent for a moment, looking expectantly at the stream and listening to sounds of the creatures in the underground stream. Her big eyes went even wider. "The wallowgrumps. They followed us down the ravine."

Raxe thought back again to his introduction to a wallowgrump. The massive amphibious creature took three bullets from Raxe's high-powered nine-millimeter pistol and was more annoyed than injured. Close quarters combat with one of those things, even with Demonsbane, would be foolhardy at best. Fighting several was out of the question.

Rell Kallen must have shared the sentiment. After Azh spoke the elf immediately began to pace around the dimly lit cave, his long, narrow nose sniffing, his pointed ears twitching. Raxe did not know what Rell hoped to find. The only things he could see were the uneven rock walls, the stalagmite-riddled floor and the stalactite-riddled ceiling.

He also saw his daughter growing more agitated with each second that passed.

"Can you control wallowgrumps the way your mom could control aquatic creatures?" he asked hopefully.

"We can influence aquatic life," Azh corrected. "But wallowgrumps are amphibious. They can stay underwater for a time but not forever. They are resistant to my – and my mother's – control."

"Damn," Raxe mumbled. He used his left hand to draw Demonsbane from its frog at his right hip. With a grunt he snapped the weapon painfully into his damaged claw of a right hand. His fingers, permanently frozen into a near fist, involuntarily tightened on the handle of the enchanted battleaxe. He took a deep breath against the agony as he pulled Questblade from the sheath hanging from his weapons belt at his left hip. "How long before they get to us?"

"I don't know," Azh answered. "But from the panic stirring underwater, we do not have much time."

Raxe remembered the larger creatures he spied as his daughter transported them through the underground waterways. If *those* things let wallowgrumps pass without challenging them, those monsters were even more formidable than he thought.

He frowned and looked over at Rell Kallen, who was near the far end of the cave. He was still searching, but he started striding purposefully toward the far wall.

"Elf! We're gonna need you down here," he called.

"I think not!" Rell called back. "You need to come this way. I've found our egress!"

Raxe and Azh sprinted toward Rell Kallen's end of the rectangular cave. All Raxe could see was a solid wall. Its surface was irregular but straight for the most part. There was no time for doubt, though, and no reason for the elf to mislead them. With his superior senses, Rell Kallen could have easily detected something that Raxe could not.

They were about thirty yards away from Rell when they heard loud splashes behind them. Raxe looked over his shoulder and saw the wallowgrumps leaping from the stream. The creatures' large, bulbous eyes lighted upon the trio even before their clawed webbed feet slapped against the stone floor. They immediately gave chase.

4.2

THE DUNGEONS OF LORR PALACE

The female prisoner's head snapped up when she heard the loud metallic clink of her cell door unlocking. Long, dark, unkempt hair streaked with gray fell across her eyes and she had to brush them away with pale, slender fingers. A strand caught in the serrated edges of her gnawed upon fingernails and she winced when it was plucked painfully from her head as she pulled her hand away.

The pain was quickly replaced by stunned confusion and more than a bit of cold fear. She could not recall the last time she had heard the lock function. The only sounds that she heard from that door since she was imprisoned three years earlier were the softer click and light grind of metal on wood when her food slot was opened and closed. And there was the occasional taunting from some of the less mature guardsmen that patrolled the musty dungeons.

Most of the time, though, there was only maddening silence. There were only two reasons the doors opened to prisoners in this dungeon: to be released or to be escorted to their execution. She was scheduled to be released in forty-two years. Based on her crime, she held no illusions that her sentence would ever be shortened.

Her dark brown eyes squinted at the sudden flood of torchlight. It was not bright but it was significantly brighter than the wan torchlight her jailers allowed to beam through the narrow eye slots the guards left open for a couple of hours each day, or when they opened the food slot at the bottom of the door.

The woman stood defiantly in her ragged gray prisoner's tunic and plain long skirt. She tried to radiate strength and gall but the attempt was thoroughly diminished by her long, skinny frame that was only a missed meal or two from appearing malnourished.

The torchlight framed the shadow of a tall, lean man dressed in modest wizard's robes with shoulder length hair.

When the woman's eyes finally adjusted to the light it was all she could do to stifle the gasp that threatened to escape. She would not give him the satisfaction.

"To what do I owe this *honor*?" she sneered.

"Glynhalla the Rainmaker," the Head Mage began without preamble. "How would you like to shorten your sentence?"

Glynalla's eyes narrowed to slits. "What would you have me do, wizard?"

"The same thing that put you here," Rionn answered evenly. "Only this time, you would be doing it *for* the kingdom and not against it."

"You want me to make it rain for you?" she asked incredulously. "Why?"

"That is none of your concern," Rionn answered with a dismissive wave. "Considering the part you played in Mardah's schemes, which is part of the reason we are in our current predicament, you should be eager to do anything to curry favor with King William and me."

"Surely you don't think I'm able to use my power in this tiny, windowless cell," she complained.

"I know you can," Rionn returned. "This cell isn't much smaller than that hovel of yours in the southern Runestones. From there, you made it rain for nearly a week in the northern regions of the Kingdom. For what I ask of you, you don't have to affect a distance nearly as far away and the area is not nearly as vast."

Glynhalla smiled and folded her arms across her spare bosom. "And why would you ask such a favor of me? You are the Head Mage, supposedly a Child of the Old Ones. Surely you or one of your flunkies can perform this feat."

Rionn Lorr frowned impatiently but managed to keep his voice steady, low, and even. "You know full well why. None of us are elementals."

"Oh, yes," Glynhalla taunted. "Of course. After three years of imprisonment I'd almost forgotten how much of a stickler you are for the 'proper' use of magic.

"Hmmm, let me see if I can recall this correctly. A nonelemental using magic to affect the weather could shift the precious balance of Nature. For that matter, it is just as dangerous to draw your magic *from* Nature, is it not?"

The way she said it caused the head mage to raise an eyebrow. Glynhalla pierced him with a knowing glare. "I am experienced enough to know full well the possible consequences for such a rash action. You did that very thing during the Cursed Opening, did you not?"

Rionn's frown deepened.

Glynhalla continued with a smug little smile. "It was the magic that you employed to transform the Tyne River into a demon-killing weapon. You cast bolts of destruction in every direction for nearly the entire length of the river. Not even you can call upon power of that magnitude from your own internal magic.

"That's right, Head Mage, even here word drifts down to me about the state of the kingdom. Guards, visitors that are allowed to see other prisoners, they speak often of what goes on beyond these walls. They speak softly but I hear them. My ears have grown more sensitive with all of the silence down in this cold cell. So perhaps you share some of the responsibility for this current predicament."

The frown upon Rionn's face faded to a cold, blank stare. "Will you help us or not, rainmaker?"

"If I do, how many years will be removed from my sentence?"

"Ten."

"Ten?" Glynhalla scoffed. "So, I'll be seventy-five instead of eighty-five when I am free, assuming I live that long. Please, mage, at least make it worth the effort. Twenty years. Surely the safety of the Kingdom that Bears Your Name is worth that."

The Head Mage scratched his square chin and regarded the female prisoner thoughtfully. "You know, Glynhalla, I am very aware of what my critics and enemies say about me. One of the biggest criticisms is that I am too kindhearted, too compassionate. I was reminded as much by the royal council when I insisted upon imprisonment as your punishment instead of...the alternative."

Glynhalla's eyes narrowed again as Rionn continued.

"Indeed." he went on. "King William himself questioned my common sense when I argued against popular opinion regarding your sentence. The fact that you are haggling with me when so much is at stake is starting to make me believe that my critics are right. Perhaps I *am* too compassionate. Perhaps my first step toward remedying this condition should be to concede to popular opinion and insist that your alternative punishment be implemented."

Glynhalla the Rainmaker was serving a sentence of forty-five years for treason. She had assisted Mar-dah by using her elemental power to cause a slow but steady rain that lasted the better part of a week. The rains flooded the rivers and made bridges impassable to slow the Royal Infantry in their defense of the Kingdom. She knew full well what the "alternative" punishment was for her actions.

"You would not…" she stopped short when she saw the cold look in Rionn's dark blue eyes.

"Rain witch," Rionn began, his deep voice frighteningly calm. "Do not underestimate the lengths to which I will go to protect my kingdom."

A fleeting yet agonizing knife of agony flashed through her head and her mind. Glynhalla winced in pain and surprise. She remembered that pain very well. It was the same assault the Head Mage visited upon her from hundreds of miles away when he discovered her causing the rains that flooded the Tyne River and its tributaries. Back then she thought for a fleeting moment that the pain would kill her. She could only imagine the pain he could inflict upon her while standing this close.

"I'll need candles," she said, "to help focus my power."

4.3

OUTSKIRTS OF RIDGELAND

Arrowhead, trailed by Little Mole, three of the locals who volunteered to help, with Hammer bringing up the rear, all followed Ethan as he trotted along the grassy base of the mountain.

"I don't understand," Hammer called ahead to Ethan through ragged gasps of breath. "Why are we running *away* from where the infected are entering the mountain?"

"We won't be able to fight our way into the mountain from the rear of their line," Ethan called back. "Not without help. We have to work our way around to the front of their ranks so that we can help Master Delthar fend them off."

"Yes!" Little Mole said excitedly as he easily kept pace with the taller adults. "I can take us through the caves from another entrance that will allow us to head them off."

"No," said Ethan. "You are not leading us into a fight. I'll take us through the caves. You are to locate Jon the Firemaster. If he's recovered enough to fight, bring him."

"You've only been in the mountain caves once," Little Mole argued.

"And you did a great job of showing me the different passages, Little Mole," praised Ethan.

"You can't possibly remember all of those paths," Little Mole said incredulously.

"Yes, he can," Arrowhead interjected. "Now do as the man says and find the Firemaster."

With a snarl, Little Mouse veered off to the left and went to find Jon.

Hammer guffawed from the end of the line of runners. "So, when exactly did Eagle Eye become a *man*?"

"Shut your mouth, you ox," Arrowhead yelled over her shoulder. "Save your breath so you can keep up!"

Several minutes of running brought them to the same fissure Little Mole took Ethan through a few days earlier. All of them slipped through easily with the exception of Hammer, who had to turn sideways and blow all of the air out of his lungs to squeeze through. Huffing and puffing, he had to sprint to catch up with the group. If not for the glow of the torch that one of them lit, he would have lost them. He knew he would not have been able to trust the fading echoes of their footfalls.

Ethan led them unerringly through the down-sloping labyrinthine interior of the mountain. The torchlight revealed the passing of several tunnels. Some of them, according to Little Mole, terminated at dead ends or turned back onto themselves to form large loops spanning more than a mile in which an unwary explorer could get lost indefinitely. Others trailed upward to eventually reach openings at ground level or in the higher elevations of the mountain face.

One of the paths terminated at an intersecting tunnel leading to the cave containing the hole that provided a distant view of the lava flows in the depths of the earth. In the opposite direction, that same tunnel led to a well-hidden opening at ground level somewhere on the other side of the mountain. That was where they expected to find Master Mage Delthar.

It took several more minutes – that in their urgency felt like hours – for them to finally find the tunnel. They were assisted by the sounds of battle. The noise was strangely absent of the sounds of normal human combat. There were no grunts of exertion; there were no roars of fear, anger or pain. The clink of metal could be heard clearly but it was not the loud bursts of metal on metal that one expected to hear in a pitched battle. It was more like the jangle one would hear during an armed march. The group did, however, hear the sounds of countless heavy footfalls, metal striking stone, and the resonating boom of exploding rock.

The tunnel they ran through ended at the perpendicular tunnel Ethan sought. It stretched and curved out of view to the left and right. Ethan turned left, the direction from which the sound carried, and rushed down a corridor that curved slowly to the right after nearly thirty yards.

The sounds grew louder as the group progressed. Bright white light flashed from around the curve. The flashes were bright enough to swallow the soft yellow glow of the torches that Ethan and one of the locals carried.

A frightening sight greeted the small group when they rounded the curve. Master Mage Delthar, looking haggard and worn, stood only a few yards away from an onslaught of the walkers. The old wizard stood straight as a young sapling, his arms lifted high and spread to either side like narrow branches. One hand was opened wide and glowing with flickering white energy. The other clutched his wand.

Bursts of whitefyre leapt from the palm of his free hand to strike and consume some of the raging creatures closing in on him. Every few seconds he would flick the wand, flinging many of the charging creatures backward and into their comrades or sending large loose rocks into the crowd to crush skulls or break legs. The ones with broken legs clawed their way forward. The ones with crushed skulls, some of them virtually headless, nevertheless continued to trudge blindly forward.

Sweat streamed from Delthar's wrinkled face, which was frozen in a grimace of exhaustion and determination. He was deathly silent but his pain was betrayed by the squinting of his icy gray eyes. His long white hair, usually thick and unruly, was pasted flat to his head from perspiration. His wizard's robe and cloak clung to his long, thin frame as if he had just emerged from a pond. His body began to shudder and sway. He did not fall but he looked as if he would keel over at any moment.

Ethan snatched the *gun* from his back while the others, save Hammer, who leveled his massive war hammer, pulled their blades. The group barely took two steps before Delthar waved them away, sending an invisible force at them that stopped them in their tracks as if they had walked into an invisible wall.

"No!" the Master Mage commanded. "Go back from whence you came. Now!"

"But Master Delthar," Ethan yelled, "You need –"

"I need nothing but your obedience!" Delthar cried, pausing to inflict more damage on the walkers.

"You cannot hope to defeat so many on your own," Ethan argued.

Delthar did not answer right away. Instead, he sent a blast of magical energy at the front lines of the infected that sent them tumbling back, the effort finally drawing a grunt of exertion from the accomplished old wizard. And then he closed his fist. In response to that action, a heavy tremor shook the cave and the surrounding tunnels.

Ethan glanced at Arrowhead and the others, who looked back at him with the same worry Ethan knew was shrouding his own countenance.

"I'm bringing down these tunnels!" Delthar warned, his strong voice resonating above the ominous rumbling within the mountain. "The cave in will bury these creatures and seal this tunnel from the outside. Unless you want to be buried with us, I suggest you run as fast as you can."

"With *us*?" Ethan echoed. "Master –"

"*GO!*" the wizard roared. The rumbling increased in volume in response to his admonishment. "I'll not have enough strength left to teleport to safety." He had to stop to draw a raspy breath through pained lungs. "Secure any other openings to these tunnels from the infected! Do not let my sacrifice be for naught!"

The group hesitated for a moment but was quickly spurred into action when dust and loose rock began to sprinkle down upon them. They turned to run back the way they came just as sound of wrenching stone echoed through the dark tunnels like the angry growl of some gargantuan beast awakening from a long slumber. Ethan glanced over his shoulder to see massive chunks of rock and soil crash down from the cave ceiling near the old wizard.

Master Mage Delthar turned and met Ethan's gaze for a fleeting instant. In that instant, Ethan did not see the legendary and proud Master Mage. What he saw was a sad and tired man who had lived a long and hard life and knew his end had come.

In the next instant, he and the walkers closing on him disappeared amid a deafening crash of falling earth.

The tunnel they ran through continued to quake violently. Ethan sprinted past the others to once again take the lead. It took him longer than he expected to overtake Hammer, who was pacing the rest of group. Ethan had never seen the big man move so fast.

As they approached the intersecting tunnel that led to their entry point, Ethan remembered that the cave with the sinister hole in the floor had a branching warren that led to another opening at ground level. A jolt of fear struck him when he thought about Delthar's last words:

Secure any other openings to these tunnels from the infected! Do not let my sacrifice be for naught!

With that thought in mind, Ethan kept going straight instead of turning right at the intersecting tunnel that would have taken them to where they entered.

"Ethan," Arrowhead called nervously through panting breaths. "This is *not* the way we came!"

Ethan called back to her, but she could not hear him over the sudden thunder that raged through the mountain. The chain reaction caused by Delthar's cave-in followed them through the tunnels, consuming the ceiling and walls close behind them. Ethan looked straight ahead and pushed himself to run faster. He was too afraid to look back again. The action would slow him down, and besides, he had no wish to see his companions crushed by a falling mountain. All he could do was run as fast as he could and pray to all of the Old Ones that both he and his group would make it to safety.

His prayers were answered.

The quaking ceased moments before their path opened into a small cave where the group stopped to catch their breath. Ethan would have thought the sudden silence would be welcome. It was anything but. The stillness allowed him to think about the sight of Master Mage Delthar being buried under the weight of massive rocks and tons of dirt that he pulled down upon himself to ensure his noble goal.

Ethan had not known Delthar very well. He saw him often after becoming a Keeper's Hound, but the Master Mage was always discussing one matter or another with commander One-shot. Delthar rarely addressed the others directly, but he was a hero. The aged and accomplished conjurer was a living legend, having served his kingdom for his entire adult life either on the battlefield or as advisor to the Head Mage or as an educator of young conjurers in his role as Headmaster of the *Chronichai Tul Myst*. Only the Head Mage Rionn Lorr was believed to be a more powerful and accomplished wizard.

The Master Mage's death, the loss of such a hero and revered life-long servant of the Kingdom of Lorr, reminded Ethan of the loss of his father.

"Are you alright, Eagle Eye?" Arrowhead whispered. She put a small but strong hand on his shoulder.

"Yes," Ethan answered.

Hearing the soft voice, Nicolette's voice, calling him Eagle Eye was a subtle reminder that this was no time for lamenting. Ethan had long ago learned to keep his emotions from his face when he needed to, and he knew he was doing it here. Arrowhead, though, could see through the mask like no one save his own mother.

Hammer, panting with his big hands resting heavily on his knees, said, "I truly hope our path to the outside of this mountain hasn't been cut off."

"That was not the only way out," Ethan assured.

"Is that it?" Arrowhead asked, staring across the cave.

"Yes," Ethan said, indicating the hole in the cave floor.

The others had already started toward it and were peeking down into the darkness. Arrowhead stepped over to it and peered down, as well.

"You can feel the heat," said Hammer, wiping away beads of sweat that had formed on his forehead.

"Do you see it?" Ethan asked. He knew his eyesight was keener than most, but he thought they would be able to see it.

"Yes," Arrowhead confirmed. "I can just see the glow, the dancing shadows. Something moving down there."

"Molten rock," breathed one of the volunteer citizens. "Little Mole spoke true."

The other two stood to either side of him as they looked down curiously. Hammer and Arrowhead rejoined Ethan, who was staring down the tunnel emerging from the opposite side of the cave and stretching away into inky blackness.

"Do you see or hear anything, Eagle Eye?" Hammer asked. The muscles in his big arms flexed beneath his tunic sleeves as he hefted his war hammer expectantly.

"Yes," Ethan answered. "I heard steel hitting steel."

Arrowhead frowned. "Do you think it's the walkers?"

"It could be our soldiers," Ethan said.

"Excuse me, Eagle Eye," called one of the locals, a tall, lean man perhaps in his mid thirties. He looked fit, but from the uncomfortable way he held his dirk, it was clear that he was no warrior.

"Yes, Adam?" Ethan answered.

A quick flutter of his eyelids betrayed to Ethan the man's surprise that his name had been remembered, and then a flash of respect. Ethan knew that those who did not know him were surprised that someone so young would be so observant. He was used to the reaction.

"I am wondering," Adam went on, "exactly what we plan to do if it *is* the walkers that are coming."

A second local, this one shorter and broader than the first, dressed similarly in peasant worker's garb, stepped forward.

"As am I," he added. "Supporting a wizard as powerful as a master mage is one thing but facing a horde of those…those *things* with just the six of us and no magic is not appealing to us at all."

The third local, dressed the same, shorter still and reed thin, nodded emphatically his agreement. He was the other one holding a torch. "I agree with Adam and Walter. But perhaps we can retrieve some mining charges and return. We have experience with explosives and could perhaps explode the charges strategically to collapse this tunnel and close off this path before the walking dead attempt to use it."

That sensible course of action never even occurred to Ethan. He had been prepared to fight them, no matter how many, to hold them off until Little Mole brought Jon the Firemaster, who could burn all of the infected to ash if their healers had been able to restore him sufficiently. The two biggest problems with his plan were that they had no chance against the walkers without a powerful conjurer; and even if Little Mole did find Jon, the Firemaster could very well still be too weak to fight.

"Great idea, Jacob," Ethan told him.

"I assume you have a plan, Eagle Eye," Hammer said expectantly.

Ethan nodded. "The infected may be coming here to simply drop their charges into the molten rock below or passing through to the caves below. We don't know if what I heard was friend or foe, but if it is foe, we will have wasted too much time confirming it to bring reinforcements in time.

"I'll take us through that smaller tunnel to the right." The young Sureblade indicated another opening Hammer would never have noticed on his own unless he was standing right in front of it. Ethan continued. "Little Mole said it leads to an opening a little higher up the mountain face. If we move fast enough, we may be able to bring soldiers back in time to engage them."

Ethan was about to lead them out when a breeze wafted in from up ahead. It was soft and humid and carried the familiar sounds of clanking metal and wooden wheels bumping along a rocky surface. The sound was accompanied by the unmistakably fetid stench of rot and human decay. The Keeper's Hounds looked at each other in dismay.

"They're already here," gasped Arrowhead.

Hammer asked, "Run or fight?"

"You hear those rumbling wheels," Ethan said. "They're bringing a load here. You saw the amount of explosives they took from the town. If they're passing through and we bring soldiers, we'll be fighting from the rear to the front, which is what we're trying to avoid. If they're dropping the explosives from here, well, it's a long fall and not all of it may reach the magma, but who knows how much it will take?"

"So we fight," grunted Hammer. He turned to the volunteers. "We'll not ask you to join this fight," the big man assured. "But we'll not turn down the help."

Without answering, Walter and Adam turned and ran parallel to the cave wall toward the opening on their right. Jacob, however, remained.

Walter stopped and turned. "Jacob? Are you coming?"

"I'll stay," Jacob said. He tossed his torch to Walter. "If the walking dead have explosives, perhaps we can use them to

101

collapse the tunnel and trap them. It should be safe enough to blow the explosives this high above the magma streams. I'll know the best location to detonate them."

Walter shrugged. "May the Old Ones be with you, then, my friend." The taller man turned and bolted after Adam.

"You're a brave man, Jacob," Arrowhead complimented as the two volunteers turned into the tunnel.

Jacob scoffed. "Let's do this done before common sense overcomes bravery."

They jogged through the mountain. The further they ran the louder and stronger the sounds and smells became. They rounded a broad turn and Ethan's torchlight revealed the enemy shuffling along a long narrow stretch of the tunnel. Their vanguard was a little over fifteen yards away and about a dozen strong. The sight was as bad as the smell. Some of the infected were empty handed while many carried an array of bladed farming and digging implements that included sickles, pickaxes, and spades. The explosives were not yet visible behind the lead force but the rumbling sound of large and heavy wheelbarrows was impossible to miss.

"We have a problem," noted Arrowhead.

"You don't say?" Hammer chuckled darkly.

Jacob shook his head worriedly. "You don't understand. Even if we are able to fight our way through to the explosives and ignite them, how do we get clear of the blast?"

Ethan's blonde eyebrows lifted. "Hammer, are you tall enough to see over the lead group to the explosives?"

Hammer stood on his toes. "Of course, shorty," he teased, trying in vain to conceal his nervousness. "I see several big wheelbarrows. Each one is filled with four barrels. I'm sure there are more being wheeled in from around the bend. The shadows hide whether the barrels contain oil or powder, though I don't think it matters much."

Ethan turned to Jacob. "Where would you say is an ideal spot to set off an explosive to trap them?"

Jacob looked around. "Anywhere within the tunnel, actually," he answered, "as long as they do not come very much closer to us."

Ethan nodded with satisfaction. "Arrowhead," he said without turning, "I'm going to need your –"

A tug from behind at his right arm and the sound of ripping cloth interrupted him. He turned to see Arrowhead tearing away the sleeve of his tunic at the elbow.

"I'm way ahead of you, shorty," Arrowhead smirked as she wrapped his sleeve tightly around the tip of an arrow.

"Bend down, ox," she ordered Hammer.

"Yes, your highness," Hammer sneered with a low bow.

"Arrowhead, wait," Ethan cautioned. "Maybe I should –"

"Stand back and let me do this?" Arrowhead finished for him as she climbed onto Hammer's broad shoulders. "I know you are an excellent shot, but I'm called 'Arrowhead' for a reason. If you think you are better with a bow perhaps later we can have a contest."

Ethan smiled. "I can think of a prize for the victor."

"Enough flirting!" blurted an almost panicked Jacob as Hammer rose to his full height. "How can you crack wise in such dire circumstances?"

Hammer shrugged his free shoulder. "This is not our first crisis. Besides, joking is better than panicking."

"Torch," Arrowhead commanded, holding the cloth-wrapped arrow down toward Ethan.

"Yes, your highness," Ethan answered with an exaggerated and deferential nod. He used his torch to light the cloth. When it was blazing satisfactorily, Arrowhead lifted it and knocked the arrow.

"When I give the word, run," she said needlessly.

Perched on Hammer's shoulder she was over eight feet above the ground and could easily spot the wheelbarrows in the flickering torchlight. After a slight pause and a deep breath, she let the arrow fly. She leapt down from Hammer's shoulder and shouted:

"RUN!"

4.4

They ran. Once again Ethan led the way and Hammer brought up the rear. They rounded the turn at a full sprint. The cave came into view in moments. They entered the cave, and just as Ethan leapt over the pit in the middle of the cave floor, the first deafening explosion rocked the mountain. It was immediately followed by a second and third.

The heat and shockwave of the explosions sent all four of them tumbling. And then the tunnel collapsed, sending a violent cloud of rubble, dust, and choking smoke pluming into the cave. The concussion blew the torch out and for a moment the cave was plunged into complete darkness.

As the companions struggled to catch their breath, their eyes began to adjust. Ethan was the first to see it, but soon, all of them could see a weak blood-red glow from the magma in the depths of the mountain emanating from the pit. It provided just enough light to see the immediate area surrounding the pit. They staggered to their feet amid several more explosions that were muffled by the stone-choked tunnel opening. Knowing that the cave could collapse at any moment, fear spurred them on.

They turned to run, but before Ethan took a step he realized someone was missing.

"Hammer!" He called.

"Down here!" came an uncharacteristically fearful cry.

Ethan, Arrowhead, and Jacob turned to look for Hammer. None of them saw him. They saw his massive war hammer lying a few feet away from the pit in the middle of the cave floor and that was all. And then Ethan started when he saw a large hand clutched desperately to the edge of the pit.

Jacob was nearest and he did not hesitate to run over and reach down grab Hammer's wide wrist. He heaved with all of his might but he was much too small and not nearly strong enough to move the big man an inch. Arrowhead and Ethan rushed over. Before they could reach the two struggling men, the earth beneath Jacob's feet began to crack and shudder under their combined weight.

"No!" Ethan shouted as he dived forward, extending his *gun* down into the pit. Hammer grabbed it just as the ground beneath Jacob gave way.

Jacob kept a two-handed death grip on Hammer's wrist as he swung down into the widened pit. Their weight dragged Ethan relentlessly forward, threatening to yank the long staff from his hands. Arrowhead slid over feet first beside Ethan and grabbed the staff. The two of them pulled for all they were worth but it was not enough.

They would have had enough trouble trying to pull only Hammer out of the pit. Ethan and Arrowhead's combined weight was not quite three hundred pounds. Hammer was three hundred pounds by himself. Jacob was not a big man, but his weight added to Hammer's mass was too much.

Despite their efforts, Ethan and Arrowhead slid toward the edge of the widened hole. The heat emanating from the molten rock in the bowels of the mountain, combined with their struggle, drenched all of them with sweat. The *gun* grew slick from the moisture and began to slide from Ethan's and Arrowhead's grip. Every one of them knew it was only a matter of time before they either lost their hold on the long metal staff or all of them were pulled down into the pit.

"At least we stopped the walkers," Jacob called. "I'll not let all of us die. All I ask is that you tell my family of my sacrifice."

He released Hammer's arm.

Hammer quickly flicked his hand around and snatched Jacob's wrist.

"Don't be a fool man!" Hammer barked. "You're an honorary Hound now! We live or die together!"

The sudden movement yanked Ethan and Arrowhead even closer to the edge, until Arrowhead's hands extended over the rim of the pit.

"Of all the ways to die," Arrowhead gasped, "I never dreamed we'd plunge into a river of magma."

"No one is dying here!" shouted a loud, nervous voice from behind.

Ethan looked over his shoulder to see Adam and Walter dashing across the cave. They crowded him and Arrowhead as they each grasped the staff and heaved with loud grunts. Blessedly, the floor around the pit held firm and they were able to slowly and carefully haul Hammer and Jacob to safety. They all collapsed on their backs on the cave floor. They were silent for long moments, just breathing heavily and silently thanking any Old One that would listen, until Arrowhead finally spoke.

"Hammer, you've *got* to lose some weight!"

Hammer's reply was a weak chuckle.

"Adam, Walter...thank you for returning," Ethan finally huffed when he regained enough of his breath to speak.

"Well," Adam said sheepishly. "We couldn't very well find our way out of the mountain without you."

They all jumped at a loud, echoing pop of breaking stone. Adam and the others looked around to see finger-width fissures snaking their way across the cave floor from the widened rim of the pit. Adrenaline instantly replaced their exhaustion. They scrambled to their feet and bolted from the cave into the narrow tunnel. Thick dust, the faint smell of sulfur, and the frightening roar of falling stone chased them yet again. This time, though, a crumbling tunnel floor pursued them as well.

The collapse moved at a blessedly slower pace than before and it ended in less than a minute. The rest of their escape was quiet and uneventful. No more collapsing earth, falling rock or walking dead followed them through the claustrophobic tunnels.

Ethan was relieved until they exited the mountain and stepped into a scene from hell.

A long and broad line of armed men, women, and children, most of them with deathly gray skin or gaping wounds that no human could survive – or both – shambled toward them at a moderate but determined pace.

4.5

DEMON'S SPINE MOUNTAINS; MAR-DAH'S LAIR

Raxe quickened his pace, knowing all too well how far and how fast the wallowgrumps' powerful legs could propel them with each bound. While Raxe was not about to break any world records, he knew he would not come in last against world-class competition in either the 40 or 100-meter sprint. Unfortunately his legs were already sore from their earlier trials and tribulations so he was not at top speed. His tired legs, however, were more compensated for by adrenaline.

With his head start he was pretty sure he could make it safely to the other end of the cave. His concern was for Azh. He quickly discovered that his concern was misplaced. Despite her skinny, much shorter legs, she not only kept pace with her father, she started to pull away from him. Raxe was both surprised and relieved. If one of them had to get caught, he preferred to be the one.

He looked over his shoulder and saw that within just a few seconds the wallowgrumps had closed over half of the distance between them. Another burst of speed brought him even with his daughter and together they approached the far wall where Rell Kallen was waiting. As they watched, the elf stepped to Raxe's left and disappeared as if he had walked through an invisible doorway. When they reached the wall Raxe saw why he had not noticed the opening.

More so than the distance, the formation of the opening made it almost impossible to see without standing at the perfect angle. The opening was little more than a slight vertical outcropping of lichen-covered stone with a narrow fissure just behind it. The fissure was roughly two feet wide and barely five feet high. Raxe thought back to the wizard Mar-dah. He was just over six feet tall and very thin, just the right size to be able to crouch and pass through the opening.

Most of the evil wizard's mercenary soldiers, at least the ones Raxe saw and fought, would never have fit whether they wore armor or not. This had to have been Mar-dah's personal, secret passage out of the mountain.

Raxe and Azh slipped through the opening with no hesitation, which led to a tubular sloping tunnel with a rough-hewn set of stairs barely visible in the blue-green tinted shadows. The treads were uneven, shallow, high and slick with moisture from the thick humidity within the cavern. There was no glowing lichen inside the steep stairway. The only light came from residual illumination from the lichen in the cave and, apparently, more of the same lichen just outside the top of the stairway. The middle of the steep climb was submerged in complete blackness.

Father ushered daughter up the stairs ahead of him and followed closely behind. They had taken a few hurried but careful steps up the treacherous stairs when they saw Rell Kallen emerge from the top of the pool of deep shadow just above the center of the staircase. He dashed smoothly and with incredible speed up the remaining stairs, turned right, and vanished before the two Children of the Old Ones reached the midpoint of their climb.

A moment of doubt seized Raxe. He estimated the tunnel rose nearly fifty feet high. Neither of them were as fleet of foot as the Ranger Elf. Could they possibly clear the stairway before the swift wallowgrumps reached them? The moment of doubt did not make him hesitate, though. If anything, it hastened his pace.

The sound of his and his daughter's heavy breathing, the padding of Azh's soft-soled hiking boots and the clang of his metal boots ricocheted through the narrow shaft in disconcerting echoes. Raxe's boots skid along the slick stone more than once but he managed to keep his footing. He ignored the fear that swept through him when he lost sight of Azh after she plunged into the pool of black shadow. An instant later everything went black as he followed her into it.

He heard a strange sound in the darkness. The echoes made them difficult to identify. Cold dread shot through him when he emerged from the other side of the darkness and did not see his daughter ahead of him. He stopped on a dime and spun back.

"Azh!"

"I fell," she answered worriedly.

Raxe reached into the shadows, quickly found one of her arms and then pulled her up into his. Even though she appeared to be a slight, slip of a girl, Raxe was nonetheless amazed at how little she actually weighed. He straightened up in time to see a wallowgrump, and then another, leap into the stairway. With one bound, the giant, bipedal frog creatures soared nearly a quarter of the way up.

"Shit, shit, shit, shit!" Raxe whispered. He cradled Azh in his arms, spun around and hustled up the stairs.

When the lead wallowgrumps landed, their clawed flipper-feet slipped on the wet stone and sent them tumbling down the stairs. They barreled into several of their pack mates and they all went down like bowling pins. Raxe risked a glance over his shoulder and wanted to sigh in relief but he could not spare the breath. When the wallowgrumps quickly sprang to their feet he knew the tumble gave them only the briefest of respites.

With a little extra concentration he was able to take the stairs three at a time without slipping even with Azh in his arms. He reached the top of the stairs, ducked through the opening and turned right, the same direction Rell Kallen had turned. Raxe took in his new surroundings with the speed of a camera flash.

A high wall faced him a few feet away from the top of the tunnel. A large, egg-shaped boulder that was as wide as Raxe was tall and stood twice as high, rested easily on its tapered end just outside the opening. Beyond it was the only path available to them. It was a long, narrow tunnel that stretched away into the darkness. The elf was nowhere to be seen. Raxe knew in an instant that he and Azh had no chance to escape the wallowgrumps but that was not going to stop him from trying.

"I can run," Azh assured.

"Good," Raxe said as he dropped her to her feet. They ran through the opening and Raxe saw something out of the corner of his eye that brought him to a skidding halt.

Rell Kallen was there, pushing against the massive boulder with all of his considerable strength. The boulder did not budge an inch.

"A bit of assistance would be appreciated, offworlder," Rell Kallen grunted.

"No problem," Raxe said, pulling Demonsbane from its frog. The high-pitched hum of the metal handle sliding against the metal ring of the axe frog on his weapons belt rang melodiously in the confined space, but not loud enough to drown out the hissing and thumping of the wallowgrumps rushing up the tunnel.

Raxe stepped forward and gave a powerful diagonal swing from right to left from the opposite side of the boulder toward the elf. The cut started at a height level with Rell Kallen's mid thigh. Demonsbane sliced easily through the dense stone and emerged just to the left of the center of the boulder's rounded tip.

The axe blades were not large enough to cut completely through the broad stone with one swipe so he followed the first cut with another. The angle at which he sliced gave the elf just enough leverage. The base of the massive chunk of rock fell away, causing the boulder to tilt and then topple over just as two wallowgrumps entered the portal.

The boulder fell over the opening with a loud crash and a stunted, high-pitched scream of death. Dark, viscous blood sprayed out from under the fallen boulder and splashed against opposite the wall. The boulder crushed one of the wallowgrumps but its pack mate shot safely through the opening. It flashed through at an angle, from the left side of the tunnel to right wall, bounced off the wall and turned. The animal's filmy, saucer-sized eyes did not immediately see the offworlder and the elf where they stood behind the fallen boulder. Instead, they quickly locked onto the girl.

In the blink of an eye, its tail coiled like a spring against the wall, its reverse-articulated, jackknifed legs bent deeply and it launched itself at Azh. Its long slit of a maw gaped hungrily, baring short dagger-tipped teeth.

Even while Raxe's mind was trying to process what he was seeing his body was in motion. He dived forward to intercept the beast, swinging Demonsbane at the same time. The wallowgrump moved so fast that it flew right past Raxe. The offworlder barely managed to hook the curved bottom edge of one of the axe blades into the wallowgrump's long tail. The beast's momentum yanked Raxe violently off of his feet and towed him through the air.

The extra weight was enough to drag the wallowgrump to the ground a foot short of its prey. It snatched its tail free of the axe blade, drawing a long line of blood and cloven flesh in the process, and turned angrily toward this new bit of meat. It leapt at Raxe as he tried to scramble to something resembling a defensive stance. Raxe was just barely able to lift Demonsbane in front of his face horizontally, his left hand at the end of the metal haft and his right hand clutched painfully at the base of the gem from which the axe blades protruded, when the amphibian predator barreled into him.

The impact drove him to the ground, on his back, with the wallowgrump, which was twice as heavy as he was, on top of him. Raxe managed to brace Demonsbane's haft against the back of the wallowgrump's open mouth and struggled to hold it back. His visor, impenetrable as it was, would do him no good if the massive jaws engulfed his entire head. The wallowgrump's maw was so wide that its upper palate could plunge sharp teeth into Raxe's exposed crown while its lower jaw drove into Raxe's uncovered chin and possibly even his neck.

Raxe focused all of his strength into his arms. His biceps and forearms and injured right hand burned from the effort but he managed to inch the creature away. He was unable to extend his arms fully, though, and was unsure how long he could keep the beast at bay. The wallowgrump snapped at his head with the sound of a bear trap. It snapped with so much force that it shattered its back teeth against the unbreakable metal of the battleaxe haft.

The pain made the wallowgrump angrier and even more aggressive. Thick, acrid slobber oozed down on Raxe's face. Hot breath that smelled of rancid flesh and bile assaulted Raxe's nostrils. The searing pain in his right hand sent white noise screaming through his mind.

And then the wallowgrump went to work with its claws. The vicious, four-digit appendages at the end of its short arms raked Raxe's exposed deltoids and triceps while its legs continued to push its rear upward, levering its head and torso down with even more force upon Raxe.

The offworlder had to stop breathing for fear of inhaling and choking on the sputum dripping and splashing down on him. The lack of air started to make him light headed. Sharp pain in his lacerated arms distracted him. He had a fleeting, selfish moment of regret for not using the titan's ore for a chain mail shirt to wear beneath his cuirass as the dwarf Bartok had suggested instead of using it to craft Ethan's enchanted *gun*. His elbows throbbed. The wallowgrump's deadly snapping jaws started to inch back down toward its prey's head.

In a last ditch effort of quickness and strength fueled by desperation, Raxe yanked Demonsbane to the left in a tight arc. The crescent blades sliced neatly through the wallowgrump's head, severing it right at the hinge of its jaw. Its top palate and the top of its broad head bounced off to the side while the bottom jaw and torso slumped lifelessly down on top of him. Raxe pivoted and shoved the heavy corpse away. He sprang to his feet coughing and spitting and cursing. He wanted to wipe his face but his hands were as filthy with thick sputum and black blood as his head.

"Fucking…nasty…*arrgh*!!" Raxe roared coarsely as he shook his head and arms like a wet dog. "SHIT!"

"Wait, father," Azh bade, slightly raising her left hand toward him.

In his current state of excited disgust, he almost missed the word 'father.' Almost. The words coming from her sweet voice calmed him and he went still.

Azh's long hair wafted almost imperceptibly. Raxe marveled at how the sickening fluids that coated his face, upper body, hands, and forearms lifted off of and away from him in foul little globules that floated slowly down to stain the stone floor around him.

"Wow. Thanks, sweetheart," Raxe said. The relief and gratitude in his tone were at odds with the deep, gravelly rumble of his damaged voice.

The Ranger Elf snorted. "Are the two of you quite finished?"

"*I* could've used a bit of assistance you little bastard," Raxe snarled.

Rell shrugged. "I only need one of you alive to help me find the Hell Key, offworlder."

Raxe sneered. "I'll keep that in mind."

"We must hurry," Azh interjected. "And we should barricade every threshold we can."

"Why?" Rell asked.

"Yeah," Raxe concurred, surprised that he agreed with the Ranger Elf. "How will we get back out of here if we close off the path behind us?"

"If the wallowgrumps work together," Azh explained, "and they probably will, they will be strong enough to move anything we can put in their way."

"Are you kidding me?" Raxe asked. "That boulder weighs tons. Mar-dah had to have used magic to move it."

The boulder began to tremor with a deep rumbling sound. Snarls could be heard on the other side of the massive rock.

"Ok." He said, and joined the other two, who had already broken into a brisk jog.

"'Tis a shame it takes wallowgrumps on your arse to make you two move at something that passes for a decent pace," Rell Kallen grumbled as they trotted into the darkness.

4.6

THE KINGDOM OF CARTHA – CARTHAN PALACE

Queen Lairen Stefania Vergoth *tul* Cartha was the full name and honorific of the woman seated at an office desk to the right of a younger man. The man shared enough of the woman's features to make it fairly obvious that they were closely related. The woman skimmed official documents while the man waited patiently with a quill in his left hand. On his right burned a red candle scented with Sweet Autumn Clematis and the official seal of the Kingdom of Cartha.

The queen passed a document to her son, King Gregor Vergoth *tul* Cartha the Second, and then she started skimming the next document from the dwindling stack of papers. The young king, with a bored expression, signed the document passed to him, folded it, and placed it in the envelope. When he finished dripping the wax and stamping the royal seal, the queen was still less than halfway through the next document. King Gregor tapped the quill on the table while he waited.

"Mother," he said with a sigh. "I never knew being king would be so tedious. Perhaps if you allow me to read the documents I would not be so bored."

The queen smiled. "Believe me, son, this process would be even *more* tedious if you had to read these documents as well as sign them. Your father certainly thought so."

"Father," Gregor said softly.

His face ran through several emotions in a matter of seconds. First there was the sadness of his father's passing, and then there was the anger at the manner of his father's passing. Finally there was the guilt and frustration he felt from not being there to help.

"If only I had been there…"

Queen Lairen shook her head. "The Head Mage and his First Advisor used powerful magic to kill your father," the queen lied. "It's only by the grace of the Lord Ascendant that your talented guards were able to surprise the wizards and strike them down. If they had not, the wizards would likely have come after you and me next."

Those were all lies. By the queen's direction, the royal guards killed King Gregor Vergoth *tul* Cartha the First. Two of those guards, in fact, were standing sentry in that very room on either side of the door.

The king had already killed the Carthan Head Mage and ordered the guard to kill the wizard's First Advisor.

The former king of Cartha and his queen had never truly loved one another but they enjoyed a mutually beneficial relationship. The king was the symbol of power because his was the blood of the royal family. His was the beloved face of the monarchy. The people of Cartha were drawn to him. They were captivated by his confidence and his magnetic personality. The queen, on the other hand, had been the intelligence behind the throne. She was the king's primary counsel, and in some of their more clandestine endeavors, she was his only counsel. The Kingdom of Cartha grew and flourished under their partnership.

However, shortly after they launched their campaign to weaken the Kingdom of Lorr, Gregor the First drifted away from her to make decisions without her counsel. It all came to a head with the murder of their Head Mage and his First Adviser, the two highest-ranking wizards in the kingdom. Queen Lairen could no longer trust her husband so he had to die, as well. Now their son was king.

They both fell into thoughtful silence as the queen finished reading a document. Instead of passing it to her son for his authorizing signature, she crumpled it into a ball and dropped it into a wastebasket next to the desk.

"What was that one, mother?" Gregor asked.

"As waste of time," she answered.

Gregor frowned. "I would like to have seen it. The king should review all of his proposals and petitions. Perhaps –"

"Do you not trust me, son?" the queen asked.

"Of course I trust you mother," Gregor assured. "And I realize that all of this is new to me, but I must take more direct responsibility at some point. The sooner I start the faster I will learn."

"I'm proud of your dedication," the queen said sincerely. "But this set of documents is all outstanding entreaties and expired petitions that your father and I had already decided upon. Believe me when I tell you that I am saving you valuable time. After this set of documents, though, I promise that your input will be critical."

"I thank you, then, mother," Gregor conceded.

Gregor the Second shared the elder Gregor's charisma. The people of Cartha loved the son as much as the father. He also had his mother's intelligence and work ethic. Fortunately for the queen, he was sharp enough to realize that her help during the transition would be invaluable. He trusted his mother but she knew that at some point he would outgrow the necessity of her counsel.

That was why the queen insisted on reviewing these documents. Some of them were indirectly related to their campaign against Lorr. The new king was clever enough to spot the connections. He knew nothing of the plot against Lorr and would not approve of it if he had. Gregor the Second had his father's charm and his mother's intellect but was sorely lacking in the one trait his parents shared.

He had not inherited their ruthless ambition.

A knock at the door pulled their attention away from the paperwork. One of the guards pulled open the door, spoke briefly to one of the guards outside, and then opened the door wider to admit a man wearing an unadorned lavender robe with soft gray hems. He wore a golden chain around his neck attached to a fist-sized amulet made up of a silver circle containing a silver five-pointed star. Within each point was a symbol of one of the five elements. A small woolen bag with a long strap was slung over his shoulder. In his right hand he carried a wooden staff half as long as he was tall.

At the sight of a wizard in the royal study, King Gregor surged to his feet and drew his straight sword all in one motion. His mother grabbed his sword arm to stop him from vaulting the desk and attacking.

"Stay your hand," the queen bade. "This is Mage Homer Allred, the new First Advisor to our new Head Mage."

Gregor glared at his mother in wide-eyed disbelief.

"Mother, how can you trust *any* wizard after what happened to father?"

"Your father selected the former Head Mage and his First Advisor against my counsel," she lied yet again. She had actually investigated and confirmed both men. She had also approved the Second High Advisor, Stratham Glund, who was the Head Mage now that his two superiors were dead.

"I never trusted Tilsworth or Roderick," she continued. "I appointed Glund and Allred. I trust them unreservedly."

Mage Allred, who had frozen when the king threatened to attack, looked to the king and the queen regent.

"May I continue?" he asked. "Or should I leave?"

"Come, good wizard," the queen commanded. "King Gregor," she said in a cajoling tone, "my son, please sit."

King Gregor's dark gaze lingered on the wizard while he sheathed his sword and sat back down next to his mother.

Mage Homer continued his approach to the desk. "The new Head Mage wishes to report to you, my king and queen. This bag contains the means for him to do so. Will you allow me to contact him?"

"Please," Queen Lairen insisted with a beckoning wave.

The wizard made his way to the desk. The queen moved the paperwork aside to give him room to set down his bag. He opened it and retrieved a shallow silver bowl with runes etched around the rim, a slender stoppered beaker of water, and a capped vial of blue powder. After filling the bowl to the halfway point with water, Homer opened the vial of powder and set it to the side. Homer whispered several unintelligible words and made a few intricate hand gestures.

The amulet hanging from the chain around his neck began to glow, as did the runes carved into the rim of the bowl. Homer then sprinkled a pinch of the blue powder into the bowl in a circular motion. King Gregor and Queen Lairen leaned over to peer into the shallow bowl. The water began to swirl slowly in the same direction in which the wizard sprinkled the powder.

The swirl soon became a light simmer and then a gentle boil. The boil only lasted a few seconds before the water settled and took on a deep, blood red hue. The crimson color lasted about as long as the short boil and then the color changed again. This time the one color separated into to several different cloudy colors that quickly resolved into a clear image. The sharp and handsome visage of the newly promoted Carthan Head Mage, Stratham Glund, stared at his king, queen and First High Advisor.

"My sincere condolences on the loss of King Gregor Vergoth the First," Stratham Glund said immediately. "He was a good king, and he will be greatly missed. I will do all I can to atone for the treachery of my predecessors."

"You had better," growled the new king.

A frantic knock sounded at the door. When the guards opened it, a messenger rushed into the room.

"My king, my queen," the young messenger panted. "Admiral Toth has sent word that an envoy from S'Zan has arrived at the shores of Oceana City. They seek an audience with the queen mother and the new king."

"An envoy from S'Zan?" the queen asked incredulously. "The S'Zan almost never take to the sea. It must be important if they would send an envoy instead of a letter. I'll see them straightaway."

Gregor raised his hand. "No, mother. You stay here and receive the message from Glund. I'll see to the envoy."

"Alone? Are you sure, Gregor?" the queen asked. "This is but a periodic report. The envoy seems important."

"All the more reason for me to hurry," King Gregor contended. "I am a man grown, and the king. It won't do to always have my mother at my side like some young pup."

Queen Lairen sighed. "I suppose you're right," she conceded. "You go. I'll be along once Glund has completed his report."

Gregor nodded and strode to the door with the messenger at his heels. He stopped and looked at both guards in turn.

"I want one of you at the queen's side," he ordered. "If that wizard so much as looks at mother inappropriately, kill him immediately."

"As you wish, my king," the guards answered in unison.

Satisfied, the young king exited the room with the messenger in tow. A few seconds after his departure the queen's bored expression became stern and impatient. She glared down at Stratham Glund's image.

"Make this quick, Glund."

"What a coincidence that the S'Zan Rho envoy arrives just as I am to give my report," Glund noted.

"I leave nothing to coincidence," the queen replied. "I've known about that envoy for days and timed it just so. That boy has clung to my skirts like a babe since his father's death, his nose in every bit of business to which I've attended. I needed an issue of seeming import to shake him free." Queen Lairen paused to sigh. "How convenient it would be if he had his father's love of the trappings of royalty and the same disregard for the actual work."

Stratham Glund smiled. "He gets his work ethic from his lovely mother, no doubt."

"Enough banter," the queen snapped, not impressed by her Head Mage's attempt at flattery. "I've feared the worst since my late husband did away with Tilsworth and Roderick in his fit of impulsive stupidity. How are things progressing in the south of Lorr?"

"Precisely as planned," Glund answered. "We're most fortunate that their machinations were already in place and well under way at the time of their deaths.

"The *Ken d'Zanir* will be there to intercept the offworlder and elf whether they recover the Hell Key or not. As formidable as both of them are, they cannot hope to defeat a host of *Ken* elite. The desert witch, in the meanwhile, is nearing Lake Onyx to have done with the water witch."

"You sound very confident, mage," the queen observed.

"I am," Glund admitted. "I liken our progress to an avalanche rolling down a steep slope. Its momentum cannot be stopped. Our enemies will soon be buried beneath it."

The queen was incredulous. "Do you really believe Shara Dune can best Sabrina, the *Mistress of the Sea,* in the water elemental's own home?"

Stratham Glund's image nodded with certainty. "The dark wizard has assured us that the groundwork...or, to put it more accurately, the *water work* has been laid."

The mention of the "dark wizard" brought a scowl to the queen's face. "You and your predecessor have mentioned this dark wizard before. Tell me, do you know his – or her – true identity?"

"I do not," Glund confessed. "I received all of my instructions directly from the previous Head Mage. My understanding was that Mage Tilsworth was in direct contact with the dark wizard and then relayed instructions to Mage Roderick and myself."

"Do you know, Mage Glund, why I am so concerned about the dark wizard's identity?"

"I do not, my queen."

Queen Lairen leaned closer to the bowl of water. "There are whispers that a *demon* is the mastermind of all of that has transpired regarding this campaign. Have you heard these whispers?"

She could see the surprise and concern in both wizards' eyes. Mage Homer Allred gasped while something resembling guilt flashed across the face of the wizard looking at her from the water.

"I must admit that I have heard some of the whispers," Glund said. "I dismissed them as the ramblings of ignorant peasants. These Lorrian southerners like to attribute anything beyond their limited understanding to demonic forces. There is powerful magic at work, indeed, but if the dark wizard was a demon, surely a mage as learned and powerful as Tilsworth would have known."

"Is that why you never mentioned these whispers to me or the king?" the queen questioned.

"I…I…" stammered Glund, the nervousness in his eyes was poorly hidden. "I discussed this very issue with Mage Tilsworth more than once. He and I were of the same opinion. I assumed he would inform you himself if he thought there was any truth to the rumors."

The queen held his gaze for several more uncomfortable seconds before she spoke again.

"Keep your ear to the ground, wizard," she commanded. "While I am not as impetuous as my husband, my tolerance has its limits. You are to keep me informed. My concern is that a demon that could coordinate such an endeavor without detection would obviously not be a mindless beast like the ones Mar-dah released in the Cursed Opening. It would be immensely cunning and have the ability to effectively conceal itself. If there is indeed any truth to these rumors, it is best we know about it sooner rather than later."

"Perhaps we should pull out of this endeavor now," Glund suggested. "I would think the mere possibility that we could be in league with an intelligent demon is too big a risk to take. You are too important to the prosperity of the Carthan Kingdom."

"Your concern is noted and appreciated, my Head Mage," the queen said. "But it is as you say. The avalanche is in mid-fall. There is no stopping it now. There is nothing left for us to do. All I need is for you to remain in Lorr just long enough to confirm that our enemies have indeed been buried."

The Carthan Head Mage nodded and said, "With pleasure, Queen Vergoth."

"Good," the queen approved. "Now, I must see to the envoy. They know better than to go into too much detail with the boy, but I must find another way to dismiss him so that the S'Zan and I can discuss matters of *actual* importance."

Chapter 5: Weapons of Power

Ethan, Arrowhead, Hammer and the three volunteer citizens of Ridgeland were the only things standing between the walking dead and the entrance to the mountain. They had trapped the group of walkers that had approached the pit from the other part of the mountain, but the path to the lower levels from the entrance they had just passed through was made even easier by the collapsed floor. They dropped their torches and raised their weapons. Ethan turned a grim stare to the short volunteer as he doused his torch.

"So much for sending someone to plant more explosives, eh Jacob?" the young Sureblade asked.

"Indeed," Jacob agreed as he hefted his broadsword.

Arrowhead touched his shoulder as she spoke excitedly. "Unless *they* get here in time!"

Ethan turned to see mounted soldiers riding hard around a bend. Judging by their numbers as they continued to stream around the mountain, an entire company had been sent. Two-dozen riders broke away from the main column to race toward the front of the enemy line.

And then the wind shifted.

The smell almost buckled Ethan's knees. He saw all of the others either frown or jerk their head back as if they had been slapped. All of them had faced the infected before and were no strangers to the cloying and eye-watering miasma of death and rot that accompanied the hellish marchers, yet they had the same reaction every time. Such a foul stench was not something to which they could ever become accustomed.

The approach of both parties made for a weird tableau. The horrific spectacle of the motley shambling walkers was backlit by the breathtaking vista of the two suns hovering just above the western horizon. The waning light cast a golden glow halfway across the skies before fading into soft silver that stretched over their heads and vanished behind the peaks of the Runestone Mountains.

The cursed procession stretched in a straight line that drifted slowly but steadily to the northwest, up and then over a low foothill blanketed with lush green grass. Those in the distance still traversing the hilltop pushed and pulled wagons and wheelbarrows full of what they all knew to be explosives of various types.

It was the beauty of heaven and the ugliness of hell in one breathtaking panorama.

To the right, the broad column of cavalry rushed in from the east. Their charge formed a long curve that disappeared around the slope of the mountain. They drove their horses at a pace that would intercept the walkers only moments before the walkers reached the six of them. Ethan estimated that it would take just over a minute for them to converge. The time went by agonizingly slowly.

It made for a strange sight. The plague-ridden walkers approaching at an almost casual pace, many of them farmers carrying long-handled gardening tools and in complete silence other than the distant clink of metal. Some of them wore light armor but even they drug their weapons listlessly behind them or held them loosely at their sides as if they could barely lift the weight. Meanwhile the cavalry raced toward them frenetically, seasoned warriors all, with the thundering of hooves and their fierce weapons held high.

The contrast was disconcerting but short lived. When it ended, Ethan knew that torturous minute did not go by slowly enough. The moment the horses interrupted the front of the enemy lines, the seemingly disinterested walkers erupted into a violent frenzy. Shrill screams and roars of every pitch echoed through the mountains as the infected began hacking and slashing and clawing madly at the soldiers and their mounts.

The cavalry was ready. Instead of dashing headlong into the midst of the enemy, they raked across the edges of both the front and sides of the enemy lines with long-handled weapons. The mounted soldiers struck with wicked polearms, long-handled war axes and battle hammers and maces and morningstars. The severed business ends of rakes and spades and shovels, along with heads and various other human limbs went flying. Severed torsos tumbled to the ground, disconnected legs crumpled into the grass and dirt.

The walkers kept coming with no concern for their own safety. They eventually, inevitably, got past the soldier's weapons. When they did they attacked the horses, bringing them and their riders down in a tangle of fur, flesh, bone and blood. The horses' screams were louder and even more horrible than those of the soldiers.

Many of the walkers were trampled by the chargers as the soldiers attacked but more than a few of them were able to lock onto the horses' stomping legs, eventually causing them to falter and crash to the ground. The infected scrambled over the flailing men and horses, some of them hacking at the fallen warriors and mounts while others continued toward the mountainside…and the three Keeper's Hounds with the three citizen volunteers guarding the mouth of the cave.

Ethan dropped into a defensive crouch and drew a battle-won broadsword despite the warmth radiating against his back from his enchanted *gun*. The blunt-tipped staff would not do sufficient damage to stop the infected. They had to be dismembered, not pummeled. He could already feel the magic spreading through his body and knew it would help him wield the broadsword the way Raxe could. The magic whispered to him an assurance that Raxe was a master swordsman. Though the quality of this broadsword was not even close to that of his father's, it was a deadly double-edged weapon nonetheless.

Arrowhead looked over at Ethan nervously. Her straight sword was raised but she was not anxious to fight. She had fought this enemy just a day earlier and it had been the most horrifying experience of her life. She hunted, fought, and killed fourteen demons with the Keeper's Hounds. None of those confrontations shook her to her core the way her first battle against the walking dead had. Demons were harder to kill but it was easy to raise her sword against them.

Drawing steel against unarmed and, in many cases, elderly men and women, and against children, was something altogether different. For the entire time she had been in the infirmary tent having her wounds treated, she silently prayed to the Lord Ascendant and all of the Old Ones, begging them to deliver the kingdom's defenders from this awful plight.

Arrowhead soon realized they were on their own for time being. While she was loath to fight, she could clearly see that Ethan was not. The strange metal staff shimmered with a pale cyan glow. The battle lust in the teen's blue eyes was more intense than she had ever seen. His grim, almost eager aspect reminded her of when he killed Tauran.

"Ethan, we have to get these men back to town safely," she reminded. "They can find the explosives experts they mentioned and bring them to the caves. That's still our best chance to stop the infected before they place their charges."

"No!" Ethan snapped as the enemy drew nearer. "We have to help the soldiers stop these creatures here and now."

Another wave of soldiers darted in to cut down the berserker attackers that made it past the first wave, but even then, some of them, mostly children or crawlers low enough to the ground to avoid the reach of the soldiers' long handled weapons, kept coming. Hammer frowned at the pitiful yet fearsome creatures. The thought of striking children and the hobbled with his war hammer sent a chill down his spine.

"I'm not one to run from a fight, Eagle Eye," the big man started, "but on this I must agree with Arrowhead."

"Cover them, then," Ethan ordered. "I'll stay here."

"We can't make it without you," argued Arrowhead. "If you're so anxious to fight, help us fight our way out of here! There'll be plenty of them on our flanks soon enough!"

She was right. A handful of the attackers circled around the carnage to box the six of them in from the south. They had been whipped into a charging, roaring fury. They looked to tear to shreds any living thing that crossed their path, and the Hounds had to cross their path to get back to town. There was no way around them.

Arrowhead did not wait. She sprinted off toward the smaller group of attackers with the three citizens close behind. Hammer followed. Ethan grunted in frustration and bolted after Hammer.

It irked him to let the infected attacking from straight on pass unobstructed into the side of the mountain. The young Sureblade had to remind himself that their vanguard was not carrying explosives and therefore could do no real damage. The others further down the line, though, those with the explosives, were the ones that had to be stopped.

Ethan's hesitation put him several yards behind the others. So when the walkers clashed with Arrowhead and Hammer, Ethan was sprinting to catch up. Hammer sent four of them flying with a swipe of his war hammer while Arrowhead severed a reaching arm of one and then ducked, spun, severed the left shin of one and the right shin of another, both just below the knee, with one deft stroke that sent them stumbling to the ground. Arrowhead and Hammer cleared the way for several more yards for the volunteers.

Five of the attackers went wide to either side, passing the people in front of Ethan, and then converged on him. The magic of the enchanted *gun* blazed through him. The skill, the agility, and even the instinct felt natural to him even though he knew it was not. He sidestepped a downward-arcing blade of a scythe while bringing up his broadsword to behead the animated male corpse that wielded it. He kept his broadsword moving to chop a shovel in half and send the blade spinning through the air.

A tall, emaciated woman, with filthy gray skin that was nearly indistinguishable from her rotting peasant dress, dove at Ethan. He ducked low and flipped the lunging woman over his shoulder and then extended his right leg to sweep the shovel wielder off of his feet. Lifting his broadsword as he sprung into a fighting stance, he deflected a swinging broadsword and snatched his blade back to sever the right arm of the walker that held it. The one-armed man advanced as if he had not been touched.

Ethan slid to right and brought his broadsword low, cutting the attacker almost completely in half at the waist. The damage to its spinal cord threw him off balance and he finally crumpled to the ground. Ethan turned just in time to see the fifth walker rushing at him with a long pike extended. He slung his broadsword expertly around to knock the deadly sharp tip of the pike wide but the attacker's momentum was not disturbed as he sailed toward him.

Ethan jumped, pivoting at the hip, and whipped his left leg up and around. The side of his left boot smashed into the man's nose. The force of the powerful kick was magnified by the attacker's forward momentum and it clotheslined him. His legs flipped into the air and he slammed into the ground back first. Ethan spun in a half pirouette and landed with perfect balance. Before the fallen man could scramble to his feet, Ethan swept his sword around and took the doomed man's head. The body floundered but went nowhere.

The young warrior turned to face the woman and tall man he had tripped only seconds earlier to find that they were no longer there. They had risen to their feet and were shambling on toward the mountainside, completely ignoring him. There were no other infected near him at the moment but he quickly saw that such was not the case for Hammer and Arrowhead. They were fifteen yards away, surrounded by the berserker infected and barely able to hold them off while they fought their way through the crowd.

The walkers pressed in, arms, tools and weapons flailing. Hammer kept them at bay almost easily, sweeping the massive war hammer left and right. Attackers flew in every direction. Arrowhead deftly stayed to his side, using his wide attack the way they had practiced for years. She treated it like a shield and stepped out in perfect synchronicity with his backswing to slash with the quickness of a cobra. They made slow progress, but each inch cost them more energy as the walkers continued to work their way around the Hounds' formidable defense.

The three citizens had to help fend them off. Before long Adam went down, leaving Arrowhead's flank partially open. The infected pressed in closer. She turned to fend off a blow from a rusted but eerily familiar longsword. She blocked and parried two more strikes and finally saw the equally familiar face of her attacker. It looked as if it might have been handsome at one time but now it was only the face of a rotting corpse. There were enough discernable features, however, for Arrowhead to make the connection.

When Arrowhead noticed that the moldering, tattered rags he wore were the sorry remnants of a uniform much like the ones she, Ethan, and Hammer were wearing, there was no question of his identity.

"Magnus," she gasped.

The realization that this had been Magnus, also known as Shadow Blade of the Keeper's Hounds, stunned her. This was the man she thought she, Ethan, and Hammer had killed weeks earlier while the Hounds crossed Lake Onyx on their return from their final demon hunt. Just behind Magnus and looking just as terrible was Lance, the other Hound that had gone berserk and was subdued by her teammates on that same ill-fated voyage. Lance had escaped by tearing through the hull of their ship with his bare hands and plunging into Lake Onyx.

Arrowhead was puzzled before concluding that the two of them had either impossibly floated ashore or walked along the bottom of the deep great lake and made their way to Ridgeland with the rest of the infected. Her shock made her falter for the briefest instant before she gathered herself and took Magnus's head. Unfortunately, the brief pause left her out of position to defend against Lance and a young boy, both of whom launched forcefully into her left side.

Ethan's heart leapt into his throat when he saw her fall. The same heartbreaking grief he felt when her sky sleigh was brought down overcame him and threatened to immobilize him. The only thing that kept him moving was his grave fear and determination.

He was rushing to her aid when a handful of the walkers burst through the wall of cavalry soldiers and ran toward him. There were way too many, he knew. Even with the *gun*'s magic, even with Raxe's martial abilities, there was no way he was going to survive the coming onslaught with only a broadsword.

The long staff flared urgently, almost painfully, against Ethan's back. He was still wondering what good the staff would do when Raxe's words came back to him.

"It's meant to be the perfect weapon for you. It will make any other weapon unnecessary. It will be every weapon you need. It will be the only *weapon you will ever need."*

THE KEY QUEST

Ethan sheathed his broadsword and pulled the shimmering *gun* from his back, willing it to be effective against his enemies. When he brought it down in front of him it was no longer the thin staff that was slightly longer than he was tall. It was even longer, and protruding from the front end of it was a wide blade reminiscent of a flat, sharp-edged, head of a shovel. He spun it around in his hand as he ran and saw a thinner but deadly blade shaped like a crescent moon protruding from the other end.

This new weapon looked as though it should have been much heavier but to Ethan it was same ideal weight and balance as the *gun*. He had never seen such a weapon in his young life yet he knew with certainty that it was called a *Fangbian Chan* in Raxe's native world, or monk spade in Raxe's native language. And Ethan knew he could use it. He held the *Fangbian Chan* high in a two-handed grip, pointing the wider blade forward as he rushed the charging enemy.

A bright, yellow-orange wall of flame leapt up in front of Ethan. The flames reached well over fifteen feet. Ethan skidded to a stop in anger and confusion. Only magic could conjure such a precise flame. He turned with his *Fangbian Chan* at the ready, expecting to see the demon itself and ready to fight it to the death.

When he saw Jon the Firemaster standing before him, a soft yellow glow hovering above his light leather armor, Ethan's confusion and frustration grew.

"What are you *doing*?" yelled Ethan. "Arrowhead and Hammer are in danger!"

Jon's frown was both sad and determined. He was still gaunt from his time spent in captivity and torture but his strength had obviously returned.

"We've been ordered to pull back, Ethan, I'm sorry. All of the conjurers are using their flames not to destroy the infected, but to hold them at bay. The creatures apparently have just enough intelligence to not walk into the flames."

"What in the seven hells has that to do with Arrowhead and Hammer?" roared the young Sureblade. "They'll be killed over there!"

"And there's nothing we can do about it," answered Jon. He sounded sympathetic but firm. "We have our orders."

"*Damn our orders*! I'll not lose them again! I'll not lose *Arrowhead* again!"

Ethan turned and sprinted toward the wall of flame. Jon watched in disbelief. He could not believe the youngster had gone mad and decided to charge through the fire, and he was correct. Jon's tired, dark brown eyes widened as he watched the strange silver weapon, with its soft pale blue shimmer, begin to shudder and change shape in Ethan's hands. The crescent moon and spade-shaped blades on either end of the weapon melted inward to form the ends of a simple staff.

Jon's disbelief grew when Ethan lifted it back over his right shoulder as if he planned on vaulting the flames. The staff was barely six feet long and would never lift Ethan high enough. But the young Sureblade plunged the forward tip of the staff into the earth anyway.

If the boy was bluffing, Jon was not going to call him on it. He was preparing to pull the flames down enough for Ethan to clear them, but amazingly, he did not have to. The six-foot staff suddenly extended into a seventeen-foot long pike as Ethan neared the apex of his vault.

The change in shape was so quick and forceful that it propelled Ethan easily over the wall of fire. He held on to the weapon, which shrank back into a staff, as he disappeared on the other side of Jon's flaming barrier.

"His father was never this impetuous," grumbled Jon, taking long swift strides towards the wall.

5.2

Ethan cried out in fear as he descended, though it was not the fall that frightened him. The scene below terrified him and broke his heart. Arrowhead, as well as Adam, Jacob, and Walter, were lying on the ground fighting madly beneath a pile of the frenzied infected. The attackers were unarmed but they bore the four of them down with biting teeth and clawing fingers and the sheer weight of their numbers.

Hammer fought his way towards them, batting the enemy away by fours and fives. The ones whose heads were not completely smashed scrambled to their feet to resume their wild attack. Jon had cast a ring of fire around them, leaving them with nowhere to run, so instead of charging the mountain they charged the defenders. The walkers were not able to get close to Hammer but Ethan knew that if the big man stumbled, or inevitably tired, he would be a dead man.

Ethan landed in a sprint and willed his *gun* back into the *Fangbian Chan*. He dove into the fray with a fierce battle cry. The *Fangbian Chan* spun impossibly fast in his hands. It was as if it had a life of its own. The wide, razor-sharp spade at one end and the crescent-shaped double-edged metal at the other formed a whirlwind of carnage.

Ethan was at the eye of that deadly whirlwind and was anything but calm. He somersaulted, spun like a top, and bent his body to impossible angles as he twirled the monk spade. The weapon changed direction smoothly and swiftly as he swung it above and below his whirling body, slicing high in the air and near the ground, shredding anything caught in the circumference of the long, awesome weapon.

Between Ethan and Hammer, the infected went down like wheat before a thresher. Thick black blood, yellowing and graying bones, and flesh at different levels of decomposition littered the air and ground around them. Within moments, not one of the walkers was left standing within the circle of fire. Some were still. Most of them squirmed without making headway. Some rolled aimlessly this way and that. None of them were intact enough to resume their attack.

Among the fallen that had gone still were the three volunteers…and Arrowhead.

Ethan fell to his knees by her side, dropped his weapon, which had shrunk back into its original *gun* shape, and gathered Arrowhead in his arms. He was silent while tears poured down his cheeks. He did not even look up when a portal opened in the wall of flame to his right just long enough for Jon the Firemaster to stride through.

"This is your fault, Firemaster," Ethan growled.

"It was not," Hammer disagreed sadly. "She had already taken too many hits even before they finally brought her down, not only with weapons, but with clawed hands and filthy teeth. She was done well before Jon cast his fire. He was only trying to save you."

"Don't defend him!" Ethan snapped. "I could have saved her. The magic would have helped me save her!"

Jon sighed. "Ethan, we don't have time –"

"No!" barked the teen. He set Arrowhead down swiftly but gently, snatched up his *gun*, and then raised it threateningly. "I could have saved her, Jon. She's dead because of you."

Jon's sympathetic expression turned dangerous. "You fight like a man, even without the magic, Ethan. But your grief is making you think like the boy you are. Your magic won't help you if you attack me."

"Do you really believe that?" Ethan challenged. "Do you think you are powerful enough to defend someone who can fight like a Child of the Old Ones?"

Jon's expression turned again, this time to cold amusement. "To answer your question: Yes, I know I can, but you misunderstand, youngster. The magic *literally* will not help you if you attack me. Look at your weapon."

Ethan did. There was no glow. There was no warmth. The magic was gone. Ethan seemed unconcerned when he looked back up at the Firemaster.

"There is no magic," he allowed. "But that only means I don't need it to best you."

"Enough of this foolishness," commanded Jon. "We have to get away from here before –"

"Before what, you tired old man?" Ethan snarled, taking a threatening step forward.

"Ethan!" Hammer bellowed, but not in time.

Ethan flew forward violently as something, no, some*one* slammed into his back. He was driven face-forward into the blood and gore-spattered earth. He cried out in pain as sharp fingernails and teeth dug into his back and arms.

He thought he heard the others screaming at him, or to him, but he could not be sure. The pain and grief were clouding his hearing and confusing the rest of his senses. They had to be, because he thought the smell of lilacs, Arrowhead's favorite scent, was filling his nostrils along with the foul smells of the battlefield. He thought he saw small, slender woman's fingers rake across his face.

With a massive effort, he was able to turn himself onto his back and fend off his attacker for an instant. In that instant he thought he saw Nicolette. Her hair was loose and tumbling down around her shoulders. Those raven locks were stained with blood and moist, fetid dirt. Her beautiful face was twisted into a snarling bestial mask.

It *could not* have been Nicolette… It had to be the grief driving him mad.

The panicked teen pushed his attacker off, whoever it was, enough to spin back to hands and knees in an attempt to escape. He expected the attack to begin again but it did not. The thought that either Jon or Hammer had dispatched his attacker, along with the fleeting, reluctant notion that the attacker was the woman he loved, brought him to a panic.

He wanted to spin around again to see what had happened but the attack had struck him numb. Ethan crumpled back down face first to the ground and could no longer move. His mouth and mind felt as if they were filled with thick cotton.

There was only agony blazing through his body, infinitely more intense and torturous than the magic that powered his *gun*. The only other thing he could feel was the burning flow of tears streaming from his face into the dirt.

Shame filled Ethan as he realized, finally and belatedly, that Jon and Hammer had been trying to warn him. His grief made him thoughtless. It made him forget, or worse yet, disregard, the extent of the danger in which he had placed himself. And now, like Nicolette, he was infected along with the rest of the walking dead.

Meldrick Sureblade would never have been so foolish.

Ethan wondered how long the Firemaster and the surviving Keeper's Hound would wait before putting him out of his memory. All he could do was hope they killed him before they finished off Nicolette.

He felt, rather than heard, a rolling clap of thunder and then rain began to fall. With the last of his strength, Ethan brought his hands under his shoulders, palms down, in a useless attempt to push himself to his knees. The attempt was for naught. His strength was gone.

When his fading consciousness took in the weird purple hue of the fat raindrops spattering against his hands in the dying light of dusk, when he felt the angry pain burning its way through his extremities start to fade beneath the cool rainfall, he was relieved.

This was it, then. He knew he was about to die. The transformation would have his body, he thought even as his mind grew even more clouded, but it would not have his soul. When Ethan thought of all he had lost, he welcomed the darkness, for he would get to see Nicolette and his father again in the afterlife.

That was more than enough for Ethan Sureblade.

5.3

The smell of lilacs and charred earth roused Ethan from complete blackness into blue-black darkness. The sound of hissing steam, like water poured on red-hot steel just pulled from a forge, almost hurt his ears. A slight, cautious turn of the head revealed to Ethan three moons in the darkness above him. And then stars started to resolve in his vision.

The young Sureblade slowly sat up on muddy ground. A slight drizzle still fell from the heavens. In the moonlight, the raindrops retained the strange violet color he noticed before he passed out. He pulled his gaze from the night sky and looked around fearfully. It did not take him long to find Nicolette. She was also sitting up and staring at him.

And she was without question Nicolette again, and not just because her hair was down. She was no longer the snarling monster that had tried to kill him. Neither was she the intense, fearsome warrior of the Keeper's Hounds. She was indeed Nicolette, but the mix of expressions on her pale, pretty face made her mood unreadable.

With a gasp, Ethan crawled to her, sloshing through the mud with a nervous smile on his face. When he smiled, Nicolette beamed. They broke out into relieved laughter, embraced each other desperately, and then fell into the mud.

"I'm sorry," Nicolette breathed into his ear. "I almost killed you…thought I *had* killed you. I couldn't stop myself."

Ethan wanted to tell her how needless her apology was, to tell her that he could not possibly blame her for what had happened, but there was only one word he managed to utter:

"How?"

Jon's deep, tired voice drifted to Ethan through the patter of the slow drizzle. "Divine rain, young one, that's how."

Ethan and Nicolette, slightly embarrassed, sat up and looked at Jon, who sat on his haunches a few yards away. Hammer loomed over him, leaning on the long handle of his war hammer, his weight pressing half of the massive hammerhead into the wet soil. A haze of steam smelling of burnt grass and dirt wafted by on a soft breeze from earth that still smoldered from the extinguished fires.

"The Head Mage found a cure," Jon continued. "He and a team of First Echelon Mages saturated the clouds with a compound that reversed the infection. They followed the walkers that had already entered the mountains and applied the cure to them, as well."

Ethan glanced around again in disbelief. Royal soldiers were carrying the three volunteers away. Ethan could see the rise and fall of Jacob's chest as he breathed fitfully. The other two, unfortunately, lay still and were not breathing.

"Not all of them made it," added Hammer, following Ethan's glance. "Some were too badly injured to survive their wounds even after they were cleansed of the plague. Most were already dead, nothing but walking corpses, really."

"That was why we were rounding up the infected instead of destroying them. That's what I was trying to tell you," said Jon. "But in your grief, you wouldn't listen."

"I'm sorry," Ethan said softly, the flush of shame easily visible in his tan skin even in the soft moons' light. "I did not act like a warrior. I acted like a child."

"You acted like a human being," Jon corrected. He gave the teen a knowing look. "Learn from it. Grow from it, from *all* of it. Become stronger. I pray to the Lord Ascendant that we never experience anything like this again, but if it is His will that we do, I know that you will act like a warrior, then. You have too much of your father in you to do otherwise."

Left unspoken between the two of them was something else. More than grief and anger made Ethan act the way he did. When Jon said "all of it" Ethan knew that "all" included his magic. Jon was well aware of how intoxicating magic could be. The Firemaster knew how magic could instill a false sense of invincibility into even an experienced wielder, and how easily and how fatally it could turn on an inexperienced one.

"Thank you, Jon," Ethan said sincerely. "I *will* learn."

5.4

DEMON'S SPINE MOUNTAINS

Mar-dah's keep was a frustrating maze. If not for the undeniable aura of the Hell Key pulling at them, Raxe, Azhju'lestra and Rell Kallen could have easily wondered the tunnels and caverns in the bowels of the mountain forever without getting any closer to the evilly enchanted greatsword.

Their one bit of good fortune was that they did not have to travel in complete darkness. After trudging through the lowest depths for a time, they ascended to a level where the walls were free of the dimly glowing lichen, but from that point on, hand-sized conical sconces supporting small torches hung from the walls in regular intervals. The Ranger Elf, ever prepared, produced a flint stone and used it to light one of the torches. He pulled it free of the sconce and used it to light other torches as they trekked through the mountain.

The pull of the dread magic often led them to dead ends. Each time they reached one Raxe tapped the rock walls firmly with Demonsbane. If the wall sounded shallow enough he would simply cut right through it. He was eager for the chance to work off his frustration. If the wall sounded too deep to risk the time cutting through, the trio would double back and find another way around.

When they could find a large enough stone or group of stones, they would barricade their passage as Azh suggested. The wallowgrumps could track them by scent, and the barricades would slow them down. Raxe used Demonsbane to score the wall, floor, or if low enough, the ceiling every few dozen yards to mark their passage. It might have been a useless exercise with the wallowgrumps trailing them. They could easily end up backtracking right into their path, but if there were no other way out the marks would be useful.

The first few times he cut "X" marks into the stone he made it a point to linger near it for a long moment to make sure the mark remained. He would never forget his trip to Infinity Isle on his first visit across the WorldGate, when he cut tree trunks in a similar fashion to find his way back to his companions through the wild forest.

The trees healed themselves mere moments after being cut and left him hopelessly lost. It was not likely that this stone would heal itself, but then again, this mountain belonged to a powerful and imaginative wizard. Better safe than sorry. He moved on only when he was satisfied the scores would remain.

They crossed many thresholds with arches seven feet high or more, through four-inch thick walls and walls so deep that the opening was more of a short tunnel than a doorway. Nearly a third of them were warded. The wards were not concealed the way the barrier outside of the mountain was. Raxe could easily see the intense pale shimmer of energy blanketing the thresholds. Azh and Rell Kallen could sense them, too.

In some instances Rell Kallen would produce another one of his small spheres and toss it into the ward. In most of those instances the marble-like talisman worked and allowed them to pass. In some instances the magic was too strong and again they had to double back and find another route. None of them knew what the wards would do if they attempted to go through them. They did know that the man who conjured them had been one of the most powerful and malevolent wizards in the Known Lands. They had no intention of finding out what the wards might do to repel them.

They passed through many chambers. There were conference rooms large and small, with blocky stone tables surrounded by blunt chairs carved from rock. They passed through libraries with high shelves cut into the rock walls. The masterful way in which much of the stone was carved reminded Raxe of the hidden nation of the Stonehammer Dwarves. The dwarves had built a small city beneath Hell's Mountains with the same skill displayed here.

Raxe thought about Rom, a teleporting dwarf and second in command to Mar-dah, and wondered if the evil wizard had employed other dwarves to build this fortress within the mountain. If so, he had probably killed them all to keep secret the location of his lair.

They walked halls lined with small cells behind thick earthen doors with small slits piercing them at eye level. They passed through rooms that were obvious torture chambers, littered with sinister looking metal devices fitted with clamps, blades, screws and spikes. Sloping troughs were cut into the floor and disappeared into holes in the chamber walls, perfect for draining off fluids. Those rooms smelled of stale sweat and old, dry blood.

Raxe's internal clock told him they had been in the mountain for nearly seven hours. It was near midnight. They had walked almost non-stop, stopping only to eat, and when they did they worried over their dwindling rations. Raxe knew their next meal would be their last. If they did not find the Hell Key soon they would have to search for a larder within the keep, delaying them that much more.

They were always going up, traversing either crude stairways or sloped corridors. Raxe and Azh used the aura of the Hell Key to keep them moving in the right direction. Rell Kallen used his keen nose, ears, and sense of direction to find the safest paths through the meandering corridors. All Raxe could smell were the occasional fetid puddles of water and small rotting carcasses hidden in pools of blackness where the torchlight could not reach. All he could see were small creatures, both insect and animal, flitting from shadow to shadow and scurrying around distant corners. All he could hear were the chittering and clicking of those same creatures as they scrambled away in the darkness.

The baleful supernatural aura intensified as the trio ascended. The sensation, while foreboding, was strangely compelling. Raxe knew full well how dreadful a talisman the Hell Key was. He fought and killed countless demons set loose from the first five levels of hell by that enchanted greatsword. But at the same time he could not deny his morbid desire to see such a terrible power with his own eyes.

His fear, wariness, and curiosity rose to a fever pitch when the elf brought them to a stop at the foot of another dark, narrow incline of roughly carved stairs. The stairwell intersected a corridor that ran perpendicular to the one through which they walked. The Ranger Elf paused as Raxe and his daughter followed him into the high-ceilinged corridor that stretched into the shadows to the left and right.

Rell turned to Raxe. "Which way now, offworld –"

He stopped short when he saw Raxe, with the whelp Child as always at the offworlder's right hand, walking hurriedly and purposefully to the right. Rell turned and quickly caught up with them, lighting torches in the wall sconces as he went. After a dozen yards or so a wide threshold crept out of the shadows on the left hand wall. The father and daughter stepped through the opening without hesitation with Rell at their heels.

They entered a long dark corridor with yet another wide threshold barely visible on the far end. There were no intersecting hallways, only a long tunnel leading to the archway. A ten second jog took them the length of the corridor and through the unprotected archway. Rell Kallen lit the small torches in the conical sconces on either side of the entrance, revealing a conference room that was larger than the others they had seen. Other than its size, it was as unremarkable as the others had been.

The elf followed the Children of the Old Ones as they strode across the wide hall to a broad stone door. The door had no handles and no locks. Only the wide arched outline of cut stone indicated the presence of the door. Raxe and Azh both stopped a few feet from the door and simply stared at it with identical frowns. Rell nudged his way between them. He studied the door, the Children's frowns, and then the door once again.

"Is it safe to assume we have finally reached our destination?"

Raxe nodded. "But I don't know how we're gonna get in there. Mar-dah must've used magic to open it. If it had handles I'm sure it'd still be too heavy to pull open even for both of us. Not to mention this door is warded pretty heavily. The spell is pouring magical energy from the door...and it stinks to high hell."

The Ranger Elf lifted his right hand, which held one of his dark green marbles between long slender fingers. With a flick, he sent the marble flying into the door. The green marble struck the rocky surface and stuck there. Rell Kallen raised an eyebrow, expecting the marble to either flash – which is what it did when it worked properly, or bounce harmlessly away if it did not work on that particular barrier spell. He did not quite know what to make of the reaction they witnessed.

A white glow, circular and about the size of a man's fist, slowly bled outward from the shiny round stone. That, Rell Kallen thought with a satisfied sneer, is what happened when the stone worked correctly. The glow would expand large enough to provide them safe passage. The offworlder could then use Demonsbane to hack his way through. Other than his ability to feel the presence of the Hell Key, the brutish work of cutting stone and wood was all the offworlder was good for.

But the glow did not expand. It stayed at the same size and intensified. And then the elf's other thin eyebrow rose as the white glow retreated back into the dark green marble, which began to shimmer with that same white glow. It began to vibrate against the stone door. The vibration grew from a slow tap to a speed so intense that the tap turned into something like the buzzing of a giant angry bee. Pale smoke wafted from the shuddering marble just before it shook itself to a small pile of emerald ashes.

Raxe looked at Rell Kallen expectantly. "So…?"

"It did not work," the elf snapped.

"Ok," said Raxe as he scratched his scalp between his dreadlocks. "Let me try something." He stepped closer to the large door while pulling Demonsbane from his hip, sending a soft hum singing through the conference room. "This blade is supposed to be forged by the Old Ones and indestructible. I damn sure hope it is." With his thick lips pursed tightly, he tapped one of the axe blades gently against door.

There was no reaction. And from the sound of the metal on the stone, the door was fairly thick.

"No problem," Raxe grinned. "This'll be a start. Maybe we'll think of some way to get through the barrier spell by the time I get this door out of the way."

He hefted the enchanted battleaxe with both hands and gave a mighty swing. When the blade struck the door a painfully bright yellow light flashed from the stone. The light blinded Raxe and a scorching hot concussive wave heaved him from his feet. A sensation of weightlessness overcame him for a moment. It was a moment cut violently short when his back slammed against something with a force that reminded him of his landing when he fell from a sky sleigh from thousands of feet in the sky.

When his vision returned he realized he was suspended several inches high and upside down, imbedded into the wall on the opposite side of the conference room. Demonsbane was still clutched tightly in his claw of a right hand.

"Ow," he mumbled.

"Are you hurt?" asked Azh as she rushed over, her light steps almost inaudible.

Raxe chuckled at the sight of her. From his orientation it seemed as if she was running across the ceiling while her hair defied gravity. With a grunt, he pulled himself from the crater and fell to his hands and knees facing the wall. He was on his feet and turned to face the door on the other side of the room by the time Azh reached him.

"I guess the ward only reacts when the door is faced with a legitimate threat," answered Raxe. "But, yeah, I'm fine."

"None of us are *fine*," Rell Kallen reminded. "The wallowgrumps are certainly tracking us. Offworlder, perhaps you can cut through the wall on either side of the door."

"No good," Raxe answered as he shook his head. "That barrier extends throughout this entire wall. I can see it. It's a safe bet that all of the perimeter walls, including the floor and ceiling, are protected in the same way."

The elf shook his head, causing his coiled blonde braid to sway from right to left. "This is not acceptable. We *must* find a way into that room."

Raxe thought for a moment. "Did either of you see that flash or feel that blowback?"

"Of course," answered Rell Kallen as if the question was absurd.

"Good," Raxe said. "That means the spell emits energy. That's good."

"What are you babbling about?" the elf snarled.

"I'll show you," Raxe answered.

He walked back over to the door. This time, he turned his back to the wall. Holding Demonsbane in both hands but low, near his belt line, Raxe bent his knees and then thrust himself onto the door. His armored back struck the stone before any other part of his body and the blinding yellow light flashed again. But unlike before, Raxe did not go flying across the room. He stuck to the wall the same way the elf's marble had. Even though his legs were fully extended, the tips of his toes hovered several inches above the floor.

A white glow outlined Raxe's torso. It expanded to about the same distance as the radius of the glow that surrounded the marble. To Azh's horror, her father started to vibrate like the marble: slowly at first but quickly gaining intensity until Raxe was shuddering with painful speed. Azh took a couple of hurried steps toward Raxe but he raised a trembling hand.

"N-N-N-N-N-O-O-O-O-O!" cried Raxe, his vibrating body making his coarse voice come out in a stuttering roar, freezing Azh in her tracks.

The white glow then bled back into Raxe's silver cuirass. Instead of smoking and vibrating the armor into ash, the glow spread from the cuirass through Raxe's arms and into Demonsbane. Raxe gave an agonized cry and brought his battleaxe up and over his head, driving one of the blades half way into the stone. There was yet another painful flash of blinding light followed by a thunderclap. When Rell Kallen and Azh regained their sight, they saw Raxe lying in pile of rubble on the other side of the threshold.

"Impressive," Rell Kallen allowed reluctantly. "Your armor absorbed the destructive energy warding the door and transferred it to your weapon, which you then used to release that energy back *into* the door."

Rell Kallen had been unaware of that particular property of Raxe's gear. It was a useful bit of information he would remember for future reference.

"I see you were paying attention," Raxe replied as he rose shakily to his feet. He looked down to brush away a bit of dust and when he looked up, both the half-faerie and the Ranger Elf were staring past him. Raxe turned to see what they were looking at. In the dim torchlight that seeped in from the conference room, his eyes instantly locked onto the Hell Key.

The enchanted greatsword rested on a large stone table in the center of the room fifteen feet away from where Raxe stood. It was as beautiful as its counterpart, the WorldGate Key. It had the same silver two-handed grip and was bound with identical strands of intricately woven gilded cord. The pommel was the same round, flat disk that resembled a large silver coin. In fact, the two blades were identical with the exception of the masterfully carved image in the long, wide, double-edged blade. Even from fifteen feet away Raxe could see the intricate and lifelike carving of a roaring dragon. He could feel the dragon's malicious glare upon him.

That was not the first time Raxe saw the Hell Key. He saw it three years earlier in a vision. In that vision, Mar-dah's pale hand with its long, manicured fingernails clutched the weapon. Only an Old One or one of their direct descendants could invoke the Keys' magic, and before Mar-dah, millennia had passed since one had done so. The contact between Mar-dah's hand and the enchanted weapon, after so many years without it being handled by someone with the ability to actually use it for its true purpose, awakened a power so profound that both Raxe and his grandfather shared the same vision even across the WorldGate.

Seeing the Hell Key through the vision, Raxe realized, was not at all like seeing it in person. The vision could not relay the awesome and fearsome energy that radiated from the talisman. Raxe had never had an addictive personality. The only fixation he ever had was with fighting. He was particularly fond of Chinese martial arts but he also studied several of the Japanese arts. Other than that, he had never been obsessed with anything.

The sinister enchantment of the Hell Key, however, called to him seductively. It had been doing so since they entered the mountain. Now that it was within his reach its pull was like nothing he had ever experienced. The conflicting sensations of attraction and repulsion warred within him and he was unsure of which sensation to embrace. His fear of the weapon was greater than his desire to possess it. His mission, however, dictated that he retrieve it.

"What in the seven hells are you waiting for?" barked the Ranger Elf. "If you are too afraid to take hold of it, I will do it for you!"

Rell Kallen stepped quickly to the doorway. As he neared it the fine hairs on the back of his neck stood on end. His next long, hurried stride would take him through the threshold, but he stopped short. He halted so abruptly that his momentum sent his long braid swinging forward. The moment it broke the plane of the doorway, there was a small but intense yellow flash of light, a surge of heat, and the tip of his braid blew back at him as smoking gray ash.

The singed edges of the braid continued to glow an angry bright red that threatened to flare into flame at any second. The Ranger Elf produced a knife and cut through the braid almost two inches away from the smoldering end. He dropped it and watched it burn to ash before it hit the floor.

Raxe looked over his shoulder as he walked toward the table. "Oh yeah, don't try to follow me in here," he called back. "I think the ward came back."

The Ranger Elf snarled while Azh giggled.

Raxe forced his reluctant legs forward. He decided to take in his surroundings as he advanced, anything to tear his gaze away from the terribly seductive Hell Key. The room was stale and stuffy, almost stiflingly so. Three years of dust rested on every surface.

The walls were set in a hexagonal pattern. The wall in which the door was set was otherwise bare but the other five walls were almost completely dominated floor to ceiling by shelves carved into the stone. The only part of those walls that did not contain shelves was the corner to the far right. A stone chair and cauldron sat in that corner.

A few of the shelves contained dusty books of varying thickness. Most of the shelves held jars and vials of mysterious liquids and powders. On other shelves rested small, weird devices of metal and glass and wood construction with functions that Raxe could not begin to guess. The room clearly served as both a library and laboratory. Raxe did not want to think about the horrific spells and experiments that were studied and perpetrated in this disturbing chamber.

As he neared the table, he got a better look at it. The base of the table was hexagonal and sat in the center of a large six-pointed star carved into the floor. The star was close to twelve feet wide. The triangles that formed the tips of the star contained large carvings of symbols that, for the most part, resembled figures he had watched his grandfather draw from time to time during the years they were running from the organization. Sometimes Dan would carve the symbol in a wooden desk, sometimes he would draw it ink or pencil on a small sheet of paper. When Raxe asked what it was, Dan always told him the drawing was a good luck charm.

But while the symbols were similar, there was a difference in the way his grandfather drew them and the way they were drawn beneath the stone table. Dan always drew a circle around the outside of a pentagon. In the spaces within the "D" shaped outlines where the circle touched the corners of the pentagon, Dan would draw symbols that represented the five elements: earth, air, fire, water and spirit.

This symbol was a six-pointed star without a circle. The triangular star points contained symbols of the five elements, but the sixth point displayed a symbol that Raxe had never seen Dan use. It was three of the symbols that represented air. They overlapped each other with two at the top and one at the bottom middle. Even with his limited knowledge of magic, Raxe knew the differences between the pentagonal and hexagonal ciphers held great significance in regard to the type of magic being employed.

The red mage Shaddor Rinn had used that symbol is his conjuring, so Raxe knew it could not be anything good. Rinn made the foolish mistake of employing a group of traitorous Lorrian soldiers to poison Raxe and kidnap Azh in order to use their blood to fortify his magic. Rinn repaid those soldiers with the same betrayal they showed to Raxe, and they were likely dead by now. Raxe took the red mage's tongue and both of his hands to make sure the little creep could never conjure again.

The memory brought a menacing smile to Raxe's lips.

He dismissed the pleasant memory when he reached the table. He got there much faster than he had hoped to, yet he did not hesitate to reach out with his left hand and grasp the two-hand sword grip. The dragon's perfectly engraved eyes seemed to shift to peer deeply into Raxe's dark brown eyes. And then everything went black.

5.5

MIDWEST USA – INTERSTATE 80

Lisa stared at herself in the mirror mounted to the sun shade. *Here comes the baby weight,* she thought. She had not started to show, at least not in her stomach, but the other subtler signs were already there. Her face was fuller, rounder than it had been. Her fingers and toes had grown a little puffy. The thought of having to do all of this traveling and running and fighting as her pregnancy progressed made her heart beat faster. In the next moment she was rubbing her forehead with her left hand.

She turned her attention from her reflection and started intently out of the front passenger side window of the stolen Ford Explorer that Dan was steering east on I-80. She scanned the southern horizon, holding her hand over her eyes to shield them from the rising sun shining through the windshield. Though she watched the southern horizon she knew their pursuers could pop up anywhere. She and Dan would be in serious trouble if they came at them from the east, cutting them off from their intended destination. And with the sun in their eyes they would be at even more of a disadvantage than they already were.

She thought about Joel again, wondered where he was, what he was doing, if he was OK. The thought of him no longer pained her. In fact, it galvanized her. Instead of allowing it to bring her despair, she used it to firm her resolve to stay alive so that she could see him again, hold him and kiss him again.

That was why she studied the skies so thoroughly. She had to be ready for anything, even if it did actually seem like Dan's magic perfume *might* be working. During the hours that they were on the road she saw a helicopter and thought they were in trouble. It turned out to be a military chopper that passed harmlessly by. A few cars passed them in both directions in the dark wee hours of the morning and during sunrise. Not once was Dan concerned. He remained wary but never worried. Lisa supposed that should give her comfort.

Comfort, however, was not forthcoming for her. She had been through far too much to let her guard down. She was nevertheless shocked, though, when the SUV started pulling to the left.

"Dan?" she asked nervously as she turned to him.

Dan gazed listlessly ahead, seemingly at nothing. He looked to be in some sort of trance, or perhaps an epileptic seizure. All he did was hold the steering wheel and stare as the Explorer drifted aimlessly from the far right lane of the wide interstate highway toward the double yellow line.

"Dan!" she snapped, reaching over and grasping the wheel. "Dan!" she cried again.

A grimace of grave discomfort flashed across his face. His head jerked forward, his eyes went wide, and he quickly righted the SUV. He turned to her and winked but he could not hide his concern.

"I'm fine," he assured.

"What the hell was that, Dan?"

He frowned, the web of creases in his dark brown face deepening. "A vision. My grandson just found the Hell Key."

Lisa's face brightened. "Why the long face? That's a good thing."

Dan shook his head slowly and thoughtfully. "There's nothing good about anything involving the Hell Key."

"You know what I mean, Dan. That was why they went over there. So the mission is pretty much over. Did you see anything about Joel?"

Dan glanced at her and shook his head. "I'm sorry. All I saw was Ryan's hand on the Hell Key. I felt an explosion of pain in my head that shot through my body. I didn't see Joel. But understand something, girl. The plan was to *retrieve* the Hell Key. Finding it is just the first part. They still have to get it to Lorr Palace."

5.6

Rionn Lorr's head snapped up. The long, narrow vial slipped from his grasp and shattered into tiny shards when it hit the floor. The alchemists sitting at the long table, each busy about the task of mixing powders and liquids, all started at the sudden movement and sound. Rionn looked down between his booted feet at the broken glass and thanked the Lord Ascendant that it was empty.

When he noticed the puzzled and concerned gazes of the men and women around him, he smiled thinly and his sun-browned face flushed.

"Worry not, people," Rionn said. "All is well. It will be even better when we are done here."

This was the second time the Head Mage experienced the sort of vision that had just assaulted him. The first time it filled him with dread, for that was when Mar-dah gained possession of the Hell Key. This time, while he knew that the offworlder's mission was far from over, the vision filled him with hope.

PART II

WRATH

Chapter 6: Immortal Fall

6.1
SOUTHERN RANGES OF HELL'S MOUNTAINS

Lieutenant Colonel Rheingold Strong stood atop the same rise the *Ken* High Chieftain had stood upon before raiding Hillview, the small village just beyond the Hell's Mountains foothills. He had already seen the town and it sickened him. Against the backdrop of the three moons just above the eastern horizon, in the deep purple and then silver and then orange-red twilight sky, gryphons and their Ryders flew in wide circles above the village, chasing away spiraling vultures and crows.

The fires had burned out but a haze of smoke still hovered over the village. Within it lingered the stench of scorched earth and flesh. The angle of the blackwood bolts protruding from the ground, buildings, animals – and in the worst cases, people – clearly indicated that they were launched from these foothills. Strong's men were down the western slopes, inspecting the hills and the valleys and dales between them.

Further north, after a day or so of travelling south from the massacre that was Port Lorrian, the invaders' path veered into the mountains. Strong's trackers wanted to follow the path but the Lieutenant Colonel knew better. The treacherous mountain trails would slow them down. There were multiple places for ambush and other traps, and the Old Ones knew they could not survive another ambush. He knew the *Ken* were going south so Strong ordered them to travel south but parallel to the mountains instead of through them. He regretted that he had to find their path again this way.

Sergeant Caleb Godson trudged back up the hill. "We can still make out the tracks from the wheeled ballistae," he reported, "and other wagons that they surely used to transport wagon-mounted spits to cook food."

"Wheeled *cooking* apparatus?" Strong asked. "They travel with rolling kitchens?"

Godson shrugged. "There were no marks of fires on the ground but the trail of bones and other leavings clearly indicated that food was cooked."

Strong grunted. "The foreigners no longer care about being followed. They no longer take care to even attempt to mask their passage."

"The bastards have some gall," came a voice from the air. Captain Zedek, the light-armored Gryphon Ryder, swept down silently, the gryphon's giant eagle's wings spread wide as the bird-cat lighted softly on the crest of the hill on padded paws. "They flaunt their lack of concern for us."

Strong turned to his friend. "You've seen the village."

Zedek shuddered. "I've seen too much of the village. This was different than Port Lorrian."

"I noticed," Strong said. "Port Lorrian was savage vengeance."

"And this," Godson added, waving a hand at both the town in the distance and down the hill, "was a food and supply raid."

"It was just as savage," Zedek growled. "Just as heartless. They didn't just kill people. The survivors said they took *people* the same way they took livestock. Food for their hellish land dragon mounts, no doubt."

"At least they left survivors," Godson noted. "There were bloody few of them left at Port Lorrian. Fewer than here, and that town was five times the size of this tiny village."

"That's true," Strong agreed. "This was rushed. They left no message this time. They left no taunts or threats. I know they do not rush out of fear of us, though they should, now that we are better prepared." He glanced down at the end of his company and their recently built war machines. "They were rushed for a different reason."

"A blessing, that was," Zedek said. "Otherwise there would not be a soul left here. But that begs the question of *why* they rushed."

Lieutenant Colonel Strong cast a dire gaze to the south. "Because they're close to their goal," he surmised. "That means we must move even more swiftly." He looked at his companions, glancing at each one in turn. "How is morale among our men?"

"They're pissing mad," Godson declared. "They're ready to take steel to these giant western savages."

"As are my Gryphon Ryders," Zedek assured.

The Lieutenant Colonel was just as ready. He knew they could very well lose the confrontation, but all they had to do was delay the *Ken* from fulfilling their charge of killing the offworlder and his team. The delay had to slow the enemy down long enough for their reinforcements to arrive.

Most importantly, though, Strong was determined to kill as many of the *Ken d'Zanir* as he could before he died.

6.2

Heaven and hell.

That was what Raxe felt. Or at least that how he thought heaven must feel…if he assumed heaven was the granting of every carnal wish and dark desire he ever had.

He *had* seen hell – his own personal hell – many, many times. That feeling was nothing new. It was painful beyond imagining. It was indescribable despair. It was paralyzing fear and brain numbing loathing. But it was nothing new.

Another weapon forged by the Old Ones, his very own battleaxe, Demonsbane, in fact, had shown him the hell that awaited him as recompense for his many sins, especially the murders he committed as an organization assassin.

The first time he saw hell was when he gave in to the magic of his enchanted battleaxe. He saw it in his dreams almost every night for longer than he cared to remember. The dreams were less frequent now but he never forgot one detail. Whenever it seemed he was on the verge of forgetting any minute detail, the nightmares would return.

That hellish feeling was so familiar to him that it did not bother him nearly as much as the "heavenly" feeling. As rapturous as the sensation felt, heaven could not be a warm, moist whisper promising him everything he had ever lusted after, be it money, power, or sex. Heaven would not pledge to kill all of his enemies or make him a god on earth…would it? Not that he knew a lot about heaven. Because of his mother's untimely death, he spent most of his teenage and adult years rejecting the notions of God and heaven.

And then he took into consideration that he was indeed a Child of the Old Ones. The power of the Hell Key was made for the Children to control. Mar-dah had been able to not only free the demons but control them as well, at least to some degree. Why could Raxe not do the same? He already knew how to invoke the power. The magic was in the blood. The Hell Key would work the way the WorldGate Key worked. This he knew instinctively.

Or perhaps it was the Hell Key telling him so.

The Keys were twins of a sort, after all. They were different sides of the same coin. Although once they were used, the result would be markedly different.

Raxe would have to do some studying of magic in order to direct the demons, but hell, he had over two hundred years of memories straight from the mind of a master sorceress. He could... No, he *would* find a way to release those memories. He had to. The power of the Hell Key was far too great to ignore. It was a sinister weapon, but used correctly, Raxe was convinced it could be used as an instrument for good.

Mar-dah simply did not use the magic correctly. He freed the demons en masse, used them as a blunt weapon to distract the Royal Army and weaken the Head Mage to make them all easier to conquer. The malicious wizard used the Hell Key toward a wicked purpose. It was only a matter of time before that wickedness would have turned against him. That was the nature of evil.

Raxe, on the other hand, would fight fire with fire. He could use the demons against evil. He would use them in a more subtle way.

Lower level demons were the easiest to control. One or two of them, placed strategically, would make the perfect assassins. They would be especially useful in his world against the organization. Demons were very hard to kill by conventional means. Raxe knew from first-hand experience that even high caliber ammunition had little to no effect on even lower level demons. They have to be hacked to pieces, or beaten to a pulp, or blasted to bits, or burned to ash. Not even organization agents casually carried those kinds of weapons around.

The most advanced forensics would be completely stumped. How would they be able to identify or trace genetic evidence left over by creatures not of their world? And with Demonsbane, Raxe could easily send them back to hell when their jobs were done.

All he had to do was use the Hell Key correctly. He could already slay demons. Why not control them as well?

He was of divine blood, a Child of the Old Ones. He was the direct descendant of the Gatekeeper and his son…

RAXE!

Yes, his son, Raxe.

This power was meant for him, for he was…

RAXE!

Indeed. In this world, he *was* Raxe. It was more than just a moniker. It was more than a simple way to differentiate him from the Head Mage because their names, Ryan and Rionn, sounded so much alike. He was a…

Father?

Raxe shook his head and turned. He saw his daughter standing outside the wide doorway. And then he noticed the worried and irritated glare of the Ranger Elf.

"Are you going to put the weapon away now, foolish Child?" Rell Kallen snapped.

Raxe noticed the razor sharp edge of the enchanted greatsword resting on the bicep of his right arm. His left hand held the sword grip in a trembling clutch. It was a wonder he had not already drawn blood. He pulled the sword away and released the breath that he did not realize he was holding.

The Ranger Elf could see the longing and the cold cunning that the malevolent Hell Key stirred up within the offworlder. That was exactly why a Child of the Old Ones should never possess the Hell Key. This was precisely the reason the Elven Queen Eleshaë sent him to find the Hell Key and bring it back to the Elf Lands of Thâlstrën.

"We must leave here quickly," Rell continued. "The racket you've raised has attracted something's attention."

"I know," Raxe said breathlessly, his gravelly voice breaking with the effort. He made sure to keep his eyes averted from the Hell Key as he slipped it into the empty sheath hooked a few inches behind Questblade on his weapons belt. "The wallowgrumps have found us."

"No, not wallowgrumps," Rell said. His pointed ears shifted slightly to pick up sounds that the two Children of the

Old Ones could not yet hear. "What's coming now can be just as bad, though, and perhaps even worse."

Raxe strode toward the doorway. "What is it, then?"

Raxe was answered by a strange sound that he could not quite place. It floated to them from beyond the long corridor that led to the conference room. It sounded like…tapping? It was a lot of tapping, thousands of sharpened blade tips tapping and scraping against a rough, hard surface.

He saw the source of the sound just as he reached the threshold and gasped. A flood of small dark shapes came boiling into the far end of the long corridor. They covered every surface: floor, walls and ceiling. They skirted the small torches that hung on the walls the way a shallow stream flows around a large rock. They clicked and clacked and scraped as they came.

There was nowhere for the trio to run. The corridor the creatures approached through was the only way out.

The weak yellow glow of the wall sconces did not reveal many details but Raxe could see that the shapes were covered with dull gray fur. They were roughly the size and shape of raccoons. Their legs, however, were arachnid: long, spindly, barbed, and multi-jointed. Instead of ending in mammalian paws, their legs ended with needlepoints that clacked upon the stone of the cavern surfaces. They had way more than four legs, more than eight, in fact. The exact number was impossible to discern because there were too many of the creatures with too many overlapping legs and they were moving too damned fast.

Their eyes were visible, too. Their misshapen heads were dotted with a jumble of small optical orbs that flickered evilly as they reflected the torchlight. All of those wicked little eyes were fixed hungrily upon the three intruders.

"Step back!" called Raxe.

He turned his back to the warded doorway and bent his knees. Instead of jumping through the protected threshold as he did earlier, he tilted his head forward, away from the ward, and then leaned his back into it so that the upper back of his cuirass crossed the threshold first. The magic jolted him forcefully and the blinding yellow light flared yet again.

This time, both the elf and the half faerie held their heads down and shielded their eyes with their hands. When they looked up Raxe was suspended in the doorway, leaning back on his heels and propped up against the transparent barrier. The shuddering convulsions started again and the pale white light shimmered through his body. When they looked over their shoulders they saw the wave of dull, rough-furred monsters with their click-clacking claws and flickering eyes coursing up the corridor only seconds away from the conference room. The creatures were so close now that the torchlight could be seen gleaming off of their countless, disproportionately long and chattering fangs.

A ringing crash brought Rell Kallen's and Azh's attention back to Raxe, who had finally fallen roughly to the floor on their side of the threshold. He was still glowing as he quickly rolled over onto his knees, thrust Demonsbane forward with his left hand and roared in pain.

"DOWN!" he bellowed, his ruined voice booming like an avalanche of sandstone blocks.

Rell and Azh fell to the floor flat on their stomachs just as broad, jagged bolts of bright yellow energy erupted from Demonsbane's silver crescent blades. The bolts split, separated and branched out at different angles, but all of them raced through the archway and down the corridor.

The bolts tore into the charging surge of multi-legged creatures, causing a cacophony wet pops and high-pitched shrieks as the small monsters burned and exploded. The devastating energy poured from the enchanted axe blades for several seconds before it abruptly ceased.

Raxe pitched forward but managed to catch himself with his damaged right hand before his face hit the floor. Sharp, searing pain from his hand all the way up his arm was the reward for the effort. He gnashed his teeth and pushed himself to his feet to join his daughter and the elf, already back on their feet. He exhaled heavily and lowered Demonsbane tiredly to his side so that the axe blades pointed at the floor. The hall was clear for the moment.

Only dark smoke and the acrid stench of burning hair floated into the conference room. The long corridor was clear, but the sound of clicking, tapping, and scraping, however, still echoed in the distance and grew steadily louder and closer.

Rell Kallen, as always, had his angular face set in an annoyed grimace. "Fool!" he barked. "You've only bought us a few useless seconds. We can't make it to the other end of that corridor before we're overrun. You should have saved that blast to –"

Another flash of yellow light cut the Ranger Elf's words short as more powerful bolts shot from the head of the enchanted battleaxe. Raxe was still pointing the crescent blades downward so the bolts would smash into the floor. Rock, pulverized into coarse dust, and gray smoke plumed while a four-foot circular hole opened in the stone floor.

Raxe looked up at Rell Kallen. "So I could do that?" the offworlder asked tiredly. "Why not do both?"

Rell Kallen glared at him and jumped down into the hole.

"Your turn, Azh," Raxe commanded.

His daughter smiled up at him and followed the Ranger Elf with a graceful leap. Raxe saw another swarm of the creatures just entering the far end of the corridor as he dropped through the opening. As it turned out, He had blown a hole through two floors, making it a nearly thirty-foot drop. There was a moment of surprise when he realized the fall was twice as long as he expected and it took another moment for him to orient himself.

The elf landed on his toes and ran. Azh landed in a smooth crouch and stepped aside to wait for her father. Raxe landed more steadily than he expected. His armored boots absorbed the brunt of the impact and he collapsed into a skilled roll that brought him to his feet in an instant. Without a word, father and daughter took off in a sprint after the Ranger Elf Rell Kallen.

"Where are we going?" Raxe called after Rell between puffs of breath. "This isn't the direction we came."

"I know," called the Ranger Elf in return. "My way is quicker. Stay close! I can't risk jogging any slower!"

"Jog," Raxe grumbled between puffs of breath. "Little son of a bitch."

The elf was only a couple of inches shorter than Raxe, taller than Raxe had expected from his limited knowledge of elves. But he enjoyed the insult anyway.

Azh was a few paces ahead of him. Raxe suspected she might have been able to stay with the elf if she were not trying to stay close to him. They followed Rell Kallen through the myriad twists and turns of the labyrinthine corridors. Raxe could not keep himself from looking over his shoulder from time to time, expecting to see the little sharp-edged nightmares materializing behind them.

"What are those things?" Raxe yelled ahead.

"Spider rats!" Rell allowed. "They are large, twelve-legged rodents that will eat anything and everything. They prefer living flesh, blood, and bone. The only thing they don't eat is stone, which they can burrow through with tooth and claw when necessary. Now save your breath and run!"

They ran in silence for several minutes. Raxe pushed himself to keep Rell Kallen in sight, which was sometimes impossible because some of the halls were so short. In those instances Azh would run far enough ahead to see the elf but close enough for Raxe to follow the sound of her footfalls.

The Ranger Elf finally slowed his "jog" to what was for him a slow lope. His ears twitched as he listened carefully, filtering out the sounds of the Children's footfalls and focusing his acute hearing as sharply as he could.

There. He heard it. The skittering of hundreds of claws rapidly tapping against stone was unmistakable. His slowed his pace allowed Raxe and Azh to finally catch up to him. Raxe saw the look of intense concentration on elf's face.

"What's wrong?" Raxe asked.

"The spider rats are coming…quickly."

"Then we've gotta pick up the pace," Raxe said. "I recognize this area. We're almost back to the stairwell. We can block it off and buy ourselves more time."

"That would be an excellent plan if the wallowgrumps were not in the stairwell," Rell Kallen noted, his pointed ears twitching slightly. "They are almost to this floor."

"Damn," Raxe breathed.

He could not decide which threat he would rather fight. The spider rats were comparatively small and probably easy to kill individually but there were far too many of them. On the other hand, there were only a handful of wallowgrumps. But those beasts were nearly impossible to kill. Rell Kallen padded on in silence until he came to an intersecting corridor. He turned to his right and picked up his pace.

"Follow!" he commanded as he pulled away.

Raxe and Azh rounded the corner and labored once again to keep the Ranger Elf in sight. He turned left at an intersecting corner and was gone.

"Slow down, dammit!" Raxe called.

Rell's jog was almost equal to Raxe's sprint, so when the elf sprinted, Raxe had to go all out just to keep from losing him completely. The offworlder was almost surprised that Azh could move so fast with such short legs...*almost* surprised. She had amazed him more than once and he was becoming less and less startled by her abilities.

A few seconds later, they turned left where they saw the Ranger Elf turn. To their relief he was standing with his back to the wall at the end of the corridor roughly twenty yards away. Raxe's heart jumped initially because in the gloom it looked like the hall stopped abruptly at a dead end. But as they neared the elf, he could see that a perpendicular hall branched off to the right and left.

"Nice of you to wait for –" Raxe started sarcastically before Rell silenced him with a raised finger.

"We need to go that way," Rell Kallen said, pointing left down a hall so long that shadow swallowed its far end. "But that path makes another turn and then dead ends."

"How could you know that?" Raxe asked.

"I can hear the air flowing through the corridors and I can trace its direction, where it turns and where it switches back at dead ends," the elf explained impatiently in a whisper. "With *silence*, I can find a safe path."

Raxe gave the Ranger Elf an annoyed glare but remained silent. He had to struggle to keep the toe of his armored boot from tapping nervously on the stone floor. He heard a tapping sound nonetheless and glanced curiously down at his boots to make sure that they were indeed still. The tapping he heard grew louder and more numerous until it was a cacophony of skittering and scraping. He looked down at Azh and found her looking up at him, her aqua-blue eyes even wider than usual and a worried frown on her tiny face.

She nodded. "Yes, I hear them, too, father."

Raxe turned his nervous gaze back to Rell Kallen. The elf put a finger to his lips before Raxe could speak. "I know, offworlder. And the wallowgrumps are even closer. They move more silently because they are on the hunt."

Raxe looked back over his shoulder as the harsh chittering echoed down the dark corridors along with the sound of spider rats' claws on the stone ceiling, walls and floors. When he turned back to implore the elf to hurry, the elf was gone. He turned and saw the elf padding silently and swiftly down the shorter corridor.

"Son of a *bitch!*" he swore as he took Azh's hand and followed.

Fortunately for them, Rell Kallen kept a slow enough pace for them gain on him. They followed him as he turned right and caught sight of him just as he turned right again and disappeared down yet another corridor. Raxe and Azh followed down a short distance and crossed a stony threshold into a small atrium formed by several intersecting corridors.

Pale light flooded the atrium from somewhere above. Raxe followed the illumination to its source and saw that it was being reflected from a huge mirror set into the high ceiling at an angle that allowed the light to brighten the entire area. The reflected light came from a wide hole bored into the rock ceiling across from the mirror. Raxe wondered how many mirrors were used and how complex the system of tunnels must have been to provide this much light.

They found Rell Kallen kneeling in shadow in a corner of the atrium, just out of the reflected light, his head lowered and hands folded. The two of them ran up to Rell. Raxe bent down to the kneeling elf's eye level.

"I know we're in a bad spot, man," the offworlder began. "But this ain't the time to stop and pray!"

"Take my arm," Rell Kallen ordered. "And, girl, take your father's arm. Whatever the two of you do, *don't let go.*"

Both Children of the Old Ones did as instructed without hesitation. Raxe looked into Rell Kallen's slender, folded hands and noticed a string of blue pearls hanging from them. He did not know what to expect, but he hoped whatever was supposed to happen would happen quickly.

Raxe looked down the corridor opposite to the one they came from and saw the wallowgrumps explode around the far corner and bound their way. When he looked down the corridor that brought them to the atrium he saw the spider-rats pouring into the hallway. The disgusting creatures were so numerous that they engulfed every surface as they came on in a foul current of bristling fur and tiny sharp, chattering teeth. It was all Raxe could do to keep himself from shaking the Ranger Elf to hurry him up.

The wallowgrumps hissed in excited anticipation of a meal. The ever-increasing volume of the approaching spider-rats' approach made Raxe's hair stand on end.

The wallowgrumps leapt into the atrium just as the spider-rats surged in from the other side. Raxe was about to let go of the elf's arm to draw Demonsbane when the three of them suddenly fell as if a trap door opened beneath them. But there was no trap door.

Raxe's confusion turned into fear as the three of them plummeted toward the hard stone floor of the level just below them. He held both Azh and Rell Kallen tighter as he braced for impact. To his surprise, they all passed right through that floor as if it was as immaterial as air. In the next second Raxe noticed he could not actually *feel* himself falling.

There was no upward rush of air. His stomach had not lurched the way it always did when he found himself falling long distances, which happened far too often for his liking during the last three years or so.

They fell through several levels more in the same fashion before Raxe realized that it was not the floors that had turned immaterial. They had. The string of blue pearls clutched in the elf's hands shimmered with bright lavender light that spilled from between his fingers and illuminated the darkness of the rooms they passed through as they plunged through the mountain. They fell faster and faster, until the rooms flew by too quickly to count. It was as if they were riding in a free-falling elevator made entirely of transparent glass.

As they fell through one room with an unusually high ceiling, the pearls' glow revealed a massive rock badger just beneath them. The five and a half foot long badger stood tall on its hind legs, raised its wickedly curved claws and bared its needle-sharp teeth in what looked to Raxe like an evil, hungry smile. This time Raxe resisted the urge to release the elf's arm to reach for Demonsbane. Instead, he held on tighter as he passed right through the suddenly confused animal. Raxe saw a flash of internal organs and bones before they were falling through the next level.

Several more levels flashed by before they finally fell through the high ceiling of the subterranean chamber through which they entered Mar-dah's mountain keep. Rell Kallen pulled his right hand away from the shimmering pearls and reached for the coiled rope at his waist. He snatched it from the loop that held it to his belt and tossed it upward. The rope was as immaterial as the rest of them and its tip passed right through ceiling. The moment the elf released the pearls with his other hand, the lavender glow faded. Raxe suddenly felt the air rushing past him.

They were solid again, he realized, and so was the rope, which went taught just as it merged with the stone ceiling.

Their fall came to a jarring halt that tore Raxe's grip from Rell Kallen's arm. He and Azh fell toward the cold hard floor of the chamber. Raxe knew his armor would allow him to survive the impact but doubted his daughter would.

Raxe saw her only chance. He thrust out his right arm and smashed his titan's ore-coated fingers into a big stalactite hanging from the ceiling. The move halted his fall and the pain turned his vision into white noise. He tightened his left-handed grip on Azh's arm and swung her like a pendulum two times before heaving with all of his might.

Azh tumbled head over heels through the air but had straightened her willowy frame like an arrow just before sliding into the narrow stream that cut through the chamber. Raxe grunted in anticipation of the sting and tore his right hand free of the stalactite. His boots hit the ground with a loud crash of metal as he landed in a deep crouch.

Raxe rose shakily to his feet, his face dripping with sweat. He checked his weapons belt to make sure that Demonsbane still hung from the axe frog on his left hip and that both Questblade and the Hell Key were still in their sheaths hanging from his right hip. Azh stood easily atop the surface of the stream, the water churning beneath her feet.

Rell Kallen had climbed to the top of the rope. He pulled a dagger from his weapons belt and with a flick of the blade, cut the lasso just below the ceiling. He fell the thirty or so feet, landed gracefully, and retrieved the string of blue pearls from the cave floor.

"You're just full of surprises, aren't you?" Raxe asked.

"Yes," Rell Kallen answered. "And you would do well to remember that. Let us leave this blasted place."

They rushed over to the stream where Azh waited. She held out a beckoning hand to them and neither wasted a moment stepping out onto the stirring water to either side of the half-faerie. As it did earlier, the water supported them as if they stood on solid ground.

Raxe said, "Come out at a different place, Azh, the opposite side of the mountain from the way we came in."

Rell Kallen shook his head. "We'd have to circle back around the mountain to head north. We've no time for that."

"Call me superstitious," Raxe said. "But if I can help it, I never leave a place the same way I went in."

Rell grunted in response. He understood the offworlder's logic but the Ranger Elf seemed to be the only one who understood how precious their time really was.

Azhju'lestra lowered them into the stream using another air bubble. In about ten minutes the trio emerged from the stream just outside of Mar-dah's deadly barrier. It was time for the extended trek back to Hargathall's cleft.

"Damn, it's nice to be outta there," Raxe said, taking a deep breath of the mountain air. It was not as fresh as it would have been if the area had not been littered with animal carcasses, but it was still better than the oppressive atmosphere inside the mountain. "Is everyone else as ready to leave this mountain range behind as I am?"

"Stupid question," Rell Kallen spat as he jogged away.

Raxe scoffed and turned to his Azh. "What about you?"

"Yes, father," she answered, grinning.

The father and daughter trotted off after the elf yet again. They had to navigate carefully over the rocky terrain with its many rises and sudden drops. They did not, however, have to follow the Ranger Elf to find their way. Raxe had taken note of the landmarks, the unique outcroppings of rock and sparse plant life that sprouted from the hard-packed earth here and there. Once they got to the north side of the mountain he would not need to follow the elf back to Hargathall's Cleft.

But to the offworlder's surprise, when they rounded a curved path bordered on both sides by high rock walls, they saw Rell Kallen walking slowly. He stopped, reaching over his shoulder to draw his long straight sword from its baldric and turned smoothly to face the two Children.

Raxe and Azh stopped short. Raxe put a hand on Azh's shoulder and moved her behind him.

"So this is it?" he asked, sliding Demonsbane free. "Is this where you try to kill us and take the Hell Key?"

The offworlder was not looking forward to fighting the formidable Ranger Elf. In truth, he was not sure if he could win, but he was prepared to find out.

"Perhaps later," Rell replied, his wide, canted, dark green eyes scanning the landscape suspiciously. "Assuming we survive the attack from the *Ken d'Zanir* surrounding us."

"Oh, shit," Raxe growled in a rough whisper. He looked at the top of the twenty-foot rock walls to either side of them.

Four of the towering warriors stepped into view at the top edge of the rock walls. The *Ken* warriors he faced back at Lakeside stood anywhere from six feet four inches to six feet seven inches tall. The shortest of the *Ken* standing atop the rock walls was at least six feet ten inches. The tallest stood over seven feet.

Raxe's shoulders slumped. "They're all as big as the freaking Finder," he said with annoyance.

Raxe had never seen the giant mercenary without his black, heavy armor, but he moved in it so easily that Raxe was sure the Finder had been a fairly bulky man. These *Ken*, he realized, were not as heavy as the Finder, but their limbs were longer and their bare arms were chiseled with lean, corded muscle. Raxe knew from experience that they were much quicker than the Finder. The *Ken* were much quicker than anyone as big as them had any right to be.

"Their elite forces, you think?" Rell Kallen asked. He cracked an unnerving smile that lent an even keener edge to his severely sharp features.

The four warriors on each ridge began to climb nimbly down. They found hand and foot holds that Raxe could not even see, and they descended much faster than he would have liked. His first instinct was to run, and then four more of the elite assassins, broad-shouldered and cloaked, as tall as or taller than the others, stepped from around the turn in the path to block the way.

A glance over his shoulder revealed four more nearly identical warriors creeping up on them from behind.

"Can you say overkill?" rumbled the offworlder.

6.3

Sabrina the Mistress of the Sea streaked north along the Bountiful River dozens of yards below its calm surface. She sped through the deep waters at twice the speed of sound on her desperate flight from the Ocean Crystalline to Lake Onyx. Even though she flew against the current, for swimming was not at all the word for the way she moved, the waters barely stirred in her passing. The myriad creatures that populated the broad river parted to give their mistress a wide berth, heeding the psychic song of distress she cast for miles ahead of her approach.

She knew the time was not right for her to return. The plan was to stay far away from the Bountiful River and Lake Onyx until this crisis passed. She called those waters home, so when the demon eventually targeted her, as she knew it would, the Bountiful and the Great Lake would be the first places it would search. She also stayed away from the Sea of Spirits, the areas of the Ocean Crystalline that bordered the Continent of Lorr, and the Ascendant's Heart Sea because of their proximity to Lake Onyx and the northern regions of the continent. The demon would have had to work to find her.

The Mistress of the Sea dearly wanted her daughter by her side. Unfortunately the Old Ones had whispered to the water faerie through the tides months earlier, telling her that Azhju'lestra's sire would need her in a quest to locate the Hell Key and thwart the demon Dierglyorr. Had Sabrina been human or a follower of the Leader Old Ones, selfishness would have overcome duty and she would have kept her daughter hidden and safe. As a creature of faerie and a devout follower of the Protector Old Ones, she had no choice but to send her daughter with the offworlder.

Since then Sabrina spent her time in the western and southern expanses of Gods' Gate Ocean and the eastern extremes of the Ocean Crystalline. She went as far as the oceans of the Unknown Lands, where she had escorted the last Phillosith.

Phillosith were majestic aquatic beasts. They were also ancient friends and a cherished aid to Sabrina in her ministrations as overseer and protector of the waters of her Sphere. She escorted the last Phillosith to ensure his safety from the demon. Even though he was of the last of his kind, Sabrina knew that as long as there was life, there was hope.

It pained her now to separate herself from her good friend, but Sabrina had confirmed that her sister Phillosith had been killed by the demon. Once she saw the wounds on the body of the dead Phillosith with her own eyes she recognized the claw and teeth marks of a dierglii. Dierglii had been extinct for thousands of years, so the dead Phillosith had to have been killed by the demon.

Dierglii had savaged countless humans and beasts during Heaven's War until the near-divinely powerful First and Second Generations of Children of the Old Ones finally expunged them from existence. Only one dierglii survived until the end of the War. It had managed to survive so long only because it had been fused with a changeling and a human to form the demon Dierglyorr.

When the Dierglyorr finally fell at the Battle of the Bountiful Forest, a battle that transformed the vast and beautiful forestland into the cursed Forsaken Desert, it had managed to take two Old Ones with it. The offworlder's own ancestors, the Gatekeeper and his son Raxe, gave their very lives to hold off the Dierrglyor's terrible hordes long enough to send Raxe's Children, along with Demonsbane and the Keys, to safety.

Now that the sixth level demon was back, Sabrina knew it would eventually come after the last Phillosith as well as her. They were allies of its enemies and too powerful to leave alive. She also realized the futility of confronting the demon. Their best hope of surviving and helping the Head Mage Rionn Lorr was to stay out of the demon's reach. That, however, did not stop her from staying abreast of the crisis in the Kingdom of Lorr.

Sabrina, a water faerie, could communicate with sea creatures across great distances. The giant whales of the

Known and Unknown Lands – black, silver, blue, red, and mottled – all acted as information couriers from sea to sea to create a reliable network that encompassed the entire Sphere. That network brought information to the eastern expanses of the Ocean Crystalline so critical that she risked getting closer to the likely location of the sixth level demon in order to get more details.

She got very useful details. Sailors talk. They talk at sea while standing at ship railings when no one else is near enough to hear. They whisper secrets and share confidential information near portholes a few yards above the surface of the water. They talk as they walk along piers or walk the decks of ships at port. Though there may not be humans near enough to pluck their secrets, there are always aquatic creatures or sea birds near. Sometimes, there is even Sabrina herself, the Mistress of the Sea of Spirits and the only full-blooded water faerie on her Sphere.

Her network brought to her news of a plot hatched by several kingdoms of the Known Lands, a plot driven – without their knowledge – by the Dierglyorr. Although she had accumulated many useful details there was still much she did not know. More information was needed so that she could provide the Head Mage Rionn Lorr with reliable intelligence for him to act upon. She fully intended to obtain that information, even if she had to use her enthralling magic on a sailor or two. As she was on her way to carry out her plan, she was assaulted by a horrific cry of pain, confusion and death that carried to her all the way from the Great Lake Onyx. Something terrible had happened to her home. Despite the obvious risk, she had to protect the great lake.

The Bountiful River flowed from Lake Onyx in the northwest region of the Kingdom of Lorr all the way to the Ocean Crystalline at the southeastern coast of the Kingdom of Lorr. Sabrina sensed something was catastrophically wrong with Lake Onyx before coming within 50 miles of the great lake.

She cast her senses far and wide, not only surveying the state of the water but also searching for any sign of the demon. There was no trace of the Dierglyorr but everything about the river water pushing against Sabrina from the northwest was tainted. First the smell, and then the taste, turned foul. At some point the usually crystal clear waters grew dark and dim. All of the tainted sensations grew steadily worse as Sabrina neared the great lake. The water soon began to sicken her.

Water faerie were not just creatures that lived under the water. She was a *part* of the water, and the water was a part of her. Her speed decreased and her perceptions grew distorted as the poisoned water poisoned her. Most horrifically, the taint had become a part of the creatures that dwelled in the river. Sabrina's most basic instincts urged her to save herself, to escape as far away from the ruined waters as she could. But she could not. She would not abandon her chosen home without at least trying to save it.

She rose from the depths and skimmed along the surface of the Bountiful River as she approached Lake Onyx. The air above was also foul in smell and taste, though it was not as heavy and impairing as the river depths.

The fumes were completely alien to her. Even in her journeys in the most dangerous waters of the Unknown Lands, in waters surrounding active volcanic isles, she had never encountered such a vile substance. Its acrid stench hung oppressively heavy in the air. Large globules of thick brown-black fluid clotted the water and choked the life out of everything within it. All manner of sea life, from fish and amphibians of all sizes to water-loving mammals, floated dead in the water.

Sabrina wept for them. Cloudy silver liquid streamed down her smooth coral-brown cheeks. The polluted waters had even tainted her tears. When she left the river and entered Lake Onyx it became immediately evident that the poison was from another world.

Large metal containers of a type she had never seen rested at the floor of the lake. A sunken vessel crafted of metal and unfamiliar materials rested at the lake bottom, as well. The containers and the vessel bore ragged holes with scorched edges. Human corpses, twisted and broken and torn, and dressed in tattered and unusual clothing, drifted in the befouled water.

Nothing like this could exist on her Sphere and escape her attention. That meant it was brought into her world from another world. That meant it had been brought through the WorldGate by the demon.

She wept even more at the giant black cloud that hung suspended in the vast lake. The oval-shaped lake spanned over two hundred nautical miles north and south and was more than three hundred nautical miles from east to west. The cloud was almost an eighth of the size of the lake. She then realized that the cloud was *not* suspended. It was spreading slowly and inexorably outward in every direction, creeping toward the Darshay'n and Tyne Rivers while already spilling into the Bountiful to be carried downriver to spread its contamination and death.

The Mistress of the Sea stopped weeping. Her dejected expression hardened to determination. This abomination would go no further.

Her full brown lips pursed tightly and her tears turned to marbles of ice. Her undulating hair rippled angrily. The flowing aquatic hues of her irises stilled and went black. She raised her arms to the sky and cried out in a shrill song that caused the current of the Bountiful River and the waves in the Great Lake Onyx to slow and then go completely still. Her song trilled on, painfully exquisite, rising and falling perfectly in pitch, tone and volume.

The current of the Bountiful River reversed. The waves in Lake Onyx reawakened but their natural flow was redirected so that the lake twirled inward into itself in a giant whirlpool. The water, however, was not flowing downward as if going down a drain. It was pulled up into a dark-clouded sphere of polluted water just above the surface of the lake.

The sphere grew larger and darker as the faerie's melody floated on and on. The level of both the river and the great lake visibly receded as the dark sphere grew. The urgent beauty of her enchanted song dipped in tone to become somber and haunting when the amphibian, aquatic, and human carcasses began to twirl into the ever-growing sphere. Fortunately, the blackness of the alien poison hid the bodies from view. The twining waters tugged at the metal containers and eventually even the alien vessel into the darkness of the ever-expanding sphere.

Within minutes the giant globe of water grew to roughly three quarters of a mile in diameter, equal in size to one of the smaller mountains bordering the north and south of the great lake. The globe continued to roil and turn, almost completely black. The waters of the river and the rest of the great lake were clear once more.

Sabrina continued to sing. Her trembling arms remained upraised. The water still whirled inward as clear water was pulled to the giant black sphere. Within another minute, the rolling globe of poison was crystal clear around the surface, like a protective shell to contain the poison. Several yards within the surface, though, it was as black as pitch.

If anyone had been watching they would have easily seen the strain on Sabrina's stunning face. A soft azure glow began to radiate from her curvaceous body. The near-transparent streamers of aquatic tint that barely concealed her otherwise nude body fluttered and undulated as intensely as her long flowing hair. That, and the glow emanating from her skin, was clear evidence of the enormous amount of magic she was employing.

As great as the endeavor was, it was made much more daunting by the otherworldly poison that had already polluted her body. Every part of her, from the very core of her heart to the tips of her flowing locks, burned painfully with the effort she put forth.

And then the pitch and tone of the Sea Mistress's song changed again.

The whirling waters began to slow. The waves in the great lake eventually stopped spinning and returned to their normal patterns. The Bountiful River resumed its lazy southeastern flow. The mountain-sized sphere of moving water continued to turn a few feet above the now-glassy surface of Lake Onyx, though the pace at which it spun decreased significantly.

Sabrina's arms grew heavy and dropped several inches but she continued to sing. The azure shimmer around her began to dim. The glow took on a gray, cloudy aspect as the poison in her system began to overwhelm her. Yet she continued to sing.

The volume of her song lowered. Exhaustion could be heard in her melodious voice but it never broke or cracked as she sang on.

She redirected part of her focus inward, surrounding the microscopic particles of poison with the water within her own body, her very essence. With a great amount of exertion she pulled the taint from her own flesh and blood in a gray cloud of mist that streamed through the air and became part the giant sphere. The effort cost her greatly and it became a struggle for her to stay conscious. Her body, nearly drained of magic and strength, threatened to shut down. Her black irises faded to a dull gray.

Still she continued to sing.

As the spinning globe of water and poison continued to slow, vapor wafted from its surface. Sabrina was grimacing now. She had removed the poison from her system but the poison, and the energy she had to use to remove it from her body, Lake Onyx and the Bountiful River had already done their damage. Her left arm dropped limply to her side while her song chimed on.

She exerted the last of her energy to push every iota of heat out of the moving water. The vapor wafting from it thickened, rising from the globe to dissipate in the air, until the water was transformed into a giant sphere of rock-hard ice that rotated slowly a few feet above the lake. It resembled a giant crystal orb encasing a slightly smaller black orb.

The water that twirled and misted beneath her perfect feet while holding her aloft a few inches above the surface suddenly went still. The Mistress of the Sea plunged clumsily into the lake. The globe of ice immediately did the same, dunking heavily into the water and sending massive waves rolling out in every direction to wash dozens of yards further than usual upon the surrounding shores. Both Sabrina and the ice sphere drifted slowly toward the bottom of the lake floor.

In her exhausted stupor, Sabrina almost failed to notice the enormously broad and impossibly long shadow that came slithering toward her through the depths.

6.4

"They're grouping in *four* four-man squads now," Rell noted with a grim smile. "Not the individual four-man squad they sent at us back at Lakeside, and they're wearing what passes for armor for them. They're taking *my* presence into account, this time."

Indeed, the earth-toned, short-tailed tunic and leggings they usually wore were sparsely covered by various pieces of leather armor. Leather gorgets protected their necks. Breastplates were strapped securely over their tunics. Thick greaves protected their knees and shins. They did not wear helms, though. They still wore their scarfs wrapped snugly around their heads with the dangling corners tucked under the scarf. One of the big warriors approaching from ahead of them cupped his hands and brought them to his mouth. He released a loud, hooting, birdcall.

"And he just called the rest of them," Raxe needlessly observed. "They must be scattered all around the mountain range waiting for us."

"With the largest force likely near our entrance point," Rell Kallen admitted, "thus your suggestion to use a different exit. I see you finally came up with a slightly helpful idea."

"*You* got any ideas?" Raxe challenged. "Any more tricks up your sleeve that'll get us out of this?"

"The ghost pearls will not help us," Rell said. "We would drop into solid rock with no idea how far we would fall and where we would end up. The Phoenix Stone can carry only one person at a time. So, all I have is this." He lifted his straight sword and pulled a long fighting dagger from his belt. "And this."

Raxe took the elf's cue. He pushed Demonsbane into his right hand until the clawed fingers snapped around the haft. He fought back a pained grimace as he drew Questblade from the sheath on his left hip, right next to the sheath that held the Hell Key.

"Good idea," he rasped.

Questblade was an enchanted short sword not made for battle, and a short sword was not Raxe's ideal fighting weapon. However, he vividly remembered his confrontation with *Ken d'Zanir* at Lakeside. He would need as many sharp-edged weapons as he could manage.

Azh reached up and grabbed Raxe's bare right triceps and squeezed. "The two of you cannot win this, father."

"We have to, baby," Raxe said without looking at her. He spoke those words aloud while his mind was already preparing for the battle. He was calming himself, breathing deeply and finding his chi. "Stay close to me when the fighting starts. I'll make a hole for you, and as soon as you get a chance, you run away from here as fast as you can."

"You and Rell Kallen are fearsome fighters," Azh allowed, "but there are too many of them. You *cannot* win."

Raxe knew she was right but what else could they do? If he could pull the teleportation spell from Shanderah's memories he could get all of them out, but he could not recall any of her memories. The Ranger Elf did not have any magic available to him that could help them escape, or so he said.

Even though there was no winning this fight he intended to make his death a costly one and give his daughter a chance to escape. He pushed Azh gently between him and Rell Kallen and then dropped into a fighting stance. When the *S'Zan Rho* climbing down the walls touched the ground, the sixteen warriors rushed them with weapons raised.

"Remember, Azh," he began, turning to his daughter one last time.

His next words were lost to him when he saw her marine-hued hair waving softly in the air as if she was under water...just like her mother's hair. Her eyes were unfocused and shimmering. Raxe could see the magical aura around her grow brighter.

He quickly turned to face the attacking warriors and was taken aback yet again. All sixteen *Ken d'Zanir* were staggering. They struggled to walk, let alone run, while many of them clutched their throats.

All of them were drenched with sweat and wore facial expressions of pained confusion. To a man, they stumbled to the ground, gagging and coughing, jerking wildly as the lean, corded muscles all over their bodies began to visibly spasm and constrict.

The ground around them darkened as moisture poured from their bodies to drench their clothing and the dry earth beneath them. Their skin grew pale and cracked. When one of them struggled to look up, Raxe saw that his lips were blue and desiccated.

In less than a minute, the *Ken* writhed on the hard, wet ground with puddles beneath them that steadily crept away from their bodies. Their appendages slowly constricted into unnatural positions. All of their faces contorted into hideous masks of agony.

That was when Raxe finally understood what was happening.

Rell Kallen's canted eyes narrowed. "The girl is… she is drawing every bit of moisture out of their bodies," he said, trying unsuccessfully to hide his awe.

6.5

Sabrina was seized by fear as the colossal shadow surged nearer, certain the demon was coming for her. At full strength she was no match for the Dierglyorr. In her weakened state she would not even be able to put up a fight. She sent a psychic cry for aid out to the creatures that lived in the surrounding waters, but those that had not been killed by the black poison had fled far and fast. Sabrina was utterly alone and at the mercy of the approaching monster.

And then something strange happened. The approaching monster answered her cry.

Fear me not, my Mistress. You have called, so I have come. I come ready to fight and die for you.

The voice and the words jogged her hazy memory. She blinked her eyes until she could see somewhat clearly. The approaching monster was not a monster at all. It was merely another of her sea creatures, a sea wyvern. It resembled a gargantuan blue and silver mottled eel with a bearded reptilian head. She could see the faint outlines of its wing-like fore fins folded tightly against the sides of its impossibly long body.

Sea wyverns normally resided in the eastern expanses of the God's Gate Ocean. Its native waters were at the fringes of the Unknown Lands, where other manner of rare and mammoth sea creatures dwelled. The beast could swim beneath water or fly above it with equally staggering speed. It was amphibious, so it never strayed far from water. It was known as the dragon of the seas, an unparalleled hunter and master of its domain. Only the far reaches of the ocean contained creatures massive enough to quell the appetite that matched the sea wyverns' size.

Sabrina had called to it when she began her journey to Lake Onyx. She feared that she was rushing into a trap set by the Dierglyorr and hoped that the gargantuan serpent could assist her in battling the sixth level demon. She made certain to relay to the giant sea creature exactly why she needed his assistance and was not sure he would answer her call. Yet here he was, after travelling thousands of miles in a matter of hours to assist her.

The sea wyvern slowly lowered his head, which was about a quarter of the size of the sphere Sabrina had just created, until it was level with the water faerie. Its round eyes were disproportionately small compared to its head, but their diameters were still twice the length of a tall human male. The beast's body was so long that it trailed completely out of view under the clear water, but Sabrina knew that it was just over four miles long. The sea wyvern coiled a small portion of its body and eased it beneath Sabrina's descending form so that she could settle softly upon it.

Thank you, she managed to project. *But, thank the Old Ones, such a great and noble sacrifice as your life is not called for. The demon is not here.*

Sabrina sensed the sea wyvern's curiosity as it replied. *What would you have me do, my queen? I am ready to serve.*

Sabrina sent him a visual of what she needed. The gargantuan creature hesitated.

What about you? He worried. *You are not well. You should not be left alone in this weakened state.*

Sabrina struggled mightily against the darkness closing in around her to manage another sentence. *The survival of these waters is more important than my own survival.*

But they are one and the same, the sea wyvern argued.

Not any longer, Sabrina promised. *I have a...daughter that... is to take my mantle should I fall. And in any case, I am not dying. I only need rest. Now that the waters have been cleansed, they will soon refortify me.*

The gargantuan creature regarded her for several seconds before nodding lightly. Never taking his huge eyes away from his Mistress, the sea wyvern coiled a sizeable section of his body around the mountainous sphere. He spared one more reluctant glance at Sabrina before streaking toward the mouth of the Tyne River West with the giant sphere.

The Tyne River West was a half mile wide, too narrow for the massive frozen globe, so before reaching the river, the sea wyvern dove to the bottom of the lake. Its belly threw up a giant cloud of mud as it scraped against the lake floor almost a thousand feet below. With a flap of its wing fins and a thrust of its slender but sinewy hind legs, it rocketed toward the surface of the water and exploded into the air.

He sailed above the lake toward the mouth of the river. The concussive wake of his passing threw out massive twin waves that cut a half-mile-wide swath across the surface of the great lake. He spread his monstrous wing fins, almost twice the width of the river below it. Another flap sent it streaking further into the sky and farther away.

The Mistress of the Sea floated to the surface to watch her charge's form shrink as it sailed into the distance. She knew that the sea wyvern could and would, in mere minutes, traverse the two hundred mile length of the Tyne River West until it flowed out into the Ascendant's Heart Sea. From there he would dive back beneath the water and take the black globe south, through the Ocean Crystalline to the southern pole of the Sphere. In that frozen environment there would be no chance of the sphere melting before she and the Head Mage could devise a method of safely and permanently ridding the world of the giant poisonous globe. She could already see the sea wyvern turning south. It was so far away it actually looked small against the vastness of the sky.

When the sea wyvern and its dangerous cargo were no longer visible, Sabrina allowed herself to sink back into the lake, which was over two miles deep where she drifted. The soft current pulled her into the Bountiful River, toward the river water that had been completely decontaminated. She could feel the waters starting to heal and replenish her. The sensation was so comforting that she started drifting into much needed sleep.

Her eyes were closed and she was nearly unconscious when she heard loud splashes from the river surface just above her. She felt the ripple of violently displaced water as she forced her eyes open.

Terror froze her color-shifting irises to stark silver orbs when she saw a weighted net rushing down upon her. She tried to swim from beneath the widely cast net but in her weakened state she was not nearly fast enough. To make matters worse, she knew the net was not simply tossed into the river. The four corners of the wide net were weighted with heavy wooden bolts that cut through the water with a speed that could only mean they were propelled by some kind of machine. Sabrina was less than ten yards from the edge of the net when it fell upon her.

The sheer weight of the net bore the weakened Sabrina deeper into the water so fast that she could not swim from under it. The net was then retrieved, binding her tightly and snatching her up toward the surface and the shore. The instant the net tightened, she knew it was not made of any rope with which she was familiar. It was made of some form of near razor-thin, but incredibly strong metal wire that cut deeply into her flesh.

As she was hauled to the surface her transparent blood, only slightly thicker than the river water and almost as clear, flowed out in a nearly invisible cloud. When she was yanked roughly from the river, the blood pouring from her many cuts was indistinguishable to the human eye from the water that dripped from her body.

The water faerie's cry of fear and pain brought all manner of sea creatures rushing to her from near and far, but they were too late. Sabrina curled tightly into a fetal position in an attempt to pull away from the torturous netting but the wire dug deeper and deeper into her coral brown flesh. It cut through the thin, sheer ribbons that partially covered her and sent the fabric drifting away downriver.

Sabrina felt herself swinging through the air and then thumping painfully onto a wooden deck of an anchored ship. The net finally loosened but Sabrina could not move. The loss of blood sapped what little strength she had regained. It took all of her concentration just to keep from falling unconscious. She managed to lift her head to see her captors standing over her.

In her enfeebled state she could barely make out the blurred outlines of a group consisting of one woman, several men, and creatures only vaguely shaped like men. They all stared intently at her. The men stood behind the woman and the creatures, and in their midst was a large apparatus similar in form to a ballista.

The base of the construction was a horizontally oriented cylinder twice the width of a whisky barrel with thick rope coiled tightly around it and large crank handles extending from either side. It was some sort of oversized reel. The device was unknown to her, but from its general design, angle of orientation, and the four ropes extending from the reel, she knew that it was the contraption used to propel the net with so much force and speed.

When Sabrina's vision began to resolve, she immediately recognized the Queen of the Forsaken Desert. Sabrina had never met her or even saw her, for Shara Dune was known to stay in her desert and away from large bodies of water. But her flaming red hair, her incredible physical beauty that nearly rivaled that of the Mistress of the Sea, and most notably the six sand creatures that flanked her, made her identity unmistakable.

Several of the sand creatures' weapons were crafted from cold iron, the only substance not of a magical or chemical nature that could do serious harm to faerie kind. She could heal the cuts from the cable netting in short order, but any wounds caused by those iron weapons would result in permanent injury.

Beyond the sand creatures stood a dozen or more humans, all armed to the teeth. They carried swords of various metals but not of iron. Their weapons could only cause her mild discomfort. When she noticed how they were gaping at her with wonder and raw, primal lust, their weapons became less of a concern. It was at that moment that Sabrina realized she was completely naked. The sheer, broad ribbons that usually covered her had been cut away by the sharp netting and washed out into the river.

She shivered with cold, her long, multihued hair splayed wildly about the deck, extending several feet away from her scalp in every direction. Her body was, for the most part, identical to a human body. Rows of curved gills pulsed on both sides of her neck just near her collarbone and beneath both of her bottom ribs. Other than that, she knew full well that the swell of her full breasts and the curve of her hips and legs were found most desirable by both humans and elves.

She remained curled in a tight ball, lying on her side and concealing as much of her breasts as she could by crossing her slender forearms across her chest and hugging her shoulders. She kept her knees clamped firmly together and pressed against her crossed arms and her feet tucked beneath her bottom. None of this did anything to ease the intense desire that overcame the men. It was evident in their dark, hungry glares.

Shara Dune glanced over her shoulders at the men and then turned back to Sabrina. The corners of her lips curved up in a cold smile. She brought up her right hand, reached behind the small bun adorning her fiery hair, and pulled free a beautiful decorative golden comb inlaid with small rubies and emeralds. The handle was long, narrow, and wickedly pointed, like a stiletto. The decorative comb had been a gift from the wizard Stratham Glund, the second High Advisor to the Head Mage of the Kingdom of Cartha – and her current employer. She kept the comb for its extravagant beauty and its many uses, one of which was torture.

"I thought *I* had a strong effect on men," purred the Queen of the Forsaken Desert. She drew a thin but deep cut down Sabrina's cheek. She marveled at the translucent blood that flowed from the wound. "You lie here broken and bleeding and still these thugs want to ravage you."

"Why are you doing this?" Sabrina gasped softly in a desperate bid to keep the desert witch talking. She needed time to regain her strength. Her exhaustion slowed the process considerably but all she needed was a few minutes.

"I do this to receive what I am due, water witch," said Shara Dune.

"But why?" Sabrina pled.

"You have been a thorn in the side of the Kingdom of Lorr's rivals for far too long. I assist those who seek to pluck that thorn for good. This is only business, I assure you. It is my destiny to rule. This is but a stepping stone to that end."

Sabrina shook her head sadly. It was impossible to mask the exertion it was taking to close her wounds. She could only hope her captors would mistake her expression for pain alone and not deduce that she was healing herself.

Her hue-shifting eyes went black. "Do you really expect a *demon* to honor any deal it has struck?"

"Demon?" Shara asked.

"You did not know?" asked Sabrina, managing to pour incredulity into her tone despite her agony and exhaustion.

"You are lying," accused Shara. "This is nothing but a useless attempt to prolong your life, water witch. I am not as easily duped as the men you so effortlessly enthrall."

"Do what you will," Sabrina said defiantly. "You and your demon master will not be successful. The Children of the Old Ones will stop it. Heed my warning, Shara Dune. You will be swept up in their retribution if you do not distance yourself from this evil plot, and that is assuing the demon does not dispose of you when he is done with you."

Shara narrowed her sandy brown eyes and grinned. "You say that with such conviction that I almost believe you."

The Queen of the Forsaken Desert looked over her shoulders at the four-tentacled monsters that surrounded her.

The sand creatures' bare barrel chests heaved with excitement. The dual cuts that served as nasal cavities in the middle of their wedge-shaped faces expanded to ovals and contracted to slits while they huffed and puffed with anticipation. Their lipless mouths pressed together into sharp lines that curved downward on both ends. The three protrusions at the top of their heads, like bulbous and stunted elephant trunks, quivered. Their piercing obsidian eyes were wide, intense circles.

"I was considering letting the men have her first," Shara said to her sand creatures. "But they look entirely *too* eager. They do not deserve such a treat. My loves, she is yours."

Sabrina had hoped Shara would let the men have her first. She would have lived long enough to regain enough strength to kill every single one of them. Instead, the sand creatures raised their weapons and stepped toward her. The last thing that Sabrina, the Mistress of the Sea of Spirits and last full-blooded water faerie thought about before she died was the Child that she and the offworlder Raxe shared.

Azhju'lestra.

6.6

"My God," Raxe breathed.

When they finally went still, the towering, muscular, bronze-skinned warriors had been reduced to graying husks that looked as if they had baked in the desert sun for days.

Man and elf looked back at the girl with slack-jawed amazement. Her long hair settled back down to her shoulders and her shimmering eyes dimmed to their normal brightness. She looked up apologetically into her father's eyes.

"I had to kill them, father. I did not know how else to –"

The words caught in her throat as she began to choke. Her eyes grew wide and she quivered from head to toe.

"Azh!" Raxe called, reaching out to hold her but not knowing if he should. "What's wrong?"

"*Mother*..." she said breathlessly before collapsing.

Raxe dropped his weapons and caught Azh before she hit the ground. He looked down at her in horror and checked her nose and neck gills to make sure she was still breathing. She was, but weakly. Raxe sighed with relief. An instant later the shimmer of magic that Raxe saw around all things vanished from around his daughter. He looked up at Rell Kallen and noticed the same phenomenon with the Ranger Elf.

"Her magic is gone," Raxe told him. "And so is yours...completely."

"That means the rest of the *Ken* are getting closer with their magic-extinguishing powers," Rell Kallen said. He thumbed the sharp edge of his straight sword. "I wish I knew which among them has that ability."

Raxe grunted. "Let's get outta here while we can."

"Let me carry the Hell Key," Rell Kallen volunteered. "It will only slow you down."

"Not a chance," Raxe snapped as he set the girl down gently to retrieve his weapons. He sheathed Questblade, slid Demonsbane into is frog and scooped his daughter up again. "Just run, elf. I'll be right behind you."

Chapter 7: The Canyon of Death

7.1

The Ranger Elf Rell Kallen stared down into the great canyon that was Hargathall's Cleft. He studied the landscape as he waited impatiently for Raxe and his daughter. He shook his head when the offworlder finally came huffing and puffing alongside him.

"The distance from here to the bottom of this canyon is close to a fourth of a mile," Rell informed, pointing to the far side of the great chasm. "From here, the shortest route to the pass will take us on a northerly angle, which will add close to another mile to reach the other side. All told, it will be nearly three miles – a quarter of it uphill."

"Still faster than going around," Raxe countered. He looked down to the unconscious little girl he held in his arms. His daughter's breathing was still uneven but it was not as ragged as it had been when she initially lost consciousness. "Obviously we go across."

"But if the *Ken* overtake us on their land dragons," Rell argued, "they could surround us at the bottom of the canyon and we'll have nowhere to go. Even if we somehow managed to drag the fight out until nightfall, blood will certainly be spilled and then we'd all be finished. You know better than anyone how dangerous that canyon floor is after dark. If we go around the canyon we will keep them from flanking us and we won't be threatened by its foul magic."

"If they were riding their land dragons," Raxe pointed out, "They would've run us down already. We wouldn't stand a chance against all of those giant lizards anyway. The land dragons must not be able to navigate the mountain terrain reliably."

"Or maybe," Rell considered, "now that they know exactly where we are, using the land dragons would not be sporting. They primarily use land dragons for long-range transportation and large-scale combat. They would not set the beasts upon us. Their warped code of 'assassin's honor' compels them to engage us on foot to fulfill their contract."

Raxe looked down at Azh's round face again before looking back up at Rell. The girl was not heavy, but he had been carrying her for a while and his arms were tiring. The big enchanted greatsword hanging from his hip was heavier than the girl, slowing his progress even more. Raxe was slowing them down and he knew it. Rell was a little smaller in stature but the elf's strength, speed, and stamina were all far superior to Raxe's. The elf could carry Azh and the sword and still out-pace Raxe at a dead run.

But the offworlder did not trust him.

Rell would be more than a match for any one or possibly even two *Ken* warriors. Against a full squad, however, not even an elven ranger would last very long. Rell could outrun them on foot, Raxe had seen that with his own eyes, but that would not do the offworlder or his daughter any good. And it did not really matter if Raxe trusted Rell with Azh or the Hell Key or not. If they did manage to outrun the assassins on foot, they would then most certainly pursue them on their land dragons. The elf could not run *that* fast.

There was simply no way they were going to escape the swift warriors whether they went around or across the canyon. They might as well take the shortest route.

"Your decision, offworlder," Rell said. "You've heard my choice, but I'll not divide us. Separated, we stand even less of a chance."

Raxe sighed as an idea came to him. He hated it, but he could not think of any other way. He turned his intense gaze to the Ranger Elf.

"I need you to make me a promise," Raxe said solemnly.

Rell tilted his head and gave Raxe a suspicious look. "Tell me what you wish me to promise and I will tell you whether or not I will."

"If I can't come with you," Raxe started, "promise me you will take Azh to Lake Onyx before taking the Hell Key to Rionn Lorr."

"If you can't come with us?" Rell asked. "What are you talking about, offworlder?"

"We both know you're strong and fast enough to carry Azh and the Key across the canyon and to the pass before the *Ken* can catch up to you on foot. I'm not. Even without the extra burden they'll still catch me. If you two stay with me, we all die. If you promise on your Ranger oath to take Azh to Lake Onyx, I'll turn over the Hell Key to you and keep the scouts busy while you escape with my daughter."

"Of course I can outrun them on foot," Rell started. "But what makes you think I can outrun their land dragons?"

"Call it a hunch," answered Raxe. "I know how resourceful you are. The Hell Key weighs much more than Azh, so if you planned to use your Phoenix stone to take the Key away, Azh's extra weight shouldn't be a problem. And if you didn't plan to use the Phoenix stone, I'm sure you have some other trick up your sleeve."

The elf smiled, but then said, "Lake Onyx will take me hundreds of miles out of the way. It is imperative that the Hell Key reaches its destination as soon as possible."

"Then we fall to the *Ken*," Raxe returned stubbornly.

Rell looked longingly at the large, beautiful greatsword hanging at Raxe's hip. "What if I just take the Key by force and go on my way?" he challenged.

Raxe showed his teeth in something that was not quite a smile. "You're welcome to try." He held his daughter cradled in his right arm and pain-wracked right hand while using the other to pull Demonsbane from where it rested in its frog at his right hip. "We can stand here and fight, or talk, for that matter, until they run right up our asses. Or you can promise to do as I ask."

Rell chuckled. "Do you think you can kill multiple *Ken* by yourself, offworlder?"

Raxe held no illusions that he would last any longer than a few minutes. However, he recalled the last thing Rionn Lorr told him via the reflection sand. The *Ken* had an obsessive hatred for anyone that did not worship the Old One S'Zan as the one true god.

Not only did Raxe not worship or even care about S'Zan, he was a direct descendant of the Gatekeeper. If he was lucky, and God knew he was due some good luck, that hatred would make the *Ken* key in on him and he could buy the elf a little more time to get his daughter to safety. Raxe would not say this to Rell, though. Instead, he simply stared hard at the elf and insisted:

"Give me your word."

Rell sighed. "I give to you this oath, on my honor as an Elven Ranger of the Blessed Kingdom of Thâlstrën. I will take your daughter safely to Lake Onyx."

Raxe was betting on his belief that a Ranger Elf's oath was unbreakable but he was still hesitant. He reluctantly handed his daughter to Rell, who gathered her easily into his powerful arms. Raxe then unstrapped the thong of leather that held the Hell Key's sheath to his weapons belt and fastened it onto Rell's leather belt.

"I have your oath, elf," Raxe warned. "Honor it."

"I have given my oath, offworlder. I have no choice."

Without further discussion, Rell turned and started down the sloping canyon wall. Raxe could not help but marvel at the speed and agility displayed by the elf as he bounded down the rocky canyon wall like a mountain goat even with all the extra weight he carried.

Having no real desire to face the warrior scouts with the precipitous drop of the canyon wall at his back, Raxe followed as fast as he could. The elf pulled away from him quickly, of course. By the time the Child of the Old Ones reached the canyon floor he was thoroughly winded. Rell, on the other hand, was more than halfway across the canyon floor and showed no signs of slowing.

After all of the running they had done the last few days Raxe could feel his body wearing down. He pushed on nonetheless, running away from the sloping canyon wall. Ordinarily he would want to fight with his back to the wall to keep his opponents in front of him and to keep them from surrounding him. That was not an option here. The wall was sloped. His attackers could still surround him *and* fight from the high ground.

Raxe jogged about a quarter of a mile before he paused to catch his breath. By then Rell Kallen was three quarters of the way up the opposite slope. He looked up and over his shoulder.

THE KEY QUEST

Four *Ken* scouts stood at the midway point of the canyon slope. They looked down at him the way a hungry airborne eagle looks down at a field mouse.

Might as well catch my breath, Raxe thought. *There's no way I'm making it to the other side before they catch me.*

He took long, deep breaths, wanting to be as rested as possible before the unavoidable confrontation. Even if they did not know his super-human abilities only came to bear when he faced demons, Raxe was fairly sure the scouts would engage him and try to bring him down before the rest of the squad arrived. It would be a matter of honor to them, perhaps even bragging rights. These warriors would come at him with everything they had.

The four *S'Zan Rho Ken d'Zanir* raised their various weapons and charged down the canyon wall, moving almost as fast and gracefully as Rell Kallen had. The bastards.

Raxe steeled himself for the coming fight. He lifted his pack's strap from his shoulders, unfastened his cloak, and tossed them both out of the way. He purposely left Questblade sheathed this time, but he pulled Demonsbane free with his left hand. The sound of the metal haft scraping against the metal ring of the axe frog was like a comforting musical note.

He glanced over his shoulder to make sure his daughter and Rell were safely away. What he saw instead infuriated him. Azhju'lestra was laying still at the top of the southeastern edge of the canyon. Rell Kallen and the Hell Key were nowhere to be seen, but the dim red glow of a fading arc of light betrayed the elf's use of the Phoenix stone to spirit him away. Anger darkened Raxe's face and throbbed in his temples. Rionn Lorr warned him not to trust the elf but Raxe was sure that if he could get Rell Kallen to swear an oath, he would honor it.

It was a stupid gamble but he did not know what else he could have done. All he could do was try to buy some time. Once Azh came to she could help him fight their way out. After seeing her kill those *Ken* warriors earlier that day, he had no doubts about her abilities. He just had to stay alive long enough for her to regain consciousness.

Raxe bent his knees slightly and balanced on the balls of his feet, watching the four warriors approach from different directions. Their shrill battle cries would bring the others in full force. He wondered if he would last long enough to see the rest of them. He had barely managed to defeat one of those warriors by himself. How would he defeat four?

Their strength dwarfed his. They all had greater reach and were at least as quick as he. And worse, they were *Ken d'Zanir* – which translated to "Blade of the Divine" in Lorrian. This meant that like him, they had trained their entire lives, sharpening their bodies, minds, and reflexes to fight. If their overall martial skill did not quite match his, their physical superiority would surely compensate.

Running was his best option but there was nowhere left for him to run. Even if there were, the long-limbed, ultra athletic men would easily run him down. Better to fight while he had his strength and wind than fight while exhausted from a chase. He had the advantage of his armor, which he did not have against the *Ken* warrior he fought back at Port Lorrian.

Worst of all, he had his oath. Three years ago, when his submission to the magic of Demonsbane laid bare to him his fate, he swore an oath to never take another human life. It seemed silly in retrospect, and keeping it under the current circumstances would only lead to a quicker defeat. The *S'Zan Rho* fought to the death. They were committed and would not stop coming at him until he was dead or they were dead or he incapacitated them severely enough to keep them down.

All of his training and all of his fighting reflexes were honed to kill. It would be so much easier for him to simply cut them down than to put forth the extra focus needed to maim without killing.

He wished they were demons. As much as he appalled the magic as it flowed through his body, it gave him superhuman physical abilities that would serve him well. More importantly, he would not have to worry about breaking his oath.

The oath, however, was binding. The mere consideration of taking the lives of the *S'Zan Rho* caused the puckered scar on his throat to burn. It was a constant reminder of his oath and his fate. The flash of pain brought him back to the memories of what he saw in the dragon king's mountain when the black-armored giant known as the Finder struck him down and sent him to hell. This time, however, the vision of past victims attacking him included these *Ken* warriors hacking at him through the flames of hell.

Raxe understood that sparing any of their lives was not a guarantee that he would escape his damnation, but all that mattered was that he tried. He would keep his oath.

At all costs? He asked himself silently as the *Ken* closed on him. *Will you keep to this silly oath even at the cost of your own life?* He knew it was common sense talking to him and he forced it away. Breaking his oath was not an option. He would find a way.

The first warrior reached him and swung a long-handled, single-bladed war axe at Raxe's neck in a quick and controlled arc. Raxe straightened from his wide legged stance and pivoted into the path of the strike. The axe blade bounced off of his armored chest as he swung Demonsbane up and around. The razor edge cut easily through the wooden shaft of the long handle just below the axe blade.

At that moment another warrior came upon him from behind, swinging a scimitar at the bit of exposed flesh behind the offworlder's right knee. Raxe lifted his leg just enough to make the sword glance off of the top of his metal boot, but not quick enough to keep the sharp edge from barely clearing the rim of his boot and slicing into his upper calf.

Raxe continued to bring his foot up and back to shatter the sword-wielding *S'Zan Rho's* shin while ducking below the splintered haft that the first warrior swung at his head. The solid wooden handle deftly stopped and changed direction and went down toward the unprotected crown of Raxe's head.

Raxe spun away from the swift attack and right into another. The other two warriors hacked at him from his left and right. The one on his left wielded a foot-long hunting knife and the one on the right a wickedly spiked mace. Raxe continued to spin away and brought up Demonsbane in an upward diagonal sweep. The knife-man had to snatch his weapon back as Demonsbane's blades whistled past to keep his hand but then he jabbed it forward into the offworlder's exposed left triceps.

Raxe deflected the mace with Demonsbane as he spun away but failed to bring it around quickly enough to slice the mace head in two or shatter it. His double pirouette took him several yards away from his attackers. Three of them slid over quickly to surround him again. The one with the ruined shin limped through the pain to rejoin the attack.

Blood oozed down Raxe's dirty, sweat soaked left arm from the gash in his triceps. He could feel the wet warmth of blood running down the back of his right leg as well. The pain was acute but he remained focused. The *Ken's* long-handled war axe was effectively out of commission and the scimitar wielder was crippled, so the long-range weapons were less of a concern. The warriors were hesitant to come into close quarters with the enchanted battle-axe. Raxe knew their hesitation would not last, though, so he used the brief respite to come up with a plan.

Raxe had been taught to fight multiple attackers. His mother and grandfather had shown him how to flow with the wave of several adversaries, how to use them against one another. He exhaled heavily and called upon his chi, the same way he had when he deadened the pain of sacrificing his right hand to forge Ethan's *gun*. He took a deep breath and let his chi wash through him as the group of *Ken d'Zanir* attacked once more. The pain in his triceps and calf was forgotten and his lessons came back to him instinctively.

Any concern about winning or losing was swept away. All that mattered was the art of combat. The battle itself, not the outcome, became his sole concern. Combat was his essence. It was his music and he was a virtuoso. His oath would be his canvas, the surface upon which he would paint a violent masterpiece.

He would break bones and hyperextend joints. He would attack nerves endings and clusters, rend muscles from ligaments and even sever limbs if he had to. But, as insane as it sounded to any logically thinking person, he would not kill.

Before the *S'Zan Rho* brought him down, Raxe would paint a portrait of martial genius they would never forget.

7.2

Joel stood at the lip of the canyon and looked down at Ryan. He could not yet bring himself to call the man Raxe. It still seemed silly. There was nothing silly, however, about what was happening at the bottom of that canyon.

Ryan was amazingly holding his own against the fierce warriors, having already hobbled the one with the scimitar and cut the blade off of another's war axe. His movements were smooth and flowing, almost like a choreographed dance concealing power within grace. The dance moved closer to the center of the canyon, with Ryan moving away to keep them from surrounding him and the *Ken* moving to keep him surrounded. The flash of blades and darting hands and feet moved so quickly that Joel could not follow most of it. What he could see, though, was that Ryan was managing to attack while simultaneously defending himself.

Joel saw Ryan block a blow from the mace by hooking it just under the head with one of the curved top edges of his battleaxe. He pivoted the axe head to clamp it between the two axe blades and tugged, pulling the weapon and the warrior off balance, and then used the trapped mace to deflect a downward swipe of another *Ken's* scimitar. He snatched his blade down and slid away quickly while the momentum of the mace wielder caused him to stumble forward. The scimitar wielder stepped back to avoid a collision with his comrade while the other two warriors came at Ryan from the rear.

Ryan performed a leaping, spinning back kick while swinging Demonsbane in front of him in a wide horizontal arc. For a moment, he resembled a spinning helicopter blade. He did not make contact with any of his attackers, who deftly stepped out of the arc of sweeping metal or ducked under it, but it halted their advance, giving Ryan enough time to hit the ground and slide away from the warriors to get them all in front of him again.

Ryan dropped into a defensive crouch as the *Ken* eased cautiously forward. The warriors tried again to surround Ryan but he continued to glide smoothly away, keeping them in front of him.

Motion at the top of the far side of the canyon pulled Joel's attention away from the fight. More *S'Zan Rho* warriors emerged from the lengthening shadows of dusk and approached the edge of the chasm. From the top of the opposite canyon wall, Joel started counting the number of warriors as they made their way down the slope. He forced himself to stop counting when he reached fifty. He looked over at Quick, who stood protectively over Azh while sniffing at the air and peering at the surrounding tracks.

"Rell Kallen went east for perhaps fifty yards and then his trail disappeared." Quick noted. "No doubt he used his Phoenix stone to escape. He's taken the Hell Key and abandoned them."

"Can you blame him?" Joel asked. "Who would face that voluntarily?"

The changeling thought for a moment. He recalled their encounter with the *Ken d'Zanir* in Port Lorrian and how Joel was tied to his bed, as if someone was deliberately trying to keep him out of the fray. His faith whispered to him that the Lord Ascendant would not put them in a situation from which there was no escape. His instincts told him that hope would come in the form of the Children of the Old Ones. Quick trusted his instincts. He trusted his faith even more.

"Will you help him, Joel?" Quick asked.

"Help him?" Joel scoffed. "You know what those bastards can do."

"You've never faced the *Ken* as we have," Quick argued. "Perhaps you can bring your power to bear if you try."

"Try to bring *your* power to bear," Joel returned. "Better yet, instead of dying for nothing, maybe we just should get the girl out of here."

The men of the *S'Zan Rho* were bigger and stronger than most any other human Joel had ever seen. The smallest of the grown men would blend in easily with power forwards in the National Basketball Association or tight ends in the National

Football League. From what Quick told him about their elite holy warriors, the *Ken d'Zanir* had trained their entire lives to fight in a style very similar to the martial arts of his world. Even with his battleaxe, armor and training, there was no way Ryan would survive against the number of *Ken* coming for him.

But what could Joel do?

"You are a Child of the Old Ones," Quick reminded.

"And so is Rionn Lorr!" Joel was growing irritated. "And he was useless against the *Ken*. Are you trying to get me to kill myself?"

Joel could make out all kinds of weapons hanging from the *Ken's* clenched fists, belts, straps, baldrics, and sheaths. The metallic chime of metal upon metal carried to him from across the canyon. Over half of the charging horde was at the bottom of the canyon and racing toward Ryan. He was already flanked so retreat was not an option. Quick wanted Joel to throw himself into that? Joel ignored the pleading gaze of the teen and stared down into the canyon, fascinated by how calm his fellow offworlder was in the face of such dire odds.

Ryan had turned this preliminary bout in his favor. He conserved energy by not dodging or deflecting blows that could be countered by his armor, which did more than repel the strikes. It must have absorbed the inertia of the powerful blows because Ryan never lost his footing. Otherwise the much taller, much heavier men would have long since knocked him off balance.

Ryan wielded the double-bladed battleaxe in his left hand like a baton, using it primarily for defense. When he did strike with Demonsbane he used the flat of the blade, all while attacking with his deformed, metal-coated right hand and both booted feet. He struck at the enemy with a series of cobra-quick jabs and hooks and sweeps. Joel wondered why Ryan did not use Questblade. It was not Demonsbane, but it appeared to be a formidable weapon just the same.

That was when he remembered Ryan's oath. It seemed fatally ridiculous for Ryan to try to keep his oath under such dire circumstances. The way he fought, though, made Joel almost believe his fellow offworlder could pull it off. The speed and height Ryan achieved on his kicks were more incredible than anything Joel had ever seen even in his favorite martial arts films. He had heard that the fighters in those movies were so quick that the directors had to slow them down in order to film them effectively. That was exactly what Joel saw on that canyon floor.

It soon became obvious that Ryan would defeat the quartet. The approaching force, however, would easily overrun him. Joel actually was tempted to charge down into the fray. He owed Ryan that much. Had Ryan not sent Ethan and Quick to search for him after the demon's forces abducted him, Joel likely would have been caught and brought back to Tauran's dungeon to rot.

But if Quick – one of Ryan's best friends in either world as well as his biggest admirer – was unwilling to go into the canyon to help, why would Joel? Joel did not think the young changeling was afraid of anything, but Quick was very afraid of the *Ken*. They had found a way to neutralize magic, and without his ability to shape-shift, Quick would be little if any help to Ryan.

Joel was not at all confident his power would work, either. If the *Ken* could take away the Head Mage's power, it could take his away. More than that, he was even more afraid of what his power would do to him if it *did* work. Even with the newfound control he developed in Eastedge, the pain of the transformation hurt like death. He imagined the fires of hell were less painful.

Even though his power made him otherwise, Joel still saw himself as an average, hard working man who only wanted to live a normal life as a husband and father-to-be. No matter what others told him, no matter what his power made him, Joel was not a fighter. Ryan was the warrior. He was the ex-soldier and assassin.

Joel moved a step away from the edge of the canyon. All of his self-preservation instincts told him to run away as fast as he could, but deeper instincts that he could not understand urged him forward. It took all of his strength to resist them.

Quick drew his straight sword and strode toward the lip of the canyon. He shot a disappointed glare at Joel before turning his attention to the battle. Ryan needed help, and even though he knew the *S'Zan Rho* could sap his magic, Quick was apparently willing to die in defense of his friend, and by extension, the Kingdom of Lorr.

"Take the girl away from here, offworlder," Quick said solemnly as he approached. "I've been through too much with Raxe to let him die alone in this manner."

Quick's brave and simple declaration brought Dan's words to Joel's mind:

There will come a time when you have to look behind you to see the path that lies ahead of you.

Joel suddenly realized the truth of those words. All he had done was look behind him to lament his bad luck, but when he looked beyond that, he knew that everything he had gone through, even before crossing the WorldGate, indicated that he had to at least try to help. More than just his life and the lives of his wife and unborn child were at risk. This world and his were at stake.

Besides, he owed Ryan. He owed the Head Mage. Rionn Lorr and his wife gave him the herbal medicine that held his asthma at bay after he lost his inhaler, and he had not had any trouble with his breathing in well over a week. So many people had helped him and all he did was look out for himself. The only exception was when he saved Dayna from yet another assault in the dungeons of Eastedge Castle.

It was time to make another exception.

He had made up his mind to help yet he could not force himself to take another step forward. As hard as he tried, self-preservation and common sense were at war with his burgeoning sense of duty.

The result was inaction, a tremulous hesitation that left Joel at the verge of both running away and fighting. He hated himself for freezing up. When he finally, actually *wanted* to help, try as he might, he simply could not move. He heard

Quick's determined footsteps coming closer and stopping just behind him. Joel would not even turn to look. He was too ashamed to meet the disapproving gaze of the young warrior.

"I'm sorry, Quick," Joel said, looking down at the dry, cracked earth beneath his feet. "I can't do this."

"Yes, you can, Joel," Quick said softly. "And you will."

There was a resolve in Quick's tone that startled Joel. He turned with a puzzled frown that turned into a look of shock and fear when he saw Quick swinging his short sword in a wide arc at his head. Joel easily ducked the whistling blade but he had to jump back when Quick brought the blade back around at his midsection.

"What the *hell*!" Joel cried as Quick came at him again.

The next swipe was as wide and fierce as the first, driving Joel back even further. Initially Joel thought the teen had lost his patience and was trying to kill him, but he had watched Quick use his blade before. The youngster was far more precise and controlled with his attacks.

When he felt his foot slip over the edge of the canyon wall Joel realized that he was not being attacked. He was being herded. Joel's arms flailed as he fought for balance but he continued to teeter over the edge. He glared at Quick as he fell slowly backward.

"Sneaky son of a bitch," Joel noted with a grim smile.

"I'm sorry," Quick whispered. "But I trust my instincts."

Joel fell over the canyon rim and rolled uncontrollably down the steep slope. He reached out in several fruitless attempts to slow or stop his fall and only succeeded in ripping skin from his fingers and palms. He was three quarters of the way downslope when the pain of his transformation overcame him. The change was not in response to Quick's assault, Joel knew. It became more obvious than ever that his magic awakened only when his life was in jeopardy.

Quick had not tried to kill him. The boy was merely driving him over the sloping edge of the canyon wall. The *Ken* would surely attack him when he reached the bottom. It was that imminent danger, and likely the violence of his roll down the canyon wall, that triggered the change.

Joel clutched his stomach and grunted breathlessly as all of his muscles seized with shocking pain. His heart felt like it was exploding. He gagged on dust and loose pebbles when he tried to scream. Fire replaced the blood in his veins and his whole body spasmed violently even as he tumbled.

He could feel the wrenching of his bones and the rending of his flesh as his body re-shaped itself in agonizing fits and starts. Somewhere in his haze of pain, he realized that during all the other times he had transformed he would have blacked out by now. The suffering lasted longer than it ever had before. It was more intense than it had ever been. Why was he not blacking out? What was he becoming?

Unconsciousness would have been infinitely better than what he felt as he rolled down that slope. For the first time since his transformations began, he *wanted* to black out, even if it meant waking up later atop a mountain of corpses.

Joel knew his transformation was complete when the pain finally ebbed. He thrust out the flat, sharp, bony appendages that were once his hands and drove them into the canyon wall to halt his tumble.

Something was significantly different. Not only was he completely conscious, he was completely under control. He pulled his right scythe hand free and willed it back to a human hand. The hand was massive, as was the arm to which it was attached, but it had five fingers and thumb and Joel had *made* it that way. With a grin and a powerful shove of his legs and arms, he launched into the air and away from the canyon slope.

7.3

The warrior with the broken shin tried to attack from Raxe's left. When he brought his scimitar around in a quick arc aimed for Raxe's neck, Raxe sliced the blade in half with a backhand flick of his battleaxe. He immediately and effortlessly reversed the path of his weapon to send it whistling toward the hobbled warrior's head. At the last moment, Ryan pivoted Demonsbane so that the flat part of one the blades broke the *Ken*'s jaw and knocked him out.

The knife-wielding *Ken* attacked from Raxe's right, his unarmed side, with another jab at the offworlder's triceps. Raxe reached up with his metal-coated fingers and snapped the clawed digits around the *Ken's* thick wrist. The agony Raxe felt in his injured hand was acute but he expected it. The *Ken,* however, did not expect the deformed hand to immediately contract and crush his wrist. The big man paused momentarily, shocked by the unexpected pain.

Raxe, using the pain from his right hand to stoke his combative fire, took that fraction of a second to dart a sharp kick at the inside of his opponent's forward knee. He heard the knee shatter and the ligaments pop. He planted his feet, pulled the stumbling warrior into him, and flipped him over his hip, throwing him into the charging warrior wielding the haft of the broken war axe.

The approaching warrior caught his partner and tossed him aside, but the moment he was clear, Raxe was right there to deliver a whip-like kick between his legs with tip of his right armored boot. This evinced a high-pitched groan that Raxe immediately silenced with another cobra-quick whip-kick to the man's left temple. As the unconscious man crumpled to the ground, the last warrior came at Raxe from behind with his mace.

Raxe spun and brought up Demonsbane in one smooth motion, neatly slicing the spiked mace head in two. The warrior threw a darting jab at Raxe's exposed jaw but the offworlder ducked slightly so that the blow struck his helm and crushed the warrior's knuckles. Raxe then relieved him of his senses with a backhand blow from his damaged right hand just below the *Ken*'s ear.

Any satisfaction Raxe might have felt from his victory was instantly squelched when he looked up and around at the dozens upon dozens of *Ken d'Zanir* swarming onto the canyon floor. He had just taken four of them down without killing them, but the numbers he faced now were hopeless. A silent prayer for forgiveness went up to God for the lives he had taken before his oath and for the lives he would have to take now if he had any chance of surviving this ordeal. He held no illusions that he would survive but he was not about to lie down for them. With a deep, steadying breath, he readied himself for the coming onslaught.

A shadow, barely discernable in the waning light, fell over Raxe. He stepped aside just as a huge figure slammed to the ground beside him, throwing a cloud of dirt, pebbles and even Raxe into the air. Raxe landed awkwardly but kept his feet. The charging *Ken* slowed to a walk and proceeded much more cautiously to appraise the new arrival. When the dust and debris settled, Raxe looked upon a creature that, while humanoid in form, was as fearsome as any demon he had ever encountered.

Its head and face, both sparsely covered with matted, kinky, dark brown hair, were of a normal size, which was shockingly too small for its colossal body. When it stood to its full height, the thing was over two feet taller than Raxe, which made it eight feet of bulging muscle and pulsing veins.

The dull, light-brown skin that covered the beast was so taut that Raxe thought it would tear. Jagged, bony protrusions of various sizes jutted out haphazardly from multiple places on the creature's body, including its skull and cheekbones. Some of them were flat with razor edges while others were conical, but all of them tapered to wickedly pointed tips.

Bone blades and spikes protruded from its wrists and elbows, from the joints where its massive clavicle bones connected to its shoulders, from the knees and ankles and other random points of its tree-trunk legs.

Instead of hands, the disproportionately long arms ended in wide, flat, razor-edged sickles of bone. Those appendages, along with the familiar shape of the creature's brow that shrouded the pale glow of its milky white eyes, revealed to Raxe exactly who this creature was.

"Joel?" Raxe asked in disbelief.

The creature's mouth stretched open into what Raxe could only assume was a smirk. Teeth, like small ivory stalactites and stalagmites, jutted up and down from black gums. It was the most gruesome grin Raxe had seen since he last saw the King of the Dragon's foul rictus.

"How could you tell?" Joel asked in a voice that lowed and echoed like a war horn from the depths of hell.

Raxe jumped at the sound. He did not even know Joel could talk in his altered state. He had never heard him speak while his magic was active.

"I almost couldn't," Raxe admitted. "If I hadn't seen so many monsters over the years I'd be shitting myself right now. What are you doing here?"

"Helping you keep your oath," Joel answered.

"By killing all of them *for* me?"

"I don't have to kill them," Joel explained. "I can control it now."

Raxe looked up and down at the monstrosity that stood before him. With his size and spikes and sharp edges, he looked like death incarnate. It was hard to believe Joel could do anything *but* kill.

"Are you sure?" Raxe questioned. "Conjurers have control of their abilities, but you and me, our powers work differently. If I've learned nothing else, I've learned the price of our power is usually something we don't expect, and a lot more than we're willing to pay."

"I'm positive," Joel insisted.

In response to Raxe's incredulous gaze, the bone spikes in Joel's body receded back into his flesh with wet snapping sounds. The scythe-like appendages that emerged from his wrists shrank back into big hands with blunt fingers. Even his teeth squared off and appeared more human.

Joel reminded Raxe of the Havoks that had guarded his enchanted armor for over two thousand years back on Infinity Isle. Joel was not quite as large as Havoks, and they were more simian with shorter, stubbier legs and longer arms that caused their knuckles to drag along the ground. Even still, Joel managed to look fiercer than those beasts.

"See?" Joel said. His voice still sounded as ominous as it had when he first spoke. "Control."

Although the razor edges and points were now gone, he was still a menacing behemoth that looked as if he was capable of nothing but lethal carnage. Raxe only shrugged.

Joel caught his reflection in Raxe's eyes and almost jumped in shock. The reflection he saw was *the evil*. He did not have the glowing red eyes of the beast that pursued him in so many of his nightmares, but he was identical in every other way. After a moment he was able to compose himself. After all, he defeated *the evil* in his nightmares more than once and had no doubt that those triumphs were a sign of his growing control of his power.

"Get Azh out of here. Go find the elf and the Hell Key," Joel commanded. "Quick is waiting for you. I don't know if he can morph this close to the *Ken* but you can hoof it until he can. I'll catch up when I think you're far enough away. I can cover a lot of ground quickly in this form."

"Yeah, I'll bet," Raxe said. He looked around nervously at the approaching warriors.

The *Ken* had hesitated at the sight of Joel but resumed their full speed charge and were almost upon them. The two offworlders were completely surrounded, leaving no way for Raxe to get through them in order to get to the far canyon wall. Besides, Raxe would never have been able to outrun them to get there. The closest of the surrounding warriors were only about twenty yards away.

Raxe quickly snatched up his provision pack and his cloak, put them both on, and then turned to Joel. "Are you going to give me a piggy-back ride out of here or what?"

"Oh yeah," Joel remembered. "Let me give you a hand."

Joel reached out, wrapped one massive hand around the left side of Raxe's cuirass and the other around Raxe's armored right hip and lifted him off of the ground. With a superhuman heave, he sent the armored man flying. Raxe watched the ground rush away beneath him and felt the exhilarating sensation of flight but he knew the landing would be rough. He held his pack tightly against his stomach tucked himself into a ball to let the armor take the brunt of the landing just before he crashed to the rocky ground at the top of the far canyon wall. He stood, staggered, spit out dirt and patted the dust from his pack. Quick stood before him, holding Azh in his wiry arms.

"It's good to see you in one piece, Raxe," the changeling said as he passed the unconscious girl to her father.

"It's good to *be* in one piece," Raxe said as he took Azh into his arms. "Joel said he'd hold them off so we can escape. But before we track down that damned elf we have to take Azh to Lake Onyx. Something is seriously wrong. I think her mom is the only one who can help her."

Quick started to protest, to remind Raxe that the Hell Key was their first priority. He wanted to argue that protecting the world from the Dierglyorr and the possible carnage he could cause if he gained control of the Hell Key meant more than the life of one girl. Raxe saw Quick's hesitation, but the fierceness of the offworlder's glare stayed any objection the changeling could think to offer.

"Let us fly then," Quick surrendered. "But first, we must run. The *Ken* are stifling my magic again. We must put more distance between us and them before I can change forms."

Raxe was exhausted nearly to the point of collapse and the path they had to travel sloped upward, but he held his daughter securely and willed one foot in front of the other until he reached a slow jog. The changeling ran for about two hundred yards before he stopped and morphed into the familiar form of the gryphon. Instead of waiting the several seconds it would take for Raxe to arrive, he swooped back to them with a mighty flap of its wings.

Raxe placed Azh carefully across the gryphon's broad, furry back and then climbed on. He looked over his shoulder one last time into the canyon. They were too far away now for him to tell exactly what was happening in the dying light, but he could see that bodies were flying, collapsing, and not moving again. The sounds carried easily, though, and what he heard gave him chills. Being all-to-familiar with the nature of the magic passed down to the descendants of the Gatekeeper, Raxe doubted Joel could control his power to the extent he claimed. The monstrous roars and agonized screams from the canyon floor heightened those doubts.

He hoped Joel could get out of the canyon before it was fully dark. Small puddles of blood already littered the ground and it would get a lot bloodier during Joel's clash with the *S'Zan Rho* elite warriors. Raxe's close call with the accursed canyon was still dreadfully fresh in his mind. The *Ken d'Zanir* may have been able to stifle magic, but they could not stop Joel's power. Raxe suspected they would not be able to stifle the magic of Hargathall's Cleft, either.

Short of WorldHopper, the King of the Dragons, Joel might possibly have been the most formidable being Raxe had ever encountered. But Raxe did not believe for a moment that any of them would be able to withstand the ravenous and terrible force of nature that was Hargathall's Cleft when it awakened.

7.4

After tossing Raxe to safety, Joel stood his ground defiantly and watched the warriors approach. The strength he felt pulsing through his ropy veins and taut muscles made him shiver with anticipation. There was a tingling sensation of energy that made him almost giddy. He had not blacked out at all this time and that was fine with him. The pain of his transformation had passed and he could control his power. That knowledge brought on confidence he had never felt.

He blacked out during all of his previous transformations and always found himself standing over or near at least one butchered body when he regained consciousness. The only exception was the transformation prior to this last one. That time, when he felt the change coming on he willed himself not to kill his attackers. He saw to his delight when he came to that he had only rendered them unconscious. Now Joel could control his power and he was fully cognizant. He was excited and curious about what he could do.

A wave of *Ken d'Zanir* swarmed him from his right in what to him seemed like slow motion. The sharp tips of their pikes and the razor edges of their various blades came at him. Joel waved a massive right hand in a backhand stroke that snapped the weapons like twigs. The attackers' momentum continued to carry them forward while Joel's left hand followed closely behind his right in a roundhouse punch.

He intended to beat them back with just enough force to disable them or knock them unconscious or both. Just before his fist struck the nearest warrior, however, it involuntarily morphed back into the dreaded bone scythe.

Even though everything seemed to move at a quarter of the speed of reality, Joel could neither reverse the transformation nor stop the inertia of his blow. He watched with terror and loathing as the fist-turned-bone-scythe cut through leather armor, cloth, skin, muscle and bone as if they were air. He felt helpless as the scythe completed its deadly arc, laying low eight warriors with the one brutal strike.

The ones that came at him in a crouch were either beheaded or had their heads sheared away across their faces. Those that came at full height were sliced in two at the waist.

The second wave reached Joel from every side. Several warriors jumped on his broad back and several more thrust themselves at his legs in an attempt to trip him. Joel did not even stumble. More men hit him, more than he could count. They piled on him relentlessly, pounding and stabbing and cutting ineffectually at his rock-hard skin. The impact of the huge men and the slippery blood beneath Joel's feet disrupted his balance and finally brought him down. The warriors' savage but useless attack almost tickled Joel as he stumbled forward to the ground. But he did not laugh. There was nothing in the least bit funny about what was happening.

The combined weight of the transformed Child of the Old Ones and the huge warriors on his back and shoulders crushed the life out of the unfortunate men caught beneath his torso. He could hear the snapping of bones and the squishing of organs. The smell of blood filled his nostrils.

Joel felt the bone spikes involuntarily emerge from his toughened hide to find the warm flesh of the men clinging to him. Even their agonized screams seemed to trumpet out deeply and slowly, as if coming from a recording played too slow. Joel gathered himself and rose to his feet, willing the spikes to retract while he shook off bleeding men the way a dog shakes water from its fur. In addition to their bodies, all manner of bodily fluids, as well as chunks of flesh, sprayed out in every direction, blinding and otherwise distracting the warriors that had not yet reached him.

The next thing Joel knew, his legs were moving of their own accord and carrying him to the crowd of startled and disgusted warriors directly in front of him. He tried to stop but his legs ignored his brain's commands. He could not even make himself hesitate. Bone spikes blossomed again from his head, shoulders, elbows, chest, knees and ankles as he barreled into the crowd. At that point the *Ken* did something entirely unfamiliar to the fearsome warriors. They fled.

The scattering warriors in his dreadful path appeared to Joel as if they were running underwater. They could not get out of the way fast enough. Joel gored, trampled, or cut down every man within the circumference of his ten-foot wingspan. He repeatedly had to pull or shake free the corpse of an unfortunate victim impaled on his barrel chest or massive shoulders, only to make room for another and another and another still. He chased them down like an enraged bull, never missing the opportunity to reach out with his scythe-hands to cut down a warrior not in his immediate path.

Joel struggled to close his eyes but he could not. He felt like a disembodied apparition staring through the eyes of some vicious monster. In fact, he tried to pretend that was precisely what was happening. That was the only way he could think of to hold on to his fleeing sanity.

Unfortunately, his other senses would not allow him even that much relief. He could taste their salty sweat and coppery blood. He could smell the acrid stench of bile, urine and feces as his multi-horned head and spiked arms tore men open and apart.

The blood he accidentally swallowed caused Joel's stomach to lurch. He heaved out the contents of his stomach even as he pursued the *Ken,* yet he never slowed. The green and brown vomit steamed in the cool evening air and seared the flesh of his victims like acid. The hideous sights and sounds and smells and tastes sickened him even more.

Joel finally managed to force his eyes closed and found that sight was hardly needed. He was thankful for the loss of at least one of his senses but the rest of them were continuously assaulted. He tracked his victims by the scent of their flesh and fear. He located them by the sound of their panicked footfalls and pounding hearts. He pinpointed their location from the waves of air they displaced as they ran.

He knew their screams and stench and the visual of their gruesome deaths would be with him forever. That was when he understood what Ryan meant about the price of the Children of the Old Ones' power.

7.5

The southern plains of Lorr rushed beneath the Ranger Elf Rell Kallen a mile below. They resembled an earthen patchwork quilt with their rich tapestries of varying shades of browning pastureland, red and yellow autumn leaves in small clusters of trees and brush, and the rich greens of grasses not yet touched by the change of season.

He sat easily upon the living flames of his Phoenix without feeling any of its heat. The great speed at which they traveled never threatened to unseat him, but it lifted his single blonde braid upon the wind so that it trailed behind him the same way the Phoenix's blazing tail trailed behind them in a narrow, mile-long streak.

Such was the power of elven magic.

Less than three quarters of an hour had passed since his flight from Hargathall's Cleft. His Phoenix carried him over the Badlands, the Bountiful River and approached the Deadwood Forest, more than four hundred total miles. As far as he was concerned that was neither far nor fast enough. He was only a quarter of the way to the Palace of Thâlstrën in the northeastern regions of the Elf Lands. More than an hour could have been shaved from his journey if only he had been able to initiate his flight from the sky or a mountaintop.

His flight path was a vertically oriented arc moving directly northeast and parallel to the southeastern coast of Lorr. The arc's rise and fall added extra time and distance to his trip. The one disadvantage to the Phoenix stone was that the magical creature it conjured could not change its path mid-flight. Like an arrow shot from a bow, once his Phoenix's flight commenced it could not change its direction other than to succumb to gravity when its momentum eventually dampened.

Because the Ranger Elf had to initiate the Phoenix's flight from the ground and clear the top of the surrounding mountains, its current path was like that of a giant arch that would, in this instance, span roughly six hundred miles.

He would touch down nearly fifty miles away from the northeastern ranges of the Runestone Mountains. Another quick jump of the Phoenix to the highest peak of that mountain range would then provide him with the perfect angle for a straight-line northeastern shot to his home.

After that, the magic of the Phoenix stone would be exhausted and it would take months to replenish itself. That was fine with Rell Kallen, for he would likely have no further need of it. This mission, the acquisition of the Hell Key and its delivery to his queen, would be his last and greatest quest. The Queen would promote him to High Commander of the Rangers and he would delegate from then on.

Rell Kallen had served his queen loyally for over fifty years as the best of the most elite military force in the Known Lands. The current High Commander was old, even by elf standards, and more than ready to relinquish his post to a worthy successor. Even though Rell Kallen loved his service in the field, the time had come for him to stop all of this running around. It was time for him to advance to the next chapter of his life. That meant a promotion to a more fixed position within the Rangers, a bride and an heir.

He would always regret losing his betrothed Catherine Eleshaë to the Head Mage of the Kingdom of Lorr, but Rell had long since endeared himself to her younger sister, Steffånênlia. It would have been unseemly for him and Steffånênlia to act upon their mutual attraction too soon after Catherine's defection. However, enough time had passed to make a union between Rell Kallen and the younger princess – and current heir to the Thâlstrën throne – acceptable.

It was highly likely that Rell Kallen would be both High Commander of the Ranger Elves and king, a dual position never held in Thâlstrën's long and storied history. Thâlstrën had always been a matriarchal society, its kings relegated to an inferior role, wielding only the power granted to him by the queen. As the Rangers' High Commander and king, Rell would wield real power and be more than just a figurehead. The Thâlstrën Kingdom would be the better for it.

That was worth the misuse of his Ranger's Oath.

THE KEY QUEST

An unmistakable sting of guilt gnawed at the Ranger Elf's heart. He beat it back forcefully and kept reminding himself that he had not broken his oath...not technically, anyway. When he made his oath to the offworlder his words were chosen carefully and purposely ambiguous. He did indeed plan to take the girl to Lake Onyx. He simply did not say exactly *when* he would do it. After delivering the Hell Key to Her Majesty, the Ranger Elf had every intention of returning to Hargathall's Cleft.

Of course, the Phoenix stone would not yet be functional. As a result, the trip to Thâlstrën that would take roughly four hours upon the Phoenix would take nearly two days upon his peoples' fastest sky sleigh. But there was still a very good chance that both Azhju'lestra and Raxe would still be there when he returned. It was very likely that after killing them, the *Ken* would leave the Children wherever they fell.

Rell would gladly return the girl's corpse to Lake Onyx and even deliver the offworlder's body to the Head Mage. If the various scavengers, both winged and earthbound, left nothing of them but bones, then that is what he would return. If Hargathall's Cleft claimed them, well then, his oath would have been broken. Instead of misusing his oath Rell Kallen supposed he could have taken the Hell Key by force. That was, in fact, his initial plan. It could not have been done within Mardah's keep because of the likelihood that both of the Children's assistance would be essential to the safe extraction of the enchanted greatsword.

He considered making his move once they were outside of the mountain but he knew attacking Raxe in front of his daughter could be a potentially disastrous mistake. He had recently learned that the girl's mother was the Mistress of the Sea of Spirits, a water faerie. Creatures of faerie were unpredictable and immensely powerful. After witnessing what she did to the *Ken* who confronted them outside of Mar-dah's mountain, he knew he was right to wait.

So the elf decided to take the Key during one of the times they stopped to rest. He noticed during their travels that the

217

girl slept very soundly. So much time away from water had undoubtedly weakened her a bit and she required the extra rest. He could have taken the Key from Raxe and been away before the girl could assist her father.

That would not have been a very honorable method of obtaining the Key, though it would have been much more honorable than using his Ranger's Oath in a deceptive manner. His conscience picked at him and he was sure it would for years. If that was to be his burden to bear, if that was to be the price he had to pay for completing this most important of missions, so be it. His success in this endeavor was just that important.

And then there was his next move to consider. If the Children of the Old Ones and the Kingdom of Lorr failed to defeat the demon, which at this point seemed the most likely outcome, it would fall to the elves to stop it. He had no doubt that they could and would. In addition to acquiring the Hell Key, Rell Kallen was responsible for observing the demon's methods in order to assist in devising a strategy to defeat it. He had done just that. He was supremely confident that under his direction, the elven Kingdom's considerable forces could defeat the demon and its hordes.

Several scenarios for defeating the Dierglyorr were running through his mind when he caught movement out of the corner of his eye.

Rell Kallen turned to his right to see the approach of a great winged beast he could not immediately identify. What he could immediately identify, though, was that it was flying in from the southeast at a speed that matched and possibly exceeded the speed of his Phoenix, and at an angle that would soon intercept him.

The Ranger Elf slid his bow from his shoulder and knocked three iron-tipped arrows between his four fingers as he watched his pursuer fly ever nearer. At first, the beast's large and leathery wings made Rell think it was a dragon. He had to think again, though, because the only dragon capable of achieving such great speed was WorldHopper.

THE KEY QUEST

The approaching creature was as black as an overcast midnight. The King of the Dragons was forest green. This creature's body was sleek and serpentine. WorldHopper was bulky and reptilian. Another difference was its wings. WorldHopper had forelegs and wings that protruded from his back. This creature's arms were merged with its wings like webbed bat wings.

Rell thought with a bit of alarm that it might be a wyvern. But again, the wings were wrong, as was its color. Sea wyverns were covered with scales of aquatic hues. They were gargantuan beasts many times larger than the one approaching and they did not stray this far from the water. They might fly above a sea, lake, or river, but they would never leave their general vicinity.

Sky wyverns' colors were more varied, but their bodies were more like massive scaled birds than serpents or reptiles. They were native to the Fringelands in the rugged northwestern mountain ranges of the Westin Continent. Rell could see that the pursuing beast was not covered with scales as he had assumed from a distance, but rather short black hair with an oily sheen. Rell Kallen remembered the rock trolls that guarded the bridge near Mar-dah's mountain. Perhaps this was another such beast. Could this be another creature banished to the Unknown Lands during Heaven's War that was brought here by the demon?

That was when he realized that was exactly what he was seeing. An entire mountain range in Lorr had been named after the exiled beast that was flying toward him. Rell had learned about wyrms long ago, but like rock trolls, he had never seen one. The description as he recalled was identical to the approaching monster. But as the black, winged serpentine creature came closer with alarming swiftness, the elf's keen eyes locked in on the monster's eyes.

When he saw the two narrow vertical slits of blood-red light slicing through the gloom of the darkening skies, staring at him with utter hatred and the dark promise of mayhem, he knew his arrows would be of no use to him.

Demon

The Ranger Elf was counting on the demon being preoccupied with the Children of the Old Ones in this world and the Child in Raxe's world. He had guessed that the Hell Key had no real value to the demon other than to serve as bait to draw the Children to their deaths. The demon could not use the weapon and the key was a potentially deadly talisman to it. Rell Kallen was surprised the demon would dare to get even this close to the Hell Key.

Yet here it was. It streaked closer until it was a little less than one hundred yards to the southeast and flying parallel to the Phoenix. Rell Kallen was starting to lament the Phoenix's lack of maneuverability when the demon serpent cracked open its terrible maw impossibly wide and spit a cone of crimson flame across the sky at him.

With no other options available, Rell Kallen willed away the magic of the Phoenix Stone. The Phoenix he rode upon extinguished faster than the blink of an eye and the Ranger Elf dropped head-first out of the path of the attack. The flames missed him by several feet but the heat radiating from the demon's attack still singed the elf's thick boots.

The demon extinguished its flame and dove after the plummeting elf. With a few flaps of its mighty wings it brought itself just within one hundred yards of the elf once more. Its jaws unhinged again, the red flames streamed from its mouth again, and this time they engulfed the Ranger Elf.

Rell Kallen had already reached into his taught cloak and clutched his string of blue pearls. He had already recited the necessary spell by the time the flames poured over him. The fire passed through him as if it was only a figment of illusory magic…at first. The demon kept the flames trained upon him as they descended, bathing him in an unceasing stream.

After several seconds of this Rell Kallen actually began to feel the heat. It started as mild warmth but with each passing second the heat grew more intense. The Ranger Elf realized with despair that the magic of the demon fire was overcoming his elven magic, consuming the very power that made him immaterial.

Rell had never feared death. It was inevitable and he had cheated it more times than any being had a right to. His only regrets, as he felt the burning agony from the failing magic of his ghost pearls, were that he had failed his queen and that there were no other Ranger Elves around to witness his glorious death.

When the demon finally relented, all that was left was a cloud of black ash dispersing into the winds. From that cloud fell the Hell Key, the blade glowing bright orange from unearthly heat of the demon fire. A line of white steam trailed in its wake. Its sheath had been burned completely away but the weapon itself was unharmed. It fell toward the earth point-first like a bolt from the heavens. The demon's eyes followed the falling weapon gleaming in the dying suns' light until it buried itself into the ground all the way to the hilt. It pierced the earth only a few feet away from where a half-dozen of Shara Dune's sand creatures waited.

With a mental command from the Dierglyorr as it circled in the air several dozen yards above them, the sand creatures threw a heavy woolen sack over the protruding handle, which was still steaming. The sack was studded with beads of black crystal arranged in ancient spell forms not seen since Heaven's War. The sand creatures wrapped their tapered tentacles tightly around the covered grip and pulled the broadsword easily from the ground. They slipped the warded woolen sack completely over the Hell Key before carrying it west across the plains at a loping sprint.

The demon watched them go with more than a little satisfaction. It could trust the sand creatures more than humans in this endeavor. While running full out, sand creatures moved faster than horses and with twice the stamina. Despite their size and distinctive appearance, they knew how to travel quietly on their padded, three-toed feet. They knew how to travel stealthily even at great speeds.

They would use the cover of the Deadwood Forest and then the Badlands and then the Demon's Spine to take the Hell

Key to its final hiding place. No one or nothing short of a Child of the Old Ones, a Master Mage level conjurer, or a fully armed military troop could stop six determined sand creatures working in concert.

Even better, they were simple creatures that blindly and faithfully followed orders. Shara Dune was foolish enough to think that she was the only one capable of commanding them, but then again, Shara Dune had no idea she was the witless pawn of a sixth level demon. She had long ago ceded him power over them. As long as she did not directly oppose the demon's command – which would not happen because she was occupied with killing the Mistress of the Sea and had no idea they were assisting in this task – the sand creatures would obey the Dierglyorr unerringly.

The Dierglyorr controlled the Hell Key at last. The demon could not use it, of course. Demons could not even touch the weapon, let alone invoke its magic to free more demons. The Dierglyorr, however, was powerful. It possessed the physical might of a juggernaut and the cunning of a most devious and intelligent human with more than two thousand years of accumulated knowledge.

And as always, the Dierglyorr had a plan. Even though it could not invoke the magic of the Hell Key, it had control of someone who eventually could.

7.6

HARGATHALL'S CLEFT

The High *Ken* Rkam Lonos watched the carnage in the fading light of dusk from the rim of the canyon. His eyes were wide with disbelief as he watched his glorious *Ken d'Zanir* get cut down like so much wheat.

What happened to the power of his talisman? The dark wizard who had given it to him said it would neutralize any magic, and until now, it had done exactly that. It worked on the mages that accompanied the first two search parties. It stymied that changeling whelp agent of the charlatan Head Mage Rionn Lorr. It had even banished the magic of the Head Mage himself.

If not magic, what could be the fuel for the massacre perpetrated by *this* Child of the Old Ones?

Lonos, as well as his warriors, thought the talisman was working properly when the bone spikes retracted just before the hulking offworlder tossed Raxe from the canyon. That feat hinted that maybe the Child's magic had not yet completely dissipated, but surely the loss of the deadly protrusions had been evidence that the talisman was functional. That was why they resumed their attack. Now the Child was a living weapon. His every limb was adorned with killing edges. Even the creature's vomit was deadly, burning through limbs and torsos to dismember and kill Lonos's *Ken*.

He had never seen a unit of his *Ken d'Zanir* take this kind of loss in battle. He doubted his entire army could best this monster. The offworlder was a storm of death. He struck his victims with the quickness and ferocity of lightning. His disorienting screams and bellows were living thunder.

Now the *Ken* were fleeing, something that did not come naturally for the fierce warriors. Even then, the Child pursued to kill them, something that ran counter to what Lonos understood about the Children who defended the Kingdom of Lorr. They were known for being merciful, taking a natural life only in self-defense or to defend the lives of the innocent. This Child was almost demonic in his spirited onslaught.

The time had come for Lonos to leave this fruitless confrontation. Many of his *Ken* had escaped from the canyon but far too many more of them were still being butchered. Yes, it was indeed time to make his escape.

The fearsome Child suddenly paused in his gruesome work and looked up, directly into Lonos's eyes. Lonos turned and sprinted to his war steed. His second in command quickly followed suit, as did the fortunate warriors who escaped the bloodbath on the canyon floor. The six-legged, long-limbed, cluster-horned reptilian creatures bounded away the instant their masters were seated and situated.

Joel cleared the canyon in two powerful leaps. He did not know why, but he was being compelled – against his will – to pursue the warrior wearing the blue-furred, braided headdress. What he really wanted to do was follow Ryan and Quick, but there was something about that particular *Ken's* scent that commanded Joel's deadly attention. He noticed that no one else wore a headdress, so perhaps this was the *Ken d'Zanir* leader. Whoever he was, Joel felt sorry for the doomed man.

The offworlder landed nimbly at the rim of the canyon, right where his new target had been standing just seconds earlier. In their haste, the *Ken* left behind dozens of wheeled carts. Most of them were fitted with wood and steel constructions that reminded Joel of giant crossbows. About a half dozen of them held stacks of thick, sharpened stakes as long as he was tall. Joel peered beyond the carts and saw a group of *Ken* fleeing swiftly away atop their reptilian mounts as well as riderless land dragons whose masters had been slain. He quickly spotted the blue headdress.

The southernmost sun, higher than its counterpart this time of the year, had sunk completely below the western curve of the earth. Only a hint of a crimson glow bled weakly over the horizon. The moons were rising slowly in the east, but Joel could see through the twilight haze as if it were the height of day. From the distance and incredible speed of the sleek war steeds, Joel estimated it would take about three hops to catch blue headdress.

There was a moment of hesitation as Joel gave a mighty effort to regain control of his limbs. He made a motion to launch himself in the direction that Ryan and Quick had taken, but instead, he reluctantly turned leapt in the other direction. He sailed effortlessly through the dimming sky after the *Ken* leader.

A familiar sound came to Joel's hypersensitive ears as he soared. The flapping of hundreds of wings came at him from the south, and then the recognizable cries of scythe wings filled the air. He glanced over his shoulder as he reached the apex of his jump and saw that the scythe wings were already on him. They swarmed him in mid air, clutching and clawing with their powerful talons, pecking and grasping with their wickedly curved beaks.

Joel tore at the birds with his bone-scythe hands. Unlike the last time he faced them, he was conscious – if not in control – of his every action. Also unlike the last time, they came at him with the obvious intent of killing him instead of merely transporting him.

While airborne, Joel had no leverage to use against the giant birds. They willingly gave up their lives to drive him backward through the air and back to the canyon floor. They kept coming at him, using their weight and numbers to keep him confined to the ground, despite the fact that they were cut down by the dozens. There was something about their smell that reminded Joel of the *Ken* with the blue headdress. The smells had distinct differences but there was the slightest hint of familiarity. It was magic. Quick had said that the dangerous birds were under the influence of subtle magic, but now Joel knew for certain. He could smell it. He could almost taste it.

The offworlder slashed and hacked and punched and ripped and stomped – all in slow motion to his still-heightened perception – until the birds finally relented. Their shrill death cries, coming to him at such a slow and drawn out speed, grated at him even more than the cries the of the dying *S'Zan Rho* warriors.

The surviving flying predators finally flew away. Against his will, Joel leapt after them. As he darted into the air, he caught sight of a cloaked figure in the distance to the east. In Joel's enhanced state the distance and relative darkness did nothing to impede his vision. He recognized the familiar whistle the big man tucked into his cloak. He also recognized the man. It was T'Cheln, the *Ken* warrior that had acted as Tauran's bodyguard.

Joel turned his attention away from the corrupt baron's vassal as he caught one of the fleeing scythe wings and brought it to the canyon floor under a hail of blows from his spikes and blades. When he was finished, he rose to his feet and watched the remainder of the birds fly away. He could no longer smell, hear or feel the fleeing *Ken d'Zanir* or their steeds. Neither could he scent the magic possessed by the *Ken's* leader and T'Cheln.

Joel's body shuddered as if he was cold but he was completely numb. All he felt was dread.

The moment the offworlder turned his frightening gaze away from him to attack the last scythe wing, T'Cheln turned and sprinted off. He ran east as fast as he could for just over eight seconds, covering the one hundred yards between Hargathall's Cleft to the cluster of fallen boulders where he had left his land dragon. The *Ken* warrior was not sure if Joel could or would track him, but if he made the attempt, T'Cheln was determined to make a difficult job of it.

He found his mount where he left it. The giant six-legged lizard was chomping down the remains of a massive mountain snake with coloring identical to the gray and brown rocky landscape. From the size of its tail, T'Cheln knew the viper had been easily three times as long as the land dragon.

Not waiting for it to finish its meal, he vaulted upon the saddle strapped to the land dragon's back and snatched up the reins. With a flick and a click of the tongue, T'Cheln commanded the beast to a full run. The land dragon swallowed the last of its prey and darted away.

THE KEY QUEST

As he rode east, staying in the cover of the mountains in case the offworlder decided to follow, T'Cheln reflected on what he had witnessed down in the Cleft. He also considered what he did in response to what he saw.

He wondered if he should have even used the whistle to call the scythe wings to help his beleaguered brethren escape. Rkam Lonos had shamed himself and all of his *Ken* warriors during this campaign. His attack on Port Lorrian was vicious and completely unnecessary. The *Ken* were commissioned to capture Joel and kill the other Children of the Old Ones and any who assisted them, not slaughter women and children.

The *Ken* chieftain left a message written in the blood of their innocent victims upon the walls of Port Lorrian's town hall. The message revealed that the slaughter had been committed in the name of the Old One S'Zan. That was nonsense. The warrior god represented honor as much as ferocity in battle. There was nothing in the least bit honorable about what was done to Port Lorrian.

Joel's wrath would have been well deserved for that atrocity alone. Lonos's razing of the small town of Hillview only added to the ledger.

T'Cheln also wondered if, with his final command to the scythe wings using the magic whistle, he had done the right thing when he sent the giant hawks back to their home. He briefly considered calling them back. They were not likely out of range of the magic whistle. T'Cheln was there when the dark wizard gifted the fool Tauran with the talisman. The wizard warned that the birds would be beyond the call of the whistle's magic once fifty miles or more separated them.

T'Cheln grasped the magic whistle bouncing against his chest and lifted it, but his hand froze before the whistle reached his lips. The whistle, like the talisman within the closed leather pouch at his hip that extinguished magic, was certainly an awesome power to posses. Scythe wings were great weapons and the *S'Zan Rho* people, especially the *Ken d'Zanir*, were masters of weapons of all types.

The magic-stifling talisman and the whistle were not just weapons, though. They were instruments of magic. The *S'Zan Rho* despised and rejected magic in any form. In fact, the *S'Zan Rho* lord, who was also T'Cheln's father, initially deemed it the highest form of blasphemy to even consider the use of the reensapir heart. The dark wizard did a masterful job of explaining that the talisman was the ideal instrument for them specifically because it extinguished magic. T'Cheln believed that the generous payment of two horse carts full of gold, silver, and precious gems also had a lot to do with his father's eventual acceptance of the contract.

T'Cheln did not hesitate to use the reensapir heart when necessary but he had been loath to use the whistle. Had Rkam Lonos been the only intended victim, T'Cheln would have happily let the offworlder have him. He could not, however, allow what remained of his fellow *Ken* to be slaughtered when he had the power to save them.

Instead of putting the whistle to his lips the *Ken* snatched it and the thong from which it hung from around his neck, broke the whistle, and tossed the pieces. Satisfied that there was no pursuit, he turned north to ride clear of the mountains and continue trailing his fellow *Ken d'Zanir*.

Joel was alone, except for the few *Ken* that avoided death but sustained injuries too severe for them to escape on their own. It was only then that he began to morph back to his human form. He fought the transformation this time because his monstrous form was needed if he had any chance of catching up to Raxe, Quick and Azh. Unfortunately, as hard as he tried, it was no use. With no mortal threat in his vicinity there was no need for his inhuman form.

His head spun viciously and the terrible pain came back as his muscles and bones compressed back to normal. Each snap of bone sent a shock of raw agony through his entire body, tearing painful cries from his throat with every jolt. The loud snapping and grating of bone echoed off of the canyon walls and added to the moans of the injured and dying *Ken* in a desolate serenade to the seven hells.

As painful as it was, Joel was thankful that his reversion to human form was not quite as painful as the change into the monster. That was the only silver lining in this cloud. A glance at his surroundings revealed a mess of corpses, ripped and broken. Dismembered body parts were strewn wildly about, some still twitching. His world had become death.

Joel's bare arms and torso were coated with gore and so were the tattered breaches that hung from his waist in long strips. He wished a thick cover of clouds would come to block out the last of the fading light so he would no longer see the horrific sights surrounding him. It would be even better if those clouds brought a torrent of rain to wash away the filth that covered him and wind to sweep away the stink.

There would be no such mercy. The stench of his surroundings assaulted him anew. The sights and smells of the gross landscape made him throw up again. This time he did not stop until he could only dry heave. He continued to gag as he sloshed through the ankle-high muck of blood and gore. The living he stepped over and around made no move toward him. Each was too preoccupied with the pain of injuries or too afraid that the savage Child would finish what he started if they were foolish enough to provoke him anew.

Joel brushed and picked away as many sticky feathers and bits and pieces of bloody flesh as he could while he stumbled hurriedly to the northeast portion of the curved canyon wall. He stumbled to his knees to gag several more times but kept moving.

Panic threatened to overwhelm him. In his transformed state he felt a strange sort of detachment. The site of his massive, spike-riddled arms and his bone-scythe hands lent a feeling of disembodiment to the entire ordeal. Despite the sounds, sights, and smells, he could almost convince himself that it was not really him perpetrating the atrocities. Now that he was back in his human form he found himself alone in the midst of a waking nightmare. The view reminded him of television footage of the aftermath of mass slaughters and battlefields in war-torn countries.

This was worse. This was a killing field of *his* creation. Try as he might not to look at the mangled bodies of men and beasts, he simply could not stop himself. The knowledge that he was the cause of so much death hit him with near-paralyzing waves of fear and disgust.

Fortunately his revulsion overcame his dread. He was spurred on by a withering attack on his senses from the sights, the smells and taste of death in the air, the feel of grime on his skin and the moans of the injured and dying. An underlying reek of dark magic grew like a stench carried on a headwind to betray the approach of some foul, colossal beast. Joel prayed silently for the strength to move, dragged himself to the canyon wall and started up on his hands and knees, still too weak and too shaky to stand and walk up the slope.

The more distance he put between himself and the battle site, the less his olfactory senses registered the stench of blood and death, but the smell of the malevolent approaching magic did not subside. With each breath of fresher air his strength and clarity returned. In his mind, however, the slaughter he perpetrated replayed over and over again. He could not get far enough away fast enough. It seemed to take forever to clamber up to the northeastern rim of the canyon. By the time he emerged, all of the suns' light was gone and the three moons and countless stars had taken their place.

Joel looked up at the night sky. The silver-white light weaved wild, beautiful patterns against the darkness. For the briefest of moments Joel thought about something other than his predicament and lost himself in its beauty. And then he took a deep, exhausted breath. The lingering stench of the air in his nose and mouth quickly reminded him of the horror at the bottom of the canyon.

As he pulled himself safely away from the rim of the canyon, his despair finally got the best of him. He tried to scream in frustration but he did not have the breath or strength. Only a weak whimper escaped his lips while hot tears burned clear brown streaks down his soiled face. Silent sobs shook his body until physical and psychological exhaustion finally, and mercifully, claimed him.

Joel did not know how long he was out, but he knew it was not very long. He was awakened by the explosive sound of cracking stone and vibrations of the earth.

It was still dark and the moons and stars had not shifted very far from where they were when he last looked at them, so he knew he had been out for only a few minutes. He wished he could have rested longer but he could not even find peace in his slumber. The slaughter replayed in his mind from the time he lost consciousness until he regained it.

Joel rose shakily to his feet. His morbid fascination got the better of him and made him take one last glance at the terrible scene on the canyon floor. That, he realized was the source of the sounds and vibration that woke him from his fitful slumber.

To his shock, most of the bodies were gone. The ones that were still visible were only partly so. Joel's eyes widened when he realized that the partially visible bodies were being sucked into the canyon floor. Some of the dying struggled uselessly against the pull of the earth. Several of the injured found a fear-induced jolt of energy and dragged themselves toward the canyon wall, but their efforts were for naught. The solid earth cracked open beneath them, just wide enough to suck them in, and then snapped closed about them in a bone-crushing embrace while half of their bodies were submerged. A few torturous moments later the earth opened and closed again to swallow them down as it had the others, stifling forever their cries of horror and agony.

Joel stood at the rim of Hargathall's Cleft and stared down into the canyon in disbelief. The smell of death hung in the air like an invisible cloud. Underneath that stench Joel could smell the foul, awesome magic that emanated from the cursed canyon. Other than the smell, there was absolutely no evidence that anything had ever happened down there.

"Damn," Joel swore. His whisper sounded amplified in the eerie silence that now blanketed the landscape.

Joel turned and started to walk away. He stopped when he was struck by the realization that he was basically lost, without food or water, and nearly naked. The autumn night was cold and the temperature was steadily dropping.

Panic began to set in. His breathing became labored. For the first time since the early days of his imprisonment, his asthma flared up. He frantically checked his pockets and almost shed tears of joy when he miraculously found the small pouch of medicinal herbs in his front pocket. He had no idea how he managed to keep it after all he had been through.

His panic faded as he chewed the herbs, swallowed the juices and felt his breathing ease. He grew calmer with each breath and began to think clearly again. With renewed clarity, he surveyed his surroundings once more and exhaled in relief when he saw a provision pack and a cloak lying on the ground a few yards away. He recognized it as the pack Ryan carried at the start of their trek.

Joel told Ryan that he would be able to catch up with them in his altered form, but his fellow offworlder obviously had a suspicion that would not be the case. His respect for Ryan went up several notches. He donned the woolen cloak, lifted the pack and checked its contents to find food, water, and even a handful of gold and silver coins. He slipped the pack over his shoulder and gave a silent prayer of thanks.

At first, Joel was not sure what direction to take. After all he had been through, and considering the fact that he had never been much of an outdoorsman, he was not at all sure of his bearings. Luckily, the three moons shone full and bright. Their light, along with the light of the stars, cast just enough illumination for him to see the pass that led the way out of the mountain range. He and Quick had landed just outside the pass and the two of them walked through it to reach Hargathall's Cleft because the teen did not want to be stuck in his gryphon form if and when the *Ken* cut off his magic.

Joel took a few unsteady steps and then stepped on a rock with his bare left foot. He winced and staggered but managed to remain standing.

"Shoes..." he mumbled.

He saw a fallen *Ken* warrior that managed to climb out of Hargathall's Cleft only to bleed to death at the top of the canyon wall. His feet were easily bigger than Joel's but his boots looked sturdy. A vague memory about it being bad luck to wear a dead man's shoes flitted through Joel's mind.

"Hell, my luck can't get much worse than this," he decided before appropriating the boots.

He took the man's sleeveless tunic, as well. It was too big and filthy with sweat and dust from the battle, but the wound that killed him was a vicious gash to the thigh, so at least the shirt was not bloody. With his new gear collected, Joel made his way to the pass. When he finally reached it a renewed surge of hope gave him the energy to keep moving.

Upon emerging on the other side he found that there was not enough light to see the Forsaken Desert to the east. He knew it was there so he kept the mountain range at his back and walked north. As badly as his aching and tired body cried for rest, he knew he would not be able to until he put more distance between him and the mountain range. It was not easy, but he managed to ignore his discomfort and concentrate on taking one small step at a time.

He had no idea how long or how far he had walked when his exhaustion overcame him again. The Demon's Spine was far behind him but the rise and fall of the foothills made the trek difficult nonetheless. He stopped near a stream that meandered lazily from the northeast. Silver moons' light twinkled from its surface hypnotically, soothing Joel even closer to sleep. He considered taking a quick plunge to wash the foul stench and gore from his flesh and tattered clothes.

Exhaustion won out, and besides, the stream would be there in the morning. Joel found shelter in the lee of a great boulder protruding from the base of a tall hill roughly twenty yards west of the stream and decided that was as good a place as any to lay down to rest. Joel made himself as comfortable as he could on the hard ground and was asleep almost before his head touched the ground.

Chapter 8: The Wrath of Azh

8.1

From Hargathall's Cleft, where it sat in the northeastern arm of the Demon's Spine, the fastest route to Lake Onyx was north by northwest, skirting eastern edge of the Forsaken Desert and Hell's Mountains. The trek would likely take more than two days. It was for this reason Quick suggested first taking Azhju'lestra to Ocean Crystalline to see if those waters would restore her.

Raxe was confident that Lake Onyx was where she ultimately needed to go but the Ocean Crystalline was less than seventy-five miles south. If there was a chance the ocean waters could bring her back, the close proximity of the Ocean Crystalline made it worth the extra hour or so it would add to their trek. They were lighting on a rocky shore of a relatively calm ocean roughly forty minutes later. Raxe used a cup to catch the salt water. He looked up at Quick.

"Will salt water be ok?" he asked. "I've only ever seen her in Lake Onyx and the Bountiful."

Quick grinned. "I'm sure her mother has guided her all around this Sphere and through all kinds of waters. We can only hope the ocean helps her, but it certainly won't cause her any arm."

Raxe nodded and poured a cupful over the gills on each side of her neck. He sat up straight and his eye widened with hope when the gills fluttered and pulsed, but he was still unable to rouse her from her stupor.

"That was something, at least," Raxe acknowledged. "I'll fill a canteen and then it's on to Lake Onyx."

Quick made haste. The extra weight of Raxe and his daughter made the trip take longer than it would have if he had been flying alone, so the first leg of the trip took two days. Raxe urged the changeling not to over exert himself. As badly as he wanted to get his daughter to Lake Onyx, the effort would be pointless if the changeling killed himself from exhaustion.

On three occasions during their trek near the desert, Quick touched down so they could eat from Quick's provisions of dried fruits, breads and cheeses. During those times, the changeling cast spells to pull enough moisture from the air to quench their thirst. Raxe continued to apply the ocean water, and each time her gills fluttered in response, but that was the only response. She remained unconscious.

By late afternoon of their third day of travel, the changeling gryphon set down on the southwestern shores of the Great Lake Onyx. Raxe cradled Azhju'lestra in his arms as he approached the shoreline. Like the great lakes of North America, Lake Onyx was massive. The human eye could not see the far shores from the ground. From the air, Lake Onyx reminded Raxe of Lake Superior, the largest of the North American Great Lakes. It was quite possibly larger.

Somewhere beyond the eastern horizon of the lake was the Kingdom of Lorr. It was so close, yet to Raxe it seemed a world away. As he neared the water, the last word his daughter uttered before falling into her comatose state echoed in his mind.

Mother

Her mother, the Mistress of the Sea, had saved Raxe's life once. In the process she had also taken his seed without his consent or his knowledge and used it to conceive the girl he now carried. He had initially been resentful about that. The only emotional attachment he felt to Sabrina was the lust that the painfully beautiful water faerie evoked in every male.

As he spent more and more time with Azh, however, his resentment faded. During their short time together he had grown fond of the girl in a way he never expected to when they met. The worry he felt for her now trumped any worry he had ever felt for any human being other than his mother and grandfather. Azh's gentle little voice was so filled with anguish when she called for her mother that the mere recollection of it broke his heart.

Mother

It was obvious that Sabrina was in some sort of distress. Through the link he and Azh shared as Children of the Old Ones, Raxe caught a flash of his daughter's terrified alarm for her mother just before the girl lost consciousness. The magnitude of her distress, however, was impossible to gauge. Azh shared a link with Sabrina that he did not. All he could do was hold out hope – for his daughter's sake – that Sabrina's circumstances were not dire.

Raxe carried Azh to the spot where he had seen Sabrina last, the same spot where the Mistress of the Sea of Spirits set him ashore after nursing him back to health over three years ago. It was also the spot where she introduced him to their daughter. The great lake was beautiful. The peaceful, glassy surface of the water mirrored the azure sky and was speckled with twinkling pinpoints of reflected golden light.

Quick looked on with concern as Raxe stepped into the water. Raxe looked expectantly out across the lake, waiting for the telltale stirring of the water, the twirling mini-funnel followed by the slow, elegant ascension of the most beautiful being Raxe had ever laid eyes on. But there was nothing. The water remained still.

Something was out of place.

Quick sniffed at the air and frowned. "What is that terrible stench?" he asked.

Raxe had sensed something was wrong but he could not quite place it. He took a deep breath through his nose. He smelled it that time, just barely. The scent was much fainter to him than it was to Quick's heightened senses, but once Raxe did detect it, the source was unmistakable and it filled him with cold fear.

"Oil," he said.

"Oil?" Quick asked. "I've never smelled oil like this."

"It's crude oil," Raxe clarified. "It's a substance used in my world for…well, for all kinds of things, mainly energy and plastics. Much of my world's economic survival depends on it. But it can have catastrophic effects on the natural environment, especially in water."

Quick sniffed again and wrinkled his nose. "Death. This crude oil kills the natural environment. Your world's economy depends on a substance as foul as *this*?"

Raxe cast a worried glance out over the lake but saw no traces of oil. "It's gone now. At least it appears to be gone."

"It is," Quick confirmed. "The scent slowly fades with the wind but I fear the damage has already been done. The smell of dead lake creatures still hangs in the air along with the dying scent of the crude oil."

Raxe took another deep breath through his nose. He could barely smell it, just like the first time. He could not tell the difference in intensity, but he learned long ago to trust Quick's sense of smell. He looked down at his daughter and looked over to Quick again expectantly.

"You think it's safe to put her in?" Raxe asked.

The young changeling followed Raxe out into the lake until the water was up to his knees. He cupped his hand, scooped out a palm full of water, sniffed it suspiciously and then tasted it carefully.

After a moment, Quick nodded. "Yes. I neither smell nor taste it in the lake water. The residual odor is in the air."

Raxe stepped further into the lake until soft waves lapped against his armored upper thighs. The water was cool but soothing, allowing him to relax enough to reach out with his mind, to open himself and to simply be aware. He looked for the pale shimmer that revealed to him the presence of magic. He saw the normal shimmer of magic radiating from the great lake, not the increased concentration of energy that would have alerted him to Sabrina's presence.

It had never taken Sabrina this long to respond to him. Fear quickened heartbeat. Not knowing what else to do, he lowered his daughter into the water. Her eyes popped open the instant she touched the surface of the lake. They opened so wide Raxe thought they would bulge out of her skull. The surprise almost made him let go of her. During all they had seen and done during their perilous journey, he had never seen so much fear and anguish on her face.

The pain she felt was so acute that it flowed through Raxe as well. His knees buckled as if he had been kicked in the stomach. He saw the thin lines on her neck open slightly as the lake water washed upon her nearly invisible gills.

"MOTHER!" Azh screamed.

There was a small explosion of water just in front of Raxe. When the water settled, Azh was out of his arms and flying across the surface of Lake Onyx on a small wave that carried her northeast.

Raxe turned to call Quick but the changeling was already at his side in the form of the familiar griffin. Raxe mounted the bird cat. Quick leapt from the shallow water with a loud splash and flew out to follow her.

Azh descended as she went further out into the lake until she was completely submerged, leaving a small and shrinking wake as the only evidence of her passing. Raxe strained his eyes to keep sight of his daughter from the bird cat's back. Soon she was out of his view. Quick flew close enough to the lake's surface to keep sight of her with his keener eyesight.

No longer able to see his daughter, Raxe shifted his gaze to the horizon. He could see nothing but water and sky. Quick, on the other hand, had spotted something more. The changeling squawked and purred and grunted. Those were sounds that – to Raxe's surprise – he was able to understand. He remembered that old Shanderah understood Quick when he communicated with her in his animal forms. Raxe could only assume the residue of her memories that clung to his mind had given him the same ability.

Raft in the distance, Quick explained, *Azh's destination.*

Quick focused on the raft with relief. He no longer needed to keep sight of the half-water-faerie that had descended to a depth that had gone beyond even his sharp vision. Just when Raxe spotted the raft, a spray of water burst up beside the small floating structure. When the water settled, Azh was sitting in the boat. During their approach, Raxe saw several sea gulls circle his daughter for a few moments before continuing out across the lake.

Raxe extended his awareness to his daughter's mind, to read her thoughts as all Children of the Old Ones could read the minds of their direct descendants. What he heard scared the hell out of him. And then she cast him out, blocking his prying mind as Raxe had learned to block his grandfather. She repelled him so violently that he had to take a firmer hold with his good hand on the thick feathers of the changeling gryphon's feathered neck.

As they came nearer to Azh and the raft, a strange feeling overcame Raxe. His head started to spin and he had to fight down the urge to gag. He gripped Quick's neck even tighter. The bird cat felt the change in posture and growled his concern. Raxe could not answer. He sat stock-still on his mount with his lips pursed in an expression of bewilderment.

An act of sheer mental will pushed aside enough of the queasiness to allow Raxe to focus. He took a deep breath to clear his head and calm his stomach and then examined the sensation that had overcome him so suddenly. Psychic thrumming vibrated in his brain, down his spine, into his bones and all through his body like a subsonic reverberation. He knew the feeling was not physical because it would have affected Quick, as well. The changeling flew straight and sure, which would have been impossible if he felt the same sensations as his rider.

Raxe discerned a resonation to the psychic vibration. It came at him in quickening, powerful waves of magic. The changeling gryphon's smooth flight lurched then as he, too, finally felt the presence of the forceful magic. This surprised Raxe because Quick was usually more sensitive to magic than he was. That was when Raxe realized that the ethereal waves of energy were flowing from his daughter.

He was close enough to see that her back was to him and she was kneeling with something – no, *someone* – in her arms. Dull strips of soiled cloth spilled down from her grasp and gathered in knotted tangles on the wooden raft. Something that looked to Raxe like a gray stone carving of emaciated legs extended beyond the tousled rags.

Sorrow clenched his gut with cold, rough fingers as the gryphon set down in the raft across from his daughter.

Sabrina's battered and desiccated corpse was gathered in Azh's arms in a loving embrace.

"Mother," Azh sobbed. Her sob was not the inconsolable weeping of a child. Her voice was low and icy calm, but resonated with enough desolation to make Raxe gasp.

"Oh, mother. You did not die alone. The fish, the sea birds all bore witness to your pain. Our Phillosith brother felt it even as far as the Ocean Crystalline. They mourn your passing as deeply as I. You have ruled them well for a thousand and more years."

The thrumming of the magic grew stronger, threatening to shatter Raxe's defenses and blast him into incoherence. Quick began to shudder nervously.

"And they have told me who was responsible," the girl continued with an unsettling timbre lacing her soft voice. "I know who poisoned our home, who poisoned you, *and who took your life.*"

The raft started to tremor. The bird cat had to struggle to retain its four-legged balance. The water around the wooden raft began to seethe.

Raxe suddenly knew why he sensed the first surge of magic before Quick felt it. It was *his* magic that he felt. It was the magic of the Old Ones, passed to Azh from her father, to him from his mother and grandfather, and originally from The Gatekeeper himself, the Blacksmith to the Old Ones and the Guardian of the WorldGate. Azh was using her divine magic to bolster her considerable elemental faerie magic. The combination was at once terrible and fantastic, and Azhju'lestra was just starting to bring it to bear.

"Father…" Azh began, suddenly sounding much more serious and much older than he had ever heard.

The churning water rippled more fiercely in time to each syllable she uttered. Her tiny, beautiful face contorted into a mask of anger and agony. Her wide eyes grew impossibly wider. The beautiful, light-brown eyes with their prism of varying other colors turned into pure, shimmering white light. Her long, aqua hued locks of hair did the same.

"Leave here. Now."

Raxe started to speak but before any sound could escape, a blinding flash of silver and cyan burst from his daughter's body. A shockwave exploded from the light and blew Raxe from the gryphon's back and made Quick rear up uncontrollably. Raxe fell into the churning water and in his panic he thought the weight of his armor would drag him to the bottom of Lake Onyx.

Fortunately for Raxe, his impenetrable armor, forged by the Gatekeeper for his progeny and his progeny alone, was impossibly light for all of its invulnerability. Raxe regained his senses and kicked to the surface to grasp the edge of the raft. The blast of magical energy echoed in his ears like the tolling of a church bell and left him trembling.

"Azh!" he coughed. His eyes quickly found hers. His daughter's reply was another blast of light and another shockwave even more forceful than the first one. Before he was blinded by the second explosion, he watched his daughter's body seem to dissolve into the energy that blasted him out of the water and into the air. When the light faded, his daughter was gone.

Not only had she disappeared from view, her aura had completely vanished from Raxe's senses. It felt as if a vital piece of him had been brutally torn away. He fought back panic as he tumbled through the air. He gathered his knees to his chest and turned to right himself. He was preparing to straighten his body to hit the water feet-first when out of the corner of his eye he saw the gryphon darting in his direction. An urgent squawk told him what to do, so he lifted his legs as the bird cat swooped beneath him and an instant later he was mounted again.

"Azh is gone!" Raxe cried. "We have to find her!"

Even as he said the words he knew any attempt to find her would be fruitless. The stark emptiness in the place where he once felt his daughter left no doubt about her fate.

There was a faint roar in his ears that gradually grew louder as the thrumming magic intensified. Quick screeched and grunted to let Raxe know that they had better heed Azh's command and leave with all haste. His long feathered neck craned around to look behind them. Raxe turned to look at the northern horizon and his jaw dropped.

Quick turned and flew as fast as he could in a straight line toward the western shore of Lake Onyx.

Raxe could not take his eyes off of the awesome sight. A giant wave stretched from the western coast of the lake and swept across the horizon. Raxe was certain the wave spanned the entire latitudinal width of the great lake. The wave was far too large to have occurred naturally in a landlocked body of water, but there it was, coming right for them.

Raxe could not tell if the white motes boiling angrily from the approaching wave were a spray of mist from the rushing water or the spray of magic, but he could *feel* the difference. The wave grew in pulses that surged in time with the thrumming in his bones and the roaring in his ears and left no question about the wave's origin.

His daughter, Azhju'lestra, Child of the Old Ones and the last living water faerie, had called forth a monstrous tsunami.

Quick snapped his gaze forward and kept it riveted in that direction as if he was wearing blinders. Raxe tried to do the same but he could not. As much as he wanted to, he could not look away from the approaching phenomena for more than a few seconds at a time. The wave grew impossibly fast while the shore grew closer in what seemed like slow motion.

It became frightfully obvious to both Quick and Raxe that they would not reach the shore before the massive wall of water was upon them. Quick started to ascend with the hope of getting above the tidal wave, but the wall grew exponentially taller as it raced closer.

The roaring in Raxe's ears was deafening. His body shuddered from the unrelenting surges of magic assaulting him. The changeling gryphon, on the other hand, was undistracted. The water below them was a blur as Quick pushed himself to his limit.

Quick was high enough to avoid the massive breakers that heralded the arrival of the primary tidal wave but he struggled to maintain control. The mighty wave pushed away the air in its path. The strong swirling wind that preceded it pummeled Quick as it rolled across the Great Lake Onyx.

Raxe glanced at it again and regretted it. He was afraid to gauge the approximate height of the tsunami and knew it was irrelevant. The apex of the wave seemed to brush the underside of low-hanging clouds.

Raxe turned away as he clutched the gryphon's mane in a death grip with his left hand, and since he could not close his right, he wrapped his right arm around the griffin's neck in a grip that would have strangled Quick if the neck had not been so muscular. All temptation to look at the approaching tsunami rushed away on the ferocious winds that preceded it.

The wave was close enough now to block out the suns and cast a cloak of deep shadow over the fleeing duo. Quick drove himself even faster, attempting in vain to keep pace with rushing darkness. The shadow raced ahead of them, taking with it any hope of escape. In another instant, the wave dominated Raxe's peripheral vision on his right.

The rushing wave thundered in like a giant speeding train in a dark tunnel. Quick found yet another gear, but it was simply not enough. Raxe closed his eyes, gulped in a lungful of air, and held it just before the furious wall of water reached them.

8.2

The rays of the two morning suns beamed down on Joel from over the high peaks of the eastern expanse of the Demon's Spine. Their brightness and warmth cut through the cool autumn air and roused him from his slumber. The first thing he noticed was a vile taste in his mouth. Before opening his eyes, he searched his pockets for his pouch of medicinal herbs. His asthma was not bothering him but force of habit made him check. It made him feel better to know it was there, stuffed in the deep corner of his left hip pocket.

He opened his eyes to see a clear blue sky above, not the rocky ceiling of the hillside cave he gazed at before drifting off to sleep the previous night. At least he *thought* that was where he went to sleep the previous night. It was getting difficult to tell one day from the next, dreams from reality. Not knowing where and when he would get more food and drink once he exhausted his provisions, Joel had been careful to consume only as much as it took to keep him moving. The result was a haze of hunger and thirst, and he did not venture very far at all each day because he had been so weak.

Joel struggled to remember where he was and eventually convinced himself that his first recollection was true. He did indeed fall asleep in a small cave in a hillside the night before. This was the same area, though. The moons' light had revealed many of the same landmarks that he saw this morning, but from a different angle. Had he been sleep walking? How else could he have gone from the cave to sleeping under the open sky?

The sky above would have been a beautiful sight if not for the clutch of vultures circling curiously overhead. The soft lapping of a lazy stream seemed to be right next to him. He sat up and was surprised to find himself lying right at the shallow bank of the stream he drank from before going into the cave to rest. The water was not as fresh as the stream he found that first night after leaving Hargathall's Cleft, but it had been sufficient to quench his thirst.

As he wondered how he got from the cave to his present position he became nauseatingly aware of the stench of blood and offal. A quick inspection of his clothes revealed that his cloak was gone. Fresh gore coated the front of his tunic. It also stained his torn breeches in addition to the dried, stale stains from the nightmare in Hargathall's Cleft that he had not been able to wash out.

Joel pulled his tunic up to inspect his bare chest and stomach to confirm that the fresher blood was not his. His skin clung tightly to his ribcage and his torso was still riddled with bruises and broken-sword brands from the torture he endured during his captivity in Tauran's dungeons. Other than that there was nothing out of the ordinary..

But then again, there *was* something out of the ordinary. Even though his ribcage was visible just below his sunken chest, his belly was distended. He would have thought that malnourishment was the cause, as was the case with starving people with bloated bellies, until he realized he was not hungry. The hunger and thirst that had weakened him over the past few days were strangely absent. The sating of his thirst was understandable. He could have drunk from the freshwater stream during the night without remembering. The sating of his hunger, though, was something else.

"No," he gasped. "Did I finish off my provisions?"

With an exasperated sigh, he looked around for his pack and suddenly cried out when he saw four monsters huddled not ten yards away. They were at the halfway point between where he sat at the edge of the stream and the hillside cave where he had intended to spend the night.

The monsters were giant, nightmarish caricatures of frogs with short, spindly forelegs that ended in webbed, hands with curved claws. Long, tails that were broad at their base and tapered to blunt tips swished nervously. They crouched on long, muscular, reverse-articulated legs that sent them scrambling back several yards when Joel yelped. Despite their nervous retreat, their wide mouths remained fixed in angry sneers that exposed short but wickedly sharp teeth.

Fear cleared the cobwebs of sleep from Joel's mind and he recalled one of the conversations he overheard while riding on the doomed sky sleigh that carried him and the others from Port Lorrian. Several of the crewmen shared stories about the variety of dangerous beasts that made their home in the Demon's Spine and the southern reaches of Hell's Mountains. One such beast was called a wallowgrump. These monsters fit that description. And from the crewmen's tales, these animals were fearsome to say the least and would not hesitate to attack humans.

Joel was paralyzed with both fear and confusion. He was certainly thankful the wallowgrumps were not attacking but he was confused as to why. Ravenous hunger was evident in their wet, bulbous eyes yet they kept their distance.

The offworlder eased away from them, shuffling slowly backward on his haunches along the damp grass, moving parallel to the stream. His hands slipped on something more viscous than mere water and he fell back, his head bumping against something stiff, wet and furry. He turned to see it and yelped again, scrambling clumsily to his feet to move away from the carcass of something resembling a brown-furred badger in a pool of dark blood and clumps of flesh and fur.

This was like no badger Joel had ever seen. It was almost as long as Joel was tall. Its body was a broad cluster of muscle that intimidated even in death. And then Joel remembered the crewmen on the sky sleigh exchanging stories about rock badgers, another man-eater that lived in these mountains. It was lying still on its side, dead eyes open and staring at the sky. Had the deadly claws on its forepaws and hind paws not been curved into near half-circles, they would have easily been as long as Joel's forearm.

The beast's torso was torn open so violently that the ribs were visible. The space within those ribs, however, was nearly hollow. A length of uncoiled intestines was the only thing visible within that bloody cavity.

Joel's wife was the veterinarian, but he knew as well as Lisa would have known that there should have been many more organs in that space.

A horrible thought flashed through Joel's mind that made him gasp with alarm and stagger away from the carcass. The sudden movement drove the wallowgrumps back several more yards away from him.

"No way," he said.

Despite the likelihood that those voracious beasts would have still been working on all the muscle and sinew remaining on the carcass, Joel assumed the wallowgrumps had gotten to the rock badger. He convinced himself that his first wild assumption could not be true.

He was thankful that he was obviously sleeping when the predator came upon him. That was probably the only reason he did not remember the doomed beast's attack and his obvious and terrible response. He had too many sickening memories of his atrocities from Hargathall's Cleft. There was no need to add the slaughter of a wild animal to the list. Just seeing the aftermath was more than enough.

Joel turned his attention to the observing wallowgrumps.

"But *you* saw it, didn't you?" he demanded as if the animals would actually answer him. "And if you didn't, you're smart enough to figure out what happened. That's why you're afraid of me."

The fearsome amphibian predators stared warily at him.

"And I stink," he continued. "You can smell the death on me. You can smell the blood of a killer fiercer than you."

He spared the eviscerated carcass one more glance, surprised that the repugnant sight did not sicken him. Years ago he surprised his wife while she was on a large animal farm call. He approached her while she and a colleague were standing over a dead horse. The horse had been cut open and had its intestines spread out all over the ground. It took all of his strength to keep from vomiting on the spot and he could not eat for the rest of the day.

This sight, while not as voluminous, was far worse in its savagery yet Joel's stomach did not so much as twitch. He pulled up his shirt and looked at his distended belly again.

And then he licked his dry lips and tasted blood.

The taste woke something up in him, made a surreal situation all too real. The more he considered the possibility of what he must have done, the more his mind rejected it.

"No...I didn't," he said aloud, shaking his head maniacally. "I couldn't have. *Hell* no...I couldn't have."

Joel walked out to the stream to cleanse himself, fighting panic all the way. He paused just before stepping into the water, startled when he caught a glimpse of his reflection in the glassy surface. His cheeks, once full if not quite round, were sunken. Dark bags hung heavily under tired brown eyes. New worry lines creased his brow. Deep frown lines trailed down from the corners of his nose and vanished beneath unkempt stubble.

He never could grow a full beard and he still could not, but patches of short, tightly coiled hair dotted his jaws in an uneven path from his sideburns to the rough stubble of his dust and blood-streaked goatee.

Blood-streaked goatee... his anxiety intensified.

He forced the unthinkable away again and focused on another part of his reflection. His recently shaved head was now covered with the same coarse stubble as his face, with small inverted peaks sloping wildly away from his hairline at several places on his forehead.

"Damn," he chuckled grimly. "I need an edge-up."

The water was deeper than he thought. The cold stream rose almost to his chest when he waded to the middle of it. He moved with the current, past the carcass and away from the wallowgrumps. When he was a dozen yards downstream, the wallowgrumps scampered forward and fell hungrily upon the dead badger. The buzzards that had been circling overhead spiraled downward to join in the gruesome repast.

With the wallowgrumps out of the way Joel could see his pack still resting near the threshold of the hillside cave entrance. After taking a deep breath and holding it, he ducked down into the stream. He raked his fingers over his scalp to clean off the remains of the rock badger, causing a dark, disgusting little cloud to bloom in the water around his head.

And then he rubbed his face vigorously until he could no longer hold his breath. He crawled from the stream and made his way slowly and carefully around the feasting scavengers to retrieve his pack. The wallowgrumps shot wary, malicious glances at him but they never left their meal. As soon as he reached his pack he snatched it open, almost hoping to find it empty to confirm his hope of why his stomach was full.

His provisions of dried meat, hard cheese, and tough black bread were at the same level they had been when last he ate.

Joel shouldered his pack and strode nervously away, reflecting on the reason the wallowgrumps did not attack. They either witnessed him killing the rock badger or could tell from the aftermath that Joel had been the predator, not the prey. Instead of going after a live meal and sharing the rock badger's fate, they decided to scavenge his leftovers for an easier and safer breakfast.

The thought of him, malnourished and battered, killing and partially *eating* a giant badger and frightening away giant killer frogs was just too much. It was so ludicrous to him that he found it morbidly amusing.

And then the thought of everything he had been through since that gray, snowy day on that southern Illinois highway fell on him like a ton of warm sand, buckling his knees so that he had to struggle to keep his balance. A mixture of emotions surged with a ferocity that made him light-headed. He did not know whether to laugh at the outrageousness of it all or cry from the horror, so when the dam of emotions finally broke...

He did both.

Right there, in the middle of nowhere, in the midst of savage beasts and carrion-eaters, Joel wailed in equal parts maniacal hilarity and abject terror. He folded his arms across his full stomach and doubled over, guffawing and moaning until his ribs grew sore and his jaws ached.

The feasting wallowgrumps stopped to watch the display. The buzzards fluttered their wings nervously and hopped away from their meal momentarily.

Joel squeezed his tearing eyes shut as he had his fit. All he ever wanted was to live a nice, uneventful life in Chicago. Hell, he did not even want to live in the hustle and bustle of the city. His goal was to find a quiet suburb, to just be a husband and father and make a comfortable life for his family. Instead, this living nightmare had become his reality while the life he led on the other side of the WorldGate, the life he *wanted* to live, had become the dream.

The image of the eviscerated rock badger took the place of the darkness behind his eyelids. The vision of the badger was immediately followed by the massacre in Hargathall's Cleft. Every flesh tearing, bone-crunching blow played back through his mind with impossible speed and appalling clarity. The rest of his experiences raced back to him in reverse order in a dizzying rush.

His torture in the dungeons of the false baron Dirk Tauran's castle, where he looked into a demon's eyes and saw the very depths of hell, gave way to the attack of the sky sleighs *Cloud Chaser* and *Sundance* by the enthralled scythe wings. The giant birds carried him away a mile in the air with massive needlepoint talons that tore open his flesh.

The memories attacked more than just his mind. He felt the acute pain of every wound inflicted upon him. He tasted the tears, blood, sweat, bile, and gore of every experience. Screams of pain from those that fell to his savagery and the smug laughter of his captors threatened to burst his eardrums, but something else burst instead.

He felt something snap deep within. His laughing intensified, as did his sobs. Through it all, he searched for an escape from the flood of dark memories. The search was a short one. Suicide was the most logical escape. It would put an end to the pain, the fear and the despair.

He laughed even harder at that absurd notion. His weird power would find a way to save him no matter what he tried. He would end up kicking his own ass into unconsciousness.

And then he came to the real solution. It seemed to peek over his shoulder with every horrific recollection, just barely visible in the peripheral of his mind's eye. It whispered seductively to him as he recalled the night when the *S'Zan Rho*'s land dragons descended upon him outside the inn at Port Lorrian. It called to him during his harrowing trip through the WorldGate.

Madness was the answer.

It had to be. Joel may not have been able to kill himself but he could lose himself. Crippling insanity would be a welcome release from his living hell.

He opened himself to the sweet oblivion of a complete psychotic break, welcoming it as he relived the attack of the razor-edged shadow things that the demon Dierglyorr sent at him and Lisa back in Chicago; and the memory of how close he had come to killing his own wife while he was in the throes of a nightmare so real it triggered his power.

He recalled where it all began. It was only fitting that his sanity crash during the recollection of where and how his long nightmare started. Even though he still could not remember killing the agents posing as thugs in a failed assassination attempt, he remembered the result: two men lying dead in the slush and snow in spreading puddles of blood. Both killed by gunshot wounds to the head. That was the price he made them pay for threatening his wife.

His wife.

Lisa.

They threatened not only Joel's life, but also the lives of his wife and unborn child. That was where it all started and their lives were still in danger. If he succumbed to the madness, everything he had been through would have been for nothing. He would not let the demon win.

It took every ounce of his failing strength for Joel to force the madness away. He fell to his knees, still chuckling and sobbing, until all he could do was gasp and gag. He coughed violently for another minute and fought successfully against the urge to vomit, which was a victory in itself.

When his fit finally ended he took a moment to wipe the wetness away from his tear-soaked face and catch his breath.

While on his knees, Joel recited the Lord's Prayer and thanked Him for the vision of Lisa.

He rose to his feet and walked on with short, trembling steps. By the time he topped a medium-sized hill to look to the northern horizon, he had regained his composure. From that vantage point he could see across the top of miles of foothills as the land sloped gently to the edge of a dense forest. Even from miles and miles away, the forest appeared dark and foreboding. The Forsaken Desert was just visible in the distance to the west.

Joel looked down the other side of the hill on which he stood. At the bottom of the slope, suns' light revealed a wide path emerging from the mountain range. The path curved west on a steady decline along the foothills of the Demon's Spine. The path was not a well-worn one. He had not been able to see it in the relatively bright light of the moons but he could just make it out in the sunlight. He had no doubt that it led to Shaddiston.

Shaddiston was supposed to have been one of the stops that Raxe's expedition made on the way to Hargathall's Cleft. Joel did not know how far away it was and there was only one way to find out. He hitched the strap of his pack securely on his shoulder and made his way to the path.

8.3

Joel walked for hours and covered more ground than he had expected. His unlikely, and blessedly un-remembered repast had fortified him for a time although he was growing hungry again.

His clothes dried quickly in the soft, cool autumn breeze and warm sunlight. Unfortunately his shirt was so damaged and stained he knew he would better off without it. If he happened upon any travelers he would never have been able to explain its appearance. He pulled it off and left it on the ground several miles back. Now his bare torso was covered in dust, his woolen slacks were in tatters, and his leather boots were torn and ragged.

He reached into the pack that hung by his right hip. As he walked he pulled the water skin out, took a swallow, and replaced the skin in the pack, all the while being careful not to spill a drop. Next, he retrieved a fist-sized, hardtack biscuit and took several bites. He had to remind himself not to eat too much too fast. He had no idea how long it would take to get to Shaddiston, and he had no clue what he would eat or drink when his provisions were gone.

After another couple of hours, he heard the clatter and hoof beats of a horse-drawn carriage echoing through the foothills. It was not long before the carriage was rolling by. To his relief, they stopped and offered him a ride. Joel was surprised the passengers would allow the carriage to stop for someone looking as haggard as he did but he was grateful for their kindness.

As it turned out, the passengers were missionaries. One was an older, heavyset woman wearing a fancy traveling dress with her unnaturally black hair pulled back into a severe bun. Her companion was a much younger, smartly dressed man with neatly trimmed, curly, reddish-blonde hair. They took him for a homeless vagabond, which was very much how Joel thought of himself at that moment.

Feeling compelled to do good deeds in the holy name of the Lord Ascendant, they told him they would take him to a Church sponsored shelter that they knew of in Shaddiston, and there he could get a bath and a hot meal if he was willing to do a day's worth of farm or masonry work. Joel had no interest in the work. A hot bath and a hot meal, however, sounded fantastic. He decided it was a decent trade off.

Their offer of a ride turned out to be more than a benevolent favor for an unfortunate letch. The payment was that for the duration of the journey, Joel had to listen to the Holy Word of the Lord Ascendant. The odd couple was particularly interested in explaining how the self-proclaimed Children of the Old Ones were actually powerful wizard charlatans blaspheming in order to be worshipped by the gullible people of Lorr.

Joel listened with genuine interest. He was a Christian, brought up in a Catholic group home and baptized into the Baptist faith. He was curious about how the religious doctrine of this world compared to his. It soon became obvious nothing in the way of actual doctrine was forthcoming. What he got instead were outrageous and detailed stories explaining how those calling themselves Children of the Old Ones were not true descendants of the Old Ones. They were merely beguiling sorcerers and witches who fortified the magical and military forces of the Kingdom of Lorr. Their goal was to launch an assault on the other nine kingdoms of the Known Lands in a plot to rule the world.

Joel did not have time to get know Rionn Lorr and the others very well. From the little he did know, Joel was pretty sure his current hosts' stories were more fiction than fact. He would not risk losing his ride, though, so Joel had to continuously stifle chuckles and struggle to keep his face from contorting into incredulous frowns.

They told one story that he did believe, at least some of it. There was a report that Raxe, an elf and a little girl had come through town and stole three horses. When a squad of Lorrian soldiers and a local sorcerer tried to stop them, they killed the soldiers and took both of the sorcerer's hands as well as his tongue.

Joel knew there had to be more to the story. There was no doubt about Raxe and Rell Kallen having the ability and inclination to kill and maim, but not for the reasons these people claimed. He wondered what had actually happened. If he ever saw Ryan again he would try to remember to ask.

By mid day their stories ceased to interest him. At that point he had to struggle to keep his disinterest from showing on his face. Fortunately, at the height of his boredom, they reached Shaddiston.

Joel looked through the window at the outskirts of the town. The dry, hard earth of the Demon's Spine foothills had given way to sparse grasslands. To the west the Forsaken Desert could no longer be seen but in the distance the sky itself seemed to shimmer from the heat rising up from beyond the horizon.

Joel decided that Shaddiston looked a lot like Eastedge. Instead of goats, however, cattle looked to be the livestock of choice. The cows were smaller than those Joel was familiar with and their pastureland was proportionately smaller. Countless chickens darted here and there all through streets. The carriage passed children as they herded one-horned cows up and down the grass path beside the dirt road. Silver-furred bovines that reminded Joel of smallish buffalo with pairs of bony lumps in place of horns pulled plows over fields.

The offworlder was able to successfully relegate the incessant droning of his talkative hosts to a mere background buzz but he did not know how long he could put up with them. If and when he decided to make a break for it, he wanted to have some idea of where he was. He gave an occasional nod or false look of understanding or whatever other expression he thought they might be expecting but he paid more attention to his surroundings than to them.

Soon the farms were behind them and they were passing stables and stockyards, then metal smithies and warehouses. The traffic picked up. There were more wagons and carriages and foot traffic though the streets. Joel straightened in his seat when he heard familiar voices at one of the smithies they were passing.

The woman in the carriage with him, Joel remembered her calling herself Ministress Bethelyne something or other, saw his hopeful reaction and thought it was because of her impromptu sermon.

"So you agree?" she said hopefully. "It did not seem as if you were paying us much attention."

"Oh, well, I wasn't, Beth," he said apologetically.

The woman gasped. The young man at her side put a comforting hand on her thigh. Joel thought the hand was a bit too high for the young man to be family and too familiar for a plutonic friend or servant. The foppish redhead leaned forward, the ruffled collar of his doublet swaying with the movement, and narrowed his eyes.

"That's *Ministress Hargrave* to you, vagabond," he growled. "Even a Lorrian beggar should know enough to pay more respect to his superiors."

Joel raised his hands in a defensive gesture. "I meant no disrespect," he said truthfully. "I was just distracted by familiar voices. I'm sorry, but I have to decline your kind offer of a meal and bath. I have to get off here."

"You owe us for the ride," the Ministress Hargrave insisted. "You promised your strong back and arms for the ride as well as the rest. Must I call on the city constables to force you to honor your agreement?"

Joel sighed and fished through his pack. The ministress, thinking the vagabond was reaching for a weapon, yelped in fear. The young man beside here pulled a long dagger from his polished boot as Joel pulled a closed fist from the pack.

"I would not suggest you do anything rash, beggar," the man warned, his voice somewhat higher and shakier than it was a moment earlier. He looked even less comfortable holding a blade than Joel felt when he did.

Holding back a chuckle, Joel opened his hand to reveal a palm-sized gold coin etched with the standard of the Kingdom of Lorr. He held it out to the Ministress Hargrave.

"I only wanted to compensate you for the ride, since I can't pay my debt the way we agreed," Joel said graciously. "But if you would rather me work instead…"

"Where would a filthy beggar get that much money?" the male consort demanded.

With an effort, Joel kept his face serious and straightened his shoulders. "This was given to me by Raxe, the wielder of Demonsbane and descendant of the Gatekeeper and his Old One warrior namesake. The Head Mage Rionn Lorr gave it to him for our quest. I'm a Child of the Old Ones, too. Like Raxe, I'm a descendant of the Gatekeeper. The help you've given me will help us defeat a sixth level demon that's trying to destroy the Known Lands."

The Ministress Hargrave gasped again and began to fan herself with a kerchief pulled from her ample cleavage.

The young man scowled. "Is that supposed to be humorous?" He snatched the gold coin from Joel's hand. "Be gone, you blasphemous tramp. May the Lord Ascendant curse you for your irreverence, and for stealing this gold from some unfortunate soul."

"He's already cursed me," Joel said matter-of-factly as he stepped down from the carriage, "for nothing."

Joel jogged in the direction of the voices. Two men were haggling intensely with a steel smith over the price of tools. One of the men gestured emphatically with one hand while the other arm hung from a sling. The other man interjected periodically while the smith argued with both men. Joel smiled at another uncharacteristic stroke of luck when he saw that the voices belonged to exactly whom he hoped.

"Harl Timson! Coortahn!" Joel called. Both men turned at the sound of their names.

The leathery skin of Harl's face wrinkled as he smiled in surprise. Coortahn looked much more hesitant. When Joel came closer he noticed Coortahn's apprehension but did not know why the sky sleigh co-pilot would be so unnerved by his presence.

Harl saw the tension, as well. "Can't blame old Coortahn for being uneasy," the captain explained, scratching at his injured right arm, "seeing as how you tossed him out into the blue void and all."

Joel was puzzled at first, but then his eyes widened as the memory returned. He was not conscious of his actions at the time, but Harl's words brought back the memory of Coortahn attempting to throw him from their sky sleigh when the scythe wings attacked. All Joel remembered was Coortahn reaching for him. Everything went black after that until he woke up in the talons of giant birds. It was not a pleasant memory. Apparently the prospect of being thrown from the airborne sky sleigh awakened Joel's power.

Considering how Joel's power usually worked, Joel knew Coortahn was lucky to be alive.

"Coortahn," Joel said regretfully, "I wasn't in my right mind when I did…whatever it was I did. Hell, I don't even remember doing it. That was one of the quirks of my power."

"So what happened to the rest of them?" Coortahn asked suspiciously.

Joel frowned. "As far as I know, only a few people survived: the Sureblade kid, Raxe, Quick, and six from the *Cloud Chaser* crew. The last time I saw Raxe and Quick, they were headed to Lake Onyx."

"We're headed back to Port Lorrian," Harl said. "Ride with us. What say you, Coortahn?"

"As long he stays clear of me, I've no qualms with it." Coortahn's frown betrayed the fact that he was clearly against it but he knew his captain well. Harl's request for his co-pilot and navigator's agreement was nothing more than a polite formality.

The rest of the day went by quick and peaceful, and most importantly, restfully. The next day Joel was strappping into a safety line attached to the railing of a port side cabin on the sky sleigh *Cloud Scythe*. Joel thought it an odd name considering the conclusion of their last flight together.

Harl explained with pride that the tough frame of *Cloud Chaser*'s pilot box saved his life during that ill-fated journey.

When nothing else was left of the sleigh, the claws and beaks of the scythe wings could only scratch at him through the wood and metal skeleton. It even held as he crashed down into the high cliffs of Hell's Mountains, leaving him with only a broken arm and a lot of bumps and bruises.

The grizzled captain used that very frame for the pilot box of this sky sleigh, which he bought used. He and Coortahn spent their time in Shaddiston refurbishing the used sleigh. "Cloud" came from Cloud Chaser's pilot box, and "Scythe" was chosen in defiance of the giant birds that brought them down.

Cloud Scythe flew only a few miles east of Hell's Mountains, the Lorr side. Through a port side porthole Joel saw the Serpent's Way valley creeping its way through the expansive mountain range. He thought he could barely make out the town of Eastedge proper nestled within the valley. He had bad memories of that place so he quickly turned his attention north and gasped at what he saw.

From his bird's eye view within the sky sleigh, the half-mile deep, two-mile wide valley resembled a shallow trench. Far to the north a shadow snaked its way southward through that trench. The distance and height from where he watched made it seem like the darkness was moving in slow motion. Joel, however, knew it was moving all too fast.

The valley was being flooded, and Eastedge was directly in the path of the floodwaters.

8.4

At the eastern border the Kingdom of Darshay, the newly appointed and rightful lord of the barony of Eastedge and his older cousin stood on the balcony outside of his fourth-floor common room. The balcony overlooked the small town referred to as Eastedge proper because it was the economic center of the barony. The rest of the barony surrounded Eastedge proper on the north, west, and south. It was a forested land that intruded upon an expansive break in the sprawling mountain range of Hell's Mountains the way a peninsula intrudes upon an ocean. On the eastern border of Eastedge proper, Hell's Mountain loomed like a massive barrier to another world, separating Darshay from the Kingdom of Lorr.

The valley housing Eastedge proper was actually part of the much more extensive Serpent's Way Valley. Serpent's Way snaked through Hell's Mountains from the southwestern shores of the Great Lake Onyx in the northwest fringes of the Kingdom of Lorr to where it terminated at a wall of towering crags that bordered the Forsaken Desert. Most of the valley was roughly two miles wide, narrower in some places and slightly wider in others. The part of the valley in which Eastedge proper rested, however, was considerably wider. It flared out to a width of more than three miles and spanned roughly eight miles south before it narrowed back to its initial width.

From a sky sleigh, Eastedge proper resembled a massive platter dug out of the earth. It was said that Serpent's Way once contained a mighty river and the area known as Eastedge proper had been the lake and spring that fed it.

Eastedge proper and the rest of the barony belonged to Baron David Northforest, as it had belonged to his father for two decades and more. That was before the false baron Dirk Tauran swept in with his riches and his mercenaries and his treachery to steal away the Northforest estate including the barony castle, which was built just outside of the valley, along with the entire barony.

Tauran's rule was short-lived, though. With help from the three Keeper's Hounds and their changeling companion from the Kingdom of Lorr, David and his small army of loyalists won Eastedge back for the Northforest family, and David was determined to keep it.

The young man stood next to his cousin Bartholomew and looked down into the valley, surveying the progress made in the short time David had been the baron. Under Tauran's chaotic lordship, which lasted just over two years, the bustling town of Eastedge proper quickly fell into the same grievous disrepair that plagued it before David's father took control. Back then, the stone quarries served as the town's primary economic backbone, but it had never been a strong backbone. It was an arid region not good for very much more than rock mining to supply gravel for the other parts of the Kingdom of Darshay.

With only the quarries to support it, Eastedge proper barely scraped by. It did, however, produce more income than any of the individual estates. As a result, whoever ruled the town ruled the barony by extension. It was a rugged, hardscrabble town that changed leadership with the season.

When David's father took over, he and his men happened upon a previously undiscovered water table while digging for new mining opportunities. The discovery led to the establishment within Eastedge proper of small farming communities of both crops and livestock, both of which greatly buttressed the economy. Eastedge then blossomed into a prosperous barony and an important, if not duly respected, part of the Kingdom of Darshay despite its unimpressive size.

Once Tauran pilfered the barony, he exploited its thriving economy for his own benefit. He inflated taxes so high that the agricultural commerce faltered. Farmland and pastureland gave way to taverns and brothels. Farmers, millers, smithies and stockyards went out of business in favor of gamblers, flesh peddlers, swindlers, pickpockets and other thieves. The town could not support itself with those types of ventures.

Without the agricultural business to support it, Eastedge proper collapsed in on itself in just over a year. The result was the deterioration of a thriving town to something nearly akin a ghost town. The town had supported the peasants, laborers and yeomen that formed the majority of the barony's population and they suffered greatly. The baron and the highborn lords of the other four estates of the barony only sat back and watched the town implode.

Their personal lands and livestock were maintained outside of the valley and served as the primary source of their wealth. For them, Eastedge proper provided supplemental income at best and its survival, while beneficial, was not critical to their own fortunes. They were perfectly willing to watch the town fall to ruin as long as Tauran allowed them to fill their coffers with extra wealth as it fell.

But in the week or so that Eastedge belonged to the Northforest family again, the farmers had already started returning. Brothels and taverns were immediately closed down and their proprietors ran out of town. Demolition of the structures had already begun. Honest merchants, smithies and other craftsmen began filtering back to support the farmers.

David and Bartholomew watched the activity down in Eastedge proper with much satisfaction. Bartholomew put a hand on David's shoulder.

"I imagine it won't be long before we've brought Eastedge back to its former standing."

David shrugged. "That depends on your definition of 'long,' cousin. It can't happen soon enough for my liking."

"Patience, David," the older cousin advised. "That was your father's greatest trait."

"I suppose," David conceded reluctantly. "But one can't wait too long, either. My father knew when to strike."

"As do you, David," Bartholomew noted. "That's why we're standing here now."

"Yes," David agreed, "that, and the Keeper's Hounds. I owe them as much as you owe Jon the Firemaster, his wife, and Joel."

"Don't remind me," Bartholomew grunted. "I don't care to think about the time that jackal Tauran made me spend in the dungeons beneath this castle. I cared not for the Firemaster's wife and I've never seen a man the like of that offworlder, Joel. For a man to have such power and yet be such a coward is beyond my understanding."

David nodded. "Yet we must give them their due, as much as we may have disliked the lot of them."

"Surely you didn't dislike that Nicky, did you?" Bartholomew teased.

"You mean Arrowhead," David corrected. "You're right, Bart. I didn't dislike that sweet-looking piece at *all*. Too bad she had her head so far up that Sureblade boy's arse that she had no idea what she was missing."

"Indeed," Bartholomew said with a lewd chuckle. "She missed *your* head up *her* arse!"

The cousins guffawed at that. It was the first real laughter either of them had experienced since before David was exiled and Bartholomew was imprisoned. The cousins had almost forgotten how it felt. Their laughter, however, was cut short when they both spied movement in the northeastern skies, just over the peaks of Hell's Mountains.

"What is that?" Bartholomew wondered aloud.

The approaching object resembled a small cloud but it was too low and moved far too fast. Within seconds the cloud resolved into two clouds. In a few seconds more the cousins could see *people* inside the approaching clouds.

"Bart," David snapped. "Our swords! Quickly!"

Bartholomew loved his cousin like a brother but it chafed him to be ordered around by a younger relative that he bullied when they were children. David was the baron, though, the rightful heir to his father's barony. The older cousin respected his station and followed orders.

He hurried into the common room and snatched their sheathed longswords from where they hung on hooks just inside the balcony doors. By the time he returned to the balcony the two clouds were about two hundred yards away.

"Mysts," he realized. "Those are wizards?"

"Conjurers of some sort, and powerful," David added. "Only the most accomplished of conjurers ride mysts. And judging by the direction they're coming from, they're not likely from the Kingdom of Darshay."

Bartholomew looked at his sheathed longsword with a hopeless sigh. "If they're hostiles from the Sai-Il continent or the Kingdom of Lorr, these swords won't do us much good."

"Better to die with sword in hand," David said as he drew his weapon.

Or not at all, Bartholomew thought as he considered counseling his cousin to surrender. As much as he hated imprisonment, it was infinitely preferable to death. He unsheathed his blade, though, since David already had and Bartholomew knew how stubborn the younger man could be. There was a possibility that this would not come to a fight, and if it did not, he could not risk looking the coward in the eyes of his baron and cousin.

"Wait," David said as he counted one man upon the myst to his left and a man and woman on the one to the right. "I know the girl."

Bartholomew squinted to see them more clearly and then smiled. "Speak her name and here she comes," he said. He remembered her well from the night they took Eastedge back.

"Arrowhead," David said wistfully.

"Sheathe your sword, man," called the brown-robed mage riding alone on his myst as they approached to within ten feet and stopped, hovering at the same level of the balcony. "We mean you no ill will."

"Well met, mage," David returned. He and Bartholomew did as the mage bade. He turned a wolfish gaze to the girl. "You're as striking as ever, *Nicky*," David greeted. "Though you look a bit green this time. Your first ride upon a myst, no doubt. Were you so anxious to see me again?"

Arrowhead's pretty face was impassive. "If this was a social call, I assure you I would not be here."

David grinned. "Ah, I see your tongue is still as sharp as your blade."

"I am Echelon One Mage Jonathan Markus," the man on left said, cutting short the banter between the acquaintances with urgency and a hint of admonishment. With his straight walking staff that was almost as long the rangy wizard was tall, he gestured to the other mage, who wore a light tan robe. "This is Echelon Two Mage Jason Rivers. We bring a dire message from the Kingdom of Lorr."

"I am Baron David Northforest, and this is –"

Mage Markus cut him short with a raised hand. "We know who you are, baron. Forgive my curtness but we've precious little time. It's imperative that you evacuate Eastedge proper. The valley is in grave peril."

"*Evacuate*?" Bartholomew challenged. "We've only just won the 'Proper back. You would have us evacuate? For anything less than a catastrophic natural event, a request like that would have to be made to the crown, and then only by command of King Joseph Megerathon would we evacuate."

David stepped forward. "What is this? How do we even know you are who you say you are?"

"That's why I've come," Arrowhead said. "The Serpent's Way has been flooded and the waters are coming this way. Quickly. There is no time to petition your king. Eastedge proper would be swept away while we follow protocol. These Echelon One mages are here to assist with the evacuation and I'm here as verification to you of their identity."

"You're one to verify identities," David scoffed. "You were not exactly forthcoming about your own when we met."

"Yet I saved your life more than once and helped you overthrow the false baron," Arrowhead reminded.

"For your own agenda," David argued. "Why would I –" his lips kept moving but the sound of his voice went silent.

It took him a moment to realize it, but when he did, his eyes widened. He turned to his left and saw Mage Markus with an open palm raised in his direction.

Bartholomew was appalled and frightened. "What did you do to –"

His voice promptly went silent as well.

"You've no time for this!" Arrowhead snapped. "Make sure the next words out of your mouths tell us how to raise the alarm to evacuate the town. There *must* be one!"

Both Mages looked up and to the right just before another wizard came streaking from that direction on a myst. He had a pale bald head and wore blue robes adorned with gold studs around the hem of the wide sleeves. The thin staff he carried was made of whitewood and was close to three feet long.

"There is indeed an alarm, young lady," the new arrival confirmed. "It is signaled from the bell tower in this very keep. I've already dispatched a runner to sound it."

As if on cue, a loud toll rang out. The booming peal echoed through the valley and bounced off the wall of mountains on the far side. Everyone on the balcony and hovering near it could see the already busy activity down in Eastedge proper immediately explode with urgency.

"Thanks to the Lord Ascendant," Mage Rivers swore. "It is indeed good to see you, Mage Aaron, Head Mage of Darshay. When did you find out about the flood?"

"Not so very long ago," the blue-robed wizard admitted. "I sensed a distant surge of magic, more powerful than anything I've detected since your Head Mage unleashed his demon-killing blast at the Tyne during the Cursed Opening.

"I went to investigate it. By time I arrived at the western shores of Lake Onyx, the lake waters had already breached the northern barrier of the Hells and were racing down Serpent's Way." His eyes narrowed. "Was the Head Mage the source of this surge? Surely only a Child of the Old Ones can bring such power to bear."

"I can assure you, Mage Aaron," Mage Markus said earnestly, "that Rionn Lorr was not the cause of the flood. We were all together in a briefing regarding another crises. The cause is being investigated."

The suspicious Darshay'n wizard was not impressed. "I would not expect any other response from an agent of the Kingdom of Lorr."

Mage Gilder's expression went as flat as Arrowhead's. "I'll submit to a truegaze to put the truth to my words."

Aaron dismissed the offer with a wave. "We've no time for all of that. Besides, the offer to submit to a truegaze is good enough for me. But understand, I had to ask."

"Your trust is appreciated," Mage Markus said. "And it's a good thing you sent your runner to sound the alarm *before* coming to warn the baron."

Mage Aaron shot a distasteful glance at the cousins. "We expect he'll make a fine baron. He cannot be any worse than his immediate predecessor. For now, though, he is rumored to be young, headstrong and stubborn. I see now that those rumors are well-founded."

"HOW WERE WE TO KNOW," David began, yelling so loud he startled everyone. "Oh, I didn't know I'd been given my voice back," he continued at a subdued volume. "How were we to know their warning was genuine? This could have been some trick to get us to surrender the valley again."

"To what purpose?" Aaron chastised. "The young lady had the right of it. Her presence should have been proof that they were from Lorr. Why in the name of Darshay would Lorrians risk war to possess this dusty basin?"

David grit his teeth at the insult to his home. It seemed no one truly valued the barony and Eastedge proper as he did. His anger, however, was soon overwhelmed by fear.

People were already filing hurriedly out of the valley. Some herded children up the gently sloping walls while others herded small lines of livestock with yelps and cracking whips. Others led pack animals as they hauled wagons and carts up well-worn paths. Everyone who lived in and around Eastedge proper knew that the single toll meant to evacuate with great haste and they responded accordingly.

David worried nonetheless. "Will we be able to evacuate in time?" he asked.

"With our help, yes," Mage Rivers assured.

David turned to Arrowhead. "I apologize for my mistrust. Ride with us to assist with the evacuation while the wizards do their part. We could use the help on the ground, and I'm sure they can move faster without an extra person to ferry."

Arrowhead favored him with a pretty – and sarcastic – smile. "I'm sure Mage Markus appreciates your concern but he's already assured me that it's no burden."

"Unless you fancy a very long and very violent swim, be out of that valley within the hour," Mage Markus warned.

The three wizards, with the determined young woman in tow, streaked down into Eastedge proper. By the time David and Bartholomew made their way out of the castle, onto their mounts, and into the valley, the wizards were already hard at work assisting with the evacuation effort.

Arrowhead escorted the old and feeble upon the wizards' mysts so they could be ferried to safety. She helped load wagons and carts with people and animals so the wizards could use teleportation and telekinesis spells to move them out of the valley. Goats, sheep, chickens, and small herds of cattle wondered around in confusion after they found themselves transported miles away in the blink of an eye.

The Lorrians did not assist with the transport of property. With their time constraints, lives had to be their priority, not possessions. Some were able to transport their own property. Many were not. The valley was almost clear of people and animals in less than an hour. Unfortunately, though, the valley was not completely clear.

All of the residents heard the warning toll from the bell tower. They all heard the warnings that David, Bartholomew and several of their men rode through town crying out. Yet a few of the most stubborn among them refused to believe the young baron and his foreigners. They would not leave and they would not allow their livestock to be moved. The mages, however, transported all of the children even if their bull-headed parents did not give them permission.

The stragglers made no attempt to leave until they heard a sound like the sustained roar of some gargantuan feral beast. It grew louder and louder as it rushed closer and closer. By then it was too late. The mages teleported as many as they could but they could only help those they could see. Fear kept many of the stragglers holed up in their homes in a futile attempt to ride out the flood.

THE KEY QUEST

When the floodwaters raged through Eastedge proper, the loss of life was minimal. The property damage, on the other hand, was colossal. Every wooden structure in the valley was smashed to pieces and borne down Serpent's Way in the savage current. Crops were swept away. Dirt and debris-strewn waters raced up the gently sloping valley walls, flew up into the forested lands west of the valley, and up into the mountains on the east. A few bodies, human and animal, drowned, battered and broken, accompanied the debris.

David and Bartholomew retreated back to the balcony of the castle's common room to watch carnage in sullen silence. It broke David's heart to see the loss. He thought about his father and all he had sacrificed to transform Eastedge proper from a backwater dustbowl to an economically relevant part of the Kingdom of Darshay. He thought about the men that had fallen in their successful bid to win back the barony from the thieving false baron Tauran.

The young baron raged inside at the unfairness of it all. His eyes welled up with moisture at the thought of so many people having given so much and fought so hard only to have it end in a way he was utterly powerless to prevent.

David shed tears for the stubborn but innocent people that lost their lives in the flood. Though their number was small, one life lost was one too many. Yet even in his sadness and anger, he was thankful for the arrival of the Lorrians, for the loss of life would have been exponentially greater if not for their assistance.

Chapter 9: Bait

9.1

Raxe opened his eyes and was surprised to find himself warm and dry, several feet away from a blazing hearth. He was wrapped in a soft sheet and lying upon a thick, plush rug on a hardwood floor. His entire body was sore from his recent travails but he was well rested. The smell of burning hickory soothed him, as did the smell of roasting meat from somewhere beyond his field of vision. His gaze went from the hearth to the wall in which it was built. He was in a lodging very similar to the one Annastace had rented in Port Lorrian. It was not the same room, as evidenced by the different layout, but it was similar enough to remind him of the other lodging, to remind him of her.

Just beside the fireplace he saw a tunic, breeches, and a pair of leather boots folded neatly on the floor. Just beside that were his armor and his enchanted battleaxe, blades down, leaning against the wall.

The sight of Demonsbane propped up against the wall surprised and worried him. Only he, his grandfather, and Joel could touch weapon's bare surface without suffering a fatal blast of magic. And even if someone wrapped it in something to protect against the blast, it was so heavy that it took more than one person to move. The only time those properties did not work was when the *Ken d'Zanir* warriors extinguished all magic in their vicinity.

The offworlder rose quickly to a seated position, his face a mask of suspicious curiosity, his muscles as taught as a coiled spring. An instant later he sensed the presence of someone else in the room. He looked around to see Rionn Lorr and Catherine sitting on a couch. Quick sat on a wooden chair a few feet away from the Head Mage and his wife.

Raxe sighed with relief and visibly relaxed. "Where are we?" he asked.

"A guest house on the palace grounds," Rionn answered. "We wondered when you would finally awaken. Catherine warned us that you would sleep soundly but I did not think it would be *this* long."

"How long?" Raxe asked worriedly. He started to pull the sheet off himself but thought better of it when he remembered Catherine was sitting right next to Rionn.

"Only a few hours, Raxe," Catherine chuckled as she rose from the couch. "Rionn likes to tease. Excuse me, but I must tend to dinner. Shandie and the Sureblade children are watching the food for me and they like to sample even more than Rionn." She slipped out of the sitting room, but not before Raxe caught the sly smile on her face.

"The Sureblade kids are here?" Raxe asked. "Where's their mom?"

"Raxe?" the familiar, lilting voice floated into the room followed immediately by Annastace Sureblade.

A quick smile betrayed Raxe's pleasant surprise as she rushed toward him with a worried look on her perfect face. Her expression reminded him of his promise to her about keeping her oldest son safe.

"I'm sorry, Annastace," Raxe said apologetically. "Ethan and I had to separate. I couldn't personally see to his safety, but I…"

"Ethan is fine, thanks to you," Annastace interrupted. She fell to her knees at his side and carefully grasped his right wrist with both of her small but strong hands. "I received word from Ridgeland just this morning. They say he's in too much pain to move right now but it is not serious. Apparently he has a series of strains and pulled muscles."

Raxe grinned. "Yeah, it's a temporary side effect of the weapon I gave him. If that's his only problem I promise you he's fine."

"A small price to pay for his survival," Annastace said graciously. She inspected his damaged hand and continued. "Quick told me of the sacrifice you made for my son."

"Oh," Raxe said. He forgot about the lingering pain in his hand the moment their eyes met. "It looks worse than it is."

"Not by much, I'll wager," Annastace noted just before gracing him with a smile. "The citizens of this kingdom are in your debt, I, more than most. If there's anything I can do for you, you only need to name it."

"A kiss would be nice," Raxe said immediately, without thinking. He regretted the words the instant they jumped from his lips and quickly tried to redeem himself. "But that's kind of a crude thing to ask for," he said with an awkward smile. "So your thanks are more than enough."

Annastace put a soft hand on his cheek and leaned forward. She placed a light kiss on his lips that lingered for a brief moment before she pulled away. The sweet smell of her breath lingered in Raxe's nostrils and it took him a moment to realize his eyes were closed. He opened them and had to wait another moment for the room to stop spinning. His eyes found hers and he was speechless for yet another moment.

"Thank you," was all that he could think to say.

Annastace's grateful smile tilted with what Raxe thought were equal parts embarrassment and amusement. "I will help set the table and leave the three of you to your business." She rose to her feet, glided from the room and closed the door behind her.

"What's she doing here?" Raxe asked when she was out of sight, still staring at the closed door. Her image lingered in his mind so sharply it was as if she was still there. Her skirt, as always, was conservatively loose and long. But as always, not even her dignified manner of dress could quite conceal the natural sway of her full hips.

"She's one of Catherine's best friends," Rionn answered. "And she's living at the palace now. She decided to visit Catherine while she and Shandie were here."

"Not that I'm complaining," Raxe assured. "It just seems like a pleasant coincidence."

"Coincidence," Quick chuckled.

Rionn looked incredulous. "Coincidence, indeed."

"Has Joel made it back?" Raxe asked as he pulled the sheet off and went to the clothes next to his gear.

"Joel has not returned," Rionn Lorr answered. "I was going to ask if you or Quick knew his whereabouts."

Quick shrugged. "We parted at Hargathall's Cleft. He said he would find his way back."

"I've used my magic to search for him," Rionn said. "His aura as a Child of the Old Ones is not detectable, so I used a strip of the rope the *Ken* used to bind him when they attacked us at the inn across town. I could not even detect him with my most powerful seeking spells. It is as if he is completely nonexistent to magic."

"I'm not surprised," Raxe said. "Nothing about that guy surprises me anymore. So what happened? And Rionn, how did you manage to move Demonsbane without getting fried?"

"You lost a lot of blood in the battle with the *Ken*," Quick explained. "We never had the opportunity to treat you properly. And then we traveled here with very little sleep and food without you having time to recover. The exhaustion finally caught up with you."

"We treated you while you were out," Rionn added. "I also took the opportunity to apply the antidote for the plague. With as much contact as you've had with demons, I wanted to be certain you were protected. As for Demonsbane," he lifted his hand and twirled his finger, causing the battleaxe to rise into the air and turn end over end before settling back to its original position.

Raxe nodded, silently admonishing himself for forgetting how simple it would be for a mage of Rionn's power to move something without touching it.

"I guess thanks are in order for saving Quick and me. How did you do it?"

"No thanks necessary," Rionn assured. "I felt a strong surge of magic and flew upon my myst to the source. When I saw you and Quick about to be swept away by that wave, I used a teleportation spell to get you out of harm's way."

"I suppose Quick told you what happened," Raxe said as he finished donning the tunic and breeches.

"Indeed," Rionn answered. "I had no idea how powerful Azhju'lestra really was. But then again, magic fueled by anger and vengeance is the most destructive kind there is. The tidal wave she caused was high enough to surge over and through the mountains at the northern edge of the Hell's and into the Serpent's Way valley."

"Eastedge proper is in that valley," Quick realized. "Do you think the wave was powerful enough to travel that far?"

"That far and beyond," confirmed Rionn. "But worry not for the barony of Eastedge. I sent agents there ahead of the floodwaters. The valley was almost completely evacuated before the wave struck."

Relief washed over Raxe's expression but it did not last long. "Where is she now?" Raxe asked worriedly, fearing he already knew the answer.

"Azhju'lestra appears to have been consumed by her own magic," Rionn said sadly. "I've searched for her through all means at my disposal. I cannot feel her essence and that worries me. Without Sabrina's ability to shield her aura, we should be able to feel her –"

"Unless she's dead," Raxe concluded. "I could feel her presence from the moment we crossed the WorldGate. It was faint, but I could feel it when even when Sabrina hid it from you. But now…I can't feel her at all. Her essence was snuffed out when the wave came. I watched her…I don't know. I was hoping maybe she had teleported to safety, but really, it looked like she exploded."

"Yes," Rionn Lorr said sadly. "Such is the danger of magic, especially with one as young as she. Faerie magic is the most primal and dangerous magic of all. Creatures of faerie have a different physical connection to their magic than earthly creatures. With every other race that manipulates magic, the physical body is merely a shell that contains magical energy, a conduit. The two can be separated and still exist independently."

"Such is not the case with faeries," Quick noted, recalling one of Master Mage Delthar's lessons.

"Yes," confirmed Rionn. "Magical energy is the very bond that binds the physical being of a faerie creature. One cannot exist without the other."

"That's why she collapsed when the *Ken* extinguished our magic," Raxe surmised. "Her human side must've been the only thing that kept her alive."

Quick nodded. "The shock of losing her magic and the emotional trauma of losing her mother must have kept her in that catatonic state even after our magic returned to us."

"Yes," Rionn Lorr concurred. "Azhju'lestra was too emotionally and physically immature to deal with trauma of that magnitude and then unleash the kind of magic needed to cause that tidal wave. A vessel so frail could not release such power and remain whole."

"May the Old Ones welcome her with open arms," Quick prayed.

"It was my fault," Raxe breathed.

"What?" Quick asked.

"Everything," Raxe grunted. "Her death, the destruction of Eastedge, all of it's my fault. I should never have taken her back when I did."

"Raxe," the Head Mage began, "how could you have known –"

"Because Sabrina *told* me!" Raxe snapped. He took a moment to compose himself before continuing. "She warned me not to bring Azh back until this crisis was over. She knew something bad would happen. I think she knew something like *this* could happen."

"Their connection was so strong that the shock of her mother's death put her into a catatonic state," Rionn argued. "The shock likely would have driven her to find her mother once she recovered, whether you wanted her to or not."

"It was the shock of finding her mother's remains that pushed her over the edge," Raxe said. "Her bones, the cloth she wore, they were still recognizable but I could tell they were dissolving, fading back into the elements. If I hadn't taken Azh back so soon there wouldn't have been any remains to find by the time she recovered on her own and went back to Lake Onyx."

Raxe waited for the Head Mage to counter him, to point out that there was no way Raxe could know that.

Rionn Lorr said nothing.

"So, you agree?" Raxe asked.

"I cannot deny the possibility," Rionn admitted. "Perhaps this would have happened once your daughter woke up, even if she never found Sabrina's remains, perhaps not. I know it is no consolation for your loss, but you did what you thought was right. That's all the Lord Ascendant asks of us."

There was a long moment of silence before Quick spoke again. "What do we do now?" he asked. "Rell Kallen has fled with the Hell Key. How do we find him?"

The crestfallen look on the Head Mage's face said it all. "Apparently he has a means of masking the Key from my detection. But even so, finding him should not be a problem. He would most certainly try to take the Key back to his queen in Thâlstrën."

"Can we catch him before he gets there?" Raxe asked. "I know how fast that Phoenix flies, but would he have to stop to let it recharge or something?"

Rionn shook his head. "From what I know of the Phoenix stone, Raxe, the latest he should have reached his home was the morning after he left the Demon's Spine."

"Well," Quick began hopefully, "It sounds like a trip to the Elf Lands is in order. I've never been to the Elf Lands."

"If we try to take the Hell Key back, it could very well mean war," Rionn warned.

Raxe studied Rionn closely. "You aren't even sure the elf made it back to his home, are you?" Rionn raised an eyebrow as Raxe pressed on. "You said he would 'try' to take it back. You said he 'should have' got home the next morning. Why don't you sound convinced?"

"You have the truth of it," Rionn admitted. "I'm not certain that he did, but the why of it is not yet clear to me. To use a phrase I've heard you use, Raxe, I have a *gut* feeling."

"Ok," Raxe conceded. "Where do you think it is?"

Rionn shrugged. "I have no idea, but you can tell us."

Raxe blinked. "What the hell are you talking… Oh."

The Head Mage nodded. "Oh, indeed."

With a grin of embarrassment, the offworlder stood up, walked over to where his gear rested on the floor, and pulled Questblade from its sheath. Quick chuckled the entire time while Rionn only smiled.

"What's so funny, *magic* men," Raxe groused. "I'm still not used to depending on magic they way you guys do."

Quick chuckled again. "You seem to have gotten fairly comfortable with Demonsbane."

"That's different," Raxe argued. "Demonsbane is a weapon. I'd be comfortable with this, too, in a fight," he said, lifting the enchanted short sword.

"Well," Rionn offered. "Think of this as a fight to –"

"Yeah, yeah, yeah," Raxe interrupted. "I don't need more of your wisdom, Mr. Wizard. Just give me a little quiet."

With a smirk, Rionn fell silent. Quick followed suit. Raxe appreciated the moment of levity but it was all too brief. The void in his awareness that his daughter once occupied had grown into an ache that he could only hope would not consume him.

Instead of dwelling on the emotional pain, he focused his attention on Questblade. He took a brief moment to admire the artistic engraving on the wide ivory-hued blade. The image of a man, presumably his great grandfather and crafter of the enchanted weapon, leading a small group of men and women all dressed in homespun garments from the 1860's, was so masterfully etched into the metal that it looked almost like a grayscale photograph.

When Dan gave the short sword to his grandson, he told the story of how Raxe's great grandfather used Questblade to help people held as slaves escape as safely as possible along the Underground Railroad. Dan used it in WWI and WWII to help prisoners of war escape captivity. Questblade was crafted to act as a guide to assist its wielder in finding whatever he or she sought, as long as the quest was noble. Raxe was sure this qualified.

Dan had explained that Questblade did not necessarily act like a compass or divining rod. It did not always point in the exact direction of the subject being sought. Instead, it revealed the most effective path. Raxe had used it several times and it had yet to fail him.

He held the knob-like pommel in his left hand and rested the flat part of the blade on the palm of his injured right hand. The contact of the cold blade against a patch of molten metal fused to the heel of his palm brought a sharp bolt of pain that made him wince briefly. He dismissed the pain, closed his eyes and fixed the image of Questblade and the question of the location of the Hell Key in his mind.

Both the Head Mage and the changeling could sense the magic when it ignited. A moment later, Raxe opened his eyes and set Questblade, pommel down, on the floor in front of him. The enchanted blade remained upright on the flat side of otherwise spherical pommel. It stood for a few seconds, its magic flowing through the room, before finally falling on its own accord. The tip of the short sword blade pointed in Rionn Lorr's direction.

The Head Mage looked over his shoulder. "North."

Raxe shook his head. "I think it's pointing at you, cuz."

"It can't be pointing at me," Rionn disagreed.

"Hey," Raxe argued. "It's my sword, made by my great grandfather. I've used it several times. I know how it works."

"But I have no idea where the Hell Key is."

"You sure?" Raxe asked.

"Try again," Rionn insisted.

Raxe sighed and lifted Questblade and went through the process once more. When he put the blade down, the three men waited patiently. It started falling in the same direction, but this time Rionn Lorr stepped to the left.

The blade pivoted as it fell and followed him. When the wide blade slapped against the wooden floor, it pointed directly at the Head Mage.

"Satisfied?" Raxe asked smugly.

"I would be if I knew where the hell the Key – I mean where the Hell Key – was."

The talking ceased when young Shandie entered the room through the same door the mother exited from minutes earlier. The little apron she wore was stained with wheat flour and grease. She looked like a tiny chef.

"Dinner awaits, gentlemen," she informed.

She proffered them a small curtsey, obviously repeating what her mother had instructed her to say and do, and despite the dark mood in the sitting room, the men could not help but smile at the adorable sight. She never failed to awe her father with her combination of a toddler's endearing manner and an insight far beyond her years.

…Insight beyond her years…

The thought of his daughter's *in*sight reminded him of her gift of *fore*sight. A critical realization came to him.

"Raxe," Rionn began. "Did your daughter say anything before…?"

The offworlder closed his eyes briefly against the raw memory. "Yeah. She said she knew who killed her mother. She said the sea birds and fish witnessed it and told her. But she didn't tell us."

Rionn nodded somberly. "Sabrina could talk to those creatures, too. They often acted as her spies."

"Well?" Raxe asked expectantly. "Does that mean anything to you?"

"It does," Rionn replied. "I think I *do* know where to find the Hell Key."

9.2

Deep beneath the towering dunes of shifting sands that were the Forsaken Desert, Shara Dune was angry enough to scream. She was so angry, in fact, that she could feel her frustration like a low, steady tremor in the depths of her consciousness. The burning sands above, radiating all of the searing heat of the two suns, was nothing compared to her smoldering fury.

Shara was in her element now, even if this was the last place she needed to be. This was her subterranean palace, her very throne room, and she would remain in control of herself and her situation. She would also remain in complete control of Mage Stratham Glund, the Second High Adviser to the Head Mage of the Kingdom of Cartha.

With a tremendous exertion of will, she stopped pacing across the plush, silver trimmed, teal swath of carpet that stretched from the grand entryway at the far end of the throne room to the base of the dais where her gaudy throne rested. Soft light from perfumed torches lining the walls and columns shimmered dazzlingly from her lavender and gilded silk gown for a moment after she stopped walking.

She reigned in her frustration with a deep breath, ignoring the faint but persistent buzz of barely checked fury that seemed to intensify despite her efforts of forced calm. And then her long, shapely legs carried her up the three stairs of the dais to the foot of her throne. The hip-high slits on either side of her full-length form fitting dress revealed perfect muscle tone and flawless golden skin with every step.

To either side of the dais stood a sand creature, among the tallest and bulkiest of their species. One of their four tentacles hoisted matching pentagonal iron shields while the other three tentacles hefted large, long-handled, bladed and spiked weapons of various types. They stood as still as statues, the intermittent twitch of muscle in their barrel chests and the slightly expanding and contracting of the tips of their three wide, stunted head trunks were the only things that revealed them as living, breathing creatures.

THE KEY QUEST

By the time the ornate double doors of the entryway opened and Glund was escorted into her throne room by four of the crimson armored refugees from Mar-dah's Legion Midnight, Shara Dune was seated with one leg draped seductively over the other. The wizard cast an unabashed glare at the provocative vision as he stepped through the wide threshold. Shara scoffed at the expected attention. He may have had carnal intentions upon entering her desert palace but she would make sure they did not linger.

"Do not get comfortable, Glund," Shara advised. "Neither of us will be here long. I was sorely tempted to allow you to come here alone so that my elite warriors," she indicated the sand creatures flanking her with a slender, perfectly manicured hand, "could give you a proper welcome. But I fear I may have use for you yet."

"Of course you do," the elegantly robed wizard said smugly. His escort stopped him ten feet away from the dais. He drank in her image as he continued. "Our benefactor would be hesitant to pay you should any harm befall me."

"It is past time for us to renegotiate our deal," said the Queen of the Forsaken Desert. "I have played errand girl and assassin, roles far beneath my station, for *your* benefactor, all because I believed in his goal. That ends now. I wish to tell him this to his face. I've grown weary of communicating with him through you, a lowly middleman."

If the barb insulted the prideful mage as Shara intended, he gave no sign of it. His smug expression went unchanged, serving to aggravate Shara Dune further.

"I understand your frustration," said Glund, his understanding tone in stark contrast to his arrogant grin and hungry stare. "But you must understand –"

"I understand that you are clueless!" Shara spat, snapping to her feet and pointing an accusing finger. The angry droning in her head was so strong now that the lamplight seemed to tremor in time with it. "This is the most dangerous place in the world for us to be, for *me* to be. And you arrange to have the *Hell Key* brought here, as well?"

"You have managed to stay hidden from the Head Mage all of this time," Glund countered. "Logic dictates that with you is the perfect place for the Hell Key."

"I told you when I first sought sanctuary in Cartha, my magic only conceals my son and me from seeking spells. I cannot guarantee that the magic will extend to anything or anyone else, much less a talisman as powerful as one of the Keys. If Rionn Lorr makes a concerted effort to locate the Hell Key, he may very well find it here."

Glund waved dismissively. "Our benefactor has ensured that the Children of the Old Ones are much too busy to concern themselves with your whereabouts."

"Fool," Shara snarled as she stormed down the dais stairs with perfect balance in stiletto heels that pushed her already impressive height beyond that of the average man. Her soft, straight nose was almost level with Statham Glund's aquiline nose when she stepped close enough for him to feel her hot breath upon his face.

"Do you even know who your benefactor is?" she challenged. "Do you have any idea *what* it is?"

Glund's smug expression turned into a confused frown.

"It?" he asked.

"It!" Shara shouted, her patience with his cluelessness at an end. "You have been taking your orders from a bloody demon! Apparently a powerful one, as it seems to be the mastermind behind all that has transpired."

Statham Glund shook his head incredulously. "Have you been listening to the babblings of superstitious peasants from southern Lorr? I would surely have known if –"

"You know nothing!" Shara interrupted. "You have been duped, led by the nose by this demon. Such monsters are not to be trusted. They are not to be bargained with. It will surely break any deal into which it enters. It may be controlling your Head Mage, perhaps even your king."

"Have you not heard during your travels?" Mage Glund asked. "King Vergoth is dead."

Shara Dune paused. "Dead?" she asked.

THE KEY QUEST

This was not good news. Glund was a merely stepping-stone for the Desert Queen. Her ultimate goal had been to gain an audience with the Carthan king. With the assistance she had given Glund and through her own beguiling magic, she knew she could win Vergoth's favor and finally gain the influence she needed.

With Vergoth gone, his son would now be king. Shara, however, knew enough about the royal family and Carthan politics to know that the Vergoth the second, as young and brash and inexperienced as he was, would be the ruler in name only. The queen would be the true ruler, at least until her son matured into his station. Queen Lairen was known as a ruthless and shrewd woman. Shara would have a much more difficult time controlling her than either Vergoth.

"Yes," Glund answered, pulling her attention back to him, "as are my two superiors. I am the new Head Mage. The reports are that the former Head Mage and his First High Advisor betrayed the king and murdered him. They were killed by the royal elite guard shortly afterward."

"Then perhaps Lairen is taking orders from the demon," Shara suggested. "Maybe even Prince – now King – Vergoth. It is someone from whom you take your orders, of that there is no question. I'll not throw my lot in with such a foul monster. I suggest you end your association as w–"

Her sentence was cut short by shocking pain to her cheek and the sensation of flight. When she stopped, abruptly and painfully, she was crumpled at the foot of the dais ten feet away from where she had been standing. She looked up in a daze to see Glund's right hand still raised from the blow.

Her sand creatures were already streaking toward the wizard with inhuman speed. A flash of blinding red light reduced them to charred chunks of flesh and smoldering, greasy black ash that settled onto the beautiful carpet and hard earthen floor. The crimson-clad, four-man escort went flying in every direction, their enchanted armor just barely protecting them from sharing the fate of the sand creatures. The impact rendered them all unconscious.

"Foolish whore," Stratham Glund taunted, his voice suddenly changed. The warm, smooth, honeyed tones turned cold, rough and sour in her ears.

Shara's daze gave way to shock. She had no idea he was so powerful. The sand creatures moved faster than any human could react. The time it would take even an accomplished wizard to form the words and gestures to conjure such a powerful blast, especially without some kind of focusing tool, should not have been enough to thwart her sand creatures at such close quarters. She was positive she had an accurate measure of the mage. This was not possible.

"Did you actually believe it was *your* magic that hid you from the Head Mage all these years?" the Carthan wizard continued. "You are a low-level elemental at best. Besides moving sand and dirt, the weak glamour you use upon simple-minded humans and dumb animals like sand creatures is the only real power you have.

"It is *I* who has kept you hidden, and only so that you could do *my* bidding. That protection ends now, witch."

"*Human* males? *Your* bidding?" Shara gasped, dreadful realization finally sinking in. "You?"

The wizard smiled, and the rictus stretched further than any human mouth could. The razor-sharp corners of the terrible smile almost connected with deep wrinkles snaking from his squinting eyes like cracks forming in stone.

"Yesssss," he confirmed. "And now I will take back the talisman that has kept you hidden."

He lifted a long-fingered hand, now more like an inhuman claw, and beckoned. An invisible force snatched the golden decorative comb painfully from Shara's hair and swept it into the wizard's hand. When it made contact with his skin it melted into gold, green, and red slime that formed a small puddle at his feet.

"Stratham Glund has been dead for weeks. I took his place three years ago, shortly before you arrived in Cartha seeking safe haven. I kept him alive all this time, just barely, just enough to bleed him for as much information as I could, until I no longer needed him.

"I've been manipulating the Carthan Head Mage, who in turn counseled the Carthan King, who in turn led almost all of the kingdoms in the Known Lands in a plot against the Kingdom of Lorr.

"The king's murder was not my doing, though I am not at all surprised. I've no doubt the official story of his death is a fabrication. His beloved queen had been scheming against him for years.

"And yes…all of this time you have had the honor of working for – and being defiled by – the almighty demon Dierglyorr."

"By the gods," Shara swore, gasping at the implications even as the demon wizard's eyes began to smolder with an eerie crimson glow.

The demon concurred, deliberately and threateningly. "By the gods, indeed," it taunted. "The Leader Old Ones themselves created me for the purpose of bringing this world to heel for them. But the Old Ones are dead, so I will bring this world to heel for *me*. You have assisted me admirably in this endeavor, and believe me, you are *less* than an errand girl. You are naught but bait, a tiny desert worm meant to draw much larger prey."

Shara Dune stared wordlessly. Cold dread filled her as she replayed his earlier words: *defiled by the almighty demon Dierglyorr…*

The demon tilted its head curiously. "Ah…worry not," it assured. "You will not bear a sibling for your son. When the Old Ones forged me they made sure I could not produce another like me. They obviously feared the potential of more than one demon as formidable as I."

Shara Dune, the Queen of the Forsaken Desert, pushed herself to her feet. Her long red hair tumbled madly over her shoulders and down her back. She stood straight and tall. If her fate were to die this day, it would not be in an undignified pose. She would not die groveling.

"So you will kill me now," she said, rather than asked. "Be quick about it, beast. And do the same for my son. For all of your deceptions, you owe me at least that much."

"I owe you nothing, and I almost never kill quickly," informed the demon. "For me, the killing of a creature as ravishing as you is a process, a long process that I like to savor. I prefer to taste as many tears, as many drops of blood, as many mouthfuls of flesh as possible. I must inhale every ounce of your fear when I devour you. Indeed, our many nights of human passion do not even begin to compare."

"Then you will leave us alive?" questioned Shara Dune in disbelief, too suspicious to be relieved.

The demon shrugged. "I will leave you," it promised. "Though I know not how long you will live. That trembling you've been feeling, that sound you've been hearing…"

It paused so that Shara could clearly hear the rumbling she thought was her own anger building and throbbing in her head. There was no longer any question that the shuddering lamplight came from an outside force. The sound had grown into a steady, distant shudder that grew louder by the second.

"Yes, that," the Dierglyorr revealed, "is the sound of the unleashed rage of a water faerie…one with the unstable psyche of a human and enhanced power from the blood of the Old Ones…one who has learned that you have recently murdered her mother."

"A water *faerie*," Shara gasped. "Sabrina was faerie?" The pride of an accomplishment as significant as killing a faerie was quickly dampened by fear. "And she spawned a Child of the Old Ones?"

"She has," the Dierglyorr confirmed. "So, no, I will not kill you, for there is not time enough to savor the process. Should you manage to survive what is coming, however, I may very well call upon you in the future."

The roaring, rolling tremor intensified in volume and force, causing Shara to stumble and make an effort to retain her balance. After righting herself, she looked up for the demon and saw that it was gone.

Shara Dune was on the verge of panic. Her first instinct was to flee but this was her domain. She would see what it was that threatened her desert home. She dashed into the shadows behind her throne and muttered a spell that opened a narrow secret door carved almost invisibly within the wall. A few hurried steps through a pitch-black corridor brought her into a larger room. Another spell and a flick of her hand lit the small torch sconces around the room, illuminating an earthen ceiling not quite ten feet high over an oval-shaped room roughly ten feet long by six feet deep.

The ceiling bore two circular holes, each just under four feet in diameter. A knee-high mound of sand rested on the floor beneath each hole. Similar rooms, with similar ceiling holes, were scattered all through the vast realm beneath the dunes. This room was Shara's personal exit. She ran beneath one of the holes and stepped into the sand mound.

For her sand creatures, a simple leap carried the tall warriors into the holes above, where their powerful tentacles easily dug into the walls of hard-packed sand to propel them up to the surface. Shara Dune did not possess such physical capabilities yet she could move through those burrows with far greater speed than her swiftest warriors.

With a glance, the knee-high mound of sand in which she stood collapsed and then spread along the floor fluidly under her high heels, where it spread and then compressed into the density of stone, forming a solid disk under her feet. The disk changed shape explosively, morphing into a three-foot high column with enough force to catapult her into the air.

She sailed like an arrow through the ceiling hole and speared twenty feet upward to the top of a narrow conduit. The conduit ended at a second ceiling made of densely packed mud so coagulated no moisture dripped from it. Shara lifted both hands high, punching through the membranous layer that was almost as thick as her forearm was long.

When her fists emerged into the heavy sands on the topside of the membrane, she willed the sands to grasp her and pull her through the mountainous dunes.

Her sand creatures' three head-trunks served as filters that allowed them to breathe as they literally swam upward through the dunes to emerge at the surface, sometimes to exit the subterranean keep and often to seize prey, be it an unfortunate animal or an unsuspecting human traveler. The Queen of the Forsaken Desert needed only a thought to maintain an air pocket around her head and a continuous thrust under feet to rocket her safely to the surface.

The Desert Queen's little red-haired toddler sat in the middle of his playroom in his mother's lair under the dunes. He played with his own mounds of sand, totally oblivious to the rumbling and shaking around him. This toddler did not play in the sand the way other children did. Other children drew pictures in sand and built sand castles. This boy created miniature knights, six-inch sand creatures. He built them with a wave of his hand, turning mundane piles of sand into incredibly articulated models and weapons.

With a thought, the boy made the miniatures move. He made a half dozen of them walk, run and fight against real desert scorpions. The scorpions fought valiantly but died at the point of sand swords compressed into rock-hard blades that pierced their shells.

The scorpions could not have run if they wanted to, and they definitely wanted to. They wanted to flee for safety from the boy and from the calamity that they sensed coming nearer. Running, however, was not possible, for they were being compelled to fight by the same little boy that was killing them with his animated sand models.

Real sand creatures stood to either side of the closed entrance, their eyes darting nervously in every direction. They wanted to flee as well but they had been commanded by their mistress to guard her son. They would obey the Queen of the Forsaken Desert until their dying breaths.

The door swung open and in walked Shara Dune. Her flaming red hair hung down past her shoulders, her tight emerald dress shimmered in the torchlight. Her son looked up at her, at the look of concern on her face, and his animated miniature warriors collapsed into small heaps of sand. The surviving scorpions scurried away.

"Come, my son," Shara bade. "We must be away from this place."

The boy stared for a moment and shook his head. "No," he said petulantly. "You are not my mother."

"Don't be a fool, little one," she snapped. "And don't make me say it again."

The toddler's eyes narrowed. He raised his hands and made two fists, one stacked upon the other. As soon as his fingers folded in, the Hell Key materialized within them.

"You are NOT my mother! Get away from me!"

Shara gasped and took a panicked step back. The Hell Key was taller and heavier than the boy. She knew he held it up with telekinetic magic, not strength of limb.

The silent sand creatures did not know what to do. They held weapons in each of their four tentacles but were too startled to raise any of them. How could they attack their mistress's son?

Shara Dune snarled. Her green eyes turned crimson and gleamed with an evil light. She lifted her hand to point an accusing finger, and the elegant digit stretched into a long claw that ended in a curved talon.

"Little bastard," the Dierglyorr spat.

Its plan had been to use the boy to wield the power of the Hell Key. That was obviously not an option. As badly as it wanted to rip the little boy to shreds, it dared not go near the young Child while he held the Hell Key. The enchanted greatsword was potentially fatal to the demon. The Dierglyorr was not easily surprised but it was taken aback at toddler Child's realization of his powers at such an early age.

"I do so *hate* you Children of the Old Ones," it hissed "Stay here and die with your whore of a mother, then."

The sand creatures attacked. Eight blades of varying lengths swept toward the demon with blinding speed…and cut nothing but empty air.

* * *

When the true Shara Dune burst into the air above the desert, she continued to pull and solidify the sands under her feet. She quickly gathered and compressed them while steadily stretching them skyward, constructing a living, growing column beneath her feet that elevated her high into the sky. Out in the open she realized just how muffled the sound had been beneath the desert. Above the sands the noise was deafening, like an endless roar of reverberating thunder heralding the end of the world.

A violent wind buffeted her from the north, clearing the way for something much more terrible. It almost blew Shara Dune from her ever-rising perch but she bent her knees and pulled the sand higher and more securely around her feet and shins. Her ascent did not stop until she was high enough in the air to see over the peaks of the southernmost reaches of Hell's Mountains twenty miles away. What she saw was beyond belief.

The long mountain range ended at the northern border of the Forsaken Desert, forming a jagged wall of earth nearly two hundred miles wide. Shara watched a two-mile wide explosion of water spill over that wall and boil through the spaces between the mountains, right where she knew the Serpent's Way valley ended. The massive rush poured down onto her desert like a raging waterfall and soared through the air in a white foamy spray, soaking the desert surface in every direction in an expanding surge over six miles wide.

Not sparing the time or breath for a startled gasp, Shara Dune banished the column of sand beneath her. She free fell, twisting her athletic limbs expertly until she was knifing through the air headfirst toward the desert floor. The concussive wind from the approaching tidal wave pushed her out of her straight line of descent but she continued to gain speed as she fell.

The dunes gathered beneath her and rushed up to cushion her fall. The sands enveloped her gently but quickly, pulling her back down through the membrane that separated the surface sands from her lair. She came down through the same ceiling from which she exited and landed gracefully on her feet. Her sand-brown eyes widened with terror and she finally released the gasp she had held back before.

"My son…"

The approaching roar climbed to yet another deafening pitch. Shara turned at the sounds of horrific crashing and screaming echoing through her subterranean kingdom. She wanted to go to her boy but there was no time. The nursery where he was being attended was nearly a quarter-mile south of her throne room. The Desert Queen could propel herself atop a disk of sand five times faster than her swift sand creatures could run, but that would still not get her to her son in time. There was no time left for anything.

The four crimson-armored warriors who had escorted the demon in Stratham Glund's guise to their queen had finally regained consciousness and were struggling to their feet. They tried to run, only to be thrown to the floor again by another powerful quake that tore through the earth. Gigantic fissures erupted within the high ceilings. The broad sandstone columns buckled.

The last thing Shara Dune saw as she screamed with fear and anger was white froth thundering angrily down through the cracks in the ceiling as the columns crumbled. An impossibly thick sheet of mud and water crashed into her throne room with the force of an avalanche.

9.3

Quick, Raxe, and Rionn Lorr were airborne within the hour. They would have lifted off sooner, but before they set out, Quick asked them to wait fifteen minutes while he ran an important errand. Both Children started to either protest or chide, but the adolescent changeling had transformed into a hawk and was streaking away before they could get the words out. Raxe stared at the shrinking image of the speeding bird until it was out of view.

"He does realize we're in a hurry right?" Raxe cast an annoyed glare at the Head Mage. "And what are you smiling about, man? You should be pissed."

"Yes," Rionn Lorr said. "He does realize we are pressed for time. And I'm smiling because for a moment I was, 'pissed,' as you say. But Quick is usually the one who charges into the fight first. For him to cause a delay knowing how important the circumstances are means there has to be a very good reason."

"You trust him that much?" Raxe asked.

"You do not?" Rionn returned.

Raxe looked to the spot in the sky where the hawk disappeared. Three years ago, when Quick was barely a teenager, he was even more impulsive and rash. He had also saved Raxe's life several times during the Cursed Opening. The young changeling had saved practically the entire Lorrian royal court and countless future victims when he shot and killed Mar-dah with Raxe's modified nine-millimeter pistol, and he was not even an official agent of the Head Mage or the Kingdom of Lorr at the time.

The offworlder nodded. "Of course I do."

The Head Mage and the offworlder decided to use the fifteen minutes they "granted" Quick to travel to the royal sky sleigh yard. They borrowed a mount for Raxe while Rionn Lorr rode Ebony. Halfway to the sleigh yard, Rionn turned to Raxe.

"So, what do you think of Annastace?" Rionn asked.

"I think very highly of her," Raxe admitted. "It's just too bad I can never act on it."

The Head Mage raised an eyebrow. "Why not?"

"We're from two different worlds. Literally," Raxe reminded. "And in the short time I knew Meldrick I came to think of him as a friend."

"So it would seem," Rionn agreed. "While we did not have a WorldGate between us, Catherine and I had to clear difficult obstacles to be together. Her elven heritage and her station within her kingdom was a far different world than mine, and she had been promised to another."

Raxe thought for a moment. "Don't tell me. Rell Kallen was her fiancé. That's where all the tension between you two comes from."

"Yes," Rionn confirmed. "But that's the past. I prefer to talk about the future. Do you really believe there cannot be one for you and Annastace?"

"You and the misses are quite the matchmakers, huh?" Raxe accused.

Rionn half-smiled. "It is merely curiosity on my part, offworlder, though I cannot speak for my wife."

"Let's 'speak' of something else, wizard," Raxe said flatly. "No use dwelling on things that ain't gonna happen. I'm going home when this is over. I doubt the Sureblade family will want to come with me."

"Understood," the Head Mage relented.

When they arrived at the royal sky sleigh yard they found Quick there waiting for them. Leather straps crisscrossing to form an "X" on his narrow torso held a long, cloth-covered package snugly to his back. Raxe assumed the cloth concealed a longsword or two, or perhaps fighting staffs.

"What'cha got there, kid?" Raxe asked as they boarded the sleigh.

"Something I hope we will not need," Quick answered gravely.

9.4

The two-bird sky sleigh ferried them south and slightly west. Raxe noted the direction once they were airborne and was immediately puzzled. He turned to the Head Mage, who was seated at the far end of a long bench on the other side of the cabin.

"Southwest?" Raxe asked, his raspy voice rumbling with confusion. "Thâlstrën is east. Wouldn't the Ranger Elf be heading that way? When he ran from Hargathall's Cleft the Phoenix took him northeast."

"Indeed," Rionn confirmed. "I actually felt the Hell Key in the Demon's Spine when you touched it for the first time. It was a fleeting sensation and vision, both of which faded as quickly as they materialized. I tried to focus on it more closely but I could not, presumably because of Mar-dah's concealment and barrier spell around his mountain. When I sought it out again I felt it moving, presumably when you carried it out of the mountain. After a short time it began to move quickly to the northeast. That must have been when the Ranger Elf swiped it from you. It disappeared from my perception just outside of the Deadwood Forest."

"So why are we flying southwest?" Raxe asked. "The Deadwood is southeast."

"Because the demon intercepted the elf," Rionn Lorr answered. "And though I can no longer detect its presence I am certain the Key is somewhere in the Forsaken Desert."

Raxe looked doubtful. "How do you know the demon took the key?"

"Other than Mar-dah," Rionn answered, "I know of no one with the power to conceal such a potent instrument of magic from me."

"If the demon has the Key," Raxe noted, "then Rell Kallen…"

"Yes," the Head Mage said. "The demon would not have left the Ranger Elf alive."

Raxe shrugged. "Can't say I'll miss the bastard."

"Neither will I," Rionn agreed. "But we cannot overlook his contribution. Even though everything he did was for the ultimate purpose of making off with the Hell Key, his assistance was critical. We would have never survived that first night back at Port Lorrian had Rell not been present to tip the scales in our favor."

"Sure," Raxe conceded. "He saved my life while we searched for the Hell Key. Still, I won't miss him."

"So, it's safe to assume the demon has the key," Quick said. "But how do you know where it is, Rionn?"

"Something my daughter said before all of this began," Rionn answered.

Raxe frowned incredulously. "You mean we're flying the length of the kingdom based on a three year old's comment?"

Rionn smiled and said:

"From the depths of blackness to the heat of flames, from desiccated valley to raging river, from sand to stone... A Child's wrath will span.

"That is what she said to her mother and me. It came to her in a vision."

"OK," Raxe said. "The 'desiccated valley to raging river' part I caught from my glimpse of the Serpent's Way Valley before and after my daughter..."

He paused. *My daughter. And she's gone.* He took a moment to gather himself. "What does the rest mean?"

"I received a report from a unit of Gryphon Ryders that had flown on patrol near Lake Onyx," Rionn explained. "They spoke of a thick, black, oily substance in the heart of the lake. They smelled its acrid stench from a mile away. When an Echelon Mage was sent to investigate, the blackness was gone, though the foul smell lingered."

"It was crude oil," Raxe said, "from my world. My guess is the demon used it to pollute Lake Onyx and lure Sabrina out into the open."

"I agree," Rionn returned. "That is the confirmation I needed. The 'depths of blackness' is the crude oil. The 'heat of flames' could easily refer to the temperatures of the Forsaken Desert, as could the mention of sand."

"But what about the 'stone' she mentioned?" Raxe wondered aloud.

Rionn Lorr shrugged at that. "Hell's Mountains, perhaps. After all, Serpent's Way runs through them, from the northern ranges of the Hells to the southern ones."

Raxe tapped at his helmet were it hung at his hip from the tip of one of Demonsbane's crescent blades. "Shouldn't she have said 'from stone to sand' if that was the case? 'Sand to stone' sounds like it went from the desert *to* the Hells."

"It does," Rionn agreed. "We'll be flying over the Hells on our way to the Forsaken Desert. Perhaps if we come near enough to the mountains, we'll feel the Hell Key's presence despite the demon's attempts to conceal it."

When they approached the Hells they flew just to the east of the mountain range, high enough to see the southern end of the once-dry valley that had suddenly become a river. The new river terminated against a line of mountains that formed a natural barrier north of the Forsaken Desert. A narrower valley branched off to the west from the basin at the end of the Serpent's Way and the Hell's. The new river water filled that smaller valley to overflowing.

Rionn Lorr and Quick had stepped out onto a small outer deck on the port side of the sleigh. Quick's sharp eyes followed the smaller valley, now a smaller river, until it disappeared over the horizon.

"That valley's so small that no one ever bothered to give it a name," the young changeling observed. "It ends at a high bluff that overlooks the Tul Darshay'n River. That bluff must be a waterfall now. I'm sure Serpent's Way valley will be called Serpent's Way River. The river filling the nameless valley will need a name, too. I wonder if it'll be named Serpent's Way for the larger valley or Tul Darshay'n East."

Rionn nodded absently but remained silent, watching the suns climb slowly into the eastern sky. Leaning on the railing, he gazed thoughtfully into the hazy clouds.

Raxe looked out at the wizard and changeling through the window in the hatch leading to the outer deck. He was utterly amazed at how someone could just stand out over so much empty space with no more support than a flimsy rail stopping them being swept over the side by the powerful winds buffeting the sleigh.

This is the Head Mage, he thought. *Hell, he can ride clouds. The kid can turn into a bird.*

Rionn turned and came toward the door. His gaze quickly found Raxe and he beckoned him purposefully. Raxe only gave an incredulous look. Quick looked back and smirked.

"Surely you're not afraid," the changeling called. "As many times as you have ridden flying beasts and sky sleighs, this should be nothing."

"I guess I trust a strong griffin back and the *inside* of a sky sleigh more than a rickety wooden plank."

With a look of amusement, Rionn stepped into the cabin. His young protégé followed. Raxe clutched at the wall rail tightly when a savage gust of wind whooshed through the cabin.

"Still have a bit of the sky-fright, eh?" Rionn teased.

Raxe would have flipped him off if he thought the Head Mage would understand the gesture.

"I've been puzzling over Joel," Rionn shared. "You said his magic has not been affected by the presence of the *Ken d'Zanir.*"

"That's right," Raxe confirmed. "At Hargathall's Cleft he morphed into a more powerful form than ever."

"I wondered at that, as well," Quick added. "His magic was seemingly untouched."

"The night we were attacked at Port Lorrian," Rionn posed, "Joel was not attacked the way we were. He was merely bound, correct?"

"Yes," Quick answered. His thin eyebrows lifted as he continued. "And when the sky sleigh was brought down over Hell's Mountains, he was not attacked the way the rest of us were. He was spirited away to be held captive by Tauran."

"The demon was never trying to kill him," Raxe realized. "Do you think it was trying to keep him alive to use him against us?"

"Perhaps it *cannot* kill him," Quick offered. "Perhaps the demon knows Joel's magic is too strong."

"Or perhaps the demon knows that Joel's power is not magic at all," Rionn concluded.

Both Raxe and Quick flashed puzzled frowns.

"*Not* magic?" Quick asked. "How can that be?"

"According to a volume of the Heaven's War Journals I've been studying, the *bearer* of the weapon had the charge of sending escaped demons back to the seven hells," Rionn gestured at Raxe. "But he who *would be* the weapon was charged with guarding the Hell Gate from those who would seek to have it opened. I will quote the text:"

> *"He who would be the Weapon will bear the task of the Gatekeeper, for it is this Child who must protect the Hell Gates from violation. Be it man, beast, or divinity, the Weapon will stand against all those who would breach damnation for ill purpose."*

"How does that translate into Joel not having magic?" Raxe asked.

"He who would be the Weapon has to stand against man, beast, and divinity," Rionn repeated. "He has to be able to stand against magic."

"Including anti-magic!" Quick blurted.

"The Leaders developed methods to neutralize the power of the Protectors," Rionn started. "That was a form of anti-magic, or negative magic that acts inward upon itself as opposed to outward upon the physical or metaphysical plane. They used living creatures to create voids that absorbed all magical energy within a particular radius."

Raxe nodded his understanding before he spoke. "But those voids are still a form of magic…created by divinity, no less. That means the Weapon would have to have been made to stand against that as well. And the only real counter to magic or anti-magic is no magic at all."

Quick was intrigued but unconvinced. "What power does he wield, then, if not magic?"

"I will let the offworlder explain," Rionn said.

Raxe was initially at a loss. He considered why the Head Mage, as knowledgeable as he was, would defer to him. And then the answer hit him like a bolt. There was only one thing Raxe would have knowledge of that Rionn Lorr would be clueless about.

"You know about the technology of my world, Quick."

"Yes," Quick said. "The things you've told me about technology are wonders that rival the magic of this world. But your technology is that of lifeless instruments used mainly for utilitarian or calculation purposes."

"Yes," Raxe agreed. "I told you about mechanical technology but there's another kind. There are methods of altering and manipulating the physical nature of living organisms. It's called genetic engineering." He paused to let Quick think on it for a moment before he continued.

"Genetic engineers have made accomplishments that seem like miracles even to the people of my world. Imagine what could be accomplished on a genetic level by the power and intelligence of an Old One."

"Yes," Quick acknowledged, "But would that not still be magic if performed by an Old One?"

"When Jon uses his magic to ignite a fire," Rionn contributed, "his power manipulates the elements to produce the resulting fire. The resulting flames however, are not invested with magic."

Raxe chimed in. "Remember when you froze the moisture on scythe wings' feathers, Quick? Did the water itself become a thing of magic?"

"Of course not," Quick answered. "I used my magic to turn the water into ice, but it was still only –" understanding dawned on him. "It was only frozen water."

"Living organisms are made up of trillions of smaller elements called cells," Raxe explained. "Genetic technology uses heat energy called radiation as well as chemicals to manipulate cells to alter the organisms, sometimes in small ways and sometimes in terrible ways. The Old Ones would have been able to manipulate cells in a much more precise and effective way than anything the technology of my world could. If they wanted to, I'm pretty sure they could do it without the resulting organism being infused with magic."

Rionn added. "I believe the Old Ones created the Weapon in such a way that his abilities would be passed on to his descendants, to use some inner physical or emotional catalyst independent of magic."

Quick's eyes shone. "The way a chameleon changes hue, or a firefly illuminates, or a land dragon expands to almost twice its bulk and spits acid, the Old Ones have altered Joel's bloodline to transform them into juggernauts when they are in mortal danger."

"That would explain why we can't detect his aura," Raxe deduced. "The Old Ones must have meant it to be that way. And from what I've seen, his power increases in direct proportion to the threat he's facing. If he had to go against...well, against one of *us*, his abilities would be a decided advantage for him."

"Exactly," Rionn Lorr said softly. His blue eyes settled gravely on Raxe's brown ones. "And we can only guess at the extents of his ability. If his destructive potential is in any way comparable to yours, Raxe, in the presence of demons, then I pray to the Ascendant One that we never have to face him in battle."

The spark of realization and awe in Quick's eyes suddenly darkened in realization and concern. The very thought of facing a Child of the Old Ones in combat frightened him to his core. Even though he had killed a Child of the Old Ones three years earlier, he held no illusions about his chances in another such confrontation. He managed to fatally shoot Mar-dah with Raxe's gun only because the malevolent wizard was distracted by the business of killing the Head Mage and his wife, the offworlder, and the entire Royal Court.

And in any event, such an attack would never work on Joel. His power protected him seemingly to the point of invulnerability. Quick had witnessed this with his own eyes. He had taken one more fleeting glance into Hargathall's Cleft with his keen vision as he and Raxe made their escape and was aghast at what he saw there. The vivid memory of Joel tearing through the *Ken d'Zanir* warriors like so much chaff was still disturbingly fresh in his mind.

Rionn Lorr turned slowly and stepped back onto the outer deck. Quick stared blankly out the window, Rionn Lorr's last sentence echoing in his mind.

If his destructive potential is in any way comparable to yours, Raxe, in the presence of demons, then I pray to the Ascendant One that we never have to face him in battle.

The rest of the day was blessedly uneventful. Rionn Lorr periodically went to the pilot's box to speak to the pilot and navigator. Raxe busied himself with his exercises. Quick watched him perform the same stretching exercises he had shown Ethan. Raxe also did several forms of what he called push-ups and sit-ups and fought invisible opponents, something he called shadowboxing. Quick spent much of his free time in meditation and mentally reciting spells and doing a bit of his own shadow boxing of a sort as he practiced at swordplay. He and the offworlder even sparred as the Head Mage looked on.

The two suns dipped below the western horizon while the three moons crept into the darkening eastern skies. By the time the bright white orbs were at their apex, both Raxe and Rionn Lorr were lying fast asleep on cots. None of them had slept the previous night. All of them were too excited by and consumed with their circumstances. Sleep finally caught up to them. Quick looked at them with a bit of envy. His body was tired but he could not sleep, certainly not his *true* sleep, which required him to take his original form. He would take his original form only when he was in complete solitude and safely hidden.

He trusted Rionn Lorr and Raxe and Ethan Sureblade with his life, but he would reveal his true form to no one. It was a deeply ingrained survival instinct of his species that was as essential to him as breathing.

He could rest in the traditional way of whatever form he took, though it was not as replenishing as his true sleep. Even a traditional rest was impossible at the moment. His thoughts kept drifting to Joel, and when his thoughts took that path, the worry that accompanied them wiped away any hope of sleep for the young changeling.

Quick did not trust Joel. It was not that he thought the man was evil. He simply was not a fighter and had no desire to be. The changeling did not have the confidence in Joel that he did in Raxe. Raxe was battle-tested and courageous. Joel, on the other hand, was not made for war. Quick would never trust him with his life the way he would and had with Rionn, Raxe, the late Meldrick Sureblade or Ethan.

He did not even trust that Joel would always pick the correct side on which to fight. As much as Raxe railed against the Kingdom of Lorr on his first visit, Quick could always tell that Raxe had the best interest of the Kingdom at heart. The same could not be said for his fellow offworlder. Quick thought of Joel as a coward, and under the wrong type of influence, Quick did not doubt that Joel could be turned against them. If a sixth level demon could use such a weapon for its own designs… Quick shuddered again at the thought.

9.5

Rionn, Quick, and Raxe traveled in silence for much of the remaining trip. By early afternoon of the second day, Quick and Rionn Lorr stood on the outer deck and looked expectantly to the southern horizon. They could see the vast expanse of the Forsaken desert spreading out across the southern lands. Both frowned curiously as the northern edges of the great desert came slowly into view on the far side of the wall of mountains that composed the termination point of the southern Hells.

As if the new river that ran through the once-dry valley was not strange enough, the site just to the south of the Hells was stranger still. A dark brown peninsula among the vast pale brown ocean of sand extended from the southern line of the mountain range deep into the desert. The darker, hardened area was not flat, but its irregular rise and fall was a fraction of the size of the hilly dunes surrounding it.

From the half-mile above the earth that the sky sleigh flew, cracks in the dried earth gave the hardened expanse the look of a desiccated, flaky-topped, giant mud pie that had been baked by sunlight until it was as hard as rock. The semicircular area had a width of about six miles.

"By the Gods..." Quick swore as he stared at the packed, hardened sand.

"From sand to stone," Raxe mused, looking out at the phenomenon through the open porthole door. "Rionn, that little girl of yours has a gift."

"Many gifts," Rionn corrected.

"How much water did it take to do that?" Quick asked.

"A great deal, no doubt," Rionn Lorr answered. "In fact, it took a surging wave nearly a mile high."

"Yes," Quick concurred. "But this result...it's amazing."

"Azhju'lestra was very powerful," Rionn observed. "She had the power of faerie enhanced by the magic of the Old Ones. I shudder to think of how powerful she would have become had she lived to her full maturity."

"I, too," Quick agreed.

"Prepare for descent, young one," Rionn instructed. "I must confer with the pilot for a moment.

Raxe was inside the cabin lost in thought about the last conversation he had with the Head Mage and the changeling. The exchange caused him to reluctantly consider how he would challenge his distant cousin should the need ever arise. He felt bad for Joel. Fate had been cruel to him recently. As much as he hoped he would never face Joel in combat, one of the first things he learned early in his military career, as well as his training with his mother and grandfather, was to be prepared for anything.

As he sat against a wall without windows, lost in thought, a familiar, loathing sensation swept through him. That cold dread oozed from marrow to bone to flesh and quickly turned into seething, silver heat that seeped through his skin and illuminated the air around him.

Quick walked into the cabin and immediately noticed the glow out of the corner of his eye. He turned to see Raxe sitting rigid on the bench with look of grim resignation. Rionn Lorr rushed into the cabin and stopped short when he saw the silver glow that slowly intensified around the offworlder Child.

"I see you feel it, as well," the Head Mage observed. "The Dierglyorr is near."

Rionn jerked his head down toward his cloak, startled. Raxe and Quick looked over at the wizard with alarm.

"It's nothing," Rionn assured. He reached into the collar of his robes and pulled out his speaking stone. "It's an Alliance agent with a message.

Rionn palmed the stone and his expression went blank, as though he was staring into nothingness. He spoke a few seconds later, but not to Raxe or Quick.

"Yes," Rionn said. "We feel its presence. Can you verify its location through the Eye?" Raxe and Quick looked on expectantly as Rionn listened to a voice that only he could hear through the speaking stone.

"That happens to be just where we are headed," Rionn said before going silent again. "Thank you," he concluded. "May the Old Ones guide you, as well."

He dropped his speaking stone back into his robes and gazed at the floor. The angry intensity he exuded was a palpable thing.

"What is it, Rionn?" Quick asked.

"I'm not sure yet," Rionn said thoughtfully. He said nothing else. The hard look on his face made it clear that he was not ready to discuss what he had been told.

Raxe absently thumbed one of Demonsbane's razor edges as he wondered what was said that made the Head Mage so upset. The warmth of the enchanted battleaxe's glow caressed Raxe's hand in anticipation of the confrontation with the sixth level demon.

And then, just as quickly as it came, the silver glow blinked out of existence.

A look of worry washed over the Head Mage. Quick frowned in surprise and fear. He could not feel the demon from such a distance the way the Children of the Old Ones could, but he could suddenly feel the familiar void within him that was once filled with his changeling power.

"Our magic is gone," Quick said needlessly.

Rionn Lorr stared resolutely out the window for a time before he finally spoke. "The demon is expecting us."

Raxe nodded in agreement. "This was a trap."

"So it would seem," Rionn Lorr agreed.

"How could it have known we were coming?" Quick asked. "*We* did not know we were coming until moments before we left."

"True," Rionn Lorr said. "And no one but us knew where we were going, no one besides my wife and daughter and Annastace. The crew did not even know where we were going until we were airborne. They would not have been able to send a message without us noticing. I was, in fact, monitoring them so I would know if they did."

A look of alarm came to Raxe's face. "You don't think Annastace…"

"Of course not," Rionn Lorr said with certainty. "I think it was coincidence."

Raxe sighed in relief but raised an eyebrow. "Why do you think that?"

"It would not surprise if the demon terminated its concealing spell so I would detect the Hell Key and come to retrieve it," Rionn told them. "But I could not feel the weapon's presence until after we were already more than halfway here."

Raxe's eyes widened with realization. "If our magic is gone, so should the Dierrglyor's."

"True," Rionn Lorr concurred. "But I assume it's made preparations to ensure a decided advantage for itself."

Raxe frowned. "In hindsight, we should've brought some backup." He turned to the Head Mage. "What do you think is waiting for us down there?"

"Something very unpleasant," Rionn assured.

Chapter 10: Trapped

10.1

Raxe looked out the porthole with awe at the new river – or, the resurrected river, thanks to his daughter – just before the sky sleigh began its descent. How many people died during the river's rebirth?

The sky sleigh dipped lower and swung around the southeastern edge of Hell's Mountains and touched down carefully on the hardened area of sand on the northern fringes of the desert less than a quarter of a mile away from the foot of the Hells. It was the same distance from the northeastern curve of the hardened sands. The narrow front end of the sleigh pointed south and the southern edge of Hell's Mountains was at their back. The pilot and navigator were skeptical about landing on the unfamiliar surface but the Head Mage assured them that the area was solid enough to hold the sleigh and the heavy avicaws.

Rionn Lorr started with wonder as he walked down the ramp and took in the artificial isthmus in the sea of sand. The extent of the transformation of the desert expanse was even more fascinating up close. The ground reminded the Head Mage of the dry, rough surface of the Deadwood Forest without the petrified skeletal trees. Quick, following down the ramp, shared in the Head Mage's fascination, as evidenced by his wide eyes and open mouth.

Raxe was the last to de-board. His eyes followed the hard-packed ground into the distance where it ended in a sharp line and transformed into flowing sand dunes. The view of the distant desertscape undulated from the terrible heat blazing down from the two suns and rising from the blistering sands. The only moisture to be found was the sweat that had already starting streaming from everyone's skin.

"This part is as hard as concrete, if not as smooth," Raxe observed. He wondered how many lives were lost in the creation of this stony platform among the desert sands.

One of the lives lost was quite possibly Shara Dune. Raxe had never met the Queen of the Forsaken Desert but he heard rumors of how beautiful she was. He was kind of sad about never having seen her with his own eyes. He had, however, met and fought many of her demon-spawn sand creatures. Most of the lives lost, hopefully, would have been those four-tentacled monsters.

"Concrete?" Quick asked.

"It's like mortar," Raxe explained. "It hardens to something very similar to stone."

The desert was ominously silent, though it was not exactly a hub of activity to begin with. The oppressive heat and lack of water were obvious natural deterrents. In addition to that, most sane people stayed away from it out of fear of the desert queen and her sand creatures pulling them under the dunes never to be seen again.

This was a different kind of silence. The quiet was, Raxe thought, disquieting. The pale silver shimmer of magic that he had become so accustomed to seeing around every living thing and natural landscape was conspicuously missing. That shimmer was his personal way of sensing magic, and without it, the landscape seemed utterly alien.

"Do you feel that?" Quick asked. "Can you *hear* it?"

"Feel what?" Raxe asked. "*Hear* what?"

"Vibrations," Quick told them. "As if something was –"

Rionn knelt, holding his long, crooked staff in his right hand, and put his left hand palm-down and fingers spread to the hardened surface.

"Coming from beneath the sand," he concluded.

Rionn stood and turned to wave to the pilot and navigator in the pilot box of the sky sleigh. The men saw the signal, and with deft manipulations of the reins, the avicaws took wing and lifted the sky sleigh into the air. The huge sleigh birds flew away noticeably more quickly than usual and were clearly agitated. He switched his staff to his left hand and wrapped his right around the grip of the broadsword hanging from his left hip. With their magic already gone, he knew the blade would be of more use to him than his wizard's staff.

A cold grip of fear seized Rionn for a moment. While he was more than a little disoriented by the absence of the magic that had been a part of him his entire life, the void was no longer a new sensation for him. He experienced it when the

Ken d'Zanir commenced their campaign against the Kingdom of Lorr and the Children of the Old Ones.

"I can feel it now," Raxe said worriedly. A loud pop sounded. Raxe ducked at the sound. It was similar to the report of a large caliber firearm. "And I can hear it, too!"

The ground rocked beneath their feet, causing all three men to scramble to retain their footing. Rionn and Quick drew their swords. Raxe pulled Demonsbane out with his left hand, forced it into his deformed right hand with a painful snap, and then drew Questblade.

Another loud crack followed the vibrations. And then the quaking, rumbling and cracking sounds came in long, sustained bursts. The thunderous cracking and jolting earth built to a crescendo that made it seem as if the rock-hard sand was about to explode but the hardened surface held fast. The assault from below stopped abruptly.

"What the hell *was* that?" Raxe wondered aloud.

"They couldn't break through," Rionn said with an exhalation of relief.

"*What* couldn't break through?" Raxe asked.

His question was answered when, in the distance, just past the curved perimeter of the cracked, hardened surface, the trio saw mounds of varying sizes rise up in the loose sand. There were too many of them to count, easily more than one hundred, as they swelled up just around the solid island like coarse gooseflesh on the skin of a giant.

The mounds grew until the sand fell away to reveal what was underneath: barrel-chested, barrel-bellied, spindly-legged monsters with skin the same pale yellow as the sand and four tentacles extruding from their torsos. Each tentacle brandished a different deadly weapon.

"Sand creatures," Rionn Lorr said, lifting his broadsword.

"More than just sand creatures," Quick added. Instead of lifting his broadsword, he slid it back into the sheath on his hip and loosened the buckle that held the leather straps against his torso.

"What else?" Raxe asked as he brandished his enchanted battleaxe and short sword.

The absence of Demonsbane's warm glow in the presence of the sand demons made the enchanted weapon feel as foreign to him as it did when he felt its magic for the very first time. He fought down the surge of fear that came with the unfamiliar feel of his weapon. As much as he loathed the power of Demonsbane, he had grown dependent on it, especially against sand creatures.

Raxe had no idea how well he would fare against the demon-spawn monsters without his magic to rely upon, but he resigned himself to the fact that he was about to find out. He lifted the battleaxe, letting the pain in his right hand sear his apprehension into a sharp-edged focus. He looked on the bright side. At least he did not have to resist the instinct to kill. Sand creatures were not human.

But Quick had just said there were more than just sand creatures out there.

"What else?" Raxe repeated.

"Look there," Quick said, pointing at another group of growing mounds while pulling the covered bundle from his back. Those mounds were almost as tall as the sand creatures, but not as broad. When the sand finally fell away, the men could see why.

"Oh shit," Raxe breathed. "*Ken d'Zanir.*"

"Oh *shit*, indeed," Rionn Lorr concurred.

There were only several dozen of them, close to fifty or a few more. They were the survivors of Joel's onslaught at Hargathall's Cleft. Without Quick and Rionn's magic, the several dozen of them alone were easily sufficient to overwhelm them without any assistance from the even more dangerous sand creatures.

An instant later they saw yet another group of mounds emerging in the midst of the sand creatures and the *Ken*. These mounds were three times the size of the earlier mounds. They were broader and much, much longer. Rionn Lorr knew what they were even before the sand fell away. They were the mounts of the *Ken d'Zanir*. And they outnumbered their masters more than two to one.

The suns' light gleamed from the long central horn and cluster of smaller horns atop the chameleon-like heads of the beasts. They bared black gums and razor-sharp teeth in hungry snarls. The muscles and sinew quivered beneath their thick, scaly, dark green hides. All six of their long legs twitched excitedly.

"Land dragons, *Ken d'Zanir*, sand creatures," Raxe observed. "Us with no magic. This keeps getting better."

"You have a strange perception of the word 'better,' offworlder," Rionn noted. "The only good thing about our situation is the hardened sand beneath our feet. Without it, they would already be upon us. At least we have a few moments to gather ourselves before they reach us."

Raxe shrugged. "It's kind of a compliment, when you think about it. All of this weight against little old us."

The Head Mage frowned. "I forgot how morbid your sense of humor was in combat."

"Quick," Raxe turned to the changeling, who was busying himself with the removal of the cloth covering from his bundle. "What are you doing? Are you ready, kid?"

The adolescent changeling pulled the cloth free. Raxe's eyes went wide when he saw what Quick was holding.

Rifles.

They were actually more like long-nosed, double-handled versions of the modified nine-millimeter Raxe brought with him on his first trip to the Kingdom of Lorr. The rear stock was proportionately elongated to provide support and to house the nearly foot-long cartridge that held the ammunition for this scaled-up pistol. There was also a handle added to the bottom of the barrel at the halfway point for extra support of the weapon's length and wait. The trigger was built into the rear stock.

There were other differences in addition to the expertly conceived modifications to account for the larger size of the rifles. A small scope was attached near the rear base of the barrel, a miniaturized version of the spyglass that Raxe had seen used on this side of the WorldGate. Other than those few modifications, the weapons matched his nine's design all the way up to the safety and the polished black steel that gleamed in the suns' light.

"Who made these?" Raxe demanded. His voice carried relief and admonition at the same time.

Quick saw the anger in Raxe's eyes and explained quickly. "The parts that I could not fashion on my own, I had made in several different smithies scattered around different towns and villages; in different kingdoms, even. No one knew what the strange pieces were for and none of them had enough information to discern their use. I collected the pieces over time and assembled them."

The Head Mage recognized the weapons from the one Raxe had gifted to Quick three years earlier. "You gave this a lot of thought, then?" he questioned sternly.

"Indeed, sirs," Quick assured. "I know your concerns, I share them as well. That is why I went about it the way I did, and that is why I stopped at only two of the weapons."

"I can't say I'm not happy to see those things under the circumstances," Raxe admitted. "But we have to have a talk about this later…if there is a later."

"Yes, Raxe," Quick said respectfully.

"I must admit that I am happy as well," Rionn Lorr added. He let his staff rest against his shoulder and pulled a spyglass from the folds of his robe and trained it on their enemies. He lost count of the number of warriors and monsters that had emerged from the surrounding dunes. "I only hope you have enough ammunition. From the numbers facing us, you would need an abundant supply."

Quick surveyed the dunes for a moment, frowned, and slowly shook his head. "If we felled a target – or even two – with each shot, we would decrease their number by not quite a third."

"That's not quite a third fewer we have to fight with these," Raxe said, hoisting his battleaxe and short sword. He slipped them back into their respective holders and took one of the two firearms from the changeling. "I hope you're a good shot, kid."

"I've practiced," Quick said confidently. The confident smirk turned instantly to a frown of worry. "I only wish I had another for you, Master Lorr."

"Worry not, young one," Rionn said with a strong hand on the changeling's shoulder. "I am thankful you brought what you have. You have bought us more time, and that is all that we could ask for."

"I do have this," Quick said, pulling Raxe's old modified nine millimeter pistol and releasing the safety. He held the weapon out to Rionn. Quick noticed the uncertain expression on his mentor's face. "You don't have to worry about being proficient with the weapon. Just hold it in both hands," Quick mimicked the way Rionn should hold it as he continued. "And then point and shoot. With their numbers it will be nearly impossible not to hit *anything*."

Despite their circumstances, Raxe grinned at the young changeling instructing his mentor on shooting a gun.

"What kind of range do these things have?" he asked as he hefted the weapon and aimed at the forces on the dunes. He noticed the scope did not have a crosshairs, but then again, the changeling had great eyesight and didn't need crosshairs. *And neither do I*, Raxe said to himself.

"The bullets can completely pierce the trunk of a thick oak from just over one hundred yards," Quick replied.

"Pretty good," Raxe complimented. "Too bad it's not enough to hit *that* guy," he added, gesturing with the nose of the firearm toward the peak of a distant sand dune.

The sand was falling away from one last *Ken d'Zanir*. Raxe recognized him from a brief glance at the rim of Hargathall's Cleft. It was the *Ken* with the large blue-feathered headrest and black, ugly rock hanging from a hide thong around his neck. Raxe recognized him as the leader.

Only a few yards behind the *Ken* chieftain emerged another figure from the sand. This one was not as large as the *Ken* around him. He did not wear the leather armor the sacred warriors wore. He wore a hooded wizard's robe. The heavy hood was pulled up to conceal the wearer's face in shadow. From the broadness of the shoulders, however, Raxe was fairly certain the stranger was a man. He trained his scope directly on the hood. The shadows were too deep to see the face from that distance, but the one thing in that dark hood he could see sent a chill through his body.

Twin flickers of blood red light shimmered in the darkness of the hood, right where a human's eyes would be.

"The Dierglyorr," Rionn whispered.

"I smell its rotten stench from here," Quick snarled.

Raxe remained silent and continued to look through his scope. The offworlder watched the red eyes survey the warriors, sand creatures and land dragons that spread out around the dunes. After sweeping to the left and right, the red burning orbs found Raxe from almost two hundred yards, and without a scope.

"This looks familiar, Children," the stranger called out. Even without their magic, the Children and the changeling could feel the cold evil its voice projected across the distance on the hot desert air. "Over two thousand years ago, I led a similar army against your ancestors. Of course, *that* army was much larger than this one."

"Be not a coward and join your charges in the fight," challenged the Head Mage. "I think you will find the results will be quite different this time!"

The Dierglyorr let out a blood-curdling laugh. "I've no time to waste on powerless Children! I've more pressing matters. You must realize: I am about to conquer *two worlds!*"

Raxe watched the robed demon mount the nearest land dragon and yank the reigns, causing the large six-legged lizard to rear up on its hind legs and turn. The lizard leapt away in long bounds only slightly slower in the deep sands than they would have been on solid ground.

"Coward," Rionn spat. "It won't fight without its magic, even with all of these men and beasts with him." He raised his spyglass again to watch the demon flee and then turned his gaze to the leader of the *Ken d'Zanir*.

The chieftain also had a spyglass, and he saw his prey looking back at him. *Ken* Rkam Lonos smiled.

"CHILDREN OF THE OLD ONES!" He called. His booming voice traveled to them clearly across the dry, still air. "AND YOU, MAGIC-BEFOULED CHANGELING, YOUR MAGIC IS GONE! PREPARE TO MEET YOUR GODS!"

He roared an unintelligible battle cry that sent the throngs of men and beasts surging onto the hardened sand.

10.2

Joel sat in a windowless cabin as *Cloud Scythe* touched down in the airfield at Port Lorrian. He did not mind looking out of the sky sleigh's windows when the vessel was in mid-flight anymore, but his stomach was already twisting and turning from the jostling of the landing. He had no desire to add to his discomfort the vertigo of watching the ground rise up to meet them.

When the final hard thud vibrated through the sky sleigh, followed by the creak and thump of sleigh doors being dropped, Joel stood and released himself from the safety strap. As he made his way to the exit he caught the briefest glimpse of Coortahn who, true to his word, avoided the offworlder during the entire flight. Joel imagined it would be pretty tough to feel safe around a man who tossed you off of a sky sleigh as easily as a child discards a candy wrapper.

All thoughts of Coortahn vanished when Joel started down the door-ramp and saw two of the most beautiful women he had ever seen standing to either side of a cute little girl. He immediately recognized Annastace Sureblade. She was there when he first arrived on this side of the WorldGate and she was not the type of woman one would easily forget. Large chocolate brown curls tumbled down either side of her round face, creating a perfect frame for her deep honey complexion, hazel eyes, and full lips.

Joel had never met the blonde woman and little girl, but he knew who they were. He heard Rionn Lorr talk about them during the brief time they traveled together. The woman's long pale blonde hair, which was pulled up into a neat bun, exposed her exotic features: unusually hight cheekbones, sharply arching pale blonde eyebrows, slightly but noticeably pointed ears, and pale green eyes that canted upwards at the outside corners. She had to be Catherine, the Head Mage's half-elf wife.

One glance at the girl and Joel could see both Rionn and Catherine Lorr all over her. Her naturally tanned complexion was identical to her father's. Her hair was the same pale blonde as her mother's. Her eyes, though not tilted like her mother's, were an identical shade of pale green. And even if she had not looked so much like her parents, her scent would have left no doubt. He could smell the magic on her, so much like Rionn's and somewhat like Ryan and Dan, the magic of the Children of the Old Ones.

Joel reached the bottom of the ramp and stopped before them. From the way the three females looked expectantly at him, he knew they had been waiting for him. The only thing he did not know, however, was what they were doing there. Where the hell were Raxe and Rionn Lorr?

"Hello ladies," he greeted. "Why do I get the feeling you're not here to escort me to the castle?"

"You must travel to the Forsaken Desert," Catherine said without preamble.

Joel took a step back toward the ramp. "Wait, what?" he asked. He had never been there, but he saw the vast desert in the western distance, just beyond the Demon's Spine when *Cloud Scythe* lifted off from Shaddiston three days earlier. "That's back where I came from. I thought we were supposed to meet up here."

"They've been and gone," Annastace told him. "Their search for the Hell Key has taken them back across the southwestern border."

Shandie stepped closer and looked up pleadingly at him with her big green eyes. "They need you! Their auras, both Raxe and my daddy's, are gone. They must be in trouble."

Joel shook his head. He thought about the breakdown he suffered just days earlier. Though he defeated the evil, he did not think he would be so lucky against the madness that threatened to overtake him when he woke up on that hillside. The memory of preying on a giant badger might have been lost to him, but the aftermath of it was bad enough.

The massacre at Hargathall's Cleft came vividly back to him. The ordeal had been so surreal, so unbelievable, that with a monumental effort he had almost managed to push it to the back of his consciousness like a bad nightmare.

During his trek back to Port Lorrian, riding with the Ministress Hargrave and then with Harl Timson, he was able to find distractions from the gruesome slaughter. But now, the thought of going once more into a situation that would bring his power to bear was too much for him.

The rank odors of death came back to him. The sounds of tearing flesh and crunching bone and the screams of the dying echoed in his mind. He could taste the blood again. The memories brought the bile surging to the back of his throat only slightly less quickly than it had when he was tearing those men to pieces with such terrible ease.

And then his heart began to beat faster and faster, until the thud of his pounding heart and whoosh of blood rushing through his ears drowned out the screams. The cold fear of an oncoming asthma attack from his psychological strain put him on the verge of panic, but while his breathing started to come in quick, nervous pants, it remained unrestricted.

The word "No" pushed its way to his lips but he pushed it back. His power felt like a curse, but *the Lord never gives us a burden greater than we can bear,* he reminded himself. With that reminder came the realization that his power was not a curse. It was a burden, without question, but it had saved his life. It had saved the lives of others. He took several deep breaths just to be sure he could, and fought to keep his knees from shaking.

Both Annastace and Shandie looked surprised at his hesitation. Catherine only looked sad.

"Rionn explained his theory of how your power works," she said soothingly. "I understand your trepidation, but –"

Joel cut her off with a bitter scoff. "Lady," he said, "You can't *begin* to understand. If I become that monster again, I don't think there's any way I can keep my sanity."

"I would risk it for someone I loved," argued Annastace, her pretty face rigid with concern. "I would risk it if it meant saving countless lives. What manner of man would not?"

Joel sighed. "I don't want to, but I never said I wouldn't."

The women and the girl relaxed visibly, but then a thought occurred to Joel.

THE KEY QUEST

"The desert is a long way away. If they're already in trouble, how the hell do you expect me to get there in time to help them?"

The women remained silent at that. They knew he had a point with which they could not argue. As well as Ryan could fight, the demon would have prepared for him and Rionn Lorr the same way it had prepared for Ryan at Hargathall's Cleft. Joel was the wild card then, but if they were in danger, and without their magic, a three or four-day sky-sleigh trip would hardly be of any use to them.

Annastace and Catherine cast worried glances at each other. And then the little girl beamed with a devious sparkle in her eye.

"Shandie," Catherine said worriedly, seeing her daughter's sudden smile. "No. The distance is too great. You do not have the strength."

Joel had a pretty good idea where this was going and he did not like it. He did not believe the little girl could do what they were hinting at, but at the same time, he could not dismiss the possibility. This was the Head Mage's daughter, after all.

"No," Catherine repeated. "The strain could be too much. Azhju'lestra lost her life from too great an exertion of magic. We will summon some Master Mages and –"

"There's no time," Shandie whined insistently. "They're not strong enough to send him there."

"Your mom's right," Joel added. "You might hurt yourself, and you just said you couldn't feel their presence. You wouldn't even know where to aim."

The little girl's blonde eyebrows bunched together in deep thought for a long, silent moment. Catherine saw the vacant look that fell over her daughter's countenance and recognized it at once. Shandie used farsight to keep track of her father when he was away. This time was no different.

Shandie had followed Rionn on his way to the desert until he entered the black circle and she could no longer see him. Just like the other times in the past few weeks when his presence had faded from her feelings, it made her so afraid she wanted to cry. She was almost four years old, though, and crying was for babies.

Daddy told her that when she had a problem she should not fret over it. She should find a solution. So she tried. She followed the path her father's sky sleigh traveled until she encountered the void. Once there, she looked and looked all around the edges of the black circle that hid her father from her but she could never find him inside the darkness.

There was one thing she *did* find, though.

Catherine was still shaking her head "no" while Annastace looked worriedly at both mother and daughter in turn. At first Joel did not understand Annastace's anxiety. Her son was not with the Head Mage and Ryan. Why would she be so worried? And then he recalled the way she and Ryan looked at each other.

Joel gave a mental shrug. He felt sorry for her, but there was nothing he could do if he could not get to the Forsaken Desert in time to help.

And then the little girl smiled mischievously. Her mother frowned with worry.

10.3

The long, spindly legs of the sand creatures propelled them forward at a speed that almost rivaled the swift land dragons. Rionn Lorr prayed to the Lord Ascendant that their magic would return before they ran out of ammunition, but in his heart he knew that was not to be. There were far too many of them to begin with, and the tough hides of the land dragons and sand creatures would likely make them difficult to bring down with only one or two shots.

Raxe looked on as the demon's hordes raged forward, trying to ignore the helplessness of their situation while marking their progress so that he could start shooting the moment they came into range. He had faced terrible odds before but he was almost always ready. At the very least he always made it a point to have an escape route.

The only other time he had been hopelessly outnumbered with no escape was when the organization attacked him at his Chicago apartment building. Back then Rionn Lorr had unwittingly saved him by pulling him through the WorldGate as Raxe fell from a third floor window. There would be no such rescue this time.

Raxe regretted that they realized too late that they were walking into a trap, but there was nothing to be done for it. It was a risk they had to take. He tried to content himself with the thought that he had done all he could do to atone for the lives he had taken in the past but there was no contentment to be found. How could three years of relative restraint make up for over a decade of killing? It had not been enough, though it was all he could do in the time allotted to him.

If he was to die this day, he could not think of a more interesting way to go. His only regret was that he would never see Annastace's beautiful face again.

So intent was he on the coming battle that it took a moment for him to notice the strange shadow sailing in behind them from the north. He risked a glance skyward and was equal parts relieved, shocked and puzzled by what he saw. Dozens upon dozens of long, dangerously sharpened wooden poles, some black, some red-brown and some pale brown, cut through the sky headed directly toward the approaching enemy.

The demon's forces saw it as well. The *Ken* began pointing and frantically yelling something over and over in their native language. Even though Raxe could not understand them, their reaction to the oncoming hail of death gave him a good idea of what they must have been saying.

It had to be their equivalent of "Move! Move! Move!"

And move they did. The mounted *Ken* steered their land dragons to the right, away from the approach of the deadly missiles. The land dragons without riders were smart enough to follow them. The sand creatures also scrambled, breaking from their headlong dash into a wild, scrambling attempt to dodge the incoming bolts.

The Head Mage looked up at the missiles arcing overhead and smiled. He could not see the source of their projection but he did not have to. He knew exactly who had given the command.

Lieutenant Colonel Rheingold Strong was smiling, too. His smile, however, was not a smile of relief or happiness. His was a cold smile of vengeance, a smile of joy from the promise of mayhem, of the need for retribution at last fulfilled. If a hungry wraith wolf could smile after running down an elusive doe at the end of a lengthy chase, it would be Colonel Strong's twin at that moment.

As he gave the command to launch the bolts, Strong reveled in the satisfaction of engaging the *Ken* with the same tactic that had devastated his company back at Lake Onyx. From the *Ken*'s current numbers, Strong could see that they had already been devastated by some other force, but Strong was more than happy to deal death to the remaining warriors.

For a time it seemed they would never catch the foreign invaders in time to help the Children. Strong's men were battered and bruised, reduced to a fraction of their original number by the *Ken's* surprise attack.

The *Ken* moved faster on their land dragons than Strong's forces could on their horses. Strong's forces had also been slowed by the time it took them to build the ballistae they were using to assault the *Ken* and their sand creature allies. But they were here now. They finally had the opportunity to repay the *Ken d'Zanir* in kind for their treachery and they were anxious to make the most of it.

When the last volley of wooden bolts was launched, Colonel Strong drew his straight sword and pointed the blade to the two suns.

"For our brothers who fell at Lake Onyx!" he cried.

"FOR LAKE ONYX!!" his men returned.

"For the innocents at Port Lorrian and the village of Hillview that died at their hands!" Strong continued.

"PORT LORRIAN AND HILLVIEW!!" his men cried.

"For the Blessed Kingdom of Lorr!!" Strong went on, his volume and pitch rising higher and higher.

"FOR THE KINGSOM OF LORR!!" his men raged.

"Let's show these brutal sons of bitches the meaning of BLOODTHIRSTY!!"

With a collective savage roar, the remnants of Colonel Rheingold Strong's royal company raised their weapons and charged down the mountain and into the Forsaken Desert.

Many of the *Ken*, their land dragons, and the sand creatures could not get out of the way in time as death thundered down upon them. Screams of pain, both human and inhuman, rang out across the desert. The heavy, wickedly pointed shafts with their gravity-fueled momentum easily penetrated the thick hides of sand creatures. Blackwood bolts shattered the land dragons' rock-hard scales like glass and plunged into the tough flesh beneath. The teak bolts could not penetrate the land dragons' scales but the force of impact broke bones and crippled the beasts.

Dozens of corpses of men, beasts and monsters littered both the soft and hardened sand within a few grisly seconds.

Multi-hued puddles of blood oozed together to form pools of sickly green, blue-black, and crimson.

In the next instant, a cacophony of howls and roars of battle cries erupted from overhead and behind Quick, Rionn Lorr and Raxe. The trio turned again and saw soldiers – cavalry, foot soldiers, and Gryphon Ryders – surge over a rise at the foot of the Hell's directly behind and above them. The newcomers were ragged and fatigued. Dried blood stained their scuffed, dusty clothes as well as their armor and their mounts. Even so, they charged at a breakneck pace with weapons held high and faces set in grim determination.

"Colonel Strong," Rionn Lorr exhaled. "They made it after all."

Raxe nodded. "Cool," he said, hefting his rifle. "Let's improve the odds a little more for the good guys."

Despite the differences between this firearm and the ones of his world, the feel of the gun in Raxe's hand was both comfortable and familiar. He was amazed at how expertly the dwarven smiths were able to create the components of these long-barreled rifles based on the design of the nine-millimeter handgun.

He was also worried. In his world, the simple rifle was the precursor to all manner of terrible, destructive weapons. Such weapons provided false confidence to cowards, turning them into cold-blooded killers; transformed emotionally unstable individuals, who otherwise would likely have run away from their problems or turned their rage inward, into mass murderers.

Raxe had seen it all too often in the military and civilian worlds. Guns made killing too impersonal, too easy. In this world of magic, where the weak-minded, insecure, mentally disturbed and downright evil used magic the way the same kind of people in his world used guns, another destructive weapon was the last thing the Kingdom of Lorr needed.

As Raxe expertly dropped a land dragon or sand creature with each shot, striking the middle of their heads or their eyes or their throats or even gaping mouths, he realized how hypocritical his concerns sounded.

He, who had for so many years made his living using all manner of long-range, impersonal weaponry as a sniper and a fighter pilot, had the gall to be concerned about introducing guns to this world. But that was a different time, a different place. He was a different person. Three years ago he came to realize how wrong and how damned he was for those actions and he made an oath to never take another human life. He also decided to fight to save lives.

Raxe took care to avoid shooting any of the human enemies, who stayed well behind the approaching vanguard of sand creatures and land dragons. He noticed Quick was doing the same. For someone with just a few years of experience shooting firearms, Quick was a phenomenal shot. His aim was almost as true as Raxe's. It took him no more than two shots to bring down each of his targets.

Rionn was not really aiming. He was taking Quick's advice and just pointing and shooting. His broadsword was back in its sheath and his staff lay by his feet. As he fired, a look of menacing satisfaction was set in the chiseled lines of his tanned face. Just as Quick said, it took several shots to bring most of his targets down, but almost every shot hit something or someone. Unlike Quick and Raxe, however, Rionn was not hesitant to fire upon the *Ken d'Zanir*, but try as he might, the hard-charging monsters intercepted his shots more often than not.

The sound of gunfire rang out like mini thunderclaps. Raxe felt the weight of his weapon decrease as the massive cartridge emptied. He knew that all of them would soon be out of ammunition and there would still be too many surviving attackers. Sure enough, after a few dozen more land dragons and sand creatures fell, the guns' explosions became nothing more than harmless clicks.

The three men dropped their firearms and drew their bladed weapons. Rionn Lorr stomped down on the narrow tip of his staff to make the wide end flip into the air where he caught it in his left hand.

*   *   *

This was the moment High *Ken* Rkam Lonos had longed for. The Head Mage himself and the legendary Raxe, another Child of the Old Ones, were about to die at his command. The reensapir heart pulsed on his muscular chest, its warmth reassuring him that the magic workers were powerless.

Even with their reinforcements – less than two hundred men that Lonos immediately recognized as the sorry remains of the battalion that had been devastated by his *Ken d'Zanir* at Lake Onyx – Lonos knew that his men and beasts, especially with Shara Dune's sand creatures supporting his *Ken*, would make this a quick and bloody battle.

Each sand creature was more than a match for any four or five of them. The land dragons could kill anywhere from ten to a dozen of them before the king's men could bring them down. If only the *Ken* did not have to remove the beasts' acid sacs from their gullets to train them as mounts, the land dragons could easily kill twice as many.

The *Ken* were easily better than any two of the king's warriors. And without their magic, and with their fire-spitting metal rods spent, the magic wielders had no means of any consequence with which to assist the royal soldiers.

High *Ken* Rkam Lonos would find the dark wizard and demand a larger payment from him. With all the men he had lost, he deserved more than their original agreed upon fee. He would then return to the Fringes of S'Zan a hero with great wealth for his people and the honor of slaying many powerful magic workers.

The cavalry, foot soldiers, and Gryphon Ryders swept around and above Rionn, Raxe, and Quick to engage the demon's charges. They were met with a hail of arrows and spears, which they promptly countered with spears and arrows of their own.

Several of the gryphons and their Ryders went down immediately, as did several of the *Ken* and sand creatures. When the two forces met, both mounted and infantry, the battle commenced with nightmarish war cries and a deafening toll of steel on steel.

10.4

"KILL THEM ALL!" Lonos roared. "WE WILL BATHE IN THE BLOOD OF EVERY LAST LORRIAN!"

He was answered by the echoes of what sounded like stuttered explosions from the edge of the Hell's Mountains.

Quick tilted his head at the familiar sound. "Catapults?"

The explosive snaps of catapults were immediately followed by deep, bellowing roars, but not from his or allies or enemies. The sounds came from the same general direction as the royal soldiers but a little further west along the wall of mountains, and from a higher elevation.

Those not immediately engaged turned their eyes skyward in time to see what appeared to be dozens upon dozens of squat boulders covered with spiked metal plating tumbling lazily through the air, soaring directly toward the heart of the Dierrglyor's forces. They crashed to the earth with shuddering thuds, throwing up huge plumes of sand. Raxe lost sight of the projectiles among the massive bodies of the enemy but he could easily see the mad violent scramble that took place shortly after impact.

Raxe squinted at one of the armor-plated boulders as it neared the earth. Just before it struck, it unfolded. Stubby legs like sawed-off tree trunks descended while short but incredibly muscular arms popped outward from a broad torso. One meaty fist clutched a disproportionately wide short sword. The other held a studded cudgel. The wide head was protected by a horned helm. The flat face was half covered with a dark brown beard that was not quite thick enough to hide the newcomer's fierce grin. He brought his weapons down with maniacal force just as he vanished among the embattled *Ken,* sand creatures, and land dragons.

"Dwarves?" Rionn Lorr asked.

"The Stonehammer Nation!" Quick cried hopefully.

They looked back up to the line of the Hells and saw the last of the dwarves wheeling catapults out into the open along the mountainside. The catapults, like the dwarves themselves, were compact, stout and powerful. Three-dozen armored dwarven warriors, each with a long handled war axe strapped to his back, pushed his own catapult. Each catapult had its basket winched down and secured.

With hearty guffaws and taunts to one another, they scrambled into the catapult baskets. Their efforts were not exactly synchronized but they all pulled their war axes from their backs and used the long reach of the weapons to cut the ropes securing the arms of the catapults. They released with violent force and the dwarves soared high into the sky, curled into small but dense spheres of mayhem.

One of the flying dwarves fell directly toward the waiting tentacles of sand creature. The nearly seven foot tall monster flexed its bare, barrel of a chest as its four tapering tentacles brandished a broadsword, a dirk, a four-flanged mace and another broadsword. The puckered holes at the top if its three stubby head trunks hissed in anticipation.

Each one of its tentacles flashed into motion with blinding speed and surgical precision. The falling dwarf however, never unfolded from his fetal curl, exposing nothing but steel plates and thick leather armor. The sand creature obviously misjudged the inertia and sheer mass of its would-be target. Its inhumanly powerful swipes bounced harmlessly away as the dwarf slammed right into its chest, flattening the sand creature and creating a crater in the rock-hardened sand with a sickening crunch and a splash of thick green blood.

Only then did the dwarf come out of his tuck, staggering left to right yet holding his buckle and studded mace high, bellowing a challenge to the land dragon charging him.

Another dwarf lunged out of the midst of the fighting on his left, hefting a blackwood bolt longer than he was tall and as thick as the dwarf's stump-like thighs. The sharpened point of the dense wooden bolt forced its way between the scales on the charging land dragon's muscular neck. The surprising pain and the incredible strength of the dwarf bore the land dragon to the hard-crusted sand.

The blackwood bolt sunk deeper into the lizard's neck. The dwarf held on tight as the land dragon's skid across the rough surface pulled him along for the ride. The massive lizard's six legs thrashed frantically until its long claws found purchase. It sprang to its feet and whipped its head left and right with enough force to tear the bolt free, sending it and the dwarf slamming onto the sand. Despite the black blood spurting from its ruptured neck, the land dragon gathered itself to pounce on the blackwood bolt-wielding dwarf. Before it could leap, a studded mace slammed into the side of its head. The land dragon wobbled and finally fell dead.

"Ha!" the mace-wielding warrior roared. "One blow!"

"I softened it up for ye," yelled the dwarf with the blackwood bolt. "And I'd have finished it if ye hadn't butt in ye bloody bastard!"

"Tis *my* kill!" laughed the mace wielder as he dashed off to another skirmish.

A few of the dwarves remained tucked into violent balls of muscle, leather and steel and rolled along the hardened sand for as far as their momentum would carry them, bowling over *Ken* and breaking the long spindly shins of sand creatures until they finally came to a stop. At that point they exploded into motion, unleashing a torrent of savage blows upon whatever enemy stood before them.

One of them happened to come out of his roll just as a land dragon descended upon him. The doomed warrior brought his dirk up just as the massive jaws of the lizard engulfed him. The two-foot long dirk plunged down the land dragon's throat, but the arm was so short that the land dragon was still able to snap its jaws shut over the dwarf's sword arm, shoulder, head and neck. Both fell into the sand.

The land dragon coughed and gagged. It finally went still with dead, staring eyes with the point of the dwarf's blade emerging from the base of its skull. The dwarf's body rolled away, but its head and right arm remained in the dead land dragon's maw.

The rest of the dwarven warriors were similarly engaged, battling *Ken d'Zanir* to a relative standstill. What they lacked in speed and reach they easily made up for in brute strength and raw savagery. They had a much more difficult time with the sand creatures. The speed and skill with which the sand creatures handled their weapons with all four tentacles were too much for one dwarf.

The fierce warriors took a tentacle or two but they were soon overwhelmed by the powerful and lightening fast appendages. A few dwarfs simply shielded their heads and neck as best they could and barreled headlong into the sand creatures. A few managed to run through the deadly gauntlet of flashing steel to tear into the sand creature's bulging bellies with steel, stone, and sometimes even teeth.

A grim smile adorned the face of almost every one of the dwarves as they fought, cursed, taunted, killed and died. For a time their surprise arrival halted the surge being made by the demon's warriors. However, it did not take long for them to get over their initial shock. When they did, their numbers and sheer physical speed and power began to overwhelm even the formidable dwarven fighters.

The royal soldiers began to give ground. The defensive perimeter they formed around the changeling and the Children of the Old Ones began to collapse. Raxe, Quick, and Rionn prepared to join the fray when a booming voice stopped them in their tracks.

"Ho there! Head Mage, offworlder, Quick!"

The three of them turned to see another trio approaching. Two armed men, one tall and lanky and riding a gryphon, another broad and muscular and riding a massive brown warhorse, the third a gray-robed man of medium size riding a lean stallion. They looked as tired and weatherworn as the rest of the soldiers, and just as determined and fierce.

"It's good to see you, men," Rionn Lorr greeted. "Mage Raynard, I see you put your magic to good use assisting in the building of ballistae and carving of ammunition. But where did you find enough blackwood to fashion so many of those bolts? Blackwood trees do not grow on this continent."

Mage Gilder Raynard shrugged. "I only helped with carving the oak and ash bolts," he admitted. "We only had time and materials enough to build half a dozen ballistae. We found the blackwood bolts and the additional ballistae abandoned at Hargathall's Cleft. It seems the Old Ones saw fit to convince the *Ken* to leave us a much-needed present!"

"More like a *Child* of the Old Ones," Raxe said.

This information, along with the relatively small number of *Ken* they now faced, confirmed that Joel had been devastatingly successful back at Hargathall's Cleft. He wondered where his fellow offworlder and distant cousin was. They could sure as hell use his help.

"With all due respect, Master Lorr," Colonel Rheingold Strong yelled over the thunder of hooves and the din of battle, "Enough talk! It's time for the three of you to retreat. We've ridden hard and long to protect you and fulfill our charge, not to watch you fall!"

"Ha!" Raxe scoffed. "You'll have to kill me to keep me *out* of this!"

The offworlder howled, lifting Demonsbane in one hand and Questblade in the other. Quick was right beside him, brandishing his longsword. Rionn Lorr grimaced and followed. He smirked darkly to himself at the irony of how he, widely known as the most powerful mage in the Known Lands, was about to die in battle with a blade and club and absolutely no magic.

A sound that was part hiss and part roar came at them from the right. They all turned to see a land dragon bound over a group of fighting men and beasts to charge Quick. Its eyes and mouth were open wide, its long tongue lolling.

The nimble changeling leapt to the side to avoid the bulk of the nearly horse-sized lizard but he could not quite avoid the swiping claw at the end of the land dragon's long, spindly foreleg. The wicked appendage tore three deep parallel gashes across Quick's arm and sent him tumbling head over heels. The giant lizard pivoted and prepared to pounce on its wounded prey.

Raxe started toward the land dragon to help his friend. Before he could take two strides, the land dragon turned back toward him and leapt. Raxe tried to stop short but his momentum sent his metal-booted feet skidding forward. His inability to change direction and the land dragon's speed left him no options. He let the skid and gravity take him. His heels slid forward as he dropped backward. He flicked Demonsbane in an underhand swing just when the land dragon darted through the air where his face and neck had been just an instant earlier.

Demonsbane drew a thin black line down the iron-hard scales of the land dragon's underbelly as it passed over him. Raxe watched several of its six wicked claws slash down at him. Each one screeched ear-piercingly from chest to groin down Raxe's cuirass, hammering him to the hardened crust of the desert surface with a sound like crunching stone.

His armor absorbed the impact and allowed Raxe to hustle to his feet just as the land dragon hit the surface and turned for another strike. It lost its footing, however, on the dark blood and innards spilling from the widening slit Raxe cut from the bottom of the land dragon's throat to its belly. Its clawed feet slipped out from under it and sent it crashing to its side, where it continued to thrash its powerful tail and legs while it shriek-hissed its life away.

Raxe did not wait to watch it die. He had to get over to Rionn Lorr to help against the sand creature that was bearing down on the Head Mage. Another sand creature emerged from the surrounding skirmishes to rush Raxe from his left. This one held a curved scimitar at the narrow tips of each of its four tentacles.

Raxe had fought against sand creatures before. He had killed dozens of them easily with little more than a few scratches for his efforts. That, however, was when his demon-triggered magic worked, granting him superhuman stamina, speed and strength. Without his magic, the demon-spawn sand creatures were almost as physically superior to him as he was to them when his magic was present.

He had his impenetrable armor, he had the battleaxe Demonsbane with unbreakable metal blades sharpened by the Old Ones themselves. Those properties remained with or without magic. Other than that, though, he had only his skills, athleticism and wits to bring to bear. Raxe knew he would not last long against the nearly six-feet long, deadly quick and powerful blade-wielding tentacles fighting from a distance, so he charged the sand creature head on.

Just before he came within range of the scimitar-wielding monster, he dropped his head and hunched his shoulders to protect his exposed neck and folded his arms tightly against his chest and shielded the bare parts of his arms by tucking them behind Demonsbane's wide crescent blades. He then brought up his damaged right hand – coated by the same metal used to fashion his armor and battleaxe – to cover the unprotected bottom half of his face. He ducked and spun as quickly as he could, thrusting himself into the sand creature's torso with as much force as his spinning body would allow.

The deafening chime of the scimitars striking his armor rang out. Raxe felt something cold and sharp slice across the back of his right knee and his left triceps. He also felt a powerful impact against his ore-tainted right hand that was painful enough to almost make him drop Demonsbane. He forced himself to finish his spin and then thrust Demonsbane outward as the landscape twirled madly before his eyes.

When he came out of his spin and turned to face the sand creature, he saw it staggering backward. The last foot or so of its lower left tentacle was neatly sliced away and a straight line, oozing thick green blood, was drawn from the monster's lower left rib to its massive right pectoral. It came forward and swiped its remaining three scimitars at Raxe, but the strikes were relatively slow and poorly aimed, allowing the offworlder to back away and to the side to avoid them.

The sand creature staggered another step before falling on its face onto the hardened sand. Raxe flicked Demonsbane once to rid it of the sand creature's emerald blood. He turned back to the Head Mage, praying he was not too late.

He was. The sand creature was attacking Rionn Lorr with a stone-carved single-bladed war axe, two dirks, and a flail made of a long wooden handle with a short chain connected to a rusty iron sphere nearly the size of a man's head. The sphere was studded with two-inch long spikes.

The Head Mage managed to simultaneously catch the sideswiping war axe on the broad head of his crooked staff and a downward swing of one of the dirks on his broadsword. The axe blade sunk deep into his staff. The force of the overhand blow buckled his knees, which was the only thing that saved the wizard from the other dirk that had been thrust right at his face. The point of the blade still scored a nasty cut from just below the Head Mage's left nostril, across his left cheekbone, and stopped just short of his left earlobe.

In the instant all of this took place Raxe knew Rionn Lorr was finished. There was no way to stop the oncoming flail.

And then Quick was there, barely redirecting the spiked bronze ball by catching its chain with a two-handed swing of his straight sword. The ball and chain wrapped twice around the blade and its inertia immediately tore the blade from Quick's grasp and slammed it to the hardened sand. Two dirks whipped in Quick's direction but the changeling managed to once again fling himself out of danger with less than an inch to spare. The wind of one of the dirk's passage buffeted his throat, the other cut through his tough leather jerkin and bit into the flesh of his chest as he tumbled away.

Rionn Lorr seized this brief distraction to shove his staff forward with all of his might. The war axe that his attacker held was still imbedded in the hard wooden staff, and luckily for Rionn, the sand creature had not been expecting such an attack. The hard edge of the stone axe head struck the sand creature solidly on the bridge of its flat, upturned nose.

The Head Mage did not hear the satisfying crunch of breaking bone he had hoped to hear, but he saw the monster's beady eyes briefly lose focus. He wasted no time in bringing his broadsword down and driving it forward, throwing all of his weight behind the thrust.

The point of the sword punched through the thick, sand-brown hide at the bottom of the creature's chest and just above its distended belly. Rionn heard the air rush from the sand creature's body even as it whipped the war axe forward again.

The staff ripped free of the huge axe blade and went flying, along with the Head Mage, who had stubbornly refused to release his magical talisman even though it no longer possessed magic. Rionn crashed to the hard surface, skidding and stopping next to Raxe. The sand creature crumpled as the offworlder helped his fellow Child of the Old Ones to his feet.

Quick, his longsword recovered, sprinted over to them. The trio did not even have time to sigh in relief, for a handful of both sand creatures and *Ken* warriors breached the perimeter defenders with vicious and deft strikes of metal and stone weapons.

Lonos grinned ferociously as his forces advanced on the doomed trio and their would-be rescuers. His superior fighters were already pushing the royal forces back in spite the unexpected interference from the dwarves. The *Ken* commander had advanced past the edge of the crusted sand, knowing that the time had almost come for Lonos himself to join the battle and shed the blood of these heretics alongside his men.

His smile did not last long, though. A shadow drop down behind him to envelope the one he cast. The owner of the shadow struck the earth with an impact that sent a tremor through the hardened surface. The *Ken* chieftain snarled and turned quickly, drawing his weapon out of sheer reflex.

The other offworlder Child stood there smiling a fierce smile. The rictus was filled with normal teeth, not the pointed shards he displayed at Hargathall's Cleft, yet it somehow managed to convey the same cold, mocking threat. Joel was not the terrible bone-spiked behemoth he had become back at that cursed canyon. In fact, he once again looked every bit like a small, weak human.

But along with that smile, his eyes were the same as they were at Hargathall's cleft: clouded and milky and soulless; and his hands were the same flat, curved blades of bone.

Lonos knew the reensapir heart would not work against this one. It was already obvious by those deadly scythe hands.

He also knew he could not outrun this monster. The warrior chieftain knew he was at his end, and he would meet it like a true *Ken d'Zanir*. He raised his broadsword to strike with all of his strength and speed, but before the tip could even clear his waist, the Child's right scythe-hand moved.

Lonos did not feel anything at first, but seconds later he felt a sting in his neck and warm, thick wetness running down his chest, shoulders and back. When he looked down at the blood streaming down his torso his world became a tumbling blur of colors. When it stopped, he noticed he was staring straight ahead at a pair of fur-booted feet. It was as if he had fallen in a neck-deep hole.

Just before his world went black, he realized with horror that the feet he was staring at were his own.

The reensapir heart slipped from the bleeding neck stump as the headless body crumpled. Joel reached out a bloody, human right hand to snatch the string of the falling talisman. He knew he had to be quick. He could already feel himself changing back to his normal human form. Before the transformation was complete, he put the petrified heart in his left hand and used the last of his augmented strength to squeeze it until it broke into pieces.

10.5

A blinding pale flash and a single ear-popping concussive wave caused Rionn Lorr a moment of disorientation. When the moment ended the Head Mage smiled, even in the midst of the demon's attacking force.

At the same time the Head Mage smiled, Raxe lit up with a silver glow and felt that familiar fire bloom within him.

With but a thought, Rionn Lorr sent fist-sized globes of light bursting from the wide, flat, upper end of his staff. The sand creatures and *Ken* and land dragons that breached the perimeter and had come to within a sword-swing away were incinerated instantly upon contact with the streaking light globes, transformed to black ash only slightly slower than the blink of an eye. The other spheres moved harmlessly around the royal forces and dwarves to unerringly seek out and destroy the enemy.

Rionn Lorr took no joy in killing. While he had no pity for the demon-spawned sand creatures, the land dragons and *Ken* were natural beings with as much right to life as any other of the Lord Ascendant's creations. It had been nearly five years since he had to take a human life, when he was fighting to avoid a war between humans and dragons. A young upstart wizard foolishly attacked Rionn and left him no choice.

It was not the first time Rionn had been forced to take a human life and he prayed that it would be the last. That prayer was not answered, for the *Ken* and their beasts were in collusion with a demon that threatened his kingdom. While there was joy in taking their lives, neither was there the slightest hesitation.

Raxe, with his gravelly voice, roared an unintelligible war cry, raised Demonsbane, and leapt at the nearest group of sand creatures. He wielded the enchanted battleaxe as easily as an appendage, moving almost as fast as the deadly white light from the Head Mage's staff.

In the distance, Rionn caught sight of one of the dwarven warriors as he dropped a wicked cudgel and pulled a jointed ash stave from where it was strapped to his back. Meaty fists held the stave horizontally in a wide two-handed grip and heaved the large bough over his head. His gimlet eyes glared at the enemy rushing toward him. The Head Mage could not see the dwarf's lips move beneath his thick, soiled, brown mustache and beard, but he could feel the magic that poured from the dwarf's direction.

Every *Ken*, sand creature, and land dragon within a twenty-yard radius turned to stone in mid-stride. And every dwarf in the vicinity wasted no time in reducing the stone figures to rubble with mighty blows from their massive blunt instruments and heavy bladed weaponry. Hoping he would never have to use it, the Head Mage took note of the manipulation of energies the dwarf employed to cast that potentially useful spell.

Echelon One Mage Gilder Raynard had moved nearly fifty yards to the east and stood in the middle of a small cone of harsh wind that was only visible because of the loose sand and chunks of rock-hard sand that were sucked into the whirling gale. He held his staff near one end in a close two-handed grip and thrust it through the mini cyclone. He barked a one-word spell and from the staff's opposite end he unleashed branches of pale yellow lightening that forked out in a wide, fan-like pattern easily fifty yards wide.

Like the Head Mage's spheres of deadly energy, Raynard's yellow lightening arced harmlessly around and over their allies to strike down their enemies. The blasts were strong enough to down every man and creature it touched, leaving their bodies laying still, blackened, and smoldering.

The sand creatures that eluded the wizards' assaults quickly fell at the bite of Demonsbane. Several land dragons fell victim to Raxe's enchanted battleaxe as well. If they made the mistake of attacking, or even if they simply stood between Raxe and a sand creature and failed to move, Raxe cut right through them to get to his targets.

Questblade was not made of the same unbreakable metal as Demonsbane but it did almost as much damage. With his augmented strength, Raxe drove it right through the tough scales and hides of land dragons and sand creatures alike.

Raxe still honored his oath, though, and did not kill a single human. It was not a difficult task. Even though he moved faster than the human eye could follow, he was in complete control. He easily hurtled or dodged the men he encountered. And if, as he passed by a human enemy, he could spare a moment for an immobilizing blow with Demonsbane's handle or break an arm or shatter a kneecap, he did so and let another warrior finish him off.

He was grateful to have that kind of control but he was still trying to get used to it. In the time before he allowed himself to truly accept his magic, the use of it had been a horrifying experience. It controlled him, jerked him around like a child with a ragdoll while draining his life force to fuel the effort. Once he became one with his power the experience was sheer ecstasy. It still used his life force for fuel, but Raxe's acceptance of it put him and the weapon in perfect harmony, exponentially reducing the amount of energy needed to wield Demonsbane.

The silver fire flowing through his veins, his flesh, and his bones was intoxicating. He could not imagine what it must have been like for his divine ancestors who likely felt this way all the time. It was a shame he had to be in the presence of demons or demon-spawn to feel such elation, but it was elation nonetheless, and he enjoyed it to the fullest.

The land dragons that eluded the wizards' onslaught and Demonsbane's deadly bite charged on, only to meet Quick, who had changed into a land dragon and was already puffed up and hissing. Unlike the *Ken*'s relatively domesticated beasts, however, Quick's acid sac glands were completely intact. He sprayed his acidic poison in a wide arc, searing away the scales and flesh of land dragons, sand creatures, and *Ken* who had not been able to escape the range of his attack.

Those remaining humans wasted no time in retreating. The *Ken d'Zanir* feared no human or beast but magic was another thing altogether. With their magic returned, the fierce warriors knew their intended victims gave the royal forces too much of an advantage, so they fled...

Only to be cut down by the royal soldiers and dwarves on the ground and the Gryphon Ryders from the air.

Rionn Lorr watched his fellow Child of the Old Ones and his young apprentice as they tore into the attackers. He was prepared to launch another assault that would have abruptly ended the confrontation, but the royal forces, along with the dwarves, Quick and Raxe, were doing a fine job without him. In only a few seconds longer than it would have taken him to conclude the battle himself, all of their attackers were dead, dying, too wounded to fight, or fleeing.

The sky darkened. The Head Mage looked up to see an armada of armed and armored Gryphon Ryders approaching from the north along with two sky barges, each ferried by eight avicaws. He saw their colors and knew that this was the force sent by King William to put an end to the *Ken d'Zanir* once and for all. With the walkers defeated and Ridgeland safe and settled, the king could concentrate his efforts on the threat in the south. Rionn chuckled at their timing. The battle was all but finished but at least they could finish off the remaining sand creatures and land dragons. They could also capture and imprison the surviving *Ken*.

The lieutenant colonel and his men deserved their vengeance, so Rionn let them finish their work while he conserved his energy. He knew he would need as much of his strength as he could muster. His work was far from done.

PART III

DEMON

Chapter 11: Betrayer

11.1

Joel, back in his normal human form, walked across the hardened sand, stepping over bodies and around pools of green and red and black blood. The scene reminded him of the aftermath of his battle at Hargathall's Cleft, but in his opinion, the massacre at the cursed canyon was countless times worse. The manner of death here was almost merciful compared to what he had done to the men and beasts at Hargathall's Cleft, and what the Cleft itself did to the survivors who could not get off of the canyon floor in time. Joel waved away the wafting acrid smoke rising from ashes and charred bodies with his left hand while keeping the right one clinched tightly around its contents.

Raxe was taken aback by Joel's appearance. The last time he saw him, Joel was about two feet taller, a giant made of muscle, sinew and bone and bristling with deadly spikes. To see him like this was a stark reminder of what Joel had been through. Joel, who was slightly heavier than Raxe when he came across the WorldGate, had lost close to sixty pounds by Raxe's estimate. Angry bruises and keloids from crude brands dotted his torso. Dark bags hung below his tired, bloodshot eyes but Raxe could see that Joel's eyes were as alert as ever. When he reached Rionn Lorr, he held his right hand out and opened it, revealing the six pieces of the broken, blackened, petrified heart.

"This is what's been stealing your powers," Joel informed. "I don't know what the hell it is, but you don't have to worry about it anymore."

Rionn Lorr held a wadded, blood-soaked piece of cut cloth firmly against the scar on his face as he studied the contents of Joel's hand.

"That is a reensapir heart," he said angrily.

"What would the *Ken d'Zanir* be doing with such a talisman?" Quick questioned through his teeth, which were clutching a makeshift bandage as his free hand cinched it tight around his injured arm. "They despise anything even remotely associated with magic."

"Really?" Joel asked. "They didn't have a problem with magic at Hargathall's Cleft. Another one of them had a little wooden whistle shaped like a tube. It controlled the scythe wings. He must've gotten it from Tauran. I saw him with it when they kidnapped me."

Rionn Lorr was about to respond, but before he could, a deep, hearty voice called to him.

"Head Mage Rionn Lorr!" cried a gore-spattered dwarf.

The dwarf's breastplate was dusty and sticky with drying blood but not even that mess could hide the raised crest emblazoned upon it: two ornate war hammers crossing, heads up, to form an "X" set within a wide decorative shield with three points at the top that curved smoothly down to a point at the bottom.

Muscular arms bulged beneath a leather jerkin and heavy chain mail. Bloody spiked gauntlets protected big hands that easily held the stout handle of a large double-bladed battleaxe that made Demonsbane look like a shiny child's toy. The dwarf's tree-trunk thighs were covered by plates of dense steel sewn securely to thick woolen breaches tucked into metal-plated leather boots.

A horned bascinet protected the dwarf's head. Lengths of steel extended down over the dwarf's nose and the sides of his face, and the high point of the horned helmet ended in a vicious point a foot and a half high, a point that was coated with dark blood of varying hues. A heavy, rust colored beard, streaked with pale brown sand and dark fluids, flared out from beneath the helmet.

"King Grimhammer of the Grimhammer Clan and Stonehammer Nation, I am!" boasted the dwarf. He nodded his wide face to the right. "This be General Bartok."

General Bartok, his armor almost identical to his king's with the exception of a rounded helm, touched his right fist, which still clutched a bloody broadsword that was almost as long as he was tall, to his heart in greeting.

"And this be Listwhin the Wise," the dwarf king said, nodding to his left to indicate the chain-mailed dwarf with the jointed stave. "High Mage of the Stonehammer Nation."

Rionn Lorr cast a curious glance at Quick and Raxe before nodding deeply to the approaching dwarves.

"My greetings and thanks to you, your highness," Rionn said sincerely. "I must apologize for my ignorance, for I had no idea the Stonehammer Nation continued to exist after Heaven's War."

"Ye know yer history," King Grimhammer noted. "That we ever existed at all is known only to a few. A Head Mage *should* be so learned but most of 'em ain't. Most of 'em only care about the here and now. Then again, I suppose a long-lived Child of the Old Ones like ye has more time t' study obscure history than most."

Rionn Lorr nodded his thanks as he half smiled and half frowned. "You have me at a complete disadvantage, sir," he said. "How is it you know so much about me and I know nothing of you?"

"Ye ain't s'posed t' know 'bout the Grimhammer Clan," the king said in his booming voice that was still excited from combat. "We've kept ourselves hidden from the world since Heaven's War at the behest of your ancestor, the Old One Lorr himself. We were tasked t' keep a few precious items protected over the years until they were needed." It was the king's turn to frown. "We did it well fer nearly two thousand years, but just recently, there were a couple of 'em we weren't able to protect so well."

"The Keys," Rionn Lorr realized. "The Finder took them from you?"

"Aye," the dwarf confessed. "And more pissed about it I could not be. We wanted t' go after the giant bastard but there was still something remaining that we had t' protect. We couldn't risk exposin' ourselves by goin' after 'em…but by Hargathall's blade, we damn sure wanted to!"

"What was the other item?" Rionn Lorr asked.

"Ask yer fellow Child over there," King Grimhammer said, pointing his axe blades in Raxe's direction. "Then ask 'em about the foolish thing he did with it."

Rionn Lorr turned to the offworlder. Raxe shrugged and said, "I'll tell you about it later."

"Ye kept our presence t' yerselves?" the dwarf king asked with a note of thanks in his tone. "We've nothing left t' secret, now, though. I figured it was nigh time fer the Stonehammer Nation t' come out of hiding."

"Well, King Grimhammer," Rionn Lorr returned. "I must say I'm glad you did."

The King looked skyward and smiled. "After so many years underground, it feels good t' fight under the warm light of the suns."

"Aye," Bartok growled in agreement. "And many of our Clan met glorious ends this day. T'was a good day indeed."

The king turned a mischievous grin to Rionn. "I saw ye charge into combat even when yer magic weren't workin'. Yer's is the kind of stupidity we dwarves can appreciate."

"Um…thank you?" Rionn Lorr said with grin of his own.

"This one's funny, for a wizard!" the king guffawed to his general as he clapped Rionn on the left shoulder hard enough to send him staggering a few feet to the side. "I look forward t' meeting King William in person. I hear he is a warrior, as well. T'is good, that is. Damn politicians only muck things up. Tell yer king that the Stonehammer Nation looks forward t' bartering with the Kingdom of Lorr. I've heard yer ale is almost as hearty as ours. Tell yer king t' have lots of it when we parlay!"

"You have my word on it," Rionn promised. "So what will the Stonehammer Nation do now?"

King Grimhammer finally removed his helmet. Heavy brown locks streaked with white were flattened to his head by sweat and the weight of his horned helmet. His bushy brown eyebrows twitched and the web of creases at the corners of his gimlet eyes deepened as he surveyed the corpses scattered haphazardly among the desert sands.

"Feast!" he said. "These land dragons'll make fer good eating, they will! The meat of lizards that size can be tough if it ain't cooked right, but our women know how t'tender up the toughest flesh. We'll take as many as we can carry back below the Hells and have a fine buffet! Yer all welcome t'join us, you know. The changeling and offworlder can speak t' the quality of our grub."

Raxe nodded and shrugged again. "I don't know what the hell it was I ate. I gotta admit, though, it was pretty tasty."

Rionn glanced at Raxe again before turning back to King Grimhammer. "I must decline your generosity," the Head Mage said. "Your assistance was timely to say the least and is greatly appreciated, but we still have much to do."

"Of course, of course," replied King Grimhammer. With a wave of his war axe the other dwarves went into action sheathing their weapons and seizing fallen land dragons by the tail. "Till our paths cross again, wizard."

Rionn nodded as the dwarf King and general left to find their own land dragons. Soon, all of the surviving dwarves were trudging north toward the Hells. Rionn, Quick and Raxe watched them for a time as the Royal soldiers scrambled around the battle site, checking for wounded fellow soldiers and making sure all of the fallen land dragons left by the dwarves and all of the fallen sand creatures were dead. When a few stubborn but gravely injured *Ken* tried foolishly to attack, they were quickly put down.

Seeing the *Ken* reminded Rionn of their ability to extinguish magic. "I know how the reensapir heart must have come into the *Ken's* possession," he said, returning to the conversation they were having before the dwarf king made his introductions. "And that knowledge disturbs me deeply."

"How did they get it?" Quick implored.

"We knew there was a spy in our ranks, someone who informed our enemies about the expeditions to the Demon's Spine," the Head Mage explained carefully. "The expeditions were not public knowledge but they were not top secret missions, either. Several high ranking military officers and affiliated mages knew of them."

"Any one of them could be the traitor," Joel noted.

"But what has that to do with the heart?" Quick asked.

"Simple," the Head Mage answered, anger slowly fading to sadness. His shoulders slumped as he spoke. "As I said, this shattered talisman is a petrified reensapir heart. I recognize it as one of the fossils collected from the fallen temple on Infinity Isle. Joel's description of the whistle that was used to control the scythe wings sounds very similar to another of the excavated artifacts.

"The final piece of the puzzle was revealed when I received that message through the speaking stone on the way here. The messenger was one of the Alliance mages charged with the task of monitoring Sollustre's Eye. She made a troubling statement. She said she hoped this demon wouldn't disappear before we found it. You see, they've spotted a demon many times through the Eye over the last few weeks. It would appear for a time and then disappear.

"Only the last few such appearances and dissappearances were reported directly to me. It was always too far away for you and I to feel its presence. It was always long gone by the time any kind of investigation could be mounted. Had the previous messages reached me, however, we would have noticed the pattern."

Raxe removed his helmet to wipe sweat from his brow and gave Rionn a grave stare. "They weren't reporting the earlier sightings?"

"Yes, they were," Rionn Lorr said. "They reported *every sighting*…to the only person involved with the monitoring of the eye, the Infinity Isle excavation, *and* with knowledge of the Hell Key expeditions."

Raxe waited as the Head Mage hesitated, unwilling to speak the words. He glanced back at Quick and Joel, who were both literally leaning forward with expectation.

Rionn Lorr sighed and reluctantly declared: "Master Mage Goran Delthar."

Raxe's eyebrows shot up. He had never met Delthar but he had heard a lot about him and knew he had been the Rionn's mentor.

"But he gave you the secret to ending the plague," Quick protested. "That doesn't seem like the action of a traitor. He gave his life in defense of the kingdom at the Runestones."

"How did he even know the secret of ending the plague?" Rionn challenged. "Other than providing us with a valuable sample, he wasn't involved with the research for the cure. It pains me to say this…but he could very well have been the hooded accomplice to Tauran that the Keeper's Hounds saw just outside Tohrfell's Valley."

Quick shook his head, unbelieving. Ethan had told him about the ceremony the Keepers' Hounds interrupted. It had involved sacrificing an infant. He would not allow himself to accept the Master Mage's involvement in such an endeavor.

Rionn Lorr nodded, his face a mask of disappointment. "I know it's difficult to accept, Quick," Rionn sympathized, studying the crestfallen look on the young changeling's face. "It is even more difficult for me. He has mentored me my entire life and he has been my most trusted advisor and friend. But other than the demon, Delthar is the one common link among all of the treachery that has befallen us. As for him dying, I wonder if he really did sacrifice himself. At last report his body had not yet been recovered."

"Even if he did not give his life," Quick argued, unwilling to believe the worst about someone he respected so much, "why would he give you the key to ending the plague if he helped to cause it?"

"That is a question I intend to have answered," Rionn Lorr assured. "But first we must do what we came here to do: find the Hell Key. And then I must send the offworlders back to their world to finally put an end to the Dierglyorr."

Joel's barely interested expression suddenly twisted with fear. "How do you know it's crossed the WorldGate again?"

"If it doesn't know of our victory here," Rionn explained, "it will soon. It will have to escape across the WorldGate because there is nowhere left for it to hide in this world."

"I gotta know something first," Raxe said as he turned to the other offworlder. "Joel, where the hell did you come from? I was starting to think we'd lost you."

"You almost did," Joel admitted, thinking about his brief struggle against a psychotic break. "When I left Hargathall's Cleft, I hitched a couple of rides back to the castle. I had no intention of coming back this way."

"Then why did you?" Rionn Lorr asked.

Joel gave the Head Mage a wry smile. "Let's just say the women in your family are very persuasive…and powerful."

Rionn Lorr returned the smile. His smile, though, was one of pride. "They most certainly are." His smile was replaced for a brief instant by a look of thoughtful concern. "Let me guess. Little Shandie used a teleportation spell."

"Yeah," Joel said. "It wasn't as bad as I thought it would be, except for the part where I popped up over a mile in the sky and started falling. I changed into…into that thing as I fell, so I was pretty sure I'd live, but that didn't make it fun."

"Of course," Rionn Lorr. "She's heard me speak of the effective range and shape of the *Ken's* magic void. She sent you right to the center of the void's diameter and high enough above ground to clear its circumference."

"Wait, she blinked you from the capital to here?" Raxe asked in disbelief. "I remember how teleporting people just a few miles exhausted the old Shanderah. How could that little girl send you *hundreds* of miles?"

Rionn answered. "Like me, my daughter was born with internal magic." There was pride in his voice but Raxe saw an unmistakable shadow of worry in the Head Mage's dark blue eyes. "With her Elven blood, she has unfettered access to resources in nature that are perilous for me to tap. And she is quite adept for one so young."

"You don't say," replied Joel. "Well that's cool and all, but are you saying you can't blink us back? We need to get back home. The quicker we can get back to the castle and the WorldGate Key the quicker we can go home."

"I'm sorry, Joel," Rionn returned. "I assure you it takes much more than a simple 'blink' to successfully perform a teleportation. Such a feat, even for Shandie, is a dangerous exertion of magic. Without the help of some additional talisman to significantly augment my magic, the energy it would take to transport the three of us such a great distance would deplete me too much to open the WorldGate once we reached the castle. The use of the WorldGate Key requires even more energy. I'd need at least two days of recovery before I could make the attempt."

"But that demon's probably back in our world by now," Joel protested. "My wife…Ryan's grandfather…they're in danger. We don't have two days to spare!"

"True," Rionn agreed. "That's why we will take a sky sleigh for nearly a day and then I can transport us the rest of the way from there. It will take less than half that time to replenish myself enough to send you home."

Joel thought even that was too long, but then he remembered how spent the wizard was when he brought them to this world. He relented, knowing that a day and half was better than two days or more.

"Let's get the hell outta here, then," Joel said.

"Not before we retrieve what we've come for," reminded Rionn. "The Hell Key is here. And so is the other Child."

Raxe, looked around as if he expected to find the Child only a few feet away. After a moment's consideration he went silent, closed his eyes and regulated his breathing into a slow, deep rhythm. He narrowed his focus to all of the subtle feelings that identified the presence of other Children of the Old Ones.

The faint yet distinctive psychic whispers were there. The echoes of heartbeats both near and far, each one pulsing at a unique rhythm fluttering just barely out of time with his heartbeat, were there. Like his visual recognition of magic, the feeling of the presence of other Children had become instinctive. It was always there, though he could ignore it easily and just as easily focus upon it when the need arose.

Raxe sifted through each sensation to identify the Head Mage and little Shandie. His grandfather's presence was barely pinpointed from across the WorldGate, like the ethereal memory of an all-but-forgotten dream. He had to fight off a pang of sadness and guilt at the glaring absence of his daughter, Azhju'lestra.

And then he felt it: a rhythm at once familiar and unfamiliar, a whisper that was different than the others. He could tell from its rhythm and tone that the other was young, a toddler like little Shandie, but male.

THE KEY QUEST

From the moment his magic returned, Raxe could feel the Hell Key. Its pulsating evil was a constant repulsive drone in the background of his thoughts. Its depraved allure pulled at him as compellingly as it had when he found it the first time. And, like the aura of the unseen Child of the Old Ones, the Hell Key was moving closer.

Raxe heard Quick gasp. He opened his eyes and looked up and around to follow the captivated teen's gaze. What he found was the Head Mage standing as still as a statue, holding his long twisted stave westward with the narrow end pointing down and the wide, flat end tilted skyward at roughly forty-five degrees to the ground. The rest of his body was stock-still, the only movement the soft flutter of his robes on a light desert breeze. The weapons belt cinched snugly at his hip holding the sheathed broadsword leant a warrior's aspect to the wizard's flowing robes. The weapon's long handle and egg-shaped pommel, with their ornately carved runes, was a reminder that the broadsword was as much an instrument of magic as of combat as it shimmered in the low, late autumn suns' light.

Raxe knew the others could not see magic the way he could, but from their rapt expressions they could tell that powerful magic was being employed. This power was evidenced when a spot on the hardened sand a few yards away began to tremor as it had earlier when the enemy attempted unsuccessfully to come through it.

The sand shuddered and then cracked with a sound like the crunching of dense stone. A large section of it shattered and flew away in every direction. Loose sand plumed slowly up from the resulting cavity like a man-sized mushroom cloud moving in slow motion. The stem of the mushroom cloud of sand fell back to the desert floor, leaving the cap floating unsupported in the air, undulating like a living thing.

The roiling sands started to fall away until the cloud resolved into to two distinctly shaped figures. One was over four feet long and narrow. It only took a little bit more of the sand to drop away before everyone there knew they were looking at the Hell Key.

The other shape reminded Raxe eerily of a baby in the fetal position. When the sand finally fell completely away, Raxe saw that that was almost exactly what it was. A pale complexioned male toddler with neatly cut red locks and dressed in an expensive shift, hugged his knees to his chest and held his eyes shut tight.

Raxe would have thought the boy was an albino but his flaming red hair proved that assessment false. And when he opened his frightened, coal-black eyes, Raxe did not need to feel the boy's aura to know he was a Child of the Ones. Like the red hair was proof enough that this was the son of Shara Dune, Queen of this Forsaken Desert, the eyes and the deathly white skin left no doubt that his father was Mar-dah.

The toddler and Hell Key floated to the Head Mage upon an invisible wave of magic. He pulled his left hand from his staff and held it outward the way an experienced father would beckon a child to his arms. The toddler was clearly frightened and suspicious. He remained tense and still as he settled gently into the curve of Rionn's arm.

The toddler's eyes found Rionn's. His penetrating gaze appraised the Head Mage for several seconds before the boy exhaled and relaxed a bit. He had apparently concluded that he was safe. His fear and suspicion gave way to curiosity, relief, and most of all, sadness. Tears began to stream down his pale, chubby cheeks.

"My mommy is *gone*," he whispered.

The way he emphasized the word "gone" made it obvious that he understood the truth of things. He knew his mother was not coming back.

"Worry not, young one," Rionn Lorr soothed. "We will keep you safe."

The boy nodded, feeling the sincerity of the words as well as hearing it. His little body completely relaxed and he fell asleep in Rionn's arm.

The Hell Key was left to hover before the Head Mage until his cloak, which had been lying on the ground a few feet away, lifted into the air like a ghost to gather itself around the Hell

Key. Only when it was completely wrapped and did Rionn Lorr gather the bundle under his right arm.

Raxe nodded his understanding. The memories of the sensations evoked by direct physical contact with the Hell Key were still far too vivid. He could not blame Rionn Lorr for waiting as long as he possibly could before touching it.

"No need to touch it with my naked skin yet," Rionn Lorr confirmed. "All too soon I will become more intimate with it than I could ever desire."

11.2

T'Cheln watched the last of the sky sleighs, including the one containing the Children of the Old Ones, disappear into the northeastern skies. A few feet away his land dragon slurped and smacked and crunched on the bones of a captured mountain cat. The massive lizard sported more than a few deep gouges in its hard scales from its effort to subdue its formidable meal, but they caused no apparent discomfort as it fed.

The *Ken* warrior watched the entire conflict between the demon's forces and the Children through his spyglass from his hidden perch among the high cliffs of Hell's Mountains. From the time the Head Mage's small sky sleigh touched down until the vanguard of Lorrian Royal Gryphon Ryders and a battalion of armed and armored sky barges finally arrived, T'Cheln watched and evaluated.

After his two-year assignment serving as bodyguard and trainer to the deceased Dirk Tauran ended, T'Cheln trekked through Hell's Mountains to find his *Ken d'Zanir* brethren. He followed them at a safe distance for days and considered joining them. He eventually decided firmly against joining them when he saw the devastation they left in their wake.

Rkam Lonos had lost control. The *Ken* were not petty raiders, sacking and looting and raping those lacking the strength to stop them. Those warriors, *his* warriors, tore a bloody swath through two towns that shook T'Cheln to his core. He was shocked at their blatant disregard for honor. *S'Zan Rho Ken d'Zanir* did not hesitate to kill in righteous battle and self defense. They killed covertly to fulfill the wishes of the retainer they chose to serve, as long as those wishes did not break the warriors' first rule. That rule was to never kill innocents or children. Rkam Lonos broke that rule with no regard. That was not the *Ken d'Zanir* way.

T'Cheln, however, had known Rkam Lonos for many years. Upon considering the chieftain's grim past, T'Cheln realized he probably should have expected this to happen at some point.

THE KEY QUEST

Both T'Cheln and Lonos had been devout followers of the Word of S'Zan, the warrior Old One who fought on the side of the Leaders in Heaven's War. S'Zan believed man was not worthy of magic. Lonos, however, grew more fanatical than devout. Lonos did not fight for honor. He did not fight because he enjoyed martial artistry. Rkam Lonos fought because he loved to kill. He lived to kill. T'Cheln had heard Lonos say on more than one occasion that if given the chance, he would cull the world of all those who did not except the Word of S'Zan as the One Truth.

Most of the *S'Zan Rho's* conflicts, as well as the vast majority of their contracts, were against others from the Westin Continent, where almost everyone followed the Word of S'Zan. But in these eastern lands of infidels T'Cheln knew that Rkam Lonos could finally find a release to his grand murderous urges in a way that he could justify. To make matters worse, Lonos's fanatical enthusiasm was infectious. His zeal swept men up in a gale of bloodlust that only those with the strongest conviction could resist. T'Cheln knew that the chieftain's soldiers were as passionate as their chief.

T'Cheln and Lonos had many vehement philosophical debates over the years. Some led to physical altercations, all of which were won by T'Cheln. Unfortunately, T'Cheln's station as prince did not overrule Lonos's authority in the field. Lonos was older and had been chieftain since T'Cheln was an adolescent. His seniority made their positions equal while they were on missions.

While T'Cheln could not compel Lonos to do his bidding, he could at least challenge him. His father likely realized this, which was why, when T'Cheln insisted upon being a part of this important mission, his father assigned him to the false baron Tauran, safely distant from Lonos and his men.

T'Cheln would not have been able hold his peace in the face of Lonos's savagery. He would have been compelled to confront the chieftain about his blatant misinterpretation of S'Zan's Word. Knowing Rkam as he did, T'Cheln knew that a fight to the death would be the only way to settle such a confrontation during an important campaign.

T'Cheln had no doubt that he could defeat the chieftain. However, he also had no doubt that he would never have the full loyalty of Lonos's men. They would not easily forsake their revered chieftain, so instead of rejoining his brothers once he caught up with them, he trailed them from a distance.

He documented Lonos's atrocities in order to have him removed as chieftain upon their return to the Kingdom of S'Zan. The only time he intervened was at Hargathall's Cleft. He could not stand by and watch every last one of the *Ken* slaughtered by the berserker offworlder Child called Joel. T'Cheln still possessed his own magi-stifling reensapir heart, closed up and carried within its protective leather pouch, but he decided against interfering down in the desert. By then T'Cheln had enough time to think about their mission and for whom they were ultimately working.

When T'Cheln heard the captive Dayna reveal to Tauran that the mastermind behind this conflict was a loosed demon, he believed her. He decided that the S'Zan *he* worshipped would not approve of the *Ken's* involvement. S'Zan and the other Leader Gods' goal was to make mankind submissive, not to wipe him out. They created the demons to aid them in achieving that goal. This demon, T'Cheln realized, had no Old Ones to answer to. It was like a trained attack dog let loose upon an unsuspecting world with no master to guide it.

T'Cheln would not assist Lonos in advancing the plot of a rouge demon. The offworlder Child, Joel, with his immunity to the reensapir heart, was a clear sign that this was not a war the demon was destined to win.

The *Ken* warrior knelt on the hard earth of the mountainside, facing the setting sun. His hands clasped submissively behind his back, he bent over forward at the waist so deeply that his forehead rested on the ground. He whispered several silent prayers, asking for wisdom and strength, and also for forgiveness if S'Zan found fault with his decisions. After finishing his devotions he kissed the soil gently, unfolded his long frame and rose to his feet in one smooth motion.

Rkam Lonos was dead. In his bloodlust he led almost all of his men to their deaths. Even though the chieftain had fallen, there was still a handful of *Ken* left alive. The Lorrian soldiers took as many of them into custody as they could. The survivors too gravely wounded to survive transport were simply left to die. From his elevated position T'Cheln spied several of the *Ken* elude capture by slipping into the cover of the bordering mountain range.

The *Ken* prince mounted his land dragon and trotted down the mountainside into the desert. He inspected body after body on the rock-hard sand, found none living among the first score. And then he heard a moan from somewhere behind him. He turned toward the sound and immediately recognized the *Ken* warrior trying to rise to his feet.

"L'Atir!" T'Cheln called. He raced over to the man and helped him stand. "I was about to give up on these men and go to the warriors hiding in the mountains."

"I'm glad you did not," L'Atir said gratefully. "There are a few of us still breathing out here. I can rouse them while you see to the others." He glanced around at the desert and the mountains. "Rkam Lonos?" he asked.

"Dead," T'Cheln grunted, "killed at the hand of the berserker offworlder Child of the Old Ones. His end befitted the atrocities he committed. I must be honest, L'Atir, you and the other survivors have much to answer for."

"Yes," L'Atir admitted. "Though we were only following orders. I tried to talk sense to him but the bloodlust was upon him. The rest of the men followed him blindly. As his second, I realize it was my duty to challenge him for his dishonor, to find a way to make his warriors mine. If we make it home safely, I will humbly submit to whatever punishment is due."

"You are *my* warriors now, L'Atir," T'Cheln declared. "I will see all of you safely home."

11.3

Raxe sat on the wall-mounted bench while one of the royal healers finished stitching closed the wound on his triceps. His open-topped helmet rested in his lap. The pain from the deep cut and needle piercing his flesh barely drew his notice. His attention was fixed on Joel. To Raxe's surprise, Joel spent most of the trip looking out at the sky through a starboard side porthole. That was a notable contrast to his near-terrified demeanor on his first sky-sleigh ride.

That was not the only change Raxe noticed in his fellow offworlder. Joel had lost a shocking amount of weight, but once Raxe got over the initial shock of his appearance he had to admit that Joel did not look as bad as he should have under the circumstances.

Raxe estimated that he and Joel had weighed about the same when they met, but the weight was distributed very differently. While they were both in the neighborhood of two hundred pounds, Raxe was lean and remarkably fit with broad shoulders and well-defined musculature. Joel, on the other hand, had been in the beginning stages of developing a serious beer gut and he was not especially lean or muscular. Joel's captivity made him more wiry than bony. His face was almost gaunt. His stomach was flat but not sunken. His ribs were only slightly visible.

From the look in Joel's eyes, his captivity and subsequent experiences affected him far more than just physically. The perpetual deer-in-the-headlights look that dominated Joel's countenance after crossing the WorldGate had been replaced by wariness. The flashes of fear-fueled anger he displayed before his capture were now expressed as calm annoyance. Joel had grown harder, colder.

There was, however, one thing that was the same. Joel was just as distracted as he was then. It was obvious that he had been distracted by worry for his wife back then and it was only logical to conclude that he still was. But for some reason that Raxe could not quite place, he had the feeling that Joel was distracted by something else, as well.

Raxe had been trained in behavioral analysis. He learned to tell when someone was about to engage in potentially dangerous conduct or if they were hiding something. He could tell if someone was in a state of low alert and vulnerable. Effective behaviorism was part and parcel to a successful clandestine agent and professional assassin.

Joel was doing a surprisingly good job of masking it, but he was definitely hiding something. Raxe thought he had a pretty good idea what it was. Once the healers finished stitching his wound, he walked over to Joel.

"So, what happened back at Hargathall's Cleft?"

Joel turned from the window and stared at Raxe for a moment, appraising the gleaming silver armor. "It must be a bitch going to the bathroom in that gear," he noted.

Raxe chuckled. "It's not as hard as it probably looks."

"What happened to the elf?" Joel asked. "I thought he stole the key. How did it end up in the desert?"

"The demon took it," Raxe answered. "We're not expecting to see Rell Kallen again."

"Did you get your daughter back to Lake Onyx?"

Raxe nodded slowly. "Yeah. But once we got there…she didn't make back out. The demon had her mother killed. Azh found the body and lost it, but she gave her life to point us in the direction of the Hell Key."

"Oh, man," Joel said softly. He thought about his wife and the life growing in her womb. "I'm sorry."

"I only knew her for a few weeks," Raxe continued. "I barely knew her mother."

"It still hurts, though," Joel noted with a consoling tone.

Raxe shrugged. "Yeah, it does. A lot. So, again, what happened at the Cleft?"

Joel was silent for another moment. "I killed them," he finally said with forced calm.

Raxe raised his eyebrows. "All of them?" he asked. "Well, you know what I mean, all but the ones who attacked us in the Forsaken Desert?"

"Pretty much," Joel confirmed. "The Cleft finished finished off the ones I didn't."

"Damn," Raxe swore. "It's a good thing you don't remember your episodes. That's the kind of thing that'll give you nightmares forever."

Joel said nothing. He lowered his head until his chin rested on his chest. A tremor ran visibly through his body.

"Oh hell," Raxe swore. "You *do* remember it."

"Yeah," Joel said in a voice barely above a whisper. "Every damned second of it. I thought I'd learned to control it. All I did was condition myself to remember it."

Raxe was at a loss for words, something that did not happen often. He had taken a lot of lives before he made his oath to stop killing. Joel killed more men in one afternoon than Raxe had in over a decade of military combat and making his living as one of the best assassins in the world.

"How did you do it?" Joel asked, breaking the silence. "How did you kill and kill and manage to keep your sanity?"

Raxe shrugged. "Sanity's a relative term, man. It's completely subjective. Some might say that you can't *be* sane and be a killer, at least not the kind of killer I was."

Joel scoffed. "It's taking everything I have to keep from falling apart. The only things keeping me from jumping out of this sky sleigh are my desire to get back to my wife…and the fact that I'd turn into that monster again and survive the freaking fall. I gotta know, man. How did you cope with all the killing you did?"

"I was a trained killer," Raxe reminded him. "I was conditioned to cope with it."

"What about the moral part of it?" Joel questioned. "Was that conditioned out of you? Did you ever believe in God?"

"My mom and gramps raised me to be a Christian," Raxe admitted. "I guess I believed when I was a kid. Then I lost my mom. I couldn't reconcile the kind and caring God they taught me about with a God who'd let my father ditch his family before I ever knew him and then let my mother die in a car accident. I decided He either didn't exist, in which case it didn't matter what I did; or He was a cruel hypocrite with a warped sense of humor, in which case I didn't give a damn about Him."

Joel nodded thoughtfully. "What about now?" he asked.

Raxe shrugged again. "After all I've experienced I can't help but believe." He tapped the short-handled battleaxe at his hip. "Demonsbane showed me pretty clearly that I'm going to hell. I guess that means there has to be a heaven, right? But I don't think God's a cruel hypocrite anymore."

"What do you think?" Joel asked with genuine interest.

"I think He gives us the gifts of life and free will. He leaves it up to us to decide what to do with them."

Joel cocked his head. "You believe you're going to hell but you still fight for the good guys? What's the point?"

"I once asked the same question of the lady that Rionn's daughter was named after," Raxe answered. "She told me that we shouldn't do the right thing only out of hope for reward or fear of punishment. That makes it insincere and God knows the difference. We're supposed to do the right thing because it's the right thing to do."

"I guess," Joel allowed. "Let me ask you something else. If you believe in God, how do you square the whole 'Lord Ascendant' and Old Ones with the bible?"

"I don't," Raxe said. "How do *you* do it?"

"I'm still working that out," Joel admitted. "I was raised a Catholic. I won't lie and say I was all that devout over the years but I believe in the tenets of Christianity. I believe Jesus Christ died for our sins, rose from the grave and ascended to heaven.

"I thought you and your grandfather and Rionn Lorr were crazy until we crossed the WorldGate. Now I'm wondering if I'm the crazy one. This world, these people, this whole experience raises a lot of questions for me."

Raxe nodded. "Old Shanderah told me that the same God created both worlds. They call Him the Lord Ascendant over here. The Old Ones are supposedly this world's version of angels. She said this world was created first, and God invested it with much more magic than our world.

"Assuming that's true, I wouldn't expect the authors of the bible to know about this world. Besides, I've always considered the bible more of a guide than a literal history. I try not to get too caught up in the details." Raxe grinned. "That's where the devil lurks, you know."

Raxe's contemplative gaze lingered on Joel for a few seconds. "Is that what's bothering you, Joel? You're afraid God is going to punish you for the lives you've taken?"

Joel chose not to answer. His silence and the sullen gaze he turned to the floor were answer enough.

"I don't think you have to worry about that," Raxe said. "You didn't do those things willfully."

"That's not what I'm worried about," Joel told him, shaking his head slowly. He turned a grave stare to Raxe. "The Dierglyorr paid me a visit in Eastedge."

Raxe's face went completely blank as he returned Joel's stare. He blinked once. "What did it want?"

"It wanted to make a deal with me," Joel admitted. "It told me that if I backed off, if I didn't help you guys, it would leave Lisa alone."

Raxe's expression remained unreadable. "And what happened when you told it to go back to hell?"

"I took the deal."

Raxe's left hand shot out and clutched Joel's neck before he even realized he had done it. In the next moment he slammed Joel violently against the hard wooden wall next to the porthole. He brought his face so close to Joel's that the tips of their noses almost touched. The look in his brown eyes changed from calm to a rage that bordered on lunacy. He felt a faint heat near his free hand, which was hanging at his side near Demonsbane at his hip. He attributed the warmth to the damage done to his ruined right hand. When he spoke, his already rough, raspy growl took on the sound of an ice pick crunching through a solid block of ice.

"Are you *fucking* crazy, Joel?"

Joel glanced down at Raxe's hand around his neck and then looked up to meet Raxe's maniacal gaze. Joel once again recalled his breakdown in the Demon Spine foothills.

"I could be fucking crazy," he managed as he struggled for air, "And you might want to be careful with that hand around my neck. We both know what might happen."

"I'm not trying to kill you," Raxe snarled, loosening his grip but not letting go. "I'll just beat you damn near to death. How could you do something so stupid?"

"Tell me how it makes a difference," Joel challenged. "I've already saved your ass twice since then. I'm pretty sure that was a deal-breaker. The Dierglyorr is probably going after my wife right now."

Raxe released Joel and stepped back. He shook his head briskly as if to shed water from his dreadlocks. When he went still, his eyes were calm and his voice was once again his normal rasp.

"True," he conceded. "But why make the deal at all? You couldn't have thought the demon would honor it."

"I figured I didn't have anything to lose," Joel said.

"Did *you* intend to keep your end of the deal, Joel?"

"Actually," Joel said, "yeah. I had every intention of backing off. I changed my mind back at Hargathall's cleft, though, believe it or not. I'd decided to help you. I just couldn't make myself step off the cliff."

"So how'd you get down there?" Raxe asked.

"These damn kids have a bad habit of dropping me in the middle of your fights; first Quick at Hargathall's Cleft then Shandie. They put my life in danger to spark my power."

Raxe chuckled darkly. "Serves you right."

"Morality lessons from an assassin," Joel scoffed.

"Ex-assassin," Raxe corrected. "Let's get this straight. You didn't break the deal on purpose and it's not like the demon was going to honor it, anyway. Your power is out of your control, so even the kills you've made aren't really on you. What are you worried about?"

"I made the damn deal willingly," Joel said, frustrated. "That can't sit very well with the Man upstairs."

"I guess you have some atoning to do," Raxe grumbled as he turned and left the cabin.

He stalked through two short corridors before coming upon the Head Mage, who stood in the hall thoughtfully staring out of a porthole. A thought, or more of a suspicion, came to the offworlder. He stopped and turned to Rionn Lorr.

"You didn't happen to hear our conversation, did you?"

Rionn Lorr grinned as he stared out the window. "Do you know why that thought just occurred to you?"

"I'm not in the mood for lessons, blondie."

Rionn Lorr turned to Raxe. "You know I was too far away to have heard you by natural means. You're more sensitive to magic even if you do not realize it."

"I'll take that as a 'yes' to *my* question," Raxe said dryly.

"Your reaction to Joel's admission was...intense," Rionn noted. "I've never seen your temper flare so violently."

"He made a deal with the demon," Raxe said defensively.

Rionn shrugged. "I wonder what I would have done in Joel's place, if my wife or daughter was in Lisa's place."

"Dan *is* in Lisa's place," Raxe reminded angrily. "He's right there with her. *I* would've never made a deal like that."

Rionn shook his head. "Of course you wouldn't have. "You're magic wouldn't allow it. You'd be too busy trying to kill the demon to make any deals."

"You know what I mean, smartass," Raxe sneered.

"But do you know what *I* mean?" the Head Mage asked. "If your power could be manipulated by the Dierglyorr, if it could keep your magic from working while retaining its own power and then offered you the same deal for your grandfather's safety, would you take it?"

"Why make a deal with it when I know the demon wouldn't honor it?" Raxe argued.

"For the same reason Joel did," Rionn said soberly. "You would have nothing to lose."

Raxe gave a noncommittal grunt and trudged away, still fuming. He did not speak to Joel again for the remainder of their flight, which was fine with Joel. He spent the rest of the trip lost in troubled thoughts and haunted memories.

Chapter 12: Ultimatums

12.1

Lisa sat in a comfortable recliner watching the thirty-six-inch flat-panel high-definition television while Dan sat at a desk a few feet behind her. He was back in his wheelchair and had it parked in front of a polished oak desk while he pecked at a laptop keyboard.

She was initially surprised to see him in a wheelchair again. He was in a chair when she met him. Later that night, the two-hundred-year-old man surprised everyone, including his grandson, when he stood from his chair to prove to Ryan, Joel and Lisa that he could protect her. He had been walking since that time, sometimes with a cane if it fit his disguise, but most often without any assistance.

When she saw him back in a wheelchair a few days earlier, Lisa initially assumed it was just a part of one of his many disguises. She found herself changing that assumption. Dan spent more time in the chair than out of it, even inside the hotel room. A few weeks ago that would have worried Lisa to no end. Now, though, she was relieved.

Lisa could see that he was tired. The last time she saw him walk he was so unsteady that she thought he would topple over. She could not begin to imagine how tired he was. At his age, with all of the travelling, running, and fighting they had done over the last few weeks, and all of the magic he had to perform to defend them, she was surprised he was functional at all. She had no doubt that he could still walk but he had earned the right to rest his tired legs.

She glanced back at him with a small smile. A pair of bifocals sat at the tip of his nose, each lens reflecting a miniature image of the laptop screen. He looked over at her for a moment, winked and smiled and turned back to his keyboard. Lisa knew he was worried. The wink and smile usually came after some silly flirtation or just a plain old dirty comment. Silence from Dan was a sure sign he was distracted.

Dan was very distracted. He knew that by now the demon and therefore the agency knew he and Lisa were back in Chicago. They would have tracked them as far as the cross-country bus ride and stopped the bus at some point to search it. They would know that it was no coincidence that Chicago was one of the stops.

He knew they would not be able to leave the city again. The ravenous probing magic that had dogged them across the country and back was in Chicago with them now. Dan could feel it. It crisscrossed the city every day searching for them. Dan would know when the magic located them. Back when it trailed them unceasingly he could always sense that cold, hungry focus upon him. He found a pattern in the way it tracked them. Dan analyzed the evil pursuing him and got a good feel for its movements. The patterns, the frequency of times it was idle, the speed at which it moved, were those of someone driving a vehicle.

Dan wondered what form the demon's agent was taking. Did it resemble – or had it in fact once been – human? He knew it was not the Dierglyorr but Dan could feel the touch of hell in the magic. It was like the ghost of an icy breath on the back of his neck, a foreboding weight on his shoulders that lightened from time to time but never quite went away.

There was an important difference lately. On more than one occasion Dan could feel the magic very close, within a quarter mile, but never any closer. It would eventually move past or change direction to move further away. The hunger and the eagerness was still there, as intense as they ever were, but they were no longer focused directly upon him. There was a twinge of confusion, of uncertainty, that dampened its strength. That meant Dan's concealing ward was working the way it was supposed to work.

But Dan was no fool. He and Lisa were stuck in Chicago. There was no leaving this time. The organization would have all of the highways, major thoroughfares, airports, lake and river ports, and bus and train stations covered.

They would have every one of those places, including every major intersection, outfitted with cameras complete with thermal scanning high definition facial recognition technology. The makeup and prosthetics he had been using to change his and Lisa's appearance would not work again.

THE KEY QUEST

The ward made them invisible to any magic being used to locate them, but not to visual contact or surveillance technology. He and Lisa had been lucky to get back into the city. Dan gambled that they might not have had the city locked down while they were on the run out of state. The fact that agents had not kicked down their door yet was proof enough that his gamble paid off, but he held no illusions that they would get back out of the city. They stayed close to the hotel and used the concealing ward religiously.

Lisa was skeptical about the magic at first. After more than a week in the spacious two-room suite without being found, however, she was willing to believe. Dan thought the roomy and comfortable suite was a luxury owed to Lisa for what she went through over the recent weeks. The two of them frequented some terrible dives when they began their flight and were due for some comfort. Dan knew Lisa had indulged herself with even better accommodations in Vegas and he did not blame her. His modest room in Portland was head and shoulders better than their earlier accommodations.

They kept the five candles burning within the room at all times while they were there, making sure to place them strategically to form an equilateral pentagon. The candles burned slowly and permeated the room with the concealing spell. They were not supposed to burn candles in the room, so when the housekeeping staff first noticed the scent of the extinguished hidden candles, Dan convinced them with generous tips to keep it their little secret. On the rare occasions one of them ventured out of the room or, even rarer, the building, they dabbed themselves with the liquid form of the concealing ward before extinguishing the candles and letting the housekeeping staff in the room,.

As long as the spelled particles were on their skin or in the air around them, the demon and its magic would be blind to them. For once, Lisa, a southern girl, was thankful for the cold winters of the Midwest. They did not have to worry about sweating away the dabs of liquid concealing spell when it was twenty degrees outside. Everyone was partially concealed by heavy coats and long coats with high, upturned collars and all kinds of hats and hoods and scarves. That helped them to conceal themselves, but she and Dan made it a point to not dress warm enough to sweat.

Even still, they did not dare venture too far away from the hotel. Dan made sure they never had to. That area was picked strategically. When they did go out, they always made sure to mix with the crowded streets of the Magnificent Mile during the highest traffic times, hiding in plain sight. Everything they needed could be found either in the hotel or on the same block. Everything that is, except for an obstetrician-gynecologist.

"What time is the doctor getting here in the morning?" Lisa asked.

"Ten o'clock," Dan answered distractedly in barely more than a mumble.

"She's going to have an ultrasound and everything? I've never heard of a travelling OBG-YN."

"How do you know the doctor's a woman?" Dan asked.

"She'd better be," Lisa warned. "I don't like men baby doctors."

Dan grunted. "So Joel is the only man that can fiddle around down there?"

"Don't make me slap you, Dan. So is she going to bring an ultrasound or what?"

"Don't you believe in natural medicine and childbirth?"

"I'm a veterinarian and a woman of science. I believe in drugs and technology. I want to *see* my baby and hear the heartbeat. Now answer my damn question."

Dan finally chuckled. "Yes, Lisa. *She* will have everything *she* needs. I called an MD, not a midwife from the ninetheenth century."

"Thanks, dirty-ass old man."

Dan's expression grew serious again as he turned his attention back to the laptop.

Lisa watched him for a moment with a bit of envy, wishing she could find something to occupy herself the way Dan was occupied. She was bored out of her mind. All she did all day was watch television. She would surf the net when Dan managed to pry himself from the laptop he had "acquired" from who-knew-where. Apparently that night was television night for Lisa. Dan typed away with seemingly no intention of moving anytime soon.

She never liked to do one thing for too long a time. Once a thing got monotonous to her mind would wander to Joel she would and miss him all the more. She purchased a mini library of trade paperback books and magazines, from mysteries to corny romance novels and tabloids that she had never read until now. The books and magazines eventually grew monotonous. She needed a break from reading, so she started watching the cable network news. Once they started replaying the stories on one station she would switch to another. The news programs were an effective distraction at first but soon that became as tedious as everything else.

"Dan," she called from the sofa across the room. "How long do think we can do this?"

"As long as we have to," he said doing a poor job of hiding his irritation at yet another interruption.

"That's bull," Lisa returned. "You tense up when you feel them coming closer. I don't think you have a bottomless pit of money. You have access to a lot but it can't be infinite. The wards are working now but they'll run out eventually."

"You're right," Dan said. "They may even find us before the wards run out. They're probably checking the same types of low-budget hotels and motels we used to frequent, but soon they'll start looking at hotels like this one. Hell, they may even stumble across us on the street."

"So what do we do from here?" Lisa asked. "How long do we stick around?"

"I don't know," Dan said, steadily pecking away at the keyboard. He was a pretty decent two-finger typist but he wished he were faster. It was his fault. During his two centuries of life it never occurred to him to take the time to learn how to type properly. "It wouldn't be a problem if you could just follow instructions."

"You're on that again?" Lisa sighed.

"Damn right," Dan fussed. "I was ready for them in Portland. I had everything in place to make a stand and they were coming right to me. I missed my chance because I had to go chasing after you."

"What was so special about Portland?" Lisa wondered.

"There's a lot of power there," Dan explained. "Ocean, mountains, volcanoes, the wilderness surrounding the city; all of them are natural sources to draw upon for magic."

Lisa cocked her head. "But you told me once that drawing magic from nature can be dangerous."

"Potentially," Dan said. "But I don't have to ability to pull enough energy to do any damage. The little bit of magic I can command would've been fortified by those sources. When the demon magic came near enough it would've ignited my internal magic and I'd be even stronger. I could've done some real damage in Portland.

"Now I have to find someplace in Chicago to make a stand if it comes to that. That's what I'm doing now, seeing what I can find on the net about weather patterns, air quality indexes, the locations in or around the metropolitan area best suited to maximize supernatural energies."

"Do you think you could have beaten them in Portland?" Lisa asked, suddenly feeling even guiltier than before. "The demon *and* the organization?"

"No," Dan admitted. "But I could've taken a nice big chunk outta their asses. Maybe bought you and the others a lot more time. I might've been able to force the demon to hide out somewhere and lick its wounds, but now…in this city… I just don't know."

Lisa looked confused. "Why not?"

"I love this town but it doesn't have the biggest pool of magical energy in the United States. The Great Lakes and rivers in this region have power but not nearly as much as the Pacific Ocean. There's not as much wildlife, not as many trees, and no mountains. There's more interference with supernatural energies in more densely populated cities like this. There's too much pollution, too much electromagnetic radiation filling the air from power lines, satellite dishes, radio waves."

Lisa thought for a moment. "Why come to Chicago at all, then? Why not go back to Portland or somewhere else along the west coast? Reno is right across the border from Northern California. There are mountains, wilderness and the same ocean near there."

"I had Portland scouted," Dan said. "I found the perfect spot. It would've taken too much time to find another place in that region. They were too close by then and I had to put more distance between us. We came back to Chicago because I *know* Chicago. This is my home base. There may not be as much magical energy is here but I do have other resources I can tap when the time is right. It's just gonna be a lot tougher than it would've been in Portland."

Lisa was quiet for a time. She stared at the television, barely paying any attention to it. "I couldn't let them believe I was dead," she finally said. She started channel surfing again. "When I saw my parents on the news, not knowing if I was alive or dead, it broke my heart. I know I screwed up but I couldn't do that to them."

Dan said nothing.

"So you're ignoring me now, Dan?"

Dan remained silent.

"Very mature for a two hundred year old."

Dan suddenly sat up straight and stopped typing. "What channel were you just watching?" he asked.

"One of many twenty-four hour news networks," Lisa answered. "Take your pick."

Dan swung around in his wheelchair. "Turn back to it."

His sudden urgency startled Lisa. She quickly hit the "LAST" button on the remote to jump back to the previous station. The current story was about the endless fighting in the Middle East.

"That's not the same story that was on when you changed the channel," Dan noted.

"No," Lisa confirmed. "They were showing some police chief. Why?" An even better question occurred to her. "And how did you know what they were talking about? You weren't even looking. This is the first time you've turned away from that laptop for a half hour at least."

Dan did not answer her. He turned back to the computer and started typing again. Lisa could hear him mumbling. She had no idea what he was talking about but she was able to make out words like "U.S." and "Breaking News" and "Vegas" over the loud and hurried tap of his fingers on the keys. She also heard the occasional harshly-whispered curse word followed by "backspace, backspace, delete."

And then the tapping and the mumbling went quiet and stayed quiet for close to thirty seconds.

"Come check this out, Lisa," Dan finally said in a low voice. "You need to take a look at this."

Lisa hurried over, moving silently in her long t-shirt, baggy sweatpants and soft slippers. She leaned over his shoulder and looked at the frozen video image of a huge black man who looked as wide as a pro football offensive lineman, as tall as a pro basketball player, and built like a world-class body builder. And if his sheer size was not enough to intimidate from a still photo, the maniacal look in his eyes would have done the trick.

"I never much cared for the muscle-bound psychotic type," Lisa deadpanned.

"This picture was taken in Chicago weeks ago," Dan said. "Not too long after we first met you and Joel. It's from a security camera across the street from a bar. This guy turned it inside out. Killed some people in the process. Brutally. Ryan and I were there that night."

Lisa raised her eyebrows. "I remember that story. They said he ripped people apart like an animal and then disappeared. Is he a friend of yours?"

"More like an acquaintance."

"You make some weird acquaintances, Dan."

"Now look at this," he said, sliding his finger along the touch pad and tapping a few keys.

The still image disappeared and was replaced by a web page from the same news outlet they had just watched on TV. The page showed an image of the same man. This time, though, the background caught her eye. It was different than the first still which contained people in winter coats walking by in the background. The area was very familiar, someplace she had been recently. The surrounding people were dressed for much warmer weather. From the lights and the people and the buildings Lisa recognized it as Vegas. The trunk of a palm tree on the edge of the frame looked disturbingly similar to the palm trees outside of her hotel.

Dan tapped the screen. "This guy was seen walking out of your hotel shortly before the explosion that took out your room," he said. "This still is from the news story you just flicked past. This is who the police chief was talking about."

"Is that the… is that the demon?" Lisa asked nervously.

"Yes," Dan said.

Lisa was silent while she tried to digest what she was being told. Hearing about demons was one thing. Seeing one was something altogether different. The fact that it was in the guise of a man made it seem unreal, but she knew by now that all of this was all too real. The fact that the demon had been so *close* to her in Las Vegas was almost too much for her to take. Her hand went involuntarily to her forehead and she commenced her nervous tick of rubbing her brow.

Dan clicked the "back" button on the screen to show the first still of the big man in Chicago. "But *this* isn't the demon. This is the changeling dragon I told you about. This is WorldHopper, King of the Dragons."

"Why would the demon use the same disguise as the dragon?" Lisa wondered.

"That was only one of many disguises," Dan answered. "Here's another one."

He tapped the keyboard a few times and the video of the police chief – dark gray eyes with wrinkles that looked like cracks in his overly-tanned skin, round face, thin lips and thick neck cinched tightly by a collar buttoned to the top and a bolo tie. It was a still of the same video Lisa had just watched on television. With another keystroke the still came to life. Dan paused the video feed before the man could finish his first word.

Lisa shook her head in disbelief. "How can you be sure?" she asked. "How do you know both pictures of the big guy aren't of WorldHopper? How can you possibly know the police chief is the demon?"

"Look at me," Dan ordered. "Closely. In my eyes."

Lisa did. As she did so, Dan clicked the "Back" button twice to show the image of what he claimed was the dragon from Chicago and then looked back at her. Lisa leaned down so her eyes were level with Dan's. All she saw was the glow from the laptop display shimmering from his brown eyes and dull brown skin, nothing out of the ordinary.

"What am I supposed to be looking for?" Lisa said, her hand moving back and forth on her forehead.

Dan reached up and gently pulled her hand down. "Stop that. Just keep looking."

Dan clicked the "forward" button to bring back the picture of the big man in Vegas. Lisa kept her eyes on Dan.

"I still don't see any…wait," Lisa paused. She looked more closely. The glow from the laptop screen in his eyes and from his skin was intensified.

A sideways glance at the display showed Lisa that it was not glowing any brighter than before. Dan clicked the forward button again, back to the frozen video of the police chief, and Lisa noticed that the brighter glow remained.

"Wait," she said again.

Dan's right forearm was resting on the desk less than an inch away from the keyboard. Lisa took Dan's wrist and lowered it, away from the light of the laptop screen and into the shadows beneath the desk. She noticed fearfully that his hand and wrist were still glowing. The glow was faint and pale and silver…and familiar.

She saw that glow before, only much more intensely. It was several weeks earlier when she and Dan met. He saved her life against the razor-edged, animated sheets of darkness that he called shadow-wraiths. According to Dan, the shadow-wraiths had been sent by the demon.

"That's right," Dan said when he saw realization in Lisa's eyes. "Even through a still image, even through pre-recorded video, Children of the Old Ones can feel a demon and its magic. I felt it for an instant when you were channel surfing."

"Oh God," Lisa breathed.

"You asked why the demon would use the same disguise," Dan reminded her. "To make sure it had my attention. Even if I couldn't feel its presence through a still photo or through a computer or TV, I would've eventually seen that story. That guy is too big not to notice and his picture's all over the place. You know how these national network news stations are. They all play the same stories over and over on TV and online.

"It was only a matter of time before I saw the story and pictures, and when I did I would've recognized the big bald guy instantly. I would've known it wasn't WorldHopper because blowing up buildings isn't the dragon's M.O. He just tears up shit with his bare claws and eats people."

Lisa frowned. "He *just* eats people?"

"That's what dragons do," Dan said matter-of-factly. "That leaves the only other changeling I'm aware of on this side of the WorldGate. As for the police chief, the demon must've impersonated him to send a message."

"What message?" Lisa asked, struggling to contain her nervous tick.

Dan looked at her for a long time, as if he had an answer but was debating whether or not to share it. Lisa assumed he came to a decision because he exhaled heavily and lifted his shoulders in a resigned shrug.

"Let's see," he said.

He used the touch pad to click the tiny right arrow below the frozen video to resume the feed.

We believe this is more than a coincidence, the police chief was saying with a West-Texas drawl. *This suspect destroys a tavern with his bare hands and evades the authorities. Weeks later an explosion rocks a Vegas hotel minutes after he leaves it. We've also confirmed that there is some kind of relationship between the suspect and Dan Franklin, the man believed to have disappeared with Lisa Harvey.*

Lisa gasped at the mention of her name but listened with rapt attention.

While we've yet to confirm this, we believe Mrs. Harvey, with her appearance altered and using a false identity, was a resident at the hotel. We do not, however, think she was in the hotel at the time of the explosion.

The reporter pulled the microphone away from the chief.

So are you saying you believe Lisa Harvey might have had a hand in the explosion, chief?

I'm saying nothing of the sort, ma'am, the police chief returned defensively. *I'm saying that there are other facets of this case that have to be looked into, but we honestly don't have many avenues to pursue right now.*

Her husband is also missing and he's an orphan with no next of kin that we can identify. Dan Franklin only has one family member that we know of, his grandson – who also *happens to be missing.*

The chief turned from the reporter and looked right into the camera. Lisa felt like he was looking across time and space directly at her.

We may have to re-interview Missus Harvey's friends and family. We need to know what was going on in her personal life at the time of her disappearance. We'd hate to do it at such a terrible time for them, but I'm afraid we may not have much choice.

With that, the reporter pulled the microphone away and started talking. Her voice droned on inaudibly to Lisa. All she could hear was the police chief's – no, the *demon's* – last few words echoing in her head.

We may have to re-interview Miss Harvey's friends and family...

...I'm afraid we may not have much choice.

"That's the message," Lisa said, tears streaming down her face. "If it can't find me, it's gonna go after my family."

* * *

The ugly dog sprung to its feet so quickly and so forcefully in the back seat of the moving sedan that Hunter almost cried out in surprise. Shepherd jerked the steering wheel to the right before quickly straightening out the car.

"I think it's got their scent again," Hunter said.

"No shit," Shepherd replied irritably.

The dog turned to the left and released a booming bark.

"You might want to go *that* way," Hunter advised, pointing to the left. "I'll call in backup."

Shepherd scoffed. "Do you think we need backup against an old man and a broad?"

"Have you been paying attention?" Hunter asked in disbelief. "They've been dodging us for weeks, leaving dead and injured agents in their wake. Hell, this 'old man and broad' shook a seasoned wetworks team and highjacked one of our freaking choppers. Screw ego. I'm calling for backup. And you might want to hurry up and turn left."

"Just make the call. Let me do the driving."

That horrifying glow radiated from the retriever's eyes as it released a warning growl aimed at Shepherd, who cringed for a moment before taking the first available left turn.

"If this hell hound is as tough as he is ugly," Shepherd said, "I don't think we'll need backup."

12.2
KINGDOM OF CARTHA - CARTHAN PALACE

Queen Lairen sat alone patiently at the table in her private sound-dampened conference chamber, thankful that her son was occupied with other royal business. She had not heard from her Head Mage since his last report days earlier, when he promised her that the Hell Key was in his possession and he was using it to lure Raxe and Rionn Lorr to their doom. Assuming he was telling the truth, she had no idea how he had obtained the Hell Key, and that made her uneasy.

She had a network of informants in the Kingdom of Lorr, just as she was sure the Kingdom of Lorr had a network of spies here in Cartha. She heard from more than one source that both offworlders had been seen on the Lorrian palace grounds a day earlier, so Glund's plan obviously did not work. She should have heard from her Head Mage by now.

Of course, there was always the possibility that he had been killed.

When she heard the muffled knock outside the door, she rose, went to the door and used the interior knocker to signal them permission to open the door. The thick door swung inward slowly and in walked her new First Advisor to the Head Mage. She wondered if she should call him her Head Mage now.

"I notice, Mage Homer, that you do not have your satchel with you this time. Is it safe to assume that there is no communication from Stratham Glund?"

The wizard nodded. "It is, my queen. I have some rather disturbing news."

"He failed," the queen said, rolling her eyes. "He failed and the Children of the Old Ones killed him."

"Yes and no, your majesty."

Homer paused and the queen arched an eyebrow. If he was so dull that she had to *tell* him to continue, she would have him killed as soon as he stepped out of the private conference chamber. Her reensapir heart lay uncovered in a chair on the other side of the conference table, so his magic would not be able to help him.

Fortunately for Homer, he was smart enough to read her impatient look. "Yes, he failed, apparently long before his last communication. He was most certainly killed. His body washed ashore two days ago. The state of decay indicates that he has been dead for quite some time.

"You would have been informed sooner, but the sailors who found the body could not identify it. It was too damaged for them recognize. One of the fishwives, who also works at a local brothel that Glund frequented, noticed a familiar tattoo on the dead man's back.

"No one believed her, of course, but eventually word made its way to me. I've known Glund for years, as you are aware, so I viewed the body and I also performed an identification spell. It was indeed Stratham Glund. The man we have been communicating with recently is an imposter."

The queen was silent for a long time. Her upper lip twitched with frustration. She breathed deeply and looked at her new Head Mage, who had grown visibly uncomfortable with the silence.

Bloody demon she thought.

Her first impulse was to suspect Mage Homer, but she knew he could not be the demon in disguise. While she was not a conjurer, she knew enough of her history and the arcane arts to know that a demon is a creature of pure magic. The open reensapir heart would render him helpless at this proximity. An intelligent demon would never come this close to such danger.

The Carthan queen thought about the seven sovereigns with whom her husband had conspired to remove the Kingdom of Lorr from the coveted Seat of Power. She also considered the one kingdom that refused to attend the secret meeting that commenced this ill-fated operation. The time had come for a damage-control campaign.

"Have the royal courier sent to my office," she finally said with a defeated sigh. "I suppose I have some letters to write, nine letters, to be exact."

12.3

THE KINGDOM OF LORR – LORR PALACE

The suns had long since set the next day by the time Joel, Raxe and Rionn Lorr, accompanied by Catherine and young Shanderah, met outside of a small library in one of the many high towers of Lorr Palace. Shandie had recovered from the exertion of transporting Joel the length of the kingdom much sooner than Rionn expected.

Raxe glanced around expectantly before he pursed his lips for the briefest moment. The observant wife of the Head Mage, however, did not miss that moment. Catherine's elegant lips curved up on one side as she addressed Raxe.

"Annastace wanted to be here, I assure you, but she is otherwise occupied. She is busy preparing herself and her eldest son for his knighting ceremony. She sends her apologies and her *very* fond wishes."

Raxe flushed. "Are you a mind reader, too?"

Catherine giggled. "No, Raxe, not at all. It *is* strange, though… Annastace asked me the same question."

As crestfallen as Raxe was at her absence, he thought it was probably for the best. He wanted to see her. He *really* wanted to see her, but he did not want to have to tell her good bye. He had a suspicion that she might have felt the same way. Would they ever see each other again? The likelihood that they would not irked him. He wondered if she was having the same thoughts.

And then he noticed Catherine's canted emerald eyes studying him knowingly. He knew she was not reading his mind because he would have felt it, but she was a woman, and a sharp one. She did not have to read his mind. He cleared his throat conspicuously as they crossed the threshold into the library.

"Ethan is being knighted?" he asked, changing the subject. "Good. He deserves it. I wish we could've killed that damned Dierglyorr on this side of the WorldGate. I'd have time to go to the ceremony."

And see Annastace before I left.

The library occupied an entire level set aside for the Head Mage. The room was constructed of eight walls, roughly fifteen feet long, intersecting to form an equal sided octagon. Six of the twenty-foot high walls, including the wall containing the entrance and exit door, were lined with shelves containing books of various sizes. Some of the tomes looked fairly new but most looked old and dusty. Other shelves housed rolls upon rolls of scrolls of different lengths and thickness.

A seventh wall was papered with maps, some as tall as a man and some as small as a man's hand. Adjacent to that was the eighth wall, which was bare of any objects but covered with writing. The writing was in a variety of languages and written in different colors of chalk and coal. At the bottom center of that wall was placed a simple wooden writing desk and a big, comfortable-looking, padded chair. On the desk rested a handful of rocks of different sizes and colors that matched the colors of the writing on the walls.

Raxe could see the small white droplets of magical energy drifting through the room. They radiated lazily from the surface of many of the books and scrolls, and also some, but not all, of the writings on the wall. The energy radiated most intensely from the writings closest to the ceiling. Elevating a dozen or more feet above the floor for a few minutes for Rionn Lorr.

"Are you ready?" Rionn asked, lifting the big, beautiful broadsword with the image of the Gatekeeper etched masterfully into the blade.

"Yes," Joel said quickly.

Raxe nodded. A thought occurred to him. "Rionn, how are we gonna let you know when we've killed the demon?"

The Head Mage reached into the pocket of his loose breaches with his free hand and brought out two boxes of reflection sand and handed one box to Raxe and the other to Joel.. "We can communicate the same way we did here."

Raxe's eyebrows lifted. "Those things can connect across the WorldGate?"

"They will be able to in a moment," Rionn confirmed, "thanks to the WorldGate Key." He reached into another pocket to produce one more box and handed it to his wife.

"After activating the magic of the WorldGate Key, but before I open the portal," Rionn explained, "I will use the Key to draw the necessary symbols to link the boxes instead of using the stylus. That will enable the three of us to send messages to each other, even across the WorldGate."

"You plan to *draw* with that big-ass blade?" Joel asked.

Rionn smiled. "It won't be easy, but I've been practicing since I learned of the spell a year ago. I didn't know if the opportunity would ever arise to use it, but it's always good to be prepared. I will, however, need some assistance from the two of you."

"Don't tell me," Raxe said. "You need our blood."

Joel's impatient scowl turned into a surprised one. "What?" He started to protest, to explain how he had no intention of contacting Rionn or Raxe after all of this was done. Instead, he shrugged. "If I say no we'll just waste time arguing. Let's get it over with."

"You're finally starting to get it," Raxe chuckled.

Catherine held little Shandie close to her thigh as she looked on. Catherine's concern darkened her expression. Shandie, a smaller clone of her mother, wore the same worry on her tiny round face. Both of them knew what it took out of Rionn to use the WorldGate Key and neither of them liked it.

"If you could all open the boxes," he instructed.

As Raxe, Joel and Catherine snapped open the boxes of reflection sand, Rionn Lorr opened his tunic. He pressed the fine edge of the WorldGate Key, nearly at the hilt, firmly against his chest and slid it smoothly down and across.

By the time he got to the midpoint of the blade, he pulled the enchanted greatsword away. He held it about half an inch away from his chest to minimize the visibility of the thin line of blood that snaked from his wound to the blade. He was already standing with his back to his wife and daughter to keep them from witnessing the spectacle but he did not want to take any chances.

THE KEY QUEST

Catherine had seen her husband use the Key twice before: three years earlier when he brought Raxe through the WorldGate the first time and again when he opened the portal between worlds to bring Raxe and Joel back. She wanted to be there to support her husband but she was not anxious to see it again. Neither Rionn nor Catherine knew how Shandie would react so they certainly did not want her to see it.

When enough blood was drawn, the Head Mage held the blade out toward Raxe and Joel and gave them a nod. Raxe stepped forward and ran his palm a couple of inches along the blade and pulled his hand back, holding it up a few inches away from the blade. Joel hesitated for a moment, shrugged and followed suit.

As with the Head Mage, a thin stream of blood stretched from the offworlders' upraised palms to the Key. The enchanted blade absorbed the blood greedily but only for a few seconds before it stopped. By that time, the enchanted sword was shimmering with an intense silver glow.

Rionn stepped to Joel and gestured for him to hold his box of reflection sand low enough to accommodate the length of the blade. He held the grip high with the sword pointing down and placed his free hand against the flat of the blade to keep it steady. Rionn drew the small symbols by expertly manipulating the sword grip. After approximately five seconds, he used his index finger to stir away the symbols. He then did the same to the other two boxes.

"It is done," Rionn said. "The boxes are linked to each other and to us. Now, I will send you home."

He stepped back, took the sword grip in both hands and hefted it to draw a big, blazing silver circle in mid air. The inside of the circle quickly faded to nothingness. The thin ring of sliver fire outlined the black vacuum of reality that was the WorldGate portal.

"Oh," Shandie breathed in awe.

Joel was frightened and more than a little hesitant when he first saw the open WorldGate back in Chicago. This time he did not waste a second. He snapped his box of reflection sand closed, pocketed it, and all but leapt into the void.

Raxe stared at the silver-rimmed black disk where Joel had vanished and shook his head. He closed and pocketed his small box of magical sand and turned to the Lorr family.

"Ladies, take care of this wizard, would you? And tell Annastace I said good bye, and that I *will* see her again…hopefully under pleasant circumstances."

"We will," Catherine promised, "God's speed to you."

Raxe nodded in thanks and turned to the Head Mage. "Good luck, cuz," he said to Rionn. "Be careful when you use that HellGate Key."

"I will," Rionn Lorr answered. "Thank you, Ryan, yet again, for your assistance. The Kingdom of Lorr, this entire world, in fact, is once again in your debt. May the Old Ones guide you in your search for the Dierglyorr. And worry not. Should the beast manage to escape back to this world, we will be ready for it."

"It won't be coming back," Raxe assured with a hint of ice in his rasp of a voice.

Rionn thought he saw a faint shadow pass behind Raxe's intense, dark brown eyes. He assumed it was frustrated determination, but before he could look deeper the offworlder turned and stepped into the darkness.

12.4

Shortly after Ethan Sureblade's knighting ceremony, the new young knight, his mother and Nicolette stood together at the small reception. Annastace was regaling Nicolette with one of her seemingly endless amusing tales from Ethan's childhood, bringing a flush to Ethan's cheeks and pleading looks at his mother.

Even though she was making him want to run and hide, he was happy to hear her laughing. She was melancholy when they arrived at the ceremony. Her noble attempt to hide it fooled everyone but her eldest son. Ethan knew she wished her husband and his father, Meldrick, could be there to witness the ceremony. They were both upset that Raxe was not able to attend, which made the situation somewhat awkward for Ethan. He knew his mother loved Meldrick with all of her heart and he knew that she had feelings for Raxe.

Once the knighting ceremony ended and the reception began, Ethan wanted to comfort her but he did not know how, so he said nothing about either man and tried to make small talk with her. Annastace appreciated the effort her son made and loved him all the more for it. The poor boy, however, bored her nearly to tears. Ethan's younger siblings, the pre-teen twins Arielle and August, were not there to provide their unending form of entertainment and distraction. They were at the ceremony but were chasing about with other children their age.

Nicolette's arrival was a great relief to both of them. And she was indeed *Nicolette*. Her raven hair flowed in gentle waves down to her shoulders, beautifully complimenting her soft round face and big hazel eyes. The laced bodice of her frilled ivory blouse was at once modest and alluring. It fit her tiny waist snugly but did not hug her chest audaciously. Her long burgundy skirt draped perfectly over her legs, accentuating the curve of her hips without clinging to them. Her tiny feet, clad in slender ivory shoes with a short heel, were barely visible under the long skirt.

When Ethan managed to stop staring, he introduced Nicolette to his mother. Annastace's eyes sparkled. She wasted no time in embarrassing him.

"So *you're* the young lady with whom my Ethan is so smitten!" she said. "You should see the look on his face when he talks about you. Well, it's very much like the look on his face right now."

"Mother…" Ethan began. But Annastace quited him with a playful swat on the head and the storytelling began.

Ever watchful, Ethan spotted one of the king's stewards weaving his way through the reception hall. Ethan realized he was coming their way, likely bringing a message to him or his mother. The look on the man's face was implacable. The young Sureblade could not determine if he was bringing good news or bad. By then Ethan did not care what kind of news it was as long as it quieted his effusive mother.

Mother and son were surprised when the steward told them they had been summoned to King William's private audience. Ethan was thankful…until his mother asked:

"Would the king mind if Nicolette accompanied us? I'm *so* enjoying our conversation."

"Mother," Ethan said in a tone dangerously close to a whine. "The king has summoned *us*."

"What's wrong Ethan?" Nicolette teased. "Have you grown tired of my company?"

Ethan rolled his eyes. "You know that's not the case, Nicolette. It's just that the king –"

Annastace interrupted, speaking to the steward. "Did King William specifically say we could *not* bring someone?"

"Why, no, Lady Sureblade," he answered. "He did not."

"Come with us," Annastace insisted. "If the king objects to your presence, the kind steward can escort you back here."

"Thank you Mrs. Sureblade," Nicolette said with a smile. "I've never met the king in person and I've seen him only from a distance. It would be an honor to accompany you!"

With a sigh, Ethan followed the other three as his mother talked, Nicolette chuckled, and the steward smirked.

12.5

King William sat in his private audience chamber awaiting the arrival of the Sureblades. He was not alone. King Joseph Megerathon the Third of Darshay sat in the comfortable distinguished visitor's chair at the foot of the table. The large, plush chair was immensely comfortable. King Joseph, on the other hand, was anything but. The young Darshayan King was somewhat disconcerted by his Lorrian counterpart.

Prince Graham Broadbow sat at his customary place two seats to the right of the head of the table. Both kings' personal guards stood near the exit door, two guards for each king. All of this was customary.

King William, on the other hand, had never been one to stand on ceremony if he could avoid it. He did not sit in his elevated Sovereign's chair at the head of the table, which was a smaller version of his ornate throne. William felt the audience chamber's Sovereign's chair was too elaborate for his simple tastes and he did not like looking down on people.

Instead of sitting in his chair, William filled a chair with his generous bulk only a few seats down the table to the left of King Joseph, just beyond the reach of the Lorrian King's long, massive arms. King Joseph was very nearly half William's size. He was a foot shorter and his slight build was almost comical compared to William's hulking frame. If William wished, he could probably reach over and snap the younger king's neck before Joseph's guards could make a move to stop him.

"What troubles you King Joseph?" King William asked with an easy smile. "Is your chair not to your liking?"

"This is a fine seat, indeed," Joseph answered. "I wonder, though, if there is anything wrong with *your* chair."

"Bah," William said with a dismissive wave of a beefy hand. "We're both kings. I'll not look down on you and yell the length of this ridiculous table. I save formalities for formal occasions. From the clandestine nature of your visit, this is clearly *not* a formal meeting. Am I wrong?"

Joseph grinned. "My father warned me about you," the young king said. "I assumed he was joking or exaggerating."

The prince leaned forward. "And what *exactly* did your father say about my father?"

William grinned. "Calm yourself, son. You are still but a prince. You do not address a king in such a fashion, even if he is a few years younger than you." He turned his attention back to Joseph.

"As I remember, Joseph, your father was not one for exaggerating. He was as proper as you and just as taken aback by my less than formal behavior in informal settings when first we met."

"I am my father's son," Joseph admitted. His grin turned into a scowl. "You speak true, William. This is surely not an official visit, though it is an important one."

"I expect the Sureblades will be here soon," William said. "Is this something that needs to wait for them?"

"Not at all," Joseph answered. "I'd prefer to tell you this part of it before they arrive." When King William nodded for him to continue Joseph went on. "My father once told me that, despite your disdain for proper etiquette, you were a good man. Had your paths been different you may have even been friends."

"He spoke true," agreed King William. "Your father was a good man. But alas, politics don't often allow for true friendship among sovereigns."

"I trusted my father's wisdom," Joseph continued. "I also had a great deal of faith in his judgment of others. While the first Great Directive keeps us from joining against other kingdoms of the Known Lands, we can still assist one another in other matters."

One of William's bushy, rust-red eyebrows rose in suspicion. He knew a king would not travel to another kingdom for a triviality. Prince Graham, however, spoke up before his father could, and not in a gracious tone.

"In addition to your business with the Sureblade boy, have you come to ask a favor of my father, King Joseph?"

Joseph shook his head. "Actually, Prince Graham, I've come to *repay* a favor. When I was a child, The Kingdom of Kattahn launched a surprise assault on Darshay. They captured the Northern Territories before we could mobilize a response. They planned to occupy the north and hold it against our army and navy until the bulk of their forces could cross the Gulf of Sai-Il to solidify their occupation."

"It was during the first decade of my rule," William said, realizing where this conversation was going. "I remember it well. They would have used your Northern Territories as a base of operations to launch a campaign to conquer the rest of your kingdom."

Joseph nodded gravely. "Had it not been for your assistance they would have been successful. Our modest little kingdom would have become a southern colony of Kattahn."

"Ah," King William contested, holding up a cautionary finger. "We did not actually *assist* you. That would have been a clear breach of the first Great Directive. We would not risk punishment from the Old Ones to defend one kingdom against another."

Joseph smiled a conspiratorial smile. "Of course you did not assist us. My father did not ask for assistance and you did not offer it. You merely defended yourselves. There was no collusion between us, therefore, there was no breach of the Great Directive."

"Correct," William concurred.

Joseph's grin grew wider as he continued. "Your army and navy just *happened* to be conducting exercises in the Wyrm Mountains shortly after the Kattahn occupation...the Wyrm Mountains, neutral land and dragon country, no less. Why would anyone think Kattahn's occupying force would mistake your exercises for an offensive?"

"Exactly," the king replied with an innocent expression. "We had no choice but to defend ourselves against their utterly unprovoked assault."

"Yes," Joseph agreed, "and you defended yourselves vigorously. It was just a coincidence that your spirited self-defense bought us time to assemble our own defenses and repel the invaders before the rest of their forces arrived. With our Northern Territories reclaimed and our army and navy in place, the Kattahn military called off their attack."

"Yes," the prince interjected impatiently. "The Kattahn king claimed the invaders were renegade ex-military and mercenaries trying to appropriate a kingdom of their own. He said that the larger force crossing the gulf had been tasked with capturing the renegades and returning them to Kattahn.

"No one believed him, of course, but neither could they put the lie to his words. The story is used in lessons at the academy and my father authorized the exercise. Do you think to repay this favor with an unnecessary history lesson?"

"Graham!" King William barked, his heavy baritone bouncing off of the walls. "I'll say again and one last time. This is a sitting *king* to whom you speak, in *my* audience chamber. To disrespect him is to disrespect me. You are here because I want you to learn what it is to conduct business as a king. Do not make me regret my decision."

Prince Graham huffed and scowled but went silent. He crossed his arms almost petulantly and sat back in his chair.

"Forgive my son, King Joseph," William bade. "I would blame his brashness on his youth but you are younger still, yet conduct yourself with much more maturity."

"My father chided me more than once for the same type of behavior," King Joseph admitted. "Had he not succumbed to pneumonia, he likely would still have to. The gods know I would've preferred to remain a brash youth for many more years than to have this responsibility thrust upon me in such a dire fashion."

The prince's expression softened at this. "My sincere apologies to you, King Joseph, for speaking out of turn and disrespectfully."

"Accepted, Prince Graham," Joseph said graciously. "I assure you, I was not prattling on without good reason. I told this story as a parallel to what I believe is happening now with the other eight kingdoms."

"Pray tell," William said, folding his hands on the table before him.

"As you avoided breaking the first Great Directive to assist my kingdom all those years ago, I fear several of the other kingdoms of the Known Lands have done something similar to contribute to your recent difficulties. You probably know that there was a time, several weeks ago, when the sovereigns of the other eight kingdoms were away from their palaces simultaneously."

King William nodded. "We heard whispers."

"Just before that time," Joseph continued, "I received a veiled invitation through very convoluted methods. It was disguised as a rumor, one with just enough substance to merit an investigation. The rumor stated, in essence, that nine-tenths of the Known Lands shared a common problem, and they should gather at a common table to discuss a solution."

King William's face darkened. "An unofficial meeting of the Council of Sovereignty…at the Table of Sovereigns?"

"Was this a gathering to discuss a so-called solution to the Kingdom of Lorr?" Prince Graham asked angrily.

Joseph nodded. "I don't know what else it could have been. I did not attend, of course, but from your recent troubles I can only assume that at least several of the other sovereigns did – if not all of them."

Prince Graham was aghast. "They would dare gather to plot against another kingdom at the Table of Sovereigns, the very spot that symbolizes not only unity but retribution for such an action? What blasphemy is this? Are they *trying* to draw the wrath of the Old Ones?"

"My thoughts exactly, prince," Joseph said. "I could not believe they would take such a risk. I assuming the meeting, as unprecedented as it was, had to have been a gathering to discuss cooperative ideas to enhance their kingdoms and better their chances at gaining the Seat of Power. It never occurred to me that they would actually hatch a plan to attack the Kingdom of Lorr. Had I thought that was the case I would have come to you much sooner."

The prince scratched his chin. "The parallel you spoke of. The council met to discuss a way to unleash the plague of the walkers and set the *Ken d'Zanir* upon us without actually joining forces for an outright attack."

"Yes," Joseph confirmed. "I have contemplated this quite a bit recently. The *Ken* are of the *S'Zan Rho* nation. *Rho*, as you are aware, is the S'Zan word for 'outsider.' The *S'Zan Rho* live in close proximity to the S'Zan Kingdom but are not a part of it."

King William nodded. "They could be employed by one kingdom to attack another without a risk to the Directive."

"Exactly," Joseph confirmed. "A large transport barge of unknown origin was spotted ferrying ballistae south through the Straits of Issil. Days later, another seafaring vessel moved through the same route. It was a vessel the likes of which have never been seen in the Known Lands. It was made all of metal. Upon its deck was stacked large containers also made of metal. It moved swiftly through the water as if by magic, faster than any traditional vessel, with no sails or oars to propel it."

The Head Mage had already reported the remains of that vessel had been found at the bottom of Lake Onyx. The king knew that the sixth level demon was responsible for bringing the craft across the WorldGate from Raxe's world. The demon used it to contaminate Lake Onyx.

William would not speak of it at that moment, though. Even though rumors of an intelligent demon had been running rampant for weeks, the king would not cause a panic by confirming those rumors. No confirmation would be made until he knew the demon was destroyed.

"Which monarch do you suspect is the mastermind of these schemes, King Joseph?" Prince Graham asked.

Joseph thought for a moment. "Who has the most to gain from the Kingdom of Lorr's fall?"

"King Vergoth," the prince answered at once. "But Queen Lairen sent a bird to us, and likely to all of the Known Lands. She sent the message that the Carthan Head Mage and his two advisors plotted against us without the sovereigns' knowledge. She says Tilsworth killed Vergoth the First when they were caught out."

"Indeed," Joseph agreed. "However, it would not surprise me in the least if the Carthan sovereigns were actually directing their mages and using the rumors of this demon as an excuse. Or perhaps they were knowingly working for the demon. His wife and son may continue to push the dead king's agenda."

"Perhaps," Prince Graham allowed. "But you must admit that the most direct route from the *Ken*'s Westin continent to the Kingdom of Lorr cuts directly through your kingdom."

"It does," Joseph conceded. "But I assure you that the *Ken* did not pass through the Kingdom of Darshay. It occurs to me that they could have sailed to the southern tip of this continent and come up through the Kingdom of Cartha and Hell's Mountains without being seen. Or perhaps they went north and arrived here hidden below the deck of one of the vessels that were seen travelling through the Straits of Issil.

"All the other kingdoms had to do was ignore them as they crossed their lands or sailed through their waters on their way to this kingdom. These are all ways they could have initiated an offensive of this sort without actively joining forces to challenge you."

"Or the ways they *think* they could," King William added after brooding in silence while the younger men conversed. "For all we know they have broken it already and the penalty has yet to be imposed. The first Great Directive only speaks of the penalty as 'dire chaos.' No one knows what form the Old Ones' retribution would take, or how long it would take, for that matter. It could take years. It could take seconds."

"I vow to you, King William," Joseph began, sitting straighter in his chair with a solemn countenance. "If those fools have broken the first Great Directive and unleashed the wrath of the Old Ones, the Kingdom of Darshay will stand with you to do whatever it takes to make things right. Many still underestimate my kingdom because of its size and my youth. They call me the 'Boy King' or 'Little Monarch' when I am not around. But like the death-knell serpent, while the Kingdom of Darshay is small, its strike is deadly."

King William stood, prompting the prince and the visiting king to do the same. One long stride brought the King of Lorr to within arm's length of the King of Darshay. Though he dwarfed the younger king in height and girth, there was nothing but grim resolution and confidence in King Joseph's bearing. They shook hands firmly as Prince Graham made his way down the length of the long conference table.

"Well said, King Joseph," William complimented. "I count myself fortunate to call you an ally."

"And I, you," Graham returned.

The three of them turned at a knock on the chamber door.

"The Sureblades," called the king's steward from outside the room, "and the Keeper's Hound Nicolette Walker."

The king nodded to one of his guards. The guard opened the door to admit Annastace, Ethan, and Nicolette behind the steward and one of the royal guards standing outside the chamber. The three visitors bowed deeply.

"King William, Prince Graham," Annastace greeted. The thin ringlet on the third man's head was clearly a monarch's traveling crown. She glanced up at the silk ocean blue doublet trimmed in gold with an embroidered crest on the breast. The crest was composed of a golden lion superimposed on a shield. "And King Joseph of Darshay."

Joseph nodded in greeting. Both Ethan and Nicolette stiffened at the revelation of the other's identity.

"Enough of that," King William scolded. "Let us all sit."

Prince Graham stepped near the door to greet them. "The Lady Sureblade," he welcomed, taking her hand in his and lifting it to plant a soft kiss on her knuckles. "You are as lovely as you were when I saw you last, if not more so."

"Thank you, your grace," she replied with a polite smile.

The prince turned to Ethan. "And young...well, I suppose it is *Sir* Ethan, now. Congratulations on your knighthood. That is a unique accomplishment for one so young."

"You are too kind, Prince Graham," Ethan said. The prince wore a sincere smile and spoke kind words, but Ethan could see the truth in the man's eyes. His gaze was more mocking than congratulatory.

When the prince turned to Nicolette, his gaze changed to something Ethan liked even less.

"Nicolette Walker," he said, kissing her hand as he had kissed Annastace's, but Ethan noticed that Prince Graham's lips lingered a heartbeat or two longer on Nicolette's hand. "My, but you have certainly grown into a lovey woman."

Nicolette smiled. "Why...thank you, your Grace," she said with a girlish curtsey. "You are indeed too kind."

Ethan knew Nicolette well enough to recognize that smile. It was Arrowhead's smile, the false smile she deployed to wear to charm male landowners into letting the Keeper's Hounds hunt loosed demons on their property or pass through their holdings during a hunt. He also noticed the question that flashed in her eyes for the briefest instant. He was sure her question was the same as his.

The prince's comment implied he knew her as a girl, before he left to spend four years in Cartha. Nicolette had not come north to attend the military Royal Academy until after the prince went to Cartha. The prince was either attempting to flatter her or mistaking her for someone else.

"So," King Joseph began, his face expressionless. "This is Ethan and Nicky. If only Derrick and Elbert were here...or should I say Hammer and Quick? I would be able to confront all of the outsiders that helped the rebels overthrow one of my barons."

Both teens started to protest, but they stopped short out of respect for the visiting king. King William said nothing. King Joseph said nothing. Prince Graham stood behind the two men, almost a head taller than Joseph but half a head shorter than his father. Ethan cast a nervous look at his mother, but she stood mute as well.

"Have you nothing to say to King Joseph, Ethan?" the prince taunted, finally breaking the awkward silence.

Nicolette glanced at the prince, her nervous expression going cold. Out of the corner of his eye, Ethan saw her turn into Arrowhead. "It was *I* who decided to help the rebels," she admitted, both respectful and proud. "I convinced Hammer to assist me. Ethan and Quick arrived later."

The prince scoffed. "Are you letting a *woman* take an arrow for you, *Sir* Ethan Sureblade?"

"She speaks true," Ethan said in a measured tone. "I'll not lie to my king, not even to save my pride."

King William grunted. "You were in my employ when you participated in the overthrow of a lord in a neighboring kingdom. Such a deed could be construed as an act of war."

Ethan lifted his chin and squared his shoulders. "Yes, my king, and good King Joseph, we have no excuse for our actions. We felt that was our best opportunity to free the Child of the Old Ones being held captive by the baron under the direction of the Demon Dierglyorr."

King Joseph smiled. "And rid me of that mercenary and charlatan who had taken over Eastedge in the process. You saved me the trouble of having to do it myself."

The young king turned to the elder one. "Dirk Tauran managed to curry the favor of many in my royal council. He won the support of the more influential lords in my kingdom. No doubt it was through bribery. There is still a bit of instability in my kingdom after my father's death. Some of the high lords have not yet fully committed to supporting my claim to the throne. If I had given the order to remove Tauran, it could have ignited a civil war.

"We wondered how the usurper of such a relatively insignificant barony could entrench himself so deeply into our politics in so short a time. Now that I know he had a damned demon as a sponsor, I count ourselves lucky things didn't turn out much worse. I suppose this is yet another favor I owe you, good King William."

A sly grin lifted one corner of William's mustache. "If you insist; but beware, King Joseph. I may be calling that favor in fairly soon."

"Wait," Annastace began, "your majesties," she quickly added. "The youngsters are not being reprimanded?"

"GateKeeper's beard," King William swore with a deep chuckle. "He's *thanking* them!"

King Joseph laughed. Ethan and Nicolette exhaled their relief in unison. Annastace chuckled nervously.

THE KEY QUEST

The prince yawned in boredom and continued to eye the petite, slender and lovely raven-haired girl. King Joseph beckoned to one of his guards, who stepped forward and handed the king a sheathed greatsword.

"I've also come to give you this, King William."

The Darshayan King visibly struggled with it for a moment, the burden nearly pulling him off balance. He managed to get his bearings and held the weapon forward with a hand under the handle and the other at the fat end of an ornate black scabbard bearing the shield-and-lion crest of the Kingdom of Darshay. Ethan had never seen the scabbard but he immediately recognized the cold iron crossguard and grip. He heard Nicolette gasp. She recognized it, as well.

The Darshayan king needlessly drew it out to show them a bit of the blade, which looked more like ivory or bone than metal. It didn't gleam like steel. It seemed to absorb the light more than reflect it. Ethan and Nicolette knew that the rest of the blade still hidden within the sheath was not quite as long as an average greatsword blade. It was however, longer and wider than most broadswords, even though it was not whole.

They knew all-too-well that both edges of that hidden broken blade were razor sharp, as was its jaggedly severed edge. They also knew the legend of that blade: If its keen edges did not kill, its poisonous bite surely would.

"Dragon-fang?" Ethan breathed.

"Indeed," King Joseph confirmed. "A weapon of great renown, made from a real dragon's tooth. You defeated its previous owner. You were in a hurry that evening and surely did not have time to retrieve it so we retrieved it for you." He pushed the blade completely back into the sheath.

"This is my thank you to the Keeper's Hounds for your service to the Kingdom of Darshay. I believe you, Ethan Sureblade, are the one to whom it should be presented. After all, it was you who brought down the false baron."

Ethan only stared at the proffered weapon.

"Are you going to take it?" King William asked.

Ethan blinked. "Of course, forgive me, your highness."

He took Dragon-fang to the relief of King Joseph's straining arms. Nicolette watched the muscles flexing in Ethan's shoulders and arms beneath his tunic sleeves. Out of her peripheral vision, the sharp-eyed young huntress and archer could see Ethan's mother looking at *her*. She flushed and turned her attention back to Ethan's blue eyes while purposely avoiding meeting the gaze of the leering prince.

"My sincere thanks, your highness," Ethan said. "Though I'm afraid I'm not worthy of this gift."

He really wanted to say that he detested it. Dragon-fang was more cursed than enchanted. Its last two owners were the worst kind of men. They were pawns of demons and sadistic wizards; ruthless killers of innocents, men, women and children; rapists and thieves. Worst of all, Dragon-fang was the weapon used to kill his father. Ethan wanted no part of it.

"The spoils of victory, my young knight," King Joseph insisted. "Mount it as a trophy somewhere if you would not carry it in battle. Make sure it's somewhere high, though, preferably encased in hard glass, so that the unwary won't knick a finger and have to lose an entire hand."

"Again, thank you, King Joseph," Ethan said. "But Tauran was not the true owner. The offworlder Raxe defeated the Finder, Dragon-fang's true owner. Tauran merely stole it when it was left behind. If anything, it should go to the Child of the Old Ones, to Raxe."

King William smiled and shook his head. "Blades, son, you are as modest as your father. The offworlder is going back to his world if he's not gone already."

"Nonetheless, good kings, I cannot in good conscious –"

"Alright," William conceded. "We can find a safe place for it here at the palace until Raxe comes back to claim it."

Nicolette saw the slightest shift in Ethan's posture and knew it was the tension flowing out of him. Annastace, with a practiced smile, hid her sadness at seeing the foul weapon that took her husband's life. She was very happy, however to see the relief in her son's eyes. Both women knew his relief had nothing to do with modesty.

Chapter 13: Overtaken

13.1
CHICAGO, IL

As their van sped south on Lake Shore Drive, Dan felt thankful yet again for the relatively mild winter. The snow had not been falling heavily. While the lawns and trees were frosted with snow the streets were wet but not icy. Dan was able to make good time. It was the middle of the week and late enough in the evening that Dan did not have the stop and go traffic of rush hour to fight.

"Where are we going?" Lisa asked.

"South," Dan said distractedly. "I'm trying to lead them away from the highest concentrations of people. The demon proved in Vegas that it's not concerned with collateral damage. We have to get a little further away from downtown and the museums. There's a long stretch of beaches and then Jackson Park. It's too cold for the beaches and park to be occupied. That'll minimize the danger to bystanders and we'll have a little more room."

"A little more room for what?" Lisa asked.

"Lisa," the old man said in an even voice. "You *know* what we have to do."

"I *don't* know!" Lisa snapped. "What do we have to do?"

"When we first went on the run," Dan reminded her, "I told you it would likely come to this. I told you that you would have to be ready."

"To *kill*?" Lisa demanded.

Dan turned a stern glare to her.

"To fight," Dan corrected. "They're close. They're *really* close. I felt the evil focus on me the moment we blew out those candles. It changed direction and started coming right for us. It's behind us somewhere and closing fast. If its magic has located us it's sent agents after us, too.

"Make no mistake, they're not coming to take us captive. We can go back into hiding and let them go after your family, lie down and let them kill us, or fight like hell. If we have to kill someone, well, better them than us."

"I'm so sorry," Lisa said, wiping away a falling tear.

Dan looked at her. "What are you talking about?"

"*I* did this," Lisa admitted, looking out the window to keep from making eye contact with Dan. "I had to send that damned email back in Vegas. I screwed up your plan, got all those people at the hotel killed, put my family in danger…"

"That might not be completely true," Dan said.

"Don't try to make me feel better."

"No, really," Dan said. "You asked me why I didn't use the concealing spell earlier. Your family was the reason. Joel has no family other than you. Ryan and I rarely deal with his father's family so we only have one another.

"You have parents and siblings and cousins. You're all close. I'm surprised the demon waited as long as it did to use them against us. As long as it was content to follow us using me as a beacon, I was glad to let it. I was afraid that if I used the concealing spell earlier the demon would resort to going after your family to flush us out."

"And that's exactly what happened," Lisa argued. "If I hadn't sent that email, you never would've have had to use that concealing spell."

Dan shook his head. "You're so busy feeling sorry for yourself that you're missing the point," he snapped. His sudden change of tone shocked Lisa out of her melancholy.

"Why trail us for so long if it could've just gone after your family in the first place?" Dan continued. "Because my initial assumption was true. It wasn't concerned about you, at least not at first. Then it came after you *personally* in Vegas."

"Don't remind me," Lisa said, still shivering.

"I have to," Dan said. "You have to understand. There are a lot of different ways it could've found you. It could've used hair samples or even skin flakes from your apartment in Chicago or from any of the hotels we stayed in. It could use those samples to craft a locator spell but it didn't. It wasn't concerned about you, at least not at first. But then it was."

"Why?" Lisa wondered. "What changed?"

"I don't know," Dan said. "It won't come after you now, at least not directly, because you're with me. It will send – "

The shriek of tires and a flood of blinding light from high-beam headlamps cut Dan's sentence short. A big dark sedan leapt across three lanes of traffic from the far right shoulder and bore down on the van like a guided missile.

Lisa yelped and Dan jerked the wheel to the left to avoid a crash. He was only partially successful. The angle and speed of the approaching sedan were too much for Dan to dodge cleanly, but he managed to avoid straight on t-bone to the front passenger side door, which might well have been fatal to Lisa. The sedan instead struck the rear right fender, sending the van fishtailing uncontrollably across the yellow dividing line into oncoming traffic.

There was blessedly light traffic in the northbound lane. Only two cars were coming, and though they had to break and swerve, they were both able to avoid the skidding van. Dan kept the van from spinning completely around but he could not stop the skid. The van went across the narrow northbound shoulder, hit the curb and flipped. The front windshield exploded. The roof of the van crumpled inward with the screech of twisting metal as the van went wheels-up across the wet grass. Its momentum flipped it back to its wheels. It glided almost another twenty yards before a tree finally brought it to a violent halt.

The black sedan drifted smoothly to a stop several yards away. The two agents jumped out and rushed the van. The back door of the sedan burst open as the retriever bolted out of the back seat and past the van. Hunter and Shepherd stepped to the van carefully, their guns drawn.

"No way the old guy survived that," Hunter said.

Shepherd was already in a squat taking aim inside the empty van. He did a double take before looking up at his partner with a grin.

"Are you willing to put money on that, Hunter?"

13.2

"Are you OK?" Dan asked breathlessly.

"Yeah, I think so," Lisa huffed, eyes still wide with fear.

"Good," Dan said. "Help me up."

Lisa jumped to her feet and gasped when she realized they were no longer in the van. They were less than a stone's throw away from the steep ledge of a grassy embankment that sloped sharply down to stone and then to the frosted sand of the beach. She could not even see the van, but she could see the glow of headlights from Lake Shore Drive at the top of the grass-covered slope.

"You teleported us?" Lisa asked needlessly. "I didn't even feel it that time." She grabbed Dan's left arm and helped him to his feet.

Dan had the big duffle bag slung on his right shoulder. Lisa supported him with his left arm over her shoulder as they shuffled south along the embankment.

"You didn't feel it because you were in a van turning a cartwheel," Dan huffed, still struggling to catch his breath. They went less than twenty yards before Dan said:

"Stop, Lisa."

"Why?" she asked in a near panic.

"We can't outrun them. We have to stand and fight."

"Dan, how do you expect us to –?"

"If I'm gonna die exhausted, it *won't* be from running!"

"Dan…"

"You can run if you want, girl, but it won't do you any good. They're right behind us."

Lisa stopped and the two of them turned back toward Lake Shore Drive. They did not see any organization agents. They saw something worse. It was the ugliest dog Lisa had ever seen.

It looked like a giant evil Chihuahua. Its head was flatter and wider and monstrously larger. The body shape was similar though on a larger scale. It stared at them from atop the slope nearly seventy yards away. Its bulging eyes glowed in a weird shade of purple.

The eerie glow illuminated the terrible jumble of long, jagged teeth jutting from its slavering maw. The creature glared at them hungrily, its long black tongue lolling from the side of its narrow mouth.

"Is that the demon?" Lisa stammered.

"No," Dan said. "But the demon sent it."

He quickly pulled his modified shotgun, the one that always reminded Lisa of a space-aged child's toy, from the duffle. He set the duffle on the ground and slung the shotgun strap across his shoulder. He knelt shakily, reached back into the duffle to pull the enchanted shield out and fitted it onto his right forearm.

Lisa and Dan watched in horrified disbelief as the strange doglike creature charged down the slope. Dan's heart caught in his throat when the canine started to grow. Its massive head and shoulders expanded to cartoonish proportions. It grew taller and taller as it closed on them.

Dan's initial shock was soon replaced by confidence. He felt invigorating warmth spread through his body. Lisa, standing behind him and a little to his right, noticed a soft white glow radiating from the front of Dan's face.

"Demon magic…" Lisa breathed.

"Yes," Dan said, his voice suddenly deeper and stronger.

Lisa could see the smile on his face just before he stood up straight, no longer needing Lisa's support. Dan lifted his tricked-out shotgun and opened fire. The magic coursing through Dan invigorated him. It swept away his lingering pains, cleared his focus and sharpened his aim.

The shotgun's high-caliber ammunition struck the strange morphing creature squarely between the eyes but the "retriever" did not falter. Dan even scored a shot into each of the beast's eyes yet still it charged. The horrific creature continued to grow wider and taller until its unnaturally widening skull split into three sections; even as Dan blasted bloody chunks of flesh from its head, shoulders, chest, and arms. Lisa gasped in revulsion at the gruesome sight.

The three sections of its skull quickly formed into three separate heads. The ever-broadening shoulders followed suit.

Its three heads and three sets of shoulders converged at a common torso, and with every great bound, the beast continued to pull sickeningly apart. All the while its spiky fur sloughed off all over its body, leaving behind a dark slime that oozed slowly away as the beast tore across the field.

Out of the corner of Lisa's eye, she saw the old man's smile drop away. The confident smile was replaced by a worried frown when the onrushing creature neared the midway point of the space between them. By then it had separated into three separate creatures. Each one was as tall as a man and they continued to grow as they came on.

The slime left behind from its shedding fur was shaken off to reveal softer fur of a lighter color. In the silver moonlight it was impossible to tell the exact color, but it was definitely a lighter shade, smoother and shorter than its original spiky pelt.

And then Dan's magic blinked away completely, as if someone flipped a light switch to off.

"Oh *hell*," Dan breathed, realizing what had happened.

With the strange creature's transformation complete, the demon's spell was spent. What was left was a trio of natural creatures that, even though they were not of this world, were not possessed of magic. The termination of the demon magic took with it Dan's fortifying power. He staggered heavily and Lisa had to catch him before he fell to the ground.

"Oh, no!" Lisa exclaimed. "Run!"

"Can't," Dan said tiredly. "The demon magic is gone. The teleport took too much out of me. I can barely stand."

"Then keep shooting, goddammit!" Lisa ordered. She pulled Dan's right arm over her shoulder and found the strength to support the old man. She turned enough to rush him away while at the same time giving Dan an angle to fire.

"Tygras," the elderly Child of the Old Ones realized with dreadful awe when the beasts finally stopped growing.

When they reached a pool of light beaming down from a towering light pole, Dan and Lisa could see that giant cats' legs were disproportionately long compared to their bodies, as long as Dan was tall. The rest of the hulking felines' bodies were all corded, twitching muscle. They looked pale gray in the star and moonlight but Dan knew from both Ryan and old Shanderah that the giant cats were as light blue as a clear daytime sky.

We're screwed he thought.

He kept firing and kept hitting the beasts with every shot. He wanted to go for headshots but his exhaustion and his overall weakened state made it difficult for him to aim his shotgun precisely. Even if he had time to make the adjustment, the target-lock function would not get a fix on the beasts' heads because of the swiftness with which they bobbed and swayed as they ran. So he continued to aim for the larger and easier to hit targets like their broad torsos.

Not one bullet missed its mark. Without the demon magic to fortify the beasts during the transformation from one creature to three, the shots did more damage than they had earlier. The giant cats faltered or snarled in pain with every blow but they did not stop.

"I'm slowing you down, Lisa," Dan admitted. "Get outta here. Let me try to slow *them* down. You keep the shield and run as fast as you can."

"Without the shield you'll hold them off all of two seconds," Lisa argued, even through her rising panic. "I'll take my chances *with* you. Let's use the shield together. Maybe they'll be more vulnerable up close."

They stopped and turned. Dan stood as firmly as he could manage, with the shield strapped to his right wrist and the modified shotgun in his left hand. He held both the forward handle and the trigger while his left elbow pinned the weapon against his side. He wanted to pass the shield to Lisa but there was no time. She supported his frail waist with her hip as she stood in a firm, wide-legged stance and supported his shield arm with both of her hands.

Lisa's eyebrows knitted with fear but her narrow jaw was set with determination. Dan's face was a mask of anger. The three beasts were nearly upon them.

Dan was beginning to doubt the wisdom of their strategy when he noticed a flicker of purple light under the paw of the tygra on the outside left. That tygra suddenly and inexplicably attacked the one in the middle of the trio. It veered to its side and locked its wide jaws on the neck of the other and bore it to the ground. The surprised beast fought back savagely even though it was at a severe disadvantage.

The third tygra kept coming. Dan pumped more shots into to the giant and succeeded only in making it angrier. He even scored a headshot. The high caliber ammunition struck the beast's massive head just above its brow. The slugs exploded, blowing away flesh and fur and tiny flecks of bone to reveal a bloody and scratched – but intact – skull.

And then it was on them. Lisa screamed as the roaring mass of muscle, fur, claws and teeth exploded into them. The previously invisible shield erupted into so many violent waves of energy that it looked like a solid dome of blinding light. The shield held off the tygra's attack but the ferocity of the blow sent Lisa and Dan, as well as the giant blue cat, tumbling head over heels toward the precipice of a steep embankment less than five yards away.

Seven organization agents stood outside their three cars on the west side of Lake Shore drive, directly across the street from the battered van and the organization sedan resting beside it. From where they stood, though they were slightly less than two hundred yards away, their elevation and angle allowed them to watch the show through their military grade night vision binoculars.

They watched the two freakish, giant cats in their deadly struggle. They saw the woman and the third giant cat go over the edge of the embankment and out of view. The old man did not go over with them. He went sprawling, rolled several yards and fell still.

"You think the old guy's dead?" Hunter asked Shepherd.

Both of them had crossed the highway to join the newly arrived agents. There was not a lot of traffic, and the few cars that did pass by only slowed a moment to rubberneck before speeding off, afraid that the giant cats would notice them gawking and abandon their fight to go after human prey.

"I think we should make sure he's dead," Shepherd answered. "Kill everything moving down there."

Lisa rolled down the cold, wet, rock-strewn slope. The Chicago Hawk blew an ice-cold spray from the surface of the lake, making the rough slope slick and treacherous. She finally stopped rolling when she hit the edge of the beach.

It took a moment for her world to stop spinning. When it did, her hands immediately went to her stomach and her thoughts to her unborn baby. It took all of her strength to keep from going into a full panic. She took deep, panting breaths in a futile attempt to calm her racing heart.

Lisa palpated her torso the way she would one of her four-legged patients and found to her relief that her ribs, while sore, wore not broken. There was no abdominal pain indicating harm to the fetus but she knew only a thorough exam would tell her what she needed to know. She got to her feet and tried to get her bearings. Multiple bruises and scrapes ached on her face, arms, butt, and legs but that was it. She thanked the Lord for keeping her free from injury and prayed that the baby was alright.

And then she heard a guttural snarl, along with the sound of knives scraping on hard ground. She turned to see the giant predator cat bearing down on her. Her vision was engulfed with saucer-sized feline eyes and a massive, hungry maw full of wickedly pointed teeth.

"NO!" Lisa yelled in an ear-splitting scream. She threw her hands in the air and fell back in a futile attempt to fend off certain death. As she hit the ground, the massive cat slid right over the top of her along the slick, cold surface. The beast's underside was so close that by the time it passed, Lisa knew it was a female.

Lisa rolled to her feet and turned to see the monstrous feline scramble on the slippery surface to turn and face her prey. This time, for some reason, the tygra did not charge. She glared at Lisa but did not attack. Lisa thought she could see a hint of curiosity in the beast's eyes.

"Please don't!" Lisa pled wildly, as if the giant azure cat could understand her.

The cat lowered her head in a sinister and quizzical bow as she studied Lisa. She bared her teeth and emitted a low, rumbling growl. *How can food speak to me?*

Lisa's mouth formed a large "O" when the feral rumbling formed words in her mind. The shock of hearing words from the terrible and beautiful beast almost buckled her knees.

"I...I..." she stammered. "I don't know, but please, *please* don't kill me."

Why not? Hunger hurts. You are food."

"I can... I can..." Lisa fought panic and shock and tried to think of something to say as the intrigued but hungry predator inched forward. She felt like the proverbial mouse cornered by a lion.

"I can fix your wounds!" she suddenly exclaimed. "You've been shot, you're bleeding. I can stop the bleeding and mend the wounds."

Hunger hurts more than tiny shiny rocks in skin.

The tygra edged closer still.

But then she jerked away, startled by the thunder of gunfire and agonized roars from the other tygras somewhere over the top of the embankment.

Sisters! the tygra screamed into Lisa's mind.

"Bad men are killing your sisters!" Lisa said, seizing the moment. "The bad men are bigger than me and the old man. They'd fill your belly more than we would."

The tygra looked up the embankment before turning a reluctant glare at the small human.

I save sisters and feed, she decided. *If belly not full, I come for you.*

Lisa nodded frantically as the giant cat bounded nimbly back up the embankment.

I won't be here, Lisa thought, not daring to even mutter it under her breath.

13.3

Dan's arms were tired and cramping but there was no way he would lower that shield. He rested on one knee and pressed his left hand against his right wrist to brace the shield and keep his arm from smashing against his face. Powerful slugs slammed into his shield in a concentrated stream. The continuous assault kept him pinned in place. Even in a kneeling position, his failing legs were barely able to support him. The unending explosions against his shield made it impossible for him to stand, let alone walk.

The two fighting tygras were finally lying still after succumbing to the hail of gunfire from the organization agents at the top of the slope. The cats' bodies still twitched as the occasional slug tore threw them, but most of the fire was now trained on the old man.

Dan wondered again about the brief flash of purple light beneath the dying tygra's paw that preceded it turning on its companion. That likely saved their lives, as they surely would not have survived had all three tygras attacked simultaneously. He could not think on it for more than a moment, though. He had much more pressing concerns to distract him. As he feared, the agents began to fan out to the left and right in order to flank his protective shield.

That was when Dan recognized them. They were just beyond the bright highway lights but their constant muzzle flashes provided enough light for him to see that five of them were the survivors of the group that had cornered Dan and Lisa back in Indiana. Two of those agents, with only a few yards between them, flanked out wider and wider to Dan's left. He watched the impact of their weapons against his shield. The ripples from their exploding ammunition slid ever closer to the left edge of his magical barrier.

Dan cursed himself for not ending them when he had the chance. He was about to blame Lisa for talking him out of killing them and then reminded himself that the organization would have sent more agents to replace them, and likely in greater numbers.

He had no desire to leave them alive this time, however. Unfortunately, as he reached for his shotgun, he realized that the decision was no longer his to make.

His shotgun was gone.

The light from his enchanted shield illuminated the surrounding area but his weapon was nowhere to be found. He tried to inch away but his legs were numb. The only reason he had not fallen over was because he was leaning forward behind the shield and letting the force of the withering gunfire prop him up. The shooters did not know this, but if they had stopped firing Dan would have fallen on his face. As it was, he could only watch helplessly as the left flankers came only seconds away from getting around the perimeter of his magical shield.

Dan was saying a prayer when his attention was arrested by a violent explosion of movement from the shadows behind the agents flanking from his left.

The tygra seemed to materialize from nowhere and then it was on top of both men. The giant cat bore Shepherd to the ground with a massive paw and held him there. He screamed from the long curving claws that punched easily through flesh and bone to pin him down. Hunter had no time to scream. He was cut nearly in two by the tygras' snapping jaws as the beast pressed him into the grass and savaged him.

13.4

Lisa peeked over the edge of the embankment. She was hidden in the shadows, having found a darkened area a short distance to the south of where Dan held on to his shield for dear life. Dan's highly customized shotgun was lying before her, balanced precariously at the top of the slope.

She looked to her left when the tygra rushed from the darkness to attack the two agents. Three of the remaining agents turned their gunfire to the giant predator but the other two kept firing on Dan, keeping him rooted to his spot. She could see how weak Dan was and had no doubt that his attackers would soon see it, too.

Her survival instincts screamed at her to run away from there as fast as she could.

Would you kill for him?

It was the memory of Dan's voice in her head. He asked her that question about Joel during the first few days of their life on the run.

I'm not talking if someone had a gun to his head and you had to save his life. I mean if he was nowhere around, and you knew that the only way you could ever see him again was if you killed someone. Would you kill for him?

The question frightened her then and it frightened her now. It also reminded her that Dan had killed to save her on several occasions. It reminded her that Dan was her best chance to see her husband again. She refused to entertain the thought that Joel would not come back. No way was she *not* going to be there when he did. Dan was her and her baby's best chance at survival.

Lisa climbed to the top of the embankment, hefted the modified shotgun, and slung it diagonally over her shoulder. Having practiced with it countless times, she prepared the weapon with proficient ease and a strange detachment. Even while her heart felt like it would pound right out of her chest and ears, she felt as if she was outside of her body and watching another person.

It was like she was watching an intense horror movie where the heroine struggled in slow motion to ready a weapon before the antagonist could strike. Only Lisa was not struggling. She took a deep breath of cold winter air. Her hands were numb from the cold and mostly from fear but she smoothly armed the shotgun and used the plasma display to lock in the targets with barely audible beeps.

Lisa knew there was no coming back from what she was about to do yet there was no hesitation. Taking care to stay in the pool of shadows, she braced herself on one knee, asked God to forgive her, exhaled, and pulled the trigger.

She made it a point to hold the trigger down long enough to go to spray mode and swept the barrel quickly from left to right. The shotgun burped briefly five times as she did so. The muffled sound was reminiscent of several small fists pounding rapidly against a thick metal door. She fired live ammunition yet the kickback was almost as light as it had been when she pulled the trigger in non-firing practice mode.

Lisa was fortunate she had slung the modified shotgun over her shoulder. That was the only thing that kept it from falling to the ground when she released it in horror as she watched what happened to her five targets. She saw a cloud of blood plume from each man's torso as they went airborne and vaulted backward through the air. None of them moved after they fell heavily to the ground several yards behind where they had been standing.

And then all was still and silent. The only sounds were the whistle of the wind and the lapping of waves punctuated by the occasional cry of a nocturnal bird. Even the glow of headlights from Lake Shore Drive had gone dark.

The sights, however, were ghastly. Lisa climbed unsteadily to her feet on wobbly legs and looked out over the surreal scene. In all, ten dead bodies littered the area. Seven men and three giant cats lay about unmoving in the grass. Two of the men had been mauled horrifically. The beasts as well the other five men were riddled with holes and lying in dark puddles that steamed in the cold air.

She had killed the other five men.

After watching so many die by others' hands in her defense, she had finally delivered the deathblows herself.

The sounds of the night were replaced by a hum in Lisa's ears and the booming thump of her own heartbeat. She had been running on pure adrenaline since they left the hotel. It was finally starting to fade, leaving behind increasing aches and pains from her fall down the hill.

She had talked to a giant, savage, blue cat and she had shot five men dead.

Her breath sped up and she could feel an attack of hyperventilation coming on.

"Lisa!" Dan yelled, finding enough volume to jolt her out of her shock. "Breathe! Like I told you back at the hotel."

Lisa did. This time she was able to quickly control and then slow the pace of her breathing.

"You gotta help me back to the van, OK?" Dan said, the strength of his voice fading fast. "We gotta go. I can't do another teleport right now."

"Of course," Lisa returned. She had to will her legs into motion. No matter how she tried, she could not tear her eyes away from the carnage before her.

Lisa half ran, half stumbled to where Dan kneeled in the grass. The adrenaline was completely gone now. Her arms and legs felt like burning rods of lead. She worked through the pain and helped Dan to his feet and held him up as they made their way to the van.

"How the hell did you get away from that tygra?" Dan asked breathlessly.

"You wouldn't believe..." Lisa smiled weakly. "Well yeah, I guess you would believe it. I *talked* to her, Dan. She understood me. I understood her!"

Dan managed a sincere grin. "You found your magic. Good for you, sugar."

Lisa smiled back. The smile, however, was short-lived as their predicament shoved its way back to the forefront of her attention.

"Do you think the van can still run?" she wondered.

"I damn sure hope so," Dan answered. "It's a tough van. We may have to pull it off of the tree, though. I've got some tow chains in the van. We could use the agents' sedan to pull it free. We'll roll 'em for the keys."

"*I'm* not searching those dead bodies for keys!" Lisa said quickly. She remembered the grisly work of cleaning up the corpse of a man after Dan blew half of his head away. She had no intention of dealing with another brutalized corpse.

"Don't worry," Dan chuckled. "You saved my life. I'm more than happy to handle this one."

"So, where are we going, Dan?"

Dan turned a surprisingly bright smile to her as they reached the van.

"You're gonna *love* this plan," he promised.

Chapter 14: Back Home

14.1

When Joel and then Ryan staggered out of the void, coughing and gasping and fighting to keep from vomiting, they found themselves in the place where they last crossed through the WorldGate: the suite at the Drake Hotel.

Only this time the room was not empty.

They were greeted with the sounds of a woman's screams and a man yelling frightened expletives. The two Children of the Old ones turned in surprise and saw a woman and man under the soft, thick bed sheets. The couple was already yelling in stunned surprise at the sudden appearance of the man-sized, circular, two-dimensional rift in reality. Their screams only intensified when the two strangers stumbled out of it.

"Sorry!" Raxe said as he and Joel dashed out of the room.

Ryan snatched a long leather men's trench coat from the couch as they exited. After a long and embarrassing elevator ride with several well dressed men and women – a couple of them Joel and Raxe were sure were celebrities – they sprinted through the lobby, out the front door and onto the sidewalk in front of the posh hotel.

The terrified couple in the suite had already called security but they made the mistake of mentioning the "silver-rimmed, man-sized disc of blackness" from which the strangers emerged, so security personnel did not take them seriously. As a result, the security guards were momentarily frozen in shocked amusement when the two men – one dressed like a cloaked medieval nobleman and the other wearing gleaming, stylized medieval armor beneath an oversized full length trench coat – burst out of the elevator and into the night.

The two men jogged east through the city streets. Ryan's pilfered trench coat did not only protect him from the cold. It also hid Demonsbane where it hung from one hip and Questblade hanging from the other.

The few police officers they passed along the way would surely have stopped them if they saw the weapons, but because they were hidden the police only looked on and chuckled. The duo heard a few calls of "Halloween was two months ago" and

"Nice costumes," and "Where's the party?" Thankfully, though, no one tried to stop them.

They ran until they reached North Lake Shore Drive. The traffic was light enough for them to sprint safely across the Drive to the Lakefront Trail at the edge of Lake Michigan. When they reached a small, one story structure that contained benches and public restrooms, they finally stopped.

Joel was severely winded and instinctively reached into his pocket for the small pouch of medicinal herbs to curb the expected asthma attack. To his pleasant surprise, though, he did not need it. He was only winded. His breathing was otherwise normal. He pulled his cloak tighter against the chill wind blowing in from the lake and turned to Ryan.

The smell of stale alcohol and something else Joel could not quite identify carried to his nostrils on a brisk, icy breeze. He turned and saw a raggedly dressed old homeless man wrapped in a ratty blanket at the base of a leafless tree. Thick shocks of gray hair stuck out from beneath a filthy sweater cap and wild whiskers almost completely covered his pale white face. He cast a disinterested glance at the two strangely dressed men, shifted to a more comfortable position beneath his blanket and closed his eyes.

"Ok," Joel said. "How do we find Lisa and Dan?"

Ryan glanced briefly at the old wino and wrinkled his nose. He stared out at the black, glassy waves of Lake Michigan before he answered. "They're already on the way. I contacted gramps right after we crossed the WorldGate."

Joel gave Ryan a questioning glance. "How? You don't have a cell phone."

"We can communicate telepathically," Ryan explained. "I could do the same with my daughter back in Lorr before she..." Ryan paused for several heartbeats. "I don't know if you'll be able to do that with your kid, though. You're a little different than the rest of us."

"So I've noticed," Joel said. "How long do you think it'll take them to get here?"

"Not long," Ryan answered.

He was right. Less than five minutes later a dark blue van pulled over onto a small parking area at the edge of the sand. The way Ryan looked expectantly at the vehicle, Joel knew it was Dan and Lisa. His heartbeat quickened in fear when he saw the terrible condition of the van. The way it looked made him surprised the vehicle was moving at all.

Joel thought he was dreaming when Lisa opened the driver's side door. She looked in only slightly better condition than the van. There were dark circles under her eyes. Frayed strands of hair hanging in her face made her coif look wild despite her attempt to neaten it up a bit by pulling it back and tying it into a ponytail. Her legs were unsteady and her clothes were torn in several places.

And she never looked more beautiful.

Joel ran to her and was hugging her almost as soon as her feet touched the ground. Lisa buried her face in his shoulder and squeezed him as tightly as she could. Her tears instantly soaked through his shirt. The warm moisture on his skin was the most welcomed sensation he had ever felt. At first he feared he might be dreaming, or worse, being deceived by the demon again. When he inhaled deeply and drank in her sweet, pure scent, he knew it was real.

"Oh, baby girl," Joel whispered almost breathlessly. "I missed you so much. I love you so much. I worried about you so much! I was so afraid I'd never – "

And then she was kissing him. She jumped up and wrapped her arms around his shoulders, suspending herself high enough so that her lips were level with his. She kissed him so hard it hurt, and it was a wonderful pain. When her arms finally got tired she loosened her grip and lowered herself to the ground.

"Me, too," she managed between sobs of joy. She wrapped her hands around his waist and hugged him again as if she was afraid he would leave her, again burying her face into his shoulder.

"I ain't going nowhere, baby girl," Joel promised with a soft but intense whisper in her ear. "Never again."

"Not without me," she assured in a voice muffled within his cloak.

They both pulled back and looked at each other for a long time before Joel finally spoke again.

"Are you and the baby OK?" he asked worriedly. He put a gentle hand on her stomach. "You look beautiful but you look like you could use a nap."

"Damn if that's not the understatement of the century," Lisa chuckled. She put her hand over his where it rested low on her belly. "I don't know about the baby. It doesn't feel like anything is wrong but I won't be satisfied until an OB-GYN checks me out and tells me everything is fine."

She took in the cloak, the long sleeved cotton tunic that hung to the midpoint of his thighs and cinched at his waist with a thin leather belt, the breeches tucked into knee high leather riding boots.

"That's a cute little outfit you're wearing. The way it's hanging on you makes it look like you could use something to eat. You must've lost forty pounds."

Joel shrugged. "At least my beer belly is gone."

Lisa beamed. "Let's see how long that lasts."

"Hell, I could use a cold one right now!" Joel said.

Lisa turned her head slightly and shot him an alluring, devious look. "Is that all you could use, man?"

"Wait a second, kids," Dan cut in. He was back in his wheelchair and lowering himself down the automated lift. "I know you're happy to see each other but the freaky stuff has to wait. We still have a demon to kill."

Joel gave Dan an incredulous glare. "We? You mean *you* have a demon to kill. I've met the bastard up close once. I don't want to meet it again."

Ryan frowned. "What are you talking about? You should want it dead more than any of us."

"I do want it dead," Joel agreed. His tone softened but remained full of conviction. "I was sincere when I apologized for being such an ass back in Lorr, but you gotta believe me. It's not just fear that keeps me from going after it."

Ryan's expression turned dark and suspicious. His raspy voice lowered, taking on the tone of a screwdriver slowly scraping against sandstone. "Then what is it, Joel?"

Joel knew Raxe was asking about the deal with the demon. He did not know why Ryan did not mention it aloud but he was grateful for it. He did not want to have to explain that choice to Lisa. Not only would it piss her off, it would make her feel miserably guilty for the rest of their lives together. It occurred to Joel that Ryan might be blackmailing him. Was this his way of saying: Help me or I tell your wife?

Joel shook his head. "You don't understand. That thing knows everything about me. It knows I can kill it, but only if it threatens my life. Do you know how many ways it could cripple me? It could do it in a way that wouldn't even make my power flicker. The most I can do is get in your way. It might even try to use me against you."

"He's right," Dan said. "If that's how his gift works, you can't argue with his logic."

Joel scoffed bitterly at Dan's choice of words. "*Gift*, Dan? You got a strange sense of humor."

"The Lord works in mysterious ways," Dan reminded. "Your faith has taught you that."

"Getting back to the subject," Joel said, eager to leave that particular topic behind. "I know a lot more about how my power works than I did before I went across that Gate, and I'm telling you, I wouldn't be any help in this fight. And anyway, you and your granddad are the demon killers. That's what your power is for."

"If we fail, Joel, you know it'll come after you next," Dan warned. He nodded at Lisa's stomach. "All three of you."

"And that's when I'll deal the son of a bitch," Joel promised. "That's what *my* power is for."

Joel and Ryan stared at each other for long moments as fat snowflakes began to drift lazily from the murky sky. Ryan hated to admit it, but there was no indication that Joel was being deceitful. As powerful as Joel was, Ryan was sure he had not been professionally trained in the art of lying. Even so, Ryan still had to consider the possibility that Joel could have been sincere and at the same time be flat out wrong about the way his power worked.

If Joel was right, though, a fight with a sixth level demon would not be a convenient time to find out. In the end Raxe knew he had no right to try to force Joel to help them.

Lisa looked from one Child of the Old Ones to the other with great worry. It was the Drake hotel all over again, when they left this world through the WorldGate, the uncertainty and torture of Joel's imminent decision. She gravely feared that her husband would go with Ryan, and she was just as fearful of the possible consequences if he did not.

"Sorry," Joel said, breaking the silence. "I'm not going."

"You're a Child of the Old Ones," Ryan reminded. "There's a responsibility that comes with that whether you want it or not. You can't run from it forever."

"Maybe not," Joel conceded. "But I'm gonna run my ass off tonight." He took Lisa's hand and led her away. "C'mon, baby girl. You got any cash? There's a bus stop right down the street. We'll let the CTA take us home."

"You'd really ride the bus in that outfit?" She teased but there was a clear undertone of concern in her voice. "Let's find the nearest emergency room so they can take a look at me and the baby. We'll tell them we were on the way home from a costume party and we got mugged. By the looks of us, they'll definitely believe it."

"But your clothes don't look like a costume," Joel noted.

Lisa shrugged. "You're wearing enough costume for both of us. Let's go." She looked over her shoulder at Ryan and Dan and mouthed: "I'm sorry."

A bus arrived just as the couple reached the bus stop. Before they boarded the bus, Joel turned. His expression softened to something that Dan could swear was gratitude. Joel did not mouth any words the way his wife did but his eyes met Ryan's and he nodded slowly. Ryan grudgingly returned the nod, and then Joel and Lisa climbed on the bus. The door closed behind them and then they were gone.

14.2

Ryan shook his head as he watched the bus pull away and turned to his grandfather. "Think he'll ever come around?"

"Probably not," Dan admitted. "I think maybe he's not supposed to. He'll savagely protect himself and his family but he won't go looking for a fight. With his power, maybe that's for the best."

Though Ryan was not sure if he agreed with that or not, he was not about to waste time arguing about it. "It would be nice to have a little help," he said. "Say, what was all that 'if we fail' crap you said to him? We're *not* failing."

Dan shrugged. "I thought I might be able to scare him into tagging along."

"Good try," Ryan said. "Let's go kill us a demon."

"Don't think I didn't notice that nod between you and Joel," Dan said. "I know that's universal male sign language for 'thanks' and 'you're welcome.' What was it for?"

"A secret," Ryan said as he wheeled Dan back to the van. "So don't even ask." He was still angry about the deal Joel struck with the Dierglyorr but Joel had saved his life at Hargathall's Cleft and everyone's life at the Forsaken Desert. Ryan would keep the deal between the two of them. He owed Joel that much.

"What else is on your mind?" Dan asked as he and his grandson approached the van. "It's something other than a secret between you and Joel. You're not afraid to face the Dierglyorr…or are you?"

"I'm blocking you, old man," Ryan said in an annoyed tone. "How do you still know what I'm thinking?"

"I don't hear the thoughts but I'm old and wise and I helped raise you, boy. How many times do I have to remind you of that?"

Instead of answering, Ryan turned toward the sleeping old wino under the tree a few yards away.

"What about you, dragon?" Ryan called. "Can you hear me even though I'm blocking?"

"Dragon?" Dan asked, turning toward the old homeless man that reeked of liquor and sour body odor.

The old man shrugged his way out of the folds of his tattered blanket, chuckling menacingly as he did so.

A pair of narrow, square shoulders emerged first and then he rose smoothly to a standing position, unfolding himself as fluidly as an uncoiling snake. Drifting snowflakes began to plume into tiny puffs of steam when they floated to within a few inches of him. By the time his ascension finally came to a stop he stood over eight feet tall.

A wide horizontal slit opened in the depths of the dirt-matted, shaggy whiskers that covered his face. The slit spread impossibly wide and then parted, revealing a half-moon rictus filled with terrible wedges of needle-tipped bone masquerading as teeth. His dim, bloodshot eyes ignited with a simmering yellow glow.

Ryan winced at the sight. Dan looked on in awe.

"I cannot, human," the old vagrant rumbled with a voice like the muffled roar of an industrial furnace, "unless I *really* wanted to. I am almost impressed. I've accompanied you many times during the course of your amusing travels in many guises and you have never noticed. How did you become aware of my presence this time?"

"Right after Joel sniffed you. He didn't realize what you were. I could tell he noticed *something* different about you so I paid a little closer attention."

"You trust that reluctant Child's senses more than he trusts his own," WorldHopper noted.

"You did a good job of masking your magical aura to tame it down to that of a human," Ryan added. "But it was still too strong for an old wino sleeping near the shores of Lake Michigan in thirty-something degree weather. Plus, your aura was too steady, too consistent to be human. Human auras pulse differently, more erratically. That meant you weren't human and were likely some kind of changeling. I only know of three changelings. One is on the other side of the WorldGate. The other is the demon that I can feel miles away from here. Who else could you have been?"

THE KEY QUEST

The incredibly tall vagrant turned its long bearded head to Dan. "The insolent whelp is learning, Dan. Have you been working with him?"

Dan grinned. "I've tried, WorldHopper."

"So where have you been all this time?" Ryan demanded. "Dragons and demons are supposed to be mortal enemies. Why haven't you killed it yet? Matter of fact, the Dierglyorr kind of reminds me of you. You're both arrogant-ass shape-shifters. You both have really bad attitudes. Now that I think about it, Rionn Lorr told me that before they went extinct, dierglii actually hunted dragons. Are you afraid of it or some—grrrkgh!!"

Ryan thought he saw the old vagrant twitch. In the next instant he was dangling nine feet in the air from a large smelly hand with a painfully choking grip around his neck.

"The Dierglyorr is a cheap imitation," WorldHopper snarled in a low, chilling tone. The voice resonated in Ryan's mind louder and more painfully than it did in his ears.

"When I rejected Maldarkenlynn's entreaty to fight alongside her and the Leaders in Heaven's War, she fused the last dierglii with a changeling and that fool of a politician. She breathed her befouled breath into it to give it life. So you see, the Dierglyorr is nothing more than a failed attempt to duplicate the perfection that is WorldHopper.

"And you *dare* to compare such an inferior abomination to me? Is it not enough that I allow you to think such an absurdity? Must you disrespect me by saying it aloud?"

Ryan tried to answer but he could barely breathe, let alone talk. Speech was not necessary, in any event. Under such duress Raxe had no hope of concentrating enough to shield his thoughts from either his grandfather or the dragon. He apologized profusely in his mind, knowing that both man and dragon could hear him clearly.

"An apology is not enough," WorldHopper said, "even such a sincere, fearful apology. Know this, so that you will never let such foolishness enter your feeble mind again. I have not faced the Dierglyorr for two reasons:

"First: The demon knows that it if it does not confront me I will have no interest in it. A demon's primary desire is to bring humans to heel and as you know well, dragons care less than nothing for humankind.

"The second reason is the same reason the demon has not confronted you directly. I can dispatch even a sixth level demon easily, though admittedly it would take a bit more effort than most other prey. Why expend the effort when we can let humans to do our work for us?"

Dan shrugged. "Makes sense. What do you think, Ryan?"

Still unable to talk, Ryan nodded nervously as he struggled to take another breath.

"Instead of your apology," WorldHopper continued, "I will accept your vow to never even *think* that there is anything in existence that the King of the Dragons fears."

Ryan nodded again, his bulging eyes tearing up.

"Good," the King of the Dragons growled. The simmering yellow glow in his eyes blazed brighter. In that brief flash, Ryan was buffeted with a wave of dread more vile than even his memories of hell. It struck him like a violent slap and sent a shudder through his entire body. Singing heat and black smoke wafted out of WorldHopper's flaring nostrils.

"And know this," the freakishly tall figure counseled with an icy growl. "I will kill the demon if and when it challenges *me*. Not before. And the Dierglyorr would not dare to confront me or mine until it has built an army that it believes is mighty enough to stand against the dragons.

"To do that, it must first cull every other living thing in this world and every other world to which it can travel. Those it cannot use, it will destroy. Those it does not destroy, it will enslave. Of those it enslaves, it will personally select the most powerful to assemble its army. Then and only then will it come for me.

"Dragons, you should understand, have the patience of immortals. We've no qualms with waiting for the demon to bring its sport to us. Do *you* wish to wait that long for me to kill it? Or would you rather try to stop it here and now?"

"Here and now," Dan answered for his grandson.

Ryan once again nodded frantically, the next thing he knew, he was falling onto his backside on the cold, wet, ground. The fall would have hurt if he had not been wearing his enchanted armor beneath his stolen trench coat. He coughed and wiped tears from his eyes. When his vision cleared WorldHopper was gone.

"You OK?" Dan asked, doing a terrible job of holding back a chuckle.

"Let a dragon choke you damn near to death and tell me if you feel OK afterwards," Ryan answered in a rough, breathless whisper.

"You gotta learn to stop talkin' shit to him, boy!" Dan laughed aloud. It took several seconds for him to get it all out. When he was finished his amused expression turned serious again. "So what was it you were about to tell me before you got yourself choked up? What's bothering you?"

Ryan took a deep breath as he climbed to his feet. He looked down at the disturbed icy ground and avoided his grandfather's questioning gaze. He went around to the rear of the wheelchair and started rolling Dan to the van.

"It's getting harder to keep my oath."

"Of course it is," Dan said as if he were talking to a dullard. "You've had people and monsters trying to murder you for the last several weeks. You've been a killer damn near all of your adult life. You can't just turn off that many years of conditioning and experience."

Ryan shook his head. "That's not what I mean," he explained. "I'm always tempted in those situations but I've always been able to keep it in check. I even held back on the Finder. If anyone ever needed killing, it was that bastard."

"It doesn't get any more tempting than that," Dan concurred. "But you held back. So what's the problem?"

"In Lorr, the first time I fought one of the *Ken d'Zanir*," Ryan began, "I wasn't just tempted. I took a swing at his stomach with Demonsbane's cutting edge. I tried to cut through his sword and into his chest. The only thing that kept me from killing him was *his* skill."

"It was the heat of battle," Dan argued. "You were fighting for your life. That's reflex. The bottom line is you didn't kill him."

"Is that really the bottom line?" Ryan wondered aloud.

"What?" Dan questioned. "Are you talking about original sin, the thought being equal to the action and all that?"

Ryan shrugged.

"If that's really the case," Dan chuckled, "all of us are going to hell."

"There's a difference between thought and intent," Ryan pointed out. "The thought goes through my mind every time I'm in a fight for my life. But the fight with that *Ken* was the only time I actually tried to kill someone since I took the oath, and I don't know why."

Dan shrugged. "Maybe because you're human."

"It's gotta be more than that," Ryan insisted.

"Look, boy, we may be direct descendants of gods but we're more human than anything else. This may come as a shock but you're not perfect. You can't be in complete control all the time. Chalk it up to experience and make up for the near-mistake by killing that damned shape-shifting demon. Do you understand?"

Ryan nodded reluctantly.

"Good," Dan said with sigh of relief. "Now help a tired old man into the van. I'm driving."

Dan leaned heavily on his shorter grandson's shoulder as Ryan lifted him into the seat. Ryan was alarmed at how little Dan weighed.

Dan had always been lean and lanky. He had also been in a wheel chair for almost as long as Ryan could remember so he had forgotten how tall Dan was. The first time Dan rose from the chair in Ryan's presence was right before the Head Mage, Ryan and Joel crossed the WorldGate into Lorr. Ryan was so shocked and so pressed for time that he failed to notice that Dan was taller than him by at least three inches.

As Ryan lifted his grandfather from the wheelchair, he also noticed that Dan could not have been more than one hundred and forty pounds, which was much too thin for his height.

Ryan was positive Dan was heavier than this before he left for the Kingdom of Lorr. And worse, the older man's face was noticeably more gaunt than usual. His cheeks were sunken. His breathing was labored and his eyes were tired. Alarmingly tired.

"Are you alright?" Ryan asked. "Can you drive?"

"Hell yes," Dan assured as he opened the driver's side door and slid carefully into the seat. "Stop dragging your ass and let's roll."

By the time Ryan loaded the wheelchair on the passenger side and climbed in, Dan had started the van and put it in gear. He closed the door and turned to face his grandfather.

"You know which way to go?" Ryan asked.

"Of course," Dan said. "We don't need Questblade for this. I can feel the demon's aura just like you can. It doesn't seem as concerned about concealing itself anymore. It wants to be found. It's waiting for us."

"And I'm looking forward to finding him," Ryan snarled. "We have to make a stop on the way."

14.3

SOUTH SHORE AREA – SOUTH SIDE OF CHICAGO

Lieutenant Limbo sat on the polished hardwood floor of his living room, his back resting against his big leather sofa. Even through the thick haze of burning purple Kush hanging in the air, he could smell the sweet scent of the fine little thing sitting on the couch behind him plaiting his hair. He was trying to watch television as the woman worked on his 'do but he was thoroughly distracted by the smooth chocolate brown skin of her bare legs and feet to either side of him, perfectly formed and all lotioned up with some kind of cocoa and shae butter.

What was her name again? Verona, that was it. Her knickname, however, was "Yummy." Limbo intended to find out why. The whole time she was twisting his hair Limbo was struggling to think of a way to talk Shelley, his main broad, into a three-way with him and Yummy. He knew Yummy was down. He could tell by the way she flirted with him as she worked on his fro, whenever Shelley left the room, that is. Yummy kept complimenting his big shoulders and the muscles in his back beneath his authentic black and red Chicago Bulls jersey with "Limbo" stenciled on the back above the number 1.

Yeah, Yummy was down, but Shelley was a different story. She was jealous as hell and had already threatened to cut his throat in his sleep if he tried anything with Yummy. But then again, Yummy was Shelley's friend. Shelley was the one who brought her over to braid his hair because Limbo kept complaining that Shelley left the plaits too loose. Shelley had to know her home girl was a freak. And she knew Limbo liked thick-legged chocolate brown girls.

That was when Limbo figured it out. Shelley wanted some Yummy, too. She just did not want to be the one to bring it up. She wanted a threesome but would not come right out and say it because she was living in that river in Africa.

"Denial," Limbo mumbled with a chuckle.

"What'd you say?" Yummy asked.

"Huh?" Limbo returned, not realizing he had spoken out loud. "Don't worry about it. Hey, go ask Shelley when she's g'on be done in the shower."

"Alright shuga," Yummy answered in that sweet voice.

She gave his shoulder a firm squeeze as she stood and then walked down the long hall of the apartment. He watched those chocolate legs and those big hips and that switching backside in those short-shorts as she glided down the hall. It was cold as a witch's titty outside but the heat worked fine in his crib, which was a perfect motivator for the women that came through to strip down to as little as possible…and it was about to get hotter as soon as Shelley got her fine ass out of that shower.

All he had to do now was get his street soldiers the hell out of the apartment. Three were in the kitchen eating fast food and two were pulling their shift as night watch on the roof of the two-flat. Two more were down in the first floor apartment, probably playing video games or watching porn.

Limbo had no problem with the ladies sharing him but he would be damned if he shared the ladies with these hard-legs. He did not even want them listening. Just when he was about to order the three in the kitchen to take their food downstairs, his cell phone buzzed where it rested on the floor next to his loaded Desert Eagle. He glanced at the number and saw that it was Killa Kane, one of his men on the roof.

"Whatup, Killa?"

"Don't know yet. We got a beat-up-ass van coming down the street and it's slowin' down, like it's coming here. Could be them Six-Point Hustlers tryin' to roll on us."

"You scope it?" Limbo ordered, referring to the military-grade night vision scopes attached to their shotguns. "I'll get the guns ready. If it ain't a friendly we'll light that bitch up."

"Scopin' it now…wait. Limbo, it's Hit-Man!"

"What?" Limbo asked. "I thought he was dead!"

"I don't know," Killa said. "We saw his building get shot the fuck up and we saw his ass jump out that window, but then he fell in that black hole in the air and disappeared…"

"Wild shit," Limbo said, catching a chill at the memory from over three years ago.

The man they called "Hit-Man lived on the other side of street at the end of the block. His building had been demolished about a week after the shooting, after a shitload of people he guessed were feds combed through the apartment and took away everything whether it was nailed down or not. That pissed Limbo off to no end. He figured Hit Man had some nice surveillance equipment and all kinds of weapons Limbo and his crew could have taken for their crib.

"Let's see if it's really him. It might be the feds, or whoever the hell they were, trying to get some info from us again. Hold your position. We don't want no beef with feds but get the rest of the shooters ready just in case. If somebody gets shot we ain't g'on be the last ones."

Limbo snatched up his Desert Eagle, checked the chamber, and got to his feet. Just then both Shelley and Yummy came striding down the hall wearing nothing but towels, both glistening wet with sexy smiles.

"Shit..." Limbo swore. "Gotta handle some business, ladies. We'll party when I get back. Go in the master bedroom and wait for me."

"Awww," they both pouted. But then they giggled and padded back down the hallway. Limbo watched, green with envy, thinking they would have no trouble at all entertaining themselves until he got back.

"Black Star! Crazy L! Big Hitter! Put the food down, load up and take up positions at the front window. I'm going downstairs. If any of you go near the broads I'll shoot you."

"What if they come near us?" Crazy L asked with a grin.

Limbo did not smile. "Don't mess wit'em. I ain't playin."

Dan watched Ryan walk confidently up to the vestibule doors of the two-flat, wishing he felt as self-assured as his grandson. They both spotted the gunmen on the roof as soon as they came around the corner. They saw the three others at the street-facing window on the second floor. The gunmen thought they were hiding. Amateurs.

But amateurs could be dangerous. They were young, trigger-happy gangbangers, utterly unpredictable. That made Dan nervous. He did not care that Ryan made an agreement with them to pay "rent" to live on that otherwise deserted block. That was over three years ago. A lot could change in that time, especially with unpredictable youngsters.

As subtly as he could manage, he propped up his modified shotgun in his lap enough to set the target-lock on the two on the roof, the three on the second floor, and the man with the half-plait-half-afro hairdo who opened the door. He used the heat-signature function to lock on the two gunmen hiding out of sight on the first floor stairwell.

If things went sideways, Dan would put all of them down in a matter of seconds.

Ryan looked back with nostalgia at the cleared lot where his building used to stand. He had several refuges in different parts of the city, in different parts of the world, for that matter, and he usually never allowed himself to get too attached to one location. That spot, though, had been special. Most of his refuges were simple drop-spots, hidey-holes where he could get a few hours sleep and a meal in relative safety before moving on to the next job.

The spot that had once stood on this block had been the closest thing to a home. It was in his hometown and, most importantly, it was the place in which he had invested the most money. His largest store of weapons was kept there. He had spent a fortune in surveillance and security technology there. He had also paid large sums of money for rent and protection to gangbangers who ran the neighborhood and lived in the building he was now approaching.

What grated at him the most was that he had not been able to leave on his own terms. The organization saw to that. The organization had been after Ryan even before the Dierglyorr seized a position of leadership. Nonetheless, Ryan would take out his frustration with the organization on the demon just as soon as he was done here.

Limbo pulled the door open as Ryan stepped onto the stoop. The short, wiry, but fierce-eyed man had a Desert Eagle Mark XIX tucked in the front of his jeans in plain view. He gave Ryan a suspicious once-over before speaking.

"What the hell you doin' alive?" Limbo demanded.

"Trying to borrow something I let you hold a few years ago," Ryan answered.

Limbo gave a muted nod and then held his left hand out.

Ryan scoffed. "Other hand, Limbo."

Limbo half-smiled and extended his right hand. The two men shook hands in series of complicated motions before releasing each other. Ryan knew they had newer handshakes by now, but that was the last one *he* used with Limbo. If he had used a newer one, assuming he knew a newer one, Limbo would have been suspicious.

"Had to make sure you weren't some spy in disguise," Limbo explained. "I know how you spooks do."

"No doubt," Ryan answered.

He told the thugs that he was a covert agent when he talked them into letting him use the abandoned building seven years earlier. They seemed enamored with having a spy on the block. Early on, one of them took it upon himself to test Ryan by trying to break into his home late one evening. Ryan knew the would-be burglar was a part of Limbo's gang because of the tattoo on the back of his neck.

When his clique found his lifeless body on their doorstep at sunrise with a broken neck, they gave Ryan all due respect. Ryan initially expected retaliation but none ever came. He never found out if the thug attempted the break-in as an initiation or if his crew thought he was expendable and was willing to sacrifice him to test their new tenant. Either way, they did not seem overly concerned about the loss.

He never knew the thug's name but he remembered the face well. His was one of the many faces that haunted Ryan's nightmares when hell visited him in his sleep.

Ryan thought about all of his victims. The only solace he could find was that all of the people he killed were in hell, meaning they all were bad people. Of course, that did not excuse him for killing them, but perhaps that was why he was allowed to return after the Finder struck him down.

But what about the victims who died as an indirect result of Ryan's actions? How many deaths did he unwittingly finance when he paid rent to Limbo? These gangbangers sold deadly drugs. They robbed people. They killed rival gang members over territory to which they had no legal ownership. How many of their victims were innocent marks or caught in the crossfire of their skirmishes?

"So where you crashing now?" Limbo asked, snapping Ryan out of his reverie.

Ryan shrugged. "Nowhere in particular. Not to be rude or nothing, I'm kinda pressed for time."

"I hope it ain't money you tryin' to borrow," Limbo warned. "We ain't no bank up in here."

"Not money," Ryan assured. "A piece."

Limbo raised an eyebrow. "A piece of what?"

Ryan frowned. "Don't play crazy, Limbo. I let you hold a few of my custom guns over the years. I need one of 'em."

"You ain't let me *hold* shit. Guns were part of your rent."

"Right," Ryan agreed. "But I just need to borrow one of them. I can bring it back."

"Tell you what," Limbo began. "I'll sell it back to you if you give me a price I can work with…"

The haggling commenced and did not last long. Ryan was sure he could have talked Limbo down further than he did but he was in a hurry. Within five minutes they were done.

"Yo, Crazy L!" Limbo called. "Go get Stunner!"

"You named it?" Ryan asked. "Cool."

Ryan was glad he had withdrawn enough cash from several ATMs from several of his accounts, each with a different name and code. Limbo was as greedy as he had ever been. A few minutes later Ryan and Dan were back on the road and Limbo was having his private party.

14.4

"Figures," Dan said as he slowed the van down. They were on the same street as the warehouse Ryan and he used to interrogate Clay, the organization agent assigned to conduct surveillance on Joel and Lisa Harvey.

Their destination was not the warehouse, but an unoccupied six-story structure just across the street and adjacent to an unused six level parking garage. The building was a hulking rectangular mass of dull, weatherworn concrete and broken glass. It was situated on the corner and occupied almost half the block. Large wooden planks covered the doors and windows of the first three floors. It might once have been an office building, a department store, or perhaps even a school. Whatever it had been was long gone. All that was left was a hollow shell of dust and shadows, a likely dwelling for transients and a place of concealment for those needing to conduct discrete activities under the cover of darkness.

The block, the entire neighborhood, in fact, was as deserted at night as it was in the day. At night, however, the surroundings were much more ominous. Only one streetlight was functional and that was on the far end of the block. An overcast sky hid the moonlight and plunged the rest of the street into heavy shadows. Dan and Ryan could barely see the vapor of their warm breath in the cold winter air. It was so dark they almost missed the three large black SUVs parked in the shadows between the abandoned warehouse and the empty parking garage next door.

"Figures," Dan said again, stopping the van at the curb outside the front of the building. "The demon's been sending these kinds of messages to us for a while now, letting us know that it knows where we've been and what we've been doing. I saw a news report about a young woman that had been attacked by some kind of wild animal in Houston. The woman was Synn. The manner of death, the markings, all of it was the same as what WorldHopper left behind when he went on his rampage at the tavern."

Ryan felt a pang of guilt and sorrow. "Synn..." he sighed.

Synn had been an exotic dancer by profession who would do more than dance for the right price. While no one would call her an innocent, she did not deserve to die at the tooth and claw of a demon. If Ryan had not indulged his lust that night the Dierglyorr would have had no cause to seek her out.

As he taught himself to do so many years ago, Ryan turned his sorrow and guilt into anger and determination.

"It's trying to spook us," he said, feeling his magic pulsing comfortingly within, keeping him warm in the bracing cold and urging him to charge into battle. From the silver shimmer in his grandfather's eyes he could tell Dan felt the same way.

"We're not spooked, though" Dan said. His long, gnarled fingers gripped the inner handle of the van door. "Let's go get it."

"You're joking, right?" Ryan asked. "You don't think you're going in there, do you?"

"Hell yes I'm going in there," Dan snapped.

"This is a sixth level demon, gramps."

"Exactly," Dan said stubbornly. "That's why I'm letting you come with me."

Ryan chuckled. "Funny. Look, gramps, you need to stay out of harm's way. I have this armor. The Shield of Innocents doesn't provide a complete globe of protection. The demon knows that by now. And you're exhausted. You can barely move. How are you gonna fight?"

"I can find the strength, Ryan. I can summon it, enough of it to help us through this."

Ryan looked at Dan for a long moment, seeing both the soft white shimmer of the natural magic emanated by all living things as well as the silver glow from Dan's proximity to the demon. He felt Dan's aura through their bond as both family and as Children of the Old Ones. He did not like what he saw or felt. It was weaker than it needed to be.

"I'm sure you can find the strength," Ryan conceded. "But it would probably be the last thing you did. Even if we beat the demon, the effort would kill you."

"Your concern is appreciated, Ryan. But I've lived a long life. If this is how it ends, fighting at your side to kill a sixth level demon, then that's fine with me."

"It's *not* fine with me, old man."

"How do you plan to stop me?"

"With common sense," Ryan countered, "that's how."

When he saw the stubborn defiance in the older man's tired eyes, Ryan tried again.

"Alright, then, gramps. Let's compromise."

"Make it quick, boy, and it had better be good."

14.5

Ryan's power began to grow the moment he left his grumbling grandfather at the van and stalked toward the building. The power intensified with each step as he closed on the building. The aura of demon magic was so strong it was almost as palpable as shifting air currents.

The shimmer of magical energy visible to Ryan was usually white, but the power emanating from the Dierglyorr was easy to discern from other magic. The sixth level demon's magic was stained a sickly gray and it sent a cold, slimy sensation from Ryan's skin to his bones.

He approached the front entrance of the warehouse and saw that the big wooden planks covering it were firmly secured. Ryan could easily cut through the door with Demonsbane but he wanted to move silently. The Dierglyorr knew Ryan was coming. Ryan could feel its attention riveted to him. The demon, however, was not alone. With his magic intensified, Ryan could feel the faint magical aura of people alongside the demon. He did not want to announce himself to the men under its command.

Instead of forcing his way in, he focused on the shifting currents of magic. Even though the building appeared secure, Ryan knew there had to be a secret entrance, one known to the derelicts and drug abusers that undoubtedly used the building as a temporary shelter. With all of his senses heightened by his magic, he could pick up both stale and relatively fresh scents of vermin, dogs, cats, human waste and illicit drug residue inside the otherwise abandoned structure, even through the concrete and wood. The many squatters that used this building had either found or made a way into the building. Ryan would find it.

He felt the patterns of the demonic energy that flowed heavily from the broken windows on the top floor. He could feel fainter wafts of magic filtering through the small spaces between the wooden boards covering the doors and windows. He could also detect a somewhat stronger flow coming from around the side of the building.

He followed that flow into the inky black shadows in the dark space between the boarded building and the closed parking garage. Ryan's very presence chased the shadows away. The silver glow of his magic revealed a boarded doorway. A quick inspection revealed a half-inch wide space between the edge of the boarded doorway and the metal doorframe. He hooked a finger behind the board and gave a slight tug. The plank-covered door opened easily without making a sound.

Ryan slipped in and quietly climbed the stairs to the top floor of the warehouse. The higher he climbed, the stronger he felt. He followed the demon's aura until the silver gleam of his magic lit his way to a broad iron door. The warmth of his glow rebounded off of the door and washed over him, lending him even more of its strength. He stood before the door for a moment, staring at it as if he could see through it to the inside of the room. With the power he felt raging within him he almost expected to be able to do just that.

The Dierglyorr's power was undeniable. It caused pale silver fire to pour from Demonsbane and it caused Ryan's eyes to blaze the same color. The magic was not as intense as it was at the battle at the Tyne River back in Lorr, when he fought countless demons from the first level of hell through the fifth. Back then the sheer number of demons boosted his power to seemingly godlike proportions. The magic in that warehouse, though, burned with a greater intensity than any one of those demons could have provoked. The intensity ensured Ryan that the demon waiting for him on the other side of that door was definitely from at least the sixth level. He actually hoped it was from the seventh. He would hate to face any one demon more powerful than this one.

He knew the demon and its unwitting minions were waiting for him, and even though his magic and Demonsbane wailed at him to commence, Ryan was in no hurry. In the past, Demonsbane would have forced him to charge into the room whether he wanted to or not. He could feel a difference now. Demonsbane compelled him against his will when his will contradicted the magic's purpose.

That was not the case this time. Ryan wanted to attack as badly as Demonsbane, but there was a strategic reason for his hesitation. He wanted his enemies to grow impatient, anxious, even frustrated. The more agitated they became the more likely they were to make mistakes, and the quicker he could get past any human defenses to get to the demon. The fact that neither Demonsbane nor his magic forced him to move let him know that on some level the magic understood.

Shanderah would be proud of him, he thought. That he had reached this kind of accord with his magic was proof that he really was one with Demonsbane. He would make the demon and its men wait.

The tricky part was going to be refraining from killing the humans that protected their disguised leader. That was what "Stunner" was for. Stunner came in handy when he had to infiltrate guarded facilities to carry out a termination order. He never had a problem killing a target but he drew the line at leaving a trail of corpses as collateral damage. He owned several such weapons, but the one he had given to Limbo was the only one he had in the Chicago city limits.

Ryan reached into his pocket with his left hand and pulled out Stunner, a pistol that shot powerful shock charges. It would not only give him a means of subduing the men without killing them, it would also serve as an anchor to keep him grounded in this world, his world, the world of technology, so that he would not be completely immersed in magic. His magic did not care whether or not the targets were human. As much as he wanted to lose himself in his power, Ryan knew he could not do that without risking the lives of those he swore never to kill again.

Only demons, he kept reminding himself.

The key would be to allow the magic to guide him without letting it completely overtake him. The magic was not compelling him at the moment, but Ryan was well aware of how quickly that could change in the heat of battle. He thought about Joel back at Hargathall's Cleft. The poor guy thought he had complete control over his power and was adamant about not killing.

Ryan, though, saw the start of that fight. He was thankful that he was too far away to see the bloody details, but he did see Joel's very first blow, and every one after that, was devastatingly fatal to the *Ken d'Zanir*.

He was determined to avoid Joel's fate. If Ryan was lucky, perhaps he could scare the shit out of the humans and in the confusion use Stunner a little easier. He inhaled deeply, filling his lungs and fortifying his considerable magic with the natural energy permeating the air around him, and prepared to do some killing.

Only demons…

Chapter 15: Unmasked

15.1

"What the hell is he waiting for?" Marco asked, his voice echoing in the massive space. A termination team surrounded the illegal arms dealer. A group of elite assassins had been ordered to protect him from the man outside the door. Still, Marco could not remember when he had been so nervous.

During his years working with Supervisor Johnson, Marco had witnessed things that very few living people had ever seen. Johnson, in his bid to win Marco over and then keep him as a business partner, allowed Marco to see some of the organization's amazingly advanced and eyes-only research and experiments. It worked. Marco was all-too-happy to pay the exorbitant prices Johnson demanded. In return, Johnson misused the organization's vast resources to eliminate Marco's competition in South America, the Caribbean, and southern Europe. He also assigned agents to serve as Marco's protection detail.

Having the assassination branch of a multi-national espionage and paramilitary organization as his own personal bodyguard and hit squad was great, but Marco demanded one more thing for all of the money he was paying: Access. He wanted to see firsthand what an outfit like the organization could do, the kind of resources they could tap. Johnson had no problem showing him. He let Marco tag along on a few of his rare visits to inspect the assassination branch's research and development facilities. He showed Marco recorded and even live video feeds of agents carrying out assassinations.

Marco thought about the pre-recorded video Johnson had shown him of Axe, also known as Ryan, jumping out of a third floor window and disappearing into a mini black hole. The memory still spooked him. How the hell did he do that?

Then there was the berserk man-monster Ryan and his grandfather spoke to at that tavern. The big bald man had to be some kind of prototype bio-engineered atrocity. To what kind of technology and resources did Ryan have access?

And who was the old guy tagging along with Johnson? He must have been Supervisor Johnson's boss. Johnson actually called the stranger *Mr.* Director. He had never heard Johnson call anyone else "Mister" anything. Johnson talked shit about the director when he was not around, but now that the boss man was here, Johnson was bowing and scraping as if he was professional ass-kisser.

"I didn't know Ryan had such a flair for the dramatic," said the director with a smirk. The heavyset gray-haired man stood comfortably just behind the two agents that shadowed him everywhere he went. They flanked him with their guns drawn, determined to guard their employer with their own lives if necessary.

Marco wondered how the director could be so calm under these circumstances. With the exception of Supervisor Johnson, everyone else in the sprawling room was tense, including the director's stoic bodyguards. And Marco, knowing the nervous supervisor the way he did, knew that his calm was nothing more than well-faked self control in the presence of his boss. While working his way up to the highest level of the organization, Marco figured the director had to have seen some fantastic shit, too.

There was a sharp screech of metal slicing through metal just before the steel door literally exploded inward. It flew twenty feet into the room and landed on the floor with a loud clang. Johnson was startled and took a few hurried backward paces. Several other members of the termination team backpedaled as well. They all managed to resist the urge to raise their guns and fire. The director and his bodyguards stood firm.

A man, blazing like a silver lantern, stepped into the doorway. He stood almost fifty feet away from them in the large, unfinished room, illuminating over half of the space. The light shone brightest from the eyeholes in his gleaming silver headpiece and from the short-handled double-bladed battleaxe that hung at his left hip from the belt of his closed trench coat. A small shield, or a large buckle, was strapped to his right forearm.

Silver sparks spilled from the halo of light surrounding the battleaxe's large crescent axe blades. The motes of light bounded a few feet across the floor before blinking out.

Streamers of light flitted among his thick dreadlocks that, to Marco, seemed to undulate on a soft, invisible breeze.

"The door was unlocked," Johnson deadpanned.

"I know," Ryan rasped. Even his coarse, damaged voice seemed to crackle from the energy radiating from him.

"Nice special effects," Johnson said. "Creative theatrics, but they won't do you any good here."

The full-length trench coat Ryan wore covered him from the turned-up collar covering his neck to the silvery metal boots on his feet. The coat bulged out at the shoulders, the demon knew, from the Child's enchanted and impenetrable armor. Ryan reached into his pocket with a gloved left hand and pulled out a sleek, dark pistol. His right hand was empty, and from the looks of the scar tissue and fused metal on the twisted, claw-like, appendage, the hand was useless.

"You'd be surprised, Johnson." Ryan leveled his white-hot gaze directly at the supervisor. He did not recognize the man's voice because Johnson used voice scramblers the few times they spoke on the phone. But he was the man doing all the talking, which hinted that he was the man in charge.

Ryan was somewhat surprised that no one had fired yet. They were nervous. With his magic ignited and heightening all of his senses, he could literally smell their fear. He could hear the faint thumps of their quickened heartbeats. They were shaken by the awesome spectacle he made as he shone like a silver beacon framed within the broad doorway, yet none of them raised their guns. They were disciplined and seasoned agents.

That meant they either wanted to talk for a moment or they wanted to take him alive. That was fine for the moment. This was a sixth level demon, and Ryan knew that charging madly into battle against such a powerful and cunning creature was not the wisest course of action. Instead, he resisted the magic's pull to attack and surveyed the situation,

He noticed the two big men flanking a short, pudgy, gray-haired man. Those were the same three men from the pier at Lake Michigan. Ryan spied them talking to Johnson shortly before Rionn Lorr arrived to take him and Joel across the

WorldGate. The three of them, along with the other ten men facing him, were too closely gathered for Ryan to pinpoint the exact source of the energy that caused him and Demonsbane to burn so brightly, but the calm that radiated from Johnson confirmed to Ryan that he had guessed right about the demon's disguise. Johnson was the demon.

Ryan's gleaming eyes bore into those of his former supervisor. "Been looking for you a long time," he growled.

"And we've been looking for you, Axe," Johnson answered. "No one can disappear and reappear the way you do without the help of some high-level friends. Before we terminate you, I'd like you to tell me where they are."

"Playing the role to the end, eh?" Ryan accused. "The name's Ryan, now, and you know I didn't come here to talk. I came here to destroy you, demon."

"He's not going to talk," the director interjected. "We train them that way. Just serve him and be done."

"I'm conducting this pre-termination interview," Johnson snapped unexpectedly at his superior. He turned back to Ryan. "Axe, I need you to help me get to the real threat, the one pulling your strings. And, as you well know, we have many ways to get to the truth."

"You actually think I would help you get to Rionn Lorr?" Ryan asked. "You're never leaving this room, let alone crossing the WorldGate again."

The director's face flushed with anger. "What the hell are you two talking about?"

"QUIET!" Johnson yelled.

The director's eyes widened with shock and anger. "Johnson, you must be out of your mind to talk to me like –"

He never finished his sentence because Johnson pulled his pistol and opened fire. The nine men with him, Marco included, did the same, riddling the surprised director and his bodyguards with bullets before they could react.

After the shooting was done, Johnson gave Ryan a long, cold stare. There was no passion at all. No anger, no fear, no nothing. "What a waste," he finally said. "Axe, you're an idiot. We're going to put you out of your misery."

Johnson fired first, a chest shot and a headshot in rapid succession. The others opened fire an instant later, but by then, they were already thoroughly amazed.

With only a flick of Ryan's right wrist, ripples of white energy erupted a foot in front of from him as the two perfectly aimed shots from Johnson struck the invisible barrier cast by the Shield of Innocents and ricocheted away. Multiple ripples followed, all of them a foot or so in front of Ryan's head, torso and legs as deflected slugs struck the floor, ceiling, walls, and columns all over the room.

Ryan lifted Stunner and squeezed off several shots. The ammunition passed through the barrier and found their marks. Three men quickly went down from electrically charged darts to the neck or torso. The others ducked and dodged for cover behind large columns.

"Work your way behind him," Johnson commanded his team through his mini-ear piece and microphone. "Let's get him surrounded and see if that little toy of his protects his ass as well as his front."

The men moved with well-rehearsed precision. Johnson stood with two other men in middle of their formation, stuck their guns out from behind their columns and fired. They did not risk peeking, not wanting to expose their heads or torsos even for a second. Many of the shots went wide but enough of them were close enough to force Ryan to keep his shield arm forward.

Cover fire, Ryan realized. Their concentrated gunfire did not reach him but the shooters did not present enough of a target for Ryan to return fire. He did not have as many stun shots as they had bullets and he did not want to run out. He knew what was about to happen, so he waited, and he did not wait long. Two pairs of shooters, one pair on the extreme left and the other pair on the extreme right, darted out from behind their columns.

They stayed low and ran fast, firing all the while, moving toward columns closer to the outer walls in an attempt to flank him. Without any fear of their bullets striking him, Ryan focused between the lines of rippling pale light and fired twice.

The two men on the far right dropped before they could reach cover. The other two were able to dive behind columns before he could get a bead on them. Their line remained approximately the same length as before but shifted to the left with two fewer shooters.

"Damn it!" Johnson swore. "Kill him!"

Small metal spheres roughly an inch in diameter rolled out from behind the columns. Ryan recognized them immediately and leapt forward just as the spheres exploded. A thick white smokescreen erupted into the air fifteen feet in front of the columns.

Two of the shooters in the middle, neither of them Johnson, laid down cover fire through the smoke in Ryan's direction while the two outer men moved to wider flanking positions. The outside agent fired as he ran, crouching to minimize the chances of catching a lucky shot from Axe. He gasped in surprise when the rogue agent came sailing directly toward him through the wall of smoke. The agent was both shocked and frightened. The man with blazing silver eyes seemed to be impossibly *flying* toward him.

Ryan had hurdled more than six feet above the floor, easily higher than the agents were firing. His right shield arm was held forward while he fired with his left.

The agent altered his aim but Ryan was moving much too fast. Before the agent could even finish shifting his gun hand, Ryan had squeezed off three shots to drop the trailing shooter as well as the two agents in the middle leaning out from behind their columns. The running shooter managed to get off only one shot, which bounded harmlessly off of Ryan's shimmering shield.

Ryan extended his foot as he sailed toward the running shooter. As difficult as it was for him to control his impulse to kill, he kept himself from putting his full weight behind the kick. With his magic ignited his armored boot could have easily shattered the agent's skull and broke his neck. Instead, Ryan sailed slightly past the shooter and lightly flicked his foot out as he passed. He landed deftly as the unconscious agent toppled to the floor.

Ryan caught movement out of the corner of his left eye and turned to see another of the small metal spheres hurling in his general direction. It missed him by a few feet but bounced off the wall and came back in Ryan's direction. He lifted his right arm just as the sphere exploded.

Instead of smoke, this sphere held fire and shrapnel. The shield protected Ryan from the intense heat and jagged metal slivers propelled with deadly velocity. The shockwave, however, sent him flying back through the dissipating wall of smoke to the center of the room. Ryan twirled head over heels through the air. In his enhanced state he easily gained control of his spin and landed in a crouch.

"Just you and me, now, demon," he called as he rose to his feet. "C'mon out so we can end this."

He knew which column the Johnson was cowering behind. Even in the midst of the firefight he could see the frightened man creeping from one column to another in an attempt to make its way to the exit.

It *should* cower. It should be afraid. They both knew what Ryan could do. They both knew the demon was about to die. What Ryan did not know was whether or not the demon was standing or squatting. With a toss at the right spot, though, it would not matter.

He decided to end it quickly. He pocketed the gun and pulled Demonsbane free. With a powerful backhanded throw, the Child of the Old Ones sent Demonsbane spinning horizontally through the air like a razor-edged discus. Bright silver spun off of Demonsbane in dazzling, twirling spirals of light. The streamers of arcing energy expanded away from the enchanted weapon in angry ripples as it cut through the air. If the demon was squatting or sitting, the enchanted battleaxe would take its head off. If standing, Demonsbane would cut right through its torso.

Demonsbane sliced easily through the concrete column with a sound like an electric saw cutting through soft wood. The battleaxe disappeared on the far side of the column. The sound ended within a fraction of a second later with the *thunk* of the battleaxe embedding into the wall behind the column.

Ryan stood there watching and waiting. In another couple of seconds, Johnson's head, shoulders and upper arms slid slowly from behind the right side of the column. And that was it. The only things below his triceps and ribcage were flowing blood and spilling organs. The red mess splattered as it and Johnson's upper body thudded to the floor.

Before Ryan could finish forming his disgusted frown, the bottom part of the corpse, along with the rest of the ruined arms, dropped with a squishing thud from behind the left side of the column.

"Damn…" Ryan groaned.

15.2

Something was wrong.

Ryan's silver-glowing eyes still shone through the eyeholes in his helm. His long dreadlocks continued to undulate while thin bolts of silver energy leapt from one brown lock to another. His magic was not fading even after the demon had been cut in two by his enchanted battleaxe. He waited for the shimmering sparks to lift from the demon's ruined corpse before its inevitable disintegration, but nothing happened. The remains only bled.

"What the f–" Ryan's question was cut short when he saw a blood red glow and felt a wave of heat rushing in from his blind side.

He brought the shield around to thwart the crimson fire rushing at him, but not in time to keep the foremost flames from slip past and ignite his trench coat. Ryan sprinted away from the attack and took off the burning coat, revealing not his enchanted armor underneath, but a t-shirt and blue jeans. He wore a bulky military-grade armored tactical vest instead of his silver cuirass.

"Surprised?" asked a voice Ryan heard earlier that night.

His eyes followed the sound and found the director, still riddled with bullet holes, standing behind him. A grim smile spread like a jagged slit across his round face. His pupils shimmered with pinpricks of crimson light. Smoke wafted from his nostrils.

"You thought Johnson was the demon because that is what I wanted you to think. Humans are comically easy to deceive. I even had a couple of Johnson's men chauffeur one of my beasts all over this country because of a faceless voice on a cell phone."

Ryan shrugged. I would applaud for you but I've got only one good hand and it's full."

"Your supervisor brought me here to ambush me," the director continued, ignoring Ryan's remark. "He intended to kill me in order to escape the organization. Does that sound familiar, Ryan?"

"Not at all," Ryan rasped. He could not understand how he had mistaken Supervisor Johnson for the demon, but he was determined to keep his bewilderment hidden.

"Johnson had grown weary of the discipline and sacrifice required of a man in his position," the demon said. "The freedom and indulgence of the drug and gun trade held more appeal to him. He *lured* me here by telling me we were coming to meet you.

"He thought he was lying. He did a passable job hiding his surprise when his spotters reported your approach, but I could taste his shock and fear on the air."

The demon chuckled, a sound more like the distant rumbling of thunder than anything remotely human.

"I, on the other hand, *did* expect you. I made no effort to suppress my aura to ensure you would find me if you were lucky enough to escape the Forsaken Desert." The demon slowly shook its head in mock pity. "I wonder if I was as predictable as you fools when I was but a mere human."

"How did you –?" Ryan hated to ask, but he had to know. "How did you transfer your aura to Johnson?"

The demon's crimson pupils spread until its eyes became blazing furnaces. "I am the Dierglyorr," it echoed.

Its voice went low and icy and rumbled as if escaping from a deep chasm. It was the same voice that spoke to him across the dunes of the Forsaken Desert. "*I am your end.*"

Ryan appraised his situation. Waves of magical silver energy radiated from his flesh, burning the very air around him with crackling white-hot intensity. His blue jeans, tac vest and t-shirt stood in stark contrast to the small shield strapped to his right forearm, the antiquated battleaxe, gauntlets, boots and helm. He could see the same silvery energy pulsing and dripping from Demonsbane, which was, unfortunately, over twenty feet away. Sparks bounced tauntingly and harmlessly across the floor and over the cloven corpse of the body crumpled on the dusty concrete a few feet away from it.

The *human* body.

Ryan had broken his oath. The demon tricked it into relinquishing Demonsbane *and* taking a human life at the same time.

"So Joel found his way to you?" the demon questioned. "He must have, of course. There is no other way you could have escaped my snare."

Ryan ignored the question. His anger at allowing himself to be duped into giving up his weapon urged him to attack without it. The power coursing through him gave him confidence. He believed his right hand, partially coated with Titan's Ore, would be weapon enough. But his magic and common sense made him pause. As powerful as Ryan felt in the presence of such a potent demon, he knew he was at a distinct disadvantage without Demonsbane's cutting edges.

"Your enchanted armor is missing some pieces," the demon noted with genuine curiosity.

Ryan shrugged. The simple gesture sent a few embers of silver fire trailing off in either direction. His damaged voice was a mocking, menacing growl.

"I was in a hurry."

"That was a catastrophic mistake," the demon rumbled.

Its body began to waver as if Ryan watched him through a giant fishbowl of swirling water. Ryan was vaguely reminded of Quick during one of his transitions. Morbid curiosity made him wonder what kind of creature this transformation would yield.

The top of the human head began to swell grossly, expanding to either side as if two flesh-covered balloons were being inflated side-by-side. The neatly trimmed gray hair sloughed off as the skull distended. The forehead began to broaden, causing graying eyebrows to sprinkle away. The human eyes bulged repulsively, the eyelids splitting into tattered flaps of flesh.

A sickening crunch echoed through the room as the eye sockets widened in jerking snaps of bone. A moment later the once-human eyes popped out of the head and rolled a few feet across the floor. The empty sockets were quickly filled with bulbous, angry red orbs the size of softballs. The widening brow protruded forward until it hooded the top of those terrible eyes like sharp, shelf-like arches.

When the creature's shoulders and chest began to swell and expand in the same manner as the head, as both its suit and its flesh tore away with the sound of ripping wet cloth, Ryan's common sense finally woke him from his disgusted trance and he realized he had better fetch Demonsbane.

Ryan sprinted toward his weapon but only made it a few yards before he saw something long, thick, and serpentine flash up beside him. He brought up the Shield of Innocents just in time to deflect a black, foot-long, needle-tipped point protruding from a pair of bulbous stone-hard shells covering the tip of what Ryan guessed was a tail. His guess was confirmed when several thick coils whipped up beneath the protective dome of the shield to wrap around his torso.

He brought his arms up just in time to escape the sinewy coils and thrust both hands toward the knobs at the base of the striking tail. The clawed fingers and thumb of his injured hand stretched as they snapped around one of the knobs, eliciting a grunt of pain from Ryan. His magnified strength allowed him to hold the tip of the tail at bay but the coils around his torso, pale gray and plated with sections of the same dull black shell, squeezed his chest and ribs with bone-breaking force. The tacticval vest groaned in protest. He felt like he was being crushed by an armored anaconda, except the tail was half-again as broad as the great snake.

"We're more alike than you know, *Child,*" the demon taunted. "If you wait a little while longer, you and I could rule all of the worlds *and* the seven Hells. What say you, little man?"

"Fuck you, *demon,*" Ryan rasped. "I'm not Joel or Delthar. I don't make deals with hell spawn. I was born to kill abominations like you."

"You're doing a piss-poor job of it," the demon snarled.

Securing his grip on the end of the demon's tail, Ryan used the sharp edge of the enchanted shield to chop down on one of the coils wrapped around him. His strike found a section of exposed flesh between two plates of hard shell. Even with his magically enhanced strength, the edge did not penetrate deeply enough to draw blood from the thick hide. It did, however, produce enough pain to make the demon release a pained, ear-piercing roar.

Instead of simply releasing him as Ryan hoped, the tail whip-snapped him to the far side of the large room, and further away from Demonsbane. Ryan flipped himself in mid-air until he could see the concrete wall rushing toward him. He brought up his forearm just in time to put the shield between himself and the wall. He came to a bone-jarring halt, allowing the shield's magic to absorb the impact, and fell roughly to the floor. He bounced to his feet and turned to see the final transition of the morphing demon.

Its hellish red eyes had shifted further apart, all the way to the sides of its elongated head, like a shark's eyes. The skin on its face and body was gray and ashen. Its cheekbones were impossibly wide and sharp. Its nose was like a bat's snout. Paper-thin lips pulled back to display black gums. From the gums descended a nightmarish jumble of curved fangs. The beast's pointy chin jutted forward at the end of an elongated lower jaw lined with more of the ugly fangs.

Long bony horns jutted from knobby protrusions just above its eyes. The horns radiated out to the left and right about two feet before curving forward at almost ninety degrees. The forward pointing section of the horns tapered as they extended another nine inches. Smaller shafts of horn branched out to either side at the midway point until they came to wickedly-pointed tips.

Grotesquely muscled shoulders spanned as wide as Ryan was tall. The massive chest, each of its pectorals as wide as Ryan's shoulders, rippled as it heaved. Eight pairs of abdominal muscles spanned the front of a freakishly long midsection that tapered inward below the monstrous chest and shoulders and stretched down to a sexless crotch.

Thin arms roped with cords of muscle spindled away from those broad shoulders. The length of each of its forearms was easily four feet, just a few inches longer than the span of the deltoids and upper arms combined. From its bony wrists sprouted huge, skeletal, three-fingered hands. Each digit, including the opposable thumbs, had six joints, and each fingertip was fitted with nearly foot-long curving claws that scraped against the floor.

Another pair of heavily muscled arms emerged from its sides, just above the creature's hips. The lower arms were a third the length of the upper arms and three times as broad, ending in big four-fingered hands that looked almost human.

The demon's legs had elongated and grown broader. Its feet were splayed, webbed, four-toed and clawed. The legs still resembled human legs, at least until they suddenly snapped backwards at the knees to become reverse-articulated. The change was accompanied by a popping sound like twin gunshots. They reminded Ryan of a wallowgrump's legs, minus the reptilian scales.

The length of its sectional, plated, needle-tipped tail twitched and slithered on floor around the creature's distorted legs and feet as if it had a mind of its own.

That's nasty, Ryan thought as the demon attacked.

It leapt forward with shocking speed, leading with the sharp point of its tail. Ryan again deflected the deadly point with the Shield of Innocents. The deflective magic of the shield expanded to block the keen edges of the demon's upper and lower pairs of claws. The force of the blows and the weight of the beast drove Ryan back. The demon flailed at him with claws and tail, pushing Ryan steadily in reverse.

Not wanting to be backed into the wall, Ryan began to ease to his left until his back was to a large window. When he noticed that the dangerous tail was no longer striking at him, he focused more on his peripheral vision.

And it was a good thing he did. He immediately saw the tail's needlepoint snaking behind him from his right, around the circumference of protection provided by the shield. With reflexes heightened to super-human acuity, Ryan batted the tail away with his deformed right hand. When the deadly point rebounded and came back at him, he whipped his armored right foot up and around to block the tip of tail even as it struck and stomped down, pinning the tail to the floor.

Unfortunately, the incredibly long and dexterous tail kept coming to wrap tightly around Ryan's calf. The demon once again snapped its tail to send Ryan flying across the room a second time. This time he was not able to turn his body soon enough. The right side of his body slammed high into the wall, just below the high ceiling. The air was blown roughly from his lungs and shuddering pain shot through his body.

As he rebounded from the wall and fell, Ryan could see the demon streaking across the room, its powerful legs propelling it at an impossible speed, to intercept him before he hit the floor. Ryan barely managed to bring his shield around in time to stop a vicious swipe from the claws of the demon's upper arms. The blow slammed him to the concrete floor with enough force to crack it. The demon began to pound relentlessly at the magical barrier. Explosive ripples of blinding bright energy flared madly each time the Dierglyorr brought down its claws.

Ryan grunted and gasped against the pain of his back pressing harder and harder against the floor. He was not concerned about the demon penetrating the magic barrier. He was confident that would not happen. What he did not know was whether or not his back would break before the floor did.

After several more monstrous blows he could no longer distinguish between the sounds of concrete rupturing beneath him and bones cracking within him. His arms burned and his elbows ached from the strain of keeping the shield raised.

While Ryan's inherited magic enhanced his strength, speed, stamina and pain threshold to superhuman levels, it did not make him invulnerable. He felt ribs breaking and knew some vertebrae were next. He would not be able to take much more of the Dierrglyor's attack.

Concentrating and looking within himself, he found his chi within the span of a single, deep breath. He used it to block out his pain and reinforce his effort to keep the shield raised. He narrowed his focus so that only the shield and his immediate surroundings flooded his awareness. That was when he felt a strange vibration coming from the steel-beam-reinforced concrete floor beneath him.

He pushed himself aside as the needle-tipped point of the demon's tail came bursting up through the floor. The tail tip followed Ryan's roll and arced toward the back of his exposed neck. Ryan stopped short, reversed his roll, and the sharp point shot past him. It struck the back of the Shield of Innocents, slamming it and Ryan's right forearm to the floor with so much force that the floor beneath him, already weakened, finally buckled and gave. Chunks of concrete broke away and exposed the steel joists. The joists bent enough for Ryan to fall through to the floor below.

The demon held the shield fast as Ryan fell, his wrist and hand slipping free of the shield straps. Shocking pain in Ryan's damaged right hand tore an agonized roar from him as he fell more than ten feet and landed on his back. His vision momentarily went white from the flare of pain that shot through him. Air was blasted from his lungs.

As he tried to catch his breath, he saw a length of one of the metal beams break away and fall toward him. Too stunned and winded to move, he lifted his hands and grimaced at the impact of the beam falling crossways atop him. His enhanced strength allowed him to catch the structural member but the pain in his torso, arms – and especially his right hand – buckled his elbows.

The beam came so close to smashing down onto his mouth, chin and neck that Ryan could feel his own warm breath bounce off the metal and back into his face. In his battered and exhausted state he could not push the beam away. His back was broken. He could feel it. His back and ribs were on fire. His arms had gone numb and he wondered how long it would take for paralysis to set in.

All Ryan could manage was to move the beam away from his face and hold it over his chest. The full weight of the beam pressed down on him, pinning his elbows to the floor. It took all of his waning strength to keep the beam from crushing his sternum.

When he moved the massive beam clear of his face, Ryan saw the demon glaring down at him through the hole in the ceiling. The Dierglyorr flicked the shield down at Ryan with a disdainful snap of its tail, sending the sharp edge spinning down at his neck like a circular saw. With a grunt of painful effort, Ryan shifted the beam just enough to intercept the shield. Its edge slammed against the beam with a loud clang and bounced to the far side of the large room.

Ryan tried to prepare himself for what he knew was coming next. When the demon jumped down through the hole it would land right on top of him. The combined weight of the demon and the fallen beam would surely crush him; and if it failed to crush him, the demon's claws and tail would finish him. Ryan was tempted to close his eyes to avoid seeing the instant of his demise, but for some reason he could not.

This would *not* be a good death.

15.3

As he watched the demon drop toward him, seemingly in slow motion, Ryan absently wondered if he had done enough good to atone for the lives he had taken. He doubted he had, especially after the way he so stupidly allowed the demon to trick him into breaking his oath just minutes earlier.

A ray of bright, pale blue light burst into his vision from left to right and the sound of crashing glass filled his ears. The light blasted the descending demon out of view. A second later, as small shards of glass from the window above showered him, a sheet of golden-yellow light, tear-drop shaped and about the length of a snowboard, flashed over Ryan's face from the same direction as the azure burst. He turned his head as far as he could to his right to find the demon and gaped in amazement at what he saw.

At the right-most corner of his peripheral vision, he could see the demon. It was ducking and flinching while blue light flared again and again around its malformed head. Beams of bright golden light arced in every direction while shadows danced madly in the flashing, moving light. Every few seconds the giant teardrop of yellow light would streak into and then out of view, pouring out smaller spheres of blue light at the demon all the while. The lightshow disoriented Ryan but he could not tear his gaze away.

The Dierglyorr swiped at the air with its long upper arms as if swatting at a pesky fly. It snapped at the light with its terrible maw. The demon's tail struck at the zigzagging light like a giant cobra. It even blew great gouts of demon fire at its assailant. Its movements were almost too quick for the human to follow but it was all to no avail. The yellow streak of light was too elusive.

On a few consecutive passes through Ryan's peripheral vision, the teardrop disc of light tilted enough so that its flat side was perpendicular to Ryan's vantage point. To his shock, there was a person crouched atop the disc.

The person wore a close-fitting uniform. The color of the uniform was indeterminable in the wild lighting, but the wearer was clearly female. Her arms pumped like pistons as she hurled orbs of blue light relentlessly at the demon.

The spheres of light exploded with eye-searing brightness upon contact with the Dierglyorr. Each blast visibly shook the demon. Its reverse-articulated legs, however, were spaced wide while the claws on its feet dug deeply into the concrete floor, so even though the blasts clearly affected it, the Dierglyorr held its ground and continued to strike out at its light-riding enemy.

Another shadow passed over Ryan where he lay pinned beneath the support beam. A pair of broad armored legs ending in ankle-high metal boots landed to his right. The boots struck the concrete floor with enough force to crack the surface beneath the soles. The stranger did not miss a step as he bounded into the fray. When the newcomer moved far away enough for Ryan to see the entire body, he saw that his legs were covered with copper-colored sectioned armor.

From the metal waistband at the top of the armored leggings emerged metal strips the same pale gray as his boots. The way the metal strips rose from the armored waistband, went up his back, arched over the man's wide, muscular shoulders and went down the front of his torso reminded Ryan of oversized metal suspenders.

The man did not wear anything underneath the metal arches. The muscles that bulged and flexed beneath his dark brown skin made him look like a world-class heavyweight body builder. A pair of thin metal cables sprouted from the peak of each arch. One of each pair looped around and down to the upper thigh of each of the armored leggings while the others connected to metal wristbands that encircled both of his thick wrists.

Ryan immediately recognized the newcomer. He moved much more slowly than the woman, so Ryan could see him clearly. He was the same man in a photograph shown to him by Jorgé Barboza on the same day Ryan and Joel crossed the WorldGate into to the Kingdom of Lorr. It was Kendrick Scott, AKA Pillar.

Before Scott could reach the two combatants, the demon darted its tail out and into the path of the woman astride the streaking disk of light. The thrust was perfectly timed so that the woman could not dodge it in time. The heavy tail clotheslined her, catching her across her upper chest and sending her cartwheeling violently toward the floor. A cocoon of light blossomed around her and cushioned her fall an instant before she hit the concrete. When she landed, the shell of illumination flashed and disappeared, revealing the woman kneeling on the floor and panting heavily.

The disk of light zipped wildly in every direction like a deflating balloon until it simply dissolved into stray sparks that eventually blinked out of existence. When the disc of light dissipated, the only remaining light was Ryan's silver glow. It was bright enough to light all but the far corners of the large room.

"Light Rider!" the newcomer called as he sprinted toward the demon, "Go catch your breath. I got this!"

The demon looked over at the approaching bull of a man. It hissed and shot its needle-tipped tail out to greet him. The diamond-hard point struck Pillar dead center in his uncovered barrel chest. Ryan expected to see the tail emerge from the man's back with a plume of blood. To his surprise the blow merely knocked him to his back and pinned him to the floor.

"Pillar!" called the woman as she staggered to her feet, stumbling toward a near window.

Pillar's breathless response was an emphatic, dismissive wave of his hand. "Get outta here, girl!" He gasped. He struggled against the tail but was unable to push it away.

The Dierglyorr cast its glowing crimson glare at the woman as it stalked toward Pillar.

"Listen to him, *girl,*" the demon taunted. "Fly away as fast as you can. It won't be fast enough, I assure you. I'll be done here very soon and then I'll come for you."

The woman Pillar referred to as Light Rider gave them a doubtful look before hopping out of the broken window and falling out of sight.

* * *

THE KEY QUEST

Dan stood with his back to the entrance of the multi-level parking garage and looked up at the building where his grandson battled the changeling demon. He watched the light show change from the expected silver shine of Ryan's magical aura to the familiar white of his enchanted shield to the red-orange flare of what could only be demon fire.

When completely unfamiliar shades of pale blue and sunlight-gold began to flash through the high windows, the Child of the Old Ones wrung his hands with worry. Crashes and explosions sent shockwaves all the way down to the sidewalk, adding to Dan's trepidation. Multiple shadows flitted through the chaotic lights as if others had somehow joined Ryan and the ancient demon.

Dan tugged nervously at the collar of his long winter coat and reached out to his grandson's mind with his own. He did it subtly, only listening, to keep from distracting Ryan. There was nothing to hear. Ryan kept his mind closed but his emotions open. Dan felt his grandson's pain and fear and considered rushing in to help. His temptation was tempered, however, by the prospect of running up five flights of stairs.

He could walk well enough now thanks to the fortifying magic flowing through him from his close proximity to the demon. In fact, he felt better than he had in years. But he had to be realistic about his age and physical condition. He had exerted a great deal of energy recently to keep him and Lisa safe. A five-story climb might leave him in too poor of a condition to be of any real help to Ryan against a sixth level demon. Dan was sure the demon realized that, too.

If Dan was going to help, he would have to do it the old fashioned way.

15.4

The deadly point of the demon's tail rose and fell twice more, striking Pillar with the force of a pile driver. Chips of concrete and plumes of dust shot up from beneath the big man's back as he was driven into the floor, yet there was no blood. With a third strike, the man was driven completely through the floor along with large pieces of concrete and broken steel.

The demon's ultra-dexterous tail followed Pillar through the hole as if it was a loose fishing line being pulled underwater by a large catch determined to escape. The tail suddenly stopped unreeling and went taught.

And then it began to move again. The demon spun one hundred and eighty degrees, stopping when its back was turned to the hole, and then it started to slide backward. The ropy muscles in its legs flexed and the claws on its splayed feet crunched into the concrete floor but that barely slowed its progress as it was pulled backward.

The demon's spindly but powerful upper arms extended to the floor and it dug the sharp claws of its six-jointed fingers into the hard surface, drawing deep gouges into the dense concrete as if it was sand. The demon kept sliding until its backside was lodged in the cavity. It growled in frustration as it struggled against the powerful tug at its tail. Loud crunching sounds and sharp cracks echoed as the edges of the hole crumbled away.

Ryan paused in his struggle against the section of support beam just long enough to marvel at Pillar's awesome strength. The terrible claws of the beast tore deeper into the concrete as it gave one more monstrous heave. But instead of freeing itself, the force caused an even larger portion of the floor to give way. The demon fell through the floor with a loud crash and a dense cloud of dust.

Ryan took that opportunity to renew his fruitless efforts at the beam pinning him down. He could feel his magic working to heal his broken bones and damaged nerves. The floor quaked from the battle raging on the level just below, causing the beam to tremor in a way that sent bolts of pain through Ryan's arms. He welcomed the pain. It meant his nerves were being repaired. Maybe his full strength would return next.

He could see the columns around him shudder. The building rumbled as if thunder erupted from inside the structure. Angry, bestial roars and pained human bellows accompanied the thunderous blows being delivered and absorbed by each combatant. Each tremor sent another wave of pain through Ryan's straining body.

The beam continued to push his elbows painfully into the concrete floor. The weight forced his forearms to pivot until the beam pressed against his chest. His breathing and vision were hindered by the inexorable weight and made worse by the dust that showered down on him every time the building shook. Fortunately Ryan was too weak to cough. The extra exertion and motion would have been too much to bear.

His vision started to swim but he could hear the fight clearly. He heard Pillar grunt in pain and then a deafening crash exploded near his right ear. A gray and copper-colored blur burst through the floor to his right, streaked diagonally through the room, and blasted through the north curtain wall just below the ceiling before soaring out of view.

Silence fell so suddenly that it startled Ryan. In the next instant the demon was standing over him. Its terrible maw twisted obscenely in what Ryan could only assume what was a self-satisfied grin.

Ryan did not think he would ever see a smile as terrible as the one Joel flashed him while in his bone-beast form at Hargathall's Cleft, but this changeling demon's rictus was worse by far. The long curved fangs looked like pointed fingers reaching out from tar-black gums. Some of them curved so sharply that they jutted though the upper and lower lips in several places. The perforated flesh stretched taut when the demon drew back its blackened lips to grin, causing green blood to ooze from the ripped flesh and mix with the yellow saliva that drooled from its mouth.

"Your friends have merely delayed the inevitable," it snarled. "I will finish them if they have the courage to return. I will hunt them down if they do not."

Ryan looked up defiantly all the while, knowing his eyes betrayed his fear. He pushed at the beam again, and again his exhausted arms failed to move the heavy structural member.

Bulbous, hungry, blood red eyes beamed down at Ryan from the deep recesses of the demon's jutting brow. It raised both of its long upper arms high above its head. The two stunted, heavily muscled arms below its rib cage were poised to attack as well. All four arms were crisscrossed with black veins pulsing beneath leathery gray skin. The fourteen long, six-jointed fingers were all spread wide, with black foot-long claws poised to tear. The heavily plated serpentine tail wavered hypnotically with the needle-sharp point trained on Ryan's face like the head of a cobra prepared to strike.

When the Dierglyorr spoke again, a deep grating voice infinitely more terrible than Ryan's own sandpaper-voice made his hackles rise.

"Child, I shall taste your flesh and blood and bones as I did your name-sake two thousand years agone."

Before it could bring all of its killing edges down, the Dierglyorr looked up as if something had caught its attention, and then a blinding flood of white light burst through the dim room and a thunderous horn shattered the silence.

The demon looked through the window to see a van hurtling through the air from the parking garage next door. The lights and sound distracted it long enough for the vehicle to crash through the window and slam into its chest. The van bore the Dierglyorr to the floor a few yards away from where Ryan lay pinned beneath the beam. The van's momentum continued to push the monster across the floor until they came to an abrupt stop at the far wall with a deafening crash.

Ryan's surprise turned immediately to fear when he recognized the ruined van and saw the figure slumped over the steering wheel.

"Gramps!" he cried.

The old man did not stir. The demon barked out rumbling laughter from beneath the van and tossed it aside with a mighty heave.

The van flipped sideways, rolling three times before coming to rest upside down. Ryan panicked as he watched his grandfather, aglow with his own divine magic, pitch wildly from side to side inside the tumbling vehicle like a giant silver light bulb.

The demon rose to its clawed feet and glared at the crumpled wreck.

"Dan?" it cackled. "The *Ascendant One* smiles upon me this glorious eve! I get to wipe out two-thirds of the Gatekeeper's surviving spawn in one swipe!" It took a step forward and paused. "Ah, but your flesh is old and has lost its youthful flavor. I think I shall cook you before I dine."

The Dierrglyor's twisted maw stretched wide and spewed demon fire. Red flames washed over the upended van, combined with Children's' silver glow and lit the room with a magenta illumination that took on a yellowish tint when the van caught fire. The bright lights chased all shadows from the room and made the top floor of the building light up like a beacon in the nighttime sky.

Ryan's tortured, hopeless scream was music to the demon's ears. The scream was loud and continuous, droning on in time to the roar of the flames spewing forth from the demon's gullet. The Dierglyorr was so enraptured by its victory that it took a moment for it to register the crashing sound behind it.

It turned just in time to see a monstrous male humanoid sprinting at it with superhuman speed. This new monster's arms and legs were cartoonishly long and slender. His entire body was adorned with bone spikes, even his head. His hands were giant bone scythes.

The Dierglyorr roared "JOEL?" just as the Child of the Old Ones slammed into its chest. Its roar changed from one of surprised anger to one of pain when Joel's spikes and scythes plunged into its tough flesh. Its dark green blood spurted as the two of them tumbled across the floor.

The moment Joel hit the stairway on the first floor a few seconds earlier he was determined to come face to face with the demon once again. This time, though, he would not be chained to a wall. That imminent mortal danger ignited his power immediately, and like Hargathall's Cleft, Joel was acutely aware of everything that was happening.

He roared with the embattled Dierglyorr until their monstrous bellows became indistinguishable. Joel felt the each of the Dierrglyor's teeth and claws pierce his toughened flesh but he was not afraid. The pain spurred him to fight with a savagery that dwarfed his past transformations. This was the first time Joel actually *wanted* his devastating power; the first time he actually wanted to kill.

The combatants became a blur of claws, sharpened bone, flying concrete, white dust, and spraying green and black blood. The Dierrglyor's tail rose and fell savagely, almost too quickly to see, and so did Joel's scythe hands.

And then it all stopped. When the dust cloud settled, the Dierglyorr stood in a crouch holding Joel at a distance with its tail. The powerful tail wrapped around Joel several times yet was still long enough to hold him over ten feet away. Joel, still in his monstrous form, struggled mightily but could not break free of the crushing grip. The tail kept Joel's arms pinned to his sides, denying him the leverage he needed to bring his full strength to bear. The deadly tip of the tail struck Joel again and again around his head, face and neck but failed to draw blood.

Joel shut his eyes when the barbed tip came near them but otherwise he did not appear to be bothered very much. He appeared to suffer more from frustration than from pain. The same could not be said for the demon. It seemed to suffer from both. The bone spikes all over Joel's body protruded from the demon's tail in several places and thick, emerald blood poured from the wounds onto the floor. Nevertheless, the demon held him fast.

"Did you think you could destroy me, you stupid ape?" the Dierglyorr taunted. "When I'm done feasting on you and this other useless god-spawn, your wife and incubating whelp will be my dessert!!"

Joel cracked a horrible smile. "No they won't, bitch."

The demon's right eye shifted and widened at the sight of Ryan flying toward him with Demonsbane held high in a two-handed grip. The enchanted battleaxe blazed like a small star. Waves of silver fire poured from Ryan's entire body.

With demonic speed, the Dierglyorr flicked Joel away and snapped its tail back around to spear the approaching Child in the back.

Ryan had the enchanted shield strapped to his left wrist again but he did not need it. In mid air, Demonsbane traced a brilliant pattern at the speed of thought as Ryan chopped down and behind him with his right hand to sever the tail, whipped the blade up and to the front to slice away both of the demon's groping right hands; and brought the enchanted battleaxe down again with two hands as he approached the demon. The glowing blades sliced through the top of the demon's right shoulder, diagonally across its torso, and out of the left rib cage just above the monster's lower left arm.

Ryan's momentum carried him into the severed upper torso, knocking it away from the rest of the body. Its arms flailed and the demon's head thrashed wildly as the top half of the beast tumbled to the floor. Ryan continued to soar forward until he bounded off the wall and landed on his feet. He immediately sprinted over to the flaming van.

A stranger stood near the section of beam that had pinned Ryan to the floor. The beam was cut neatly into thirds and each cut edge still glowed and sizzled. Smoke wafted up from the nose a sleek, matte-black, Y-shaped bracer on the stranger's right forearm and wrist. With thought, he switched the setting on the firing bracer cutting laser back to safety mode. He pulled the fitted cowl from his face and smiled.

A feminine voice in the stranger's mind, his constant and often unwanted companion, warned against removing the mantle. Pete O'Malley ignored her as he often did. He wanted to take a breath of unfiltered air and survey the aftermath of the battle through his natural right eye as well as his synthetic, orange-irised left eye. Having an alien artificial intelligence

467

CPU implanted in his brain connected by nano-thin wiring to his every nerve and synthetic left eye was not as cool as Pete had initially expected it would be, but at times like this he was glad he had them.

His human eye would never have caught the lightening-quick movements of the demon's tail or the armored man's battleaxe. The nanotechnology in his synthetic eye was able to follow and record the movements so they could be played back in Pete's mind at his convenience.

"Now *that* was impressive," he said aloud.

Ryan did not have time to observe his handiwork. He had to get his grandfather out of the flaming remains of the van. An unfamiliar phrase leapt unbidden from his mouth and he waved his left hand, casting a brief but powerful blast of icy air that extinguished the flames. Ryan thanked the remnant of old Shanderah for the spell as he reached the van.

Demonsbane cut the dented door away. Ryan hung the battleaxe from his belt and pulled his grandfather out of the smoking vehicle. Dan's eyes were closed and he was not moving or breathing. Ryan carried him a few yards away before his exhausted legs gave out. He dropped to his knees but held onto Dan securely and settled him to the floor while cradling his grandfather's head and shoulders in his arms.

"Gramps," Ryan said with a trembling voice.

The devastation of his mother's death returned to him. He thought back to three years earlier, to the pain he felt when Shanderah lay dying in his arms. He thought about the agony of seeing his daughter disintegrate in a blinding burst of magic. Ryan could not imagine the pain of losing his grandfather, as well. He settled Dan's head to the floor and prepared to give CPR.

"Gramps!" Ryan tried once more, choking back tears.

"What, boy? What!" Dan gasped as he sat up suddenly.

Ryan paused. The fear in his expression transformed immediately to joyful disbelief.

"You scared the hell out of me, old man," Ryan sighed.

"And you damn near gave me a heart attack, screaming like that!" Dan snapped, clutching at his chest. After catching his breath, he pulled open his black trench coat and tapped a bony knuckle to the chest of the silver cuirass. "I was shook up a little," he admitted. "But damn, this armor is gr–!"

A hellish roar cut Dan's sentence short. Ryan turned quickly, Demonsbane held ready.

The Dierglyorr snarled, "While you destroy my earthly body and cast my soul back to hell," it spat, "know that my machinations live on in the hearts of you easily corrupted humans. *My seeds have been sown...*"

The torso began to flail and silver sparks began to dance around the severed edges of the cuts. The sparks intensified and spread until streamers of sliver lightning arced in every direction across both halves of the demon's body.

The upper and lower pieces began to tremor, as did the severed tip of its tail and severed arm. The energy that radiated from the body parts was so dense that it slowly pushed the pieces off the floor and made them hover several inches in the air. The silver light, tinged with red trailers of radiance, poured out of the pieces like fluid and pushed the severed pieces higher into the air.

The dying monster turned its crimson lantern glare on Ryan one last time.

"I eagerly await your arrival on *my* plane!" it chuckled.

A stale, humid gale tore through the room like the exhalation of death itself and chilled Pete O'Malley to his bones. The silver light engulfed and then devoured the demon's crimson radiance as its gray skin charred to black. The pieces of the vanquished demon hardened, cracked, and then shook themselves into a pile of black ash as the silver light died out.

Peter's mouth dropped open in awe. "Wow."

"What the hell was that?" Joel, in his normal form, asked from across the room.

"The essence of a sixth level demon being pulled back into hell," Dan answered. And then he grunted and doubled over in pain.

"Gramps?" Ryan croaked.

Dan reached over and snatched Demonsbane from his grandson's grasp. He held it in a two-handed grip and aimed the crescent blades at the pile of ash. A second later, a cone of red flame roared from the enchanted battleaxe into the remains of the Dierglyorr. The stream of demonic flame lasted for several seconds before abruptly cutting off, leaving a large hole in the concrete floor, its edges neatly cauterized into a smooth oval.

Dan exhaled with relief. "Damn, that really *hurt*," he managed through ragged breaths.

"Oh, yeah," Ryan said, remembering the armor's ability to absorb energy attacks and then expel them through the enchanted battleaxe.

"Heads up, fellas!" Pete called. He brought up his left wrist arm, where a thin gunmetal gray cable was coiled from wrist to just beneath his elbow. The coil extended and shot across the room toward grandfather and grandson, reaching much further than the length wrapped around his forearm suggested it should have.

Dan's eyes went wide as the end of the cable shooting at them sprouted into grapple claw. With a deft flick of the wrist, the red headed stranger in the weird metallic blue body armor caused the cable to loop around the two Children of the Old Ones twice before the grapple snapped securely onto a segment of the cable. The line tightened as the stranger braced himself in a wide legged stance with his right hand clutching his left elbow.

The cable retracted quickly, yanking Dan and Ryan roughly into the air and toward the stranger. The van suddenly reignited and then exploded when Dan and Ryan were halfway across the distance between them and O'Malley. The shockwave hurled them even faster, but only the edges of the flames licked at them as they crashed into the newcomer.

The force of the blast sent all three of them through the window just behind Pete. Both Dan and Ryan yelled in surprise at the sudden free fall, but both were cut short when they fell heavily into the cushioned interior of a convertible automobile hovering a few yards below the window.

With another thought, Pete made the grapple detach and fold in on itself until it blended in with the rest of the cable. The cable then quickly shrank back to its original length and released the two Children of the Old Ones. Pete climbed over to the steering yoke while the other two righted themselves.

Ryan scrambled to a seated position in the back seat while Dan sat up in the front passenger seat. Both men peered over the side of what appeared to them to be a cross between an airplane cockpit and the interior of a large car. When they saw that the vehicle floated five stories above the street, both had the same awed expression Pete wore when he watched them fight the demon.

"What about the other guy?" Pete asked.

"Joel?" Ryan asked, not seeming concerned in the least.

"There he is." Dan pointed down to the street, where Joel, in his normal form, lay unmoving with his eyes closed in a steaming, man-shaped crater in the middle of the street. His medieval garb was tattered, torn, and scorched.

Lisa sprinted over to him and fell to her knees. She was worried to the point of crying. "Joel? Joel!"

Joel's eyes popped open and he took a few deep breaths before whispering: "If they ask, tell them you talked me into helping out."

Lisa's worry turned to joy. "OK, but why not tell them you changed your mind on your own?"

"Can't have them getting too comfortable with me helping out," Joel explained. "I'm no kind of hero or soldier and I don't want to be. I don't want them thinking they can just call me whenever they want."

Lisa smiled and kissed him on the cheek. "You're *my* hero, baby."

"That's more than enough for me," Joel said. He rose shakily to his feet and looked up at the men in the hovering car and then turned to his wife. "You know, I should probably be amazed at a flying car, but…"

"After all you've seen, it just isn't that spectacular," Lisa finished his sentence for him. "I know what you mean."

Joel turned back to the futuristic vehicle. "You're welcome, fellas!" he yelled.

Dan and Ryan chuckled. "You're wife made you come back, didn't she?" Ryan called back.

"How'd you guess?" Joel asked. "Don't expect it to happen again!"

"Wouldn't think of it!" Dan assured.

The dashboard beeped and a blue light flashed just before Pillar's face appeared on a small dashboard monitor.

"Ace, talk to me," Pillar said. "I saw the explosion, what's your condition?"

"We're in the car," Peter replied as he surveyed his passengers. "We're OK. Where's Light Rider?"

"I'm with her," Pillar said. "She's shaken and I think she has some broken ribs but she'll be all right."

"I'll come get you," Peter offered.

"No need," Pillar answered. "I'm literally a hop, skip and a jump away from the RV. We'll rendezvous there."

"See you in a couple, then," Pete returned. "Ace out."

Ryan put a hand on Pete's shoulder. "Don't tell me," Ryan said. "Barboza sent you."

"Something like that," Peter, or Ace, answered.

"Well, it's good to see you," Ryan admitted.

"Damn good," Dan agreed.

"Hey!" Joel yelled again from the street. "Can a couple get a ride to a hospital?"

15.5

The Head Mage was decidedly *not* prepared for this. He carried the Hell Key, still completely wrapped within his cloak, under his right arm. As he walked down the narrow stairway with his wife and daughter to either side of him, he could hear little Shandie whispering the spell to light the torches resting in sconces lining both walls of the stairwell. It was an almost comically simple spell so Rionn let her do it. It was fun for her and he wanted to conserve his magic.

He felt a tremor of magic near his left hip. A surge of hopeful nervousness filled him as he reached into a hidden pocket in the folds of his robe to retrieve his box of reflection sand. Rionn identified the source from the resonance of the magical energy. Holding the box in his palm, he flipped open the box with his thumb to see the message within.

We killed it cuz. The demon won't be coming back to Lorr. Joel even helped.

Catherine noticed Rionn's relieved exhalation. "Good news from across the WorldGate?" she asked.

"*Very* good news," Rionn confirmed. "The Dierglyorr has been sent back to hell."

The happiness they felt was deep but brief as their thoughts returned to the business at hand. Rionn closed the box of reflection sand, not wanting to pause for even the small amount of time it would have taken to respond. He would send Raxe a message when this task was complete, hopefully with news just as good.

The stairwell spiraled far below the dungeon levels. The chill in the air and Rionn's trepidation grew with every tread. He looked over at his wife and saw the same disquiet in her beautiful face. Shandie's expression was one of nervous but joyous anticipation. *To be a child again*, he thought.

He did not venture down into subterranean depths of the castle often. No one did, for it was not a place to be visited casually. Even still, the long descent down the cold stairwell into the bowels of the earth beneath the palace's high tower seemed longer than it had ever been.

Rionn had been worrying about Mar-dah's corpse for three years. His concern was far greater than he had ever admitted aloud, even to Catherine, and there were very few secrets he kept from his beloved wife. They all knew that the soul of a Child of the Old Ones was unlike that of other humans. The soul of a Child was more powerful, more aware. A just soul would be readily accepted into the realm of the Lord Ascendant to join Him and the Protectors that accompanied Him in Heaven. A soul as wicked as Mar-dah's, however, would be firmly rejected.

One of the higher levels of hell would eagerly welcome such a malevolent and powerful essence. Rionn did not know this for certain, but he believed the soul of an evil Child of the Old Ones might even be taken in by the sixth or seventh level. The threat was that a soul with enough power and awareness would be able rebuff hell, to resist its pull. It could exist in a state of limbo, suspended there with the hope of finding a way to continue to impose its will upon the living. Rionn had no doubt that Mar-dah's was such a soul.

To make matters worse, the iron coffin in which Mar-dah's body was confined, packed with salt and warded with considerable magic as it was, would only confine his soul for a limited amount of time. What Rionn Lorr told no one was that time had been running dangerously short. In a matter of weeks the soul would have been able to seep through the barriers put in place to contain it. If that happened, a skilled necromancer would have been able to pull the soul back into the plane of life and perhaps place it into a human vessel. That threat was about to come to an end but Rionn felt no relief. There would be no relief until this deed was done.

Catherine was at his right shoulder descending the stairs beside him. Little Shandie was at his left hand, her tiny booted feet keeping pace with her parents. The Head Mage sighed with fear, sadness, and a bit of frustration. Rionn had suggested, then commanded, then pled and finally threatened them to give him privacy in this grave endeavor. Yet there they were, walking to either side of him into the eerie depths as if they were his bodyguards.

And now they were at the heavy, oaken, iron-banded door to the chamber containing Mar-dah's preserved corpse. Rionn Lorr paused and turned a stern glare on his wife.

"Catherine, I *insist* that you and Shandie stay out here. I will call you if I need you. I promise."

"And what if you are *unable* to call to us?" Catherine countered in that calm yet commanding way of hers, her soft green eyes glaring just as sternly as Rionn's. "You've never done this before. You've no idea what to expect."

"I've studied the process thoroughly, my love."

"Of course you have," Catherine returned. "And we both know that reading about a magical process is far different from performing it."

Rionn turned to his daughter. Her small oval head nodded softly in agreement with her mother.

"We should be by your side, daddy," the little girl said.

Rionn relented only because he believed Catherine made a good point. This was dangerous ancient magic with which he was dealing. If something happened to him and he needed their help but was unable to call out to them, the results could be catastrophic. Besides, with her power and a child's impulsiveness, he did not think he could keep his daughter out of the room for long if she really wanted to enter.

He suspected his wife thought the same. That was the only reason she had not joined him in insisting that Shandie stay away. Rionn hoped his daughter would choose not to witness this, that his trepidation and outright fear would frighten her enough to turn her away. However, there was a well-known saying among the elves that a female elf with her mind made up was as immovable as a mountain.

His wife was half elf and his daughter only one-quarter elf, so Rionn could only conclude that their legendary stubbornness was a trait that did not get diluted when elven blood mixed with that of other races.

The three of them entered the circular room. Shandie whispered another spell to light the bright sconces evenly spaced along the wall. They all stared intently at the iron tomb resting in the middle of the room.

The coffin was a rectangular box of heavy, dull gray iron; seven feet long, three feet wide, and two feet deep. There were no hinges. The six-inch deep lid fit snugly over all four edges of the rim of the large container. Three latches, solid slide bolt mechanisms, were welded to every side. Instead of being secured by a lock, they were held tight and fast by broad, gleaming, seamless metal rings. The rings were an elegant silver color with a faint touch of cyan at their core, the telltale sign of unbreakable Titan's ore.

Rionn stopped at the head of the iron coffin and set the bundled Hell Key on the floor. His wife walked around and stood to one side and his daughter went to the other. Rionn knelt and whispered a spell over the sarcophagus that set the Titan's ore rings aglow. The hint of cyan within the metal grew into a bright shimmer. There was a blinding light blue flash and then the light was gone.

Rionn inspected the rings. Their light faded and each one was missing a quarter of its original shape. They hung like hooks from the lip of the upper lid. With an open hand and an exertion of will, the Head Mage lifted the lid without touching it and directed it, slowly and smoothly, to rotate one hundred and eighty degrees. The lid floated to the left, one edge settled gently to the stone floor and the other propped up against the side of the sarcophagus. Rionn, Catherine and Shandie looked into the coffin.

Mar-dah's corpse had been almost perfectly preserved within the airtight coffin and the salt that surrounded it. There were some obvious differences. The long-limbed body was much thinner than his slender body had been in life. The skin was gray instead of the almost porcelain white it had been when blood flowed through it. The white blonde hair of the face and eyebrows bore an ashen tint.

Despite the changes wrought by death, the well-preserved body seemed like it could move at any moment. Rionn Lorr glanced at his daughter, his fatherly instinct beseeching him to send her away, to keep her from seeing a dead body, but his experience as Head Mage reminded him that he had seen worse at the same tender age.

It was an inescapable part of life for a descendant of the Old One Lorr. Shandie would likely succeed him as Head Mage and guardian of the Kingdom that Bore His Name as well as the Continent of Lorr. Even though the sovereigns of the other two kingdoms on the Lorrian Continent rejected his protection, a Child of the Ones serving as Head Mage of the Kingdom of Lorr was nonetheless duty-bound to serve as the ultimate protector of the entire continent. The sooner Shandie was exposed to death, the sooner she would learn how to deal with it.

Rionn studied her expression carefully. The knit of her thin, dark blonde eyebrows betrayed equal parts curiosity and fear. She was frightened but not repulsed, morbidly curious but leery as opposed to being excited...exactly what he was hoping for.

All he saw in his wife's countenance was worry. The body in the coffin meant nothing to her. Her concern was solely for her husband and daughter. Catherine met his gaze and held it. The look in her eyes told him what they had told him countless times over the years: *Be careful, my love*...exactly what he expected.

Rionn smiled and reached for the long bundle on the floor. He opened the blanket, moving neither slowly nor quickly, and tried his best to affect a casual air despite the fluttering of his heart. He set aside the last fold and saw the sinister reptilian eyes carved masterfully into the flat of the wide blade. The dragon stared right at him, maw gaping wide, forked tongue threatening; long fangs lining the upper and lower palates. Every scale was etched with impossible precision, giving the impression of life on a lifeless surface.

Rionn sat on the floor, rolled the loose right sleeve of his robe up above his biceps, stopping at the bottom of his deltoid, and cleared his mind to everything but his purpose. The Head Mage wanted no temptation, no strong desires of any type, at the forefront of his thoughts. He wanted nothing there for the magic to latch on to and use against him.

Raxe had warned him about the seductive pull of the weapon but the warning was hardly necessary. Rionn could feel a hint of the wicked attraction even through his past psychic visions of the Hell Key.

Rionn grasped the Hell Key with his left hand and felt a jolt, cold and sharp, race through him. His daughter shuddered as a ripple of the magic raced through her. Catherine looked at them in turn, her brow furrowed with anxiety. When they relaxed a moment later, Catherine slowly began to relax as well. Shandie resumed her cautiously curious inspection of her father and the body lying in the sarcophagus. Rionn, on the other hand, remained tense and grim as he closed his eyes and began to concentrate.

His eyes still closed, Rionn lifted the greatsword. The muscles in his left arm flexed beneath the sleeve of his robe as he lifted the large weapon. He rested the blade against his right biceps. Rionn did not have to use as much of his blood when opening the WorldGate earlier because Joel and Raxe contributed. The WorldGate Key, as if realizing Rionn's intention, had halted its usual gluttonous absorption of his life force. That was the only reason Rionn had the strength to draw blood again so soon for this procedure. He tried not to think about how much blood the Hell Key would require.

Like the WorldGate Key, the Hell Key's edge was still impossibly keen despite its age and lack of attention. Rionn pulled the greatsword slowly down, cutting a thin slit into his arm. His blood immediately soaked hungrily into the blade.

Unlike the WorldGate Key, the Hell Key immediately sent shocking and burning pain through his arm and the rest of his body.

Chapter 16: To Hell

16.1

Ryan and Dan found themselves seated outside an examination room waiting for their hosts in one of the secret medical facilities belonging to the organization's Global Organizational Defense branch. Both men wore hospital scrubs. A large duffle bag containing Ryan and Dan's enchanted gear rested on the floor between Ryan's feet.

During the two hours after the Harvey's were dropped off at their apartment, scars were cleaned and bandaged, broken bones were treated, copious amounts of pain medication were taken and brief preliminary interviews took place. The doctors had taken x-rays of Ryan's damaged hand. They concluded that the Titan's Ore covering his four fingers, the back of his hand and parts of his palm was inexplicable fused to surrounding flesh as well as the bone underneath, but that was only a guess because their equipment could not penetrate the alien metal.

Both men flinched at the same time. Ryan shook his head while Dan blinked several times. They turned to one another.

"You felt that," Dan said to his grandson.

"And saw it," Ryan said to his grandfather.

"Good luck, Head Mage," Ryan whispered.

Dan continued to study Ryan. He could tell from the look on his grandson's face that something else was bothering him. He stared until Ryan could not stand it anymore.

"What?" the grandson finally asked.

"You tell me," Dan said. "You just saved the day but I can't tell from that sorry mug of yours."

"I broke my oath. I killed Johnson."

"He had it coming," Dan assured. "It was a gruesome way to take him out but that's nothing to be upset about."

"The oath I made was unconditional," Ryan argued. "I know it doesn't mean much to you but it does to me."

"I'm not trying to make light of your oath, Ryan, but look at it logically. It wasn't your fault. The demon tricked you."

"I know that's what it said, but how?" Ryan questioned. "My magic is like an arrow. It always points me right to the demons. Could the demon really have misled my magic? Or did I just want Johnson to be the demon so badly that I ignored the obvious?"

"A little bit of both, I think," Dan answered.

"What do you mean?" Ryan asked suspiciously.

"Let me show you something, youngster," Dan began. He reached his right hand into the hip pocket of his scrub pants and pulled out his fist. "I've got a nickel in this hand, OK?" Dan opened his fist so Ryan could see the nickel and then closed his hand.

"OK," Ryan acknowledged.

"Now, watch my hands," Dan instructed as he closed his left hand into a fist and held it a couple of inches away from his right fist.

"I'm watching."

Dan's eyes never left Ryan's, and Ryan's eyes never left his grandfather's wrinkled, knobby-knuckled fists. Dan smiled and said: "Alacazam," with an exaggerated flair. Ryan ignored the tease and kept watching his grandfather's hands.

"Now," Dan continued. "Which hand is the nickel in?"

"Your hands never moved," Ryan observed. "It's gotta still be in your right hand."

Dan smiled slyly.

"What?" Ryan asked. "You used a teleportation spell to move it to your left hand?"

"Wrong on both counts," Dan said as he opened both hands to show two empty palms.

Ryan gave Dan a sidelong glance. "So you made it disappear. Again, teleportation spell?"

"I made what disappear?" Dan asked.

"What are you talking about?" Ryan pushed. "You know I mean the nickel."

"What nickel?" Dan seemed genuinely curious, which irked Ryan all the more.

"The nickel you had in your hand, old man."

"There never was a nickel," Dan said. "*That* was the trick! It was a basic perception spell. It's a simple spell anyone could learn with the right training."

"How did *you* learn it?" Ryan was intrigued.

"Shanderah taught it to me years ago," Dan revealed. "She was a sorceress, remember? That means she had no internal magic."

"I remember the stories you told me as a kid," Ryan said, and then he had to correct himself. "I guess they were lessons. Only wizards have internal magic. Witches and warlocks have a natural affinity for magic. Sorcerers have neither internal magic nor an affinity for it, only an obsessive interest that causes them to study it compulsively."

"Right," Dan confirmed. "Every spell she performed could be done by anyone with enough training. She taught me a few basic spells over the years. We could only communicate on kind of a psychic phone with no pictures. She could teach me spells that required words spoken aloud or thoughts or gestures or drawings simple enough to describe verbally. The more complicated stuff would've required her to show me, which she never could."

He gave his grandson a knowing look and tapped Ryan's left temple. "Those spells are likely in the sounds *and* pictures that Shanderah passed to you before she died. You do realize that, don't you?"

"So what was the deal with this perception spell?" Ryan questioned. He purposely ignored Dan's question and brought his grandfather back to the topic at hand.

"We're gonna talk more about Shanderah's gift to you, boy," Dan promised.

"I know," Ryan said. "*Believe me*, I know. But right now I wanna know about the perception spell. I need to know how the demon tricked me."

"A perception spell manipulates the way the brain interacts with the senses," Dan explained. "It makes you sense what you expect to sense. I told you there was a nickel in my hand and you believed me. The spell used that belief to show you something that wasn't there."

"So you're saying that the Dierglyorr probably used a similar spell to confirm what I wanted to be true," Ryan realized. "But how did it know..." He cut himself short, realizing the answer. "I gave myself away. I went after Johnson from the time I stepped in the room."

"You did say that the human part of the Dierglyorr was an accomplished sorcerer," Dan recalled. "I'm sure it was familiar with that spell or one like it."

"But one of Demonsbane's magical properties is to override my judgment if I don't make the best move," Ryan pressed. "It should have driven me straight to the demon the way it always has."

"Demonsbane forces you to make the right moves," Dan corrected. "The humans were trying to kill you. You had to defend yourself against them to get to the demon. I think you were working in concert with Demonsbane's magic."

"But I *threw* the damn thing!" Ryan croaked, his damaged voice cracking with his frustration. "In the presence of a demon, I tossed the only weapon that was effective against it. How can that not be the wrong move?"

"Johnson was another threat you had to remove." Dan thought for a moment. "After you tossed Demonsbane, how long did it take to get it back?"

"I forgot to hit my stopwatch," Ryan answered dryly.

"Don't be a smart-ass," Dan chided. "I'm trying to make a point. How long did it take the demon to transform?"

"A couple seconds," Ryan said. "It seemed like forever, but it couldn't have been more than two or three seconds. What's your point?"

Dan leaned forward. "In your enhanced state, with the way your strength and quickness goes off the charts in the presence of demons, do you think you could've retrieved Demonsbane before it finished its transformation?"

Uneasy realization settled upon him like a heavy curtain. "If I'd tried," he said. "I could've gotten it back five times before the demon came after me, but I was shocked by my mistake. In my anger I just stood there seething while it even wasted time giving a dumb-ass speech."

"Exactly," Dan agreed. His tone was not reprimanding. It was patient and instructive. Ryan was reminded of his early martial arts lessons under his mother and grandfather.

482

"Yeah, it reminded me of your martial arts lessons, too," Dan said, responding aloud to his grandson's unspoken thought. In the past, that habit annoyed Ryan to no end, but that was not the case this time. Ryan was too interested in the lesson to be concerned about blocking his grandfather or annoyed at the intrusion.

"You used to get so down on yourself when you made mistakes," Dan went on. "Your mom and I had to keep reminding you that mistakes are a part of learning."

"I'm not a kid anymore, gramps. I'm a veteran, a seasoned agent. I let anger and ego cloud my judgment. That was an immature mistake that I haven't made since I joined the Air Force. I'm better than that."

"You're human," Dan reminded him. "You might get lost in your powers sometimes and feel like a god, but like I said before, you aren't perfect; and this wasn't your standard mission. You might've been a veteran covert assassin but you're a rookie to *this*. Demons and magic and traipsing from world to world? Hell, we're both rookies to this. Just be thankful we came out alive and learn from the experience."

Ryan nodded his understanding. "So how can you protect yourself against a spell like that?" Ryan hoped he would never again be in a situation that would make that knowledge necessary, but better safe than sorry.

"Simple," Dan said. "Well, it seems simple but it's one of those 'easier said than done' things. You have to remember that things aren't always what they seem, that your senses can deceive you. Divest yourself from what you want to be true and focus on what really is. From now on just remember my imaginary nickel…and the Dierglyorr."

"There's something else," Ryan went on. "Something the demon said to me. It said: 'If you wait a little while longer, you and I could rule all of the worlds *and* the seven Hells.' What the hell did that mean? It couldn't have thought I would make a deal with it."

"It tried to distract you," Dan surmised. "It tried to get you to let your guard down with a false offer that you'd never accept but would piss you off. That's what it does. It deceives. It was a dumb move but it was desperate."

Ryan shrugged. "That's all well and good, but it doesn't let me off the hook. I let myself get tricked into breaking my oath. I don't know what's worse: losing control like that or allowing myself to be manipulated so easily."

"Stop beating yourself up, boy. You had no way of knowing. Now you do."

"Yeah," Ryan agreed...replacing his mental barrier.

He knew his grandfather was right but was unconvinced that the demon was completely to blame. It was out of character for him to let his weapon leave his possession if he did not absolutely have to. His connection to his magic, as new as it was to him, should have been too strong to be affected by a basic spell.

Ryan believed he had somehow given the demon more help than simply believing Johnson was the demon. Now that he knew about perception spells he vowed never to let something like that happen again but he could not shake the feeling that he had been affected by something he could not quite identify. Something distracted him and ate away at his self-control.

"So let's talk about some of those spells in your head," Dan said eagerly, picking up on the subject that had sidetracked him earlier.

"Not now," Ryan refused. "I've got too much I'm still trying to process. I'm not ready for...for sorcery." He was not sure if he ever would be.

"Later, then" Dan conceded. He picked up and started reading an urban Hip Hop magazine while Ryan stared at him with a puzzled frown.

"Gramps," he said, "What are you doing with that? You don't like Hip Hop."

"I hate it," Dan agreed. "But I love looking at the girls."

16.2

The Head Mage roared in both agony and surprise. The blackness behind his closed eyelids turned to bloody crimson. After a moment the red was washed out by painfully sharp whiteness…infinite and depthless.

Rionn Lorr did not know how long he had been staring at that nothingness but it seemed like an eternity. The searing ache was there, a constant presence and distraction that he tried unsuccessfully to will away. He tried to open his eyes. In fact, he thought he did. He thought he could feel his eyelids lifting yet he continued to see nothing but whiteness. Beneath the pain he could feel fear starting to grip his psyche. Panic crept upon him from beyond the whiteness.

And then it was there. The familiar dragon's head, horned and bearded, this time in profile, floated into Rionn's peripheral vision from his right. The beast's beak-like snout yawed open, fleshy nostrils flared, a forked tongue flicked in and out between impressive silver fangs.

It was as silver as its graven likeness on the flat of the Hell Key blade, but unlike the engraving, this beast was unmistakably three-dimensional. Every reptilian scale was a shimmering mirror. Like its image on the Hell Key, its serpentine neck undulated hypnotically as it trailed out of view. The dragon's head turned slowly to face him, its unnerving white gaze infinitely more substantial and overwhelming than that of the frighteningly detailed two-dimensional image.

When the rest of its body sidled into view, Rionn saw that it was not a dragon at all. The dragon-like head and neck were connected to the body of a hulking jackal. Its short, bristling fur gleamed silver against the stark whiteness of the ethereal plane. Instead of canine paws, it walked on oversized silver hooves. It had no tail. Grossly dense muscles flexed and relaxed with each step as if there was something beneath it even though there was no visible floor. Nor were there any shadows cast in this vast realm of nothingness, lending it a nightmarish aspect.

The scale of the beast and its distance from Rionn were impossible to determine in the depthless background. Rionn could not tell if it was a small creature that was relatively close or an incredibly massive beast hovering in the distance. Its presence nonetheless dominated his vision and added a suffocating, claustrophobic weight to the ever-present pain radiating from the Hell Key's magic.

The beast was a visual and, when it spoke, an auditory sensation that somehow managed to convey terrible dread and excruciating beauty in equal measure.

"Moronic Child come to open my HellGate, I am the Sentinel." Its feminine voice was so melodic and sensuous that the word "moronic" rang like a seductive compliment.

"Yes," Rionn whispered in awe.

"What do you desire from an open Gate, Head Mage?"

Rionn tried to respond but the answer he thought he had imbedded into his mind was gone. He stared mutely at the splendor and dread that was the Sentinel, hoping she would supply the answer that he had somehow lost.

"But of course," the Sentinel went on. "You have come to free the demons imprisoned by your ancestors."

The statement did not ring true to the Head Mage yet he could not bring himself to disagree. The Sentinel spoke the words; therefore, they must be true.

Rionn Lorr nodded slowly but doubtfully. "Y…yes…?"

"A wise decision, Child," the Sentinel continued, "you unfortunate, beautiful man. You have been beset on all sides by betrayal. Your kindness and trusting nature have been taken for granted. Your enemies have exploited your mercy. You have grown weary of it all and now you seek to make all things right."

"Y…yes…" Rionn confirmed with more certainty.

"Indeed," the Sentinel agreed. "When commanded properly by a wizard of your power and wisdom, demons can be utilized as flawless spies or peerless warriors. Never will you need worry about who is plotting against you. You will *KNOW*. And you will *END THEM*."

"Yes," Rionn agreed without a hint of doubt.

"Make no mistake, Rionn Lorr," the beautiful voice continued, "there is no shortage of enemies within the Kingdom of Lorr and without. They hide in shadows and in plain sight. With their every breath they plot your downfall. They will do this to you no longer, for all will be known to you. You can use the demons as you see fit to bring an end to those who would bring harm to you, to your family and to the Kingdom that Bears Your Name."

"Of course," Rionn said. He silently chastised himself for not realizing such an obvious truth long ago.

"Which level do you wish to open, then, Master?" the hypnotic voice asked, now subservient. "The higher the level, the more blood you must give. This would be a daunting proposition to a lesser conjurer than you, but you are a Child of the Old Ones, a descendant of Lorr himself.

"Bear in mind that the more powerful the demons you employ, the quicker and easier will be your success. Higher-level demons will assist you in much more complex and subtle ways than lower-level demons. And if it does become necessary to use raw force, there is no more awesome a weapon to be utilized."

"Of course," Rionn repeated.

As devious as Mar-dah had been, he was just as woefully shortsighted. He used the lower-level demons like a blunt object. He used them to simply distract and exhaust Rionn Lorr so that Mar-dah would have the decided edge that he most assuredly possessed when he finally confronted Rionn face to face. The plan had almost worked, so Rionn knew if he used higher-level demons and controlled them the right way, he could be much more effective.

"How much of your life force will you sacrifice for the safety of The Kingdom That Bears Your Name, my master?"

"Life force," Rionn echoed in a whisper. He pondered the question carefully. Why not the highest levels? Why not the sixth or seventh?

The sixth level?

There was something he should have remembered about the sixth level of the seven hells. What was it?

"A seventh would be ideal," the Sentinel enticed.

It would be better, he knew, but the sixth level held his interest. What was so significant about it? His desire could not quite overcome his curiosity. Why did that number stand out to him so much?

"Only command it," the Sentinel insisted. "Command the number of *seventh* level demons you wish to release and control and it shall be done."

The number one popped into his mind. One demon was all he needed. One *sixth* level demon would be enough to...

"No!" Rionn said angrily, forcing himself to remember. "I've come to cast a soul *into* the Hells, not to free demons!"

The dragon-headed jackal leveled a malevolent glare that shook Rionn to his core. He felt the shame of an affection-starved child standing before a disappointed parent. He felt the paralyzing fear of a doe cornered by a ravenous wolf. The Sentinel's deferential and seductive bearing was aggressive and threatening.

"Foolishness," the beast snarled. "You will allow your enemies to continue to bring harm to your kingdom?"

Rionn Lorr thought about Master Mage Delthar's admonishments and accusations. This was indeed the choice that Delthar made, to work with a demon to stop a threat to his kingdom. It was this very choice that nearly led to the destruction of the Kingdom of Lorr. It was this choice that led to his mentor's downfall.

But the difference was that Delthar did not *control* the Dierglyorr. The Dierglyorr controlled him. Rionn was more gifted than Delthar and nearly as experienced. While Delthar appeared much older because of the slower aging process of Children of the Old Ones, the truth was that Delthar was not even twenty years his senior. Rionn Lorr *would* be able to control the demons he released. And he would be able to do so more effectively than Mar-dah.

Mar-dah!

"I have come to cast the soul of Mar-dah into the Hells," Rionn Lorr snapped, stubbornly pushing aside the temptation that continued to worm its way into his mind and soul.

"To which hell would you have him cast, then, Child?" the Sentinel challenged smugly. "Do you even know which Gate is the correct one to open? Tell me to which hell the soul is to be confined and I will open that Gate. If you cannot, I will relieve you of your choice and do the intelligent thing. I will choose the level of hell to open for you, and the number of demons to release."

Rionn answered without hesitation. "His soul will be pulled into the Hell to which it is destined. That decision is not mine to make. The Lord Ascendant has already decided and His will be done. My only command to you is to tell me the TRUTH of what is to be done to finalize all of this."

"You dare *command me*?" the terrible voice boomed, sending fresh waves of anguish through Rionn's entire being. "If I refuse?" The Sentinel moved threateningly toward Rionn. Her snout almost touched his nose. The creature's breath was as cold as ice and stank of death and sulfurous hellfire. "What if I compel you to release demons instead? What if I decide to banish *you* to hell?"

This time Rionn smiled. "If you wanted to, or actually *could* do either of those things, Sentinel, you would have done so already. And now I command you again: Do what it is the Gatekeeper created you to do. As a Child of the Old Ones I *command* you. You will tell me what is required to banish Mar-dah's soul to hell."

The Sentinel's gaze grew colder than her frigid breath.

"Know this and know it, well, *Child*. You cannot banish a soul to hell without opening those dread Gates and looking beyond them. To touch the Hell Gates is to touch hell itself, and you cannot touch hell without hell touching you.

"Nor can you look into the Great Abyss without the Great Abyss looking into you."

The Sentinel's glare bore into Rionn Lorr's dark blue eyes like twin blades of ice.

"After this banishment, hell will know you, Rionn Lorr, and hell never forgets."

16.3

Catherine and Shandie leapt with fear and shuffled away when Rionn suddenly sprang to his feet and opened his eyes, his face twisted with worry. He brought up the Hell Key in a two-handed grip with the tip of the blade pointing down into the coffin. With a roar of pain, fear, and defiance, he drove the Hell Key into the heart of the still corpse.

Mar-dah's dead eyes snapped open. Catherine and her daughter screamed and backed all the way to the wall.

The fallen wizard's eyes opened so wide they bulged out of their sockets. The jet-black irises, almost indistinguishable from his pupils and framed eerily all the way around by the dull gray that had once been the whites of his eyes, darted over to Rionn Lorr's startled countenance. And then Mar-dah's near-paper-thin, ashen lips cracked open with the sound of slowly tearing parchment.

"You may want to reconsider, my cousin," oozed the familiar, deep, honeyed tones. The sound, however, was distorted, as if echoing from the depths of a bottomless well. "It may be more difficult for me to be brought back from hell than from the dark realm between worlds where I've rested these last three years, but if…no…*when* I am brought back from hell I will be infinitely more powerful. The Dierrglyor's machinations will look like parlor tricks by comparison."

"You *will not be brought back*," Rionn promised. "Not while I live."

"Perhaps," Mar-dah's deep voice grew weaker, raspier. "Perhaps not. I have followers, you know. There are those who will work tirelessly to resurrect me. I *will* have my vengeance on you…"

The black orbs in their pool of sickly gray shifted to where Rionn's daughter cowered against the wall in her mother's protective embrace. His raspy voice degenerated into a spine-chilling hiss.

"…Or I will have my revenge on your spawn."

Rionn Lorr snarled. "*You. Will. Not. Be. Resurrected.*"

Rionn twisted the Hell Key and focused all of his will, all of his magic, into the enchanted greatsword.

A terrible scream exploded from the talking corpse's mouth. The sound was abruptly swept away by a superheated wind that burst forth from nowhere and spun forcefully through the small chamber. The wind doused the wall-mounted torches and cast the room in a deep gloom. The only reason the room was not cast into complete blackness was the sickly green incandescence of the whirling energy.

The source of the vortex of roaring, spinning power was the coffin itself. The gale threatened to suck the three people in as surely as an ocean whirlpool pulled seafaring vessels to their doom. Rionn struggled to remain upright but he fought a losing battle. His squinting eyes widened in fear when he saw his wife and daughter struggling against the gale. He tried to will the swirling air to a stop but nothing happened.

The pain continued to burn within him. It burned even greater when he tried to let go of the Hell Key. The foul blade was stuck in his hands. The muscles and joints of his fingers constricted involuntarily around the Hell Key's two-hand grip. The effort to remove just one finger caused a flare of pain to rage through his entire body that was worse than anything he had ever felt. He tried to pull the greatsword free of the corpse but his arms were as immobile as his hands.

Shanderah, by far the smallest of the three, was yanked violently head first toward the coffin. Catherine reacted with elven quickness and snatched the child back into her arms. The effort however, threw her off balance and then both she and her daughter were pulled toward the coffin.

With a desperate and agonized cry, Rionn Lorr tried again to toss the Hell Key aside. His body continued to defy his mind, though, leaving him on the verge of panic.

He fought back the panic and realized that he did not need to control his body. All he really needed was control of his mind. He formed the words of the teleportation spell in his head and willed his magic to fuel it. In the next instant he and sword vanished and reappeared in the direct path of Catherine and Shandie.

With the Hell Key finally free of Mar-dah's corpse, Rionn was able to sling it away. The terrible wind died and the room went completely dark.

Panic began to wash over the Head Mage once more when he lost sight of his wife and daughter. An instant later he felt them crashing into him as their momentum from the funnel of hellish energy continued to carry them across the room. Rionn gathered them in a wide embrace and the three of them tumbled awkwardly to the floor in a tangled heap at the foot of the iron casket.

Shandie wasted no time in uttering the spell to light the wall sconces. Their tired and nervous gasps were the only sounds remaining in the quiet room as they untangled themselves and returned to their feet. They all peered into the coffin at the same time and saw that it was empty. Every speck of salt was gone. The inside of the coffin gleamed as if it had been polished.

"By the gods…" Catherine whispered.

Rionn Lorr looked at the two most important people in his life and sighed. "I *told* you girls to stay outside. Maybe you'll listen the next time."

"Next time?" Shandie echoed fearfully.

"Let us pray there will not be a next time," Catherine said, hugging her daughter to her thigh and turning her gaze to the Head Mage. "But if there is, my love, we will stand by your side once again."

Rionn shuddered, as much from the thought of having to subject his family to this danger again as from the thought of almost being seduced into releasing demons from the seventh level of hell.

"Yes," he agreed. "Let us pray."

16.4
CHICAGO

Ryan sat next to his grandfather in the triage room. Dan was still flipping through his magazine, flashing past the men but lingering to ogle the women. Ryan was reading a message in his box of reflection sand.

Mar-dah has finally been laid to his true rest. Thank the Lord Ascendant.

Ryan smoothed the sand away with his finger and used the small stylus to etch his reply in the sand.

Great. I guess we're finally done.

When Ryan smoothed the sand again, another message appeared as if written by an invisible hand.

Thank the Lord, for real. I'm saying this to both of you, Ryan and Rionn. I never thanked you two, not the way I should have. I know I wasn't the easiest person to get along with during this ordeal and I'm sorry about that. It's just starting to dawn on me that we saved two worlds, and probably more. So, thank you, guys, for everything.

Ryan grinned with surprise as he cleared the message and wrote again.

Joel, did Lisa make you write this?

A moment passed before Joel's reply. *Not this time.*

How are Lisa and the baby? Ryan wrote.

They're both fine. The fetal heartbeat is strong. Lisa needs to rest heal all those bumps and bruises.

Ryan nodded. *Glad to hear that.*

Joel wrote some more. *And one more thing: Don't take this the wrong way, but I hope I never have to see either of you again!*

Rionn Lorr replied: *Do not be surprised if my wife and I take a holiday on your side of the WorldGate. I would actually enjoy seeing you all again, as long as the fate of our worlds isn't the reason for the reunion.*

Ryan laughed, and so did Dan, who had eased over and started reading the sand.

Ryan wrote *Looking forward to it. Take care fellas.*

The laughter stopped and Ryan popped to his feet when a doctor came out of an exam room. He snapped the box closed, pocketed it, and fell into step next to the briskly walking physician.

"How is she doc?" Ryan asked.

"She's got some broken ribs, a fractured right ulna, and she inhaled some pretty harsh fumes," the doctor explained. "But if her lungs react to their trauma the same way the rest of her physiology does relative to human physiology, she should be back to full strength in about two weeks."

"Compared to *human* physiology?" Ryan asked.

The doctor paused and turned to Ryan. He inspected the visitor's lanyard hanging from Ryan's neck. When he was satisfied, he looked back up.

"You must be new," he concluded. "Not to be rude, but you should have your host give you the details. I don't know if you're authorized or not."

Ryan turned back to his grandfather and saw Jorgé Barboza standing next to where Dan sat on the hard plastic chair. The two men were conversing. Barboza looked up at Ryan as he approached.

"You guys leave a hell of a mess in your wake," Barboza greeted. "We had to clean up dead humans and giant blue tiger corpses on the Lakefront. We got them out of there just a couple of minutes before Chicago PD and federal law enforcement arrived. You set off fireworks seen by half the city and caused an explosion that gutted a building on the south side. Our media specialists are spinning like tops to cover this up."

Ryan shrugged. "Could've been worse."

"I should probably thank you," Barboza admitted. "My team needed the practice. We train to handle these kinds of scenarios but, luckily, they don't happen very often. Simulations are nothing like the real thing."

"Thank *you* for the assist, Jorgé," Ryan returned. "Your team was more helpful than you know."

"Don't thank me," Barboza insisted, "Thank Raesai when she comes to. It was her call. I didn't even know about it until the team was already en route."

"Really?" Ryan asked. "I didn't think anyone on the team knew about us."

"Merge met you and Dan, of course," Barboza said. "But the rest of the team hadn't been briefed. Raesai's just a damn good soldier. She felt what she called a 'significant shift of energies' just before Merge contacted us about your reappearance at the Drake. That shift of energies worried her enough to bring the squad in full gear. I arrived later."

"She didn't have to run it by you first?" Ryan asked.

"I told you back before you disappeared on us, Ryan, I'm not too big on protocol. And you know I don't micromanage. I trust Raesai to make the right call based on her first hand knowledge. I'd trust you the same way, but I'd need you to keep a little lower profile than you did tonight."

"How did you track us so fast?" Ryan asked. "You've never told me how Merge does it when no one else can."

Barboza smiled. "Come on out, Merge."

Ryan jumped slightly when purple energy radiated from the floor near Barboza's left shoe. The tiled floor shifted like dense fluid and bubbled up within the purple glow. Ryan was alarmed until he looked at Barboza, who was not even watching the spectacle. He was watching the expression on Dan and Ryan's faces.

The liquefied white tile turned into a deep purple, grew larger and began to vaguely take the shape of a man. A young man. When the fluid turned solid and the purple glow faded, there stood the familiar teen, dressed in a short leather jacket, blue jeans, and heavy suede hiking shoes.

"Whoa…" grandfather and grandson gasped in unison.

"He didn't have to track you. He'd been shadowing Dan and Lisa since you, Joel, and the blonde guy vanished."

"I'm pissed that I missed the action at the warehouse," Merge said. "I had to for the cleanup crew at the beach."

"Eh," Ryan said. "You didn't miss much."

Merge scoff incredulously. "That's not what Pete says."

Dan thought about the purple glow he thought he spied near the tygra's paw just before it turned on its pack mate.

"I'll bet you helped us out, too," he realized. "That was you on the beach, wasn't it?"

"Yes," Merge admitted. "That was the only time. You two didn't need much help. You gotta tell me how you two took that chopper over in Indiana."

"Magic," Dan told him. "It was a teleportation spell."

"No way," Merge argued. "There's no such thing as magic. How'd you *really* do it? Was it some sort of spatial displacement tech?"

"Call it whatever you want, kid. I did a little visualization and spoke some words of power and used hand gestures."

Merge looked incredulously at Barboza, who chuckled and said: "Told you."

"Ok, Barboza," Ryan said. "You've got my attention, now. I'm interested in your team."

"No more details until you agree to join," Barboza said.

"This isn't a trade off," Ryan argued. "I'm not deciding whether or not to join you without a hell of a lot more information about your outfit."

"You're right, this isn't a trade off," Barboza agreed. "It's a condition. I've already revealed more to you than anyone outside of the organization has ever known. You've seen the team in action. That's all the disclosure you get until you're affiliated."

"Then forget it."

Ryan started to turn away but Dan grabbed his wrist. "How blind are you, boy?" He asked.

"What?" Ryan returned. "I don't trust the organization. You know more than anyone else why I shouldn't."

"Don't forget that Questblade led you to this point," Dan reminded him.

Ryan frowned. "Questblade?"

"Yes, Questblade," Dan answered. "Without Questblade you wouldn't have found out about the men who tried to kill Lisa and Joel. If you hadn't looked for them, we would've never run into Barboza. From the very first time you used Questblade, it put you on the path that led to this point."

Ryan shook his head stubbornly. "I really don't think –"

"What's your goal?" Dan interrupted.

"My goal?"

"Are you a parrot now?"

Avoiding hell, Ryan said inwardly, purposely leaving his thoughts open for his grandfather to hear.

By saving lives, Dan added telepathically. *To atone for the lives you've taken. What better way is there to do that than joining a group actively dedicated to keeping the* world *safe? Don't be a dunce.*

Barboza could not hear them but he could tell from the way their eyes met that they were communicating. Somehow.

"This is kind of rude, gentleman," Barboza interjected. "Do you want to fill me in?"

Ryan felt as if he was moving backward. All of his life he wanted to be independent, to call his own shots, to control his own destiny. He thought he had achieved that control when he broke away from the organization and survived his first trip across the WorldGate. Yet here he was again, being asked to be a part of something that would take away the independence for which he had fought so hard.

How could he do that? Why would he do that?

The answer was simple. His grandfather had just given it to him. He was a Child of the Old Ones. His bloodline was charged with the responsibility of defending the WorldGate from those who would use it to tilt the balance of the universe, saving countless lives in the process.

Ryan unconsciously ran his left thumb back and forth across the hard, puckered scar in his throat as he considered his options. The Finder killed him, sent him to hell, and Ryan was sent back. He was never told why but he knew why. More importantly, he later realized that it was not even about spending an eternity in hell. There was no guarantee that he could ever do enough to atone for his sins. Like old Shanderah told him before she died from injuries inflicted upon her by

Mar-dah: It was not about doing right in order to be rewarded or to avoid punishment. It was about doing the right thing because it was right.

"Your mom had a saying," Dan offered. "I don't know where she got it from, but she'd say, 'If you put everything in the proper perspective the choice is easy.'"

"Well?" Barboza asked patiently.

"I don't know," Ryan said. "How am I supposed to lead your team? I saw them work. Those guys have, for lack of a better word, freaking *super* powers. Unless there are demons around I'm pretty much normal."

"Bullshit," Barboza scoffed. "You're one of the two best hand-to-hand fighters I've ever seen, and I've seen a lot. You're the best I've ever seen with just about any weapon and your armor makes you nearly invulnerable. Pillar can punch a hole in a mountain and Reasai's light energy can burn through pretty much anything and they didn't even scratch the demon. My team says your axe cut through the demon's flesh like paper. Nothing about you is normal."

Dan leaned forward in his chair. *And with 'Aunt' Shanderah's memories in your head, you have access to more power than you think!*

Ryan ignored his grandfather and spoke to Barboza. "When we first talked about this you said I could quit at any time if I don't like what I see. Does that still apply?"

"Yes."

Ryan turned to his grandfather. "What would you do old man? I know you still have some fire in you but I can't see you globetrotting with this team. What are you gonna do without me to keep you line?"

"Lisa invited me to hang around with her and Joel," Dan said. "She has magic, too, you know. I offered to help her and Joel learn to control their power. In Joel's case, I may not be able to teach him to control it but maybe I can help him manipulate or direct it as much as possible."

"Joel didn't seem too interested in any of that," Ryan said. "I doubt he'd be agreeable to your company."

"He already has agreed," Dan revealed. "I got a call from Lisa while you were sparring in the warehouse. She can be pretty persuasive when she wants to be." Dan smiled that sly smile of his. "Who knows? If I'm smooth enough, I might be able to steal her away from Joel. The only question now is whether *you* can make it without me to keep you in line."

Ryan thought back to when he chose the Air Force over college, his decision to join the Special Forces, the Cutters, and later, the organization. When each decision was made Ryan sensed a resonance on a subconscious level. It was as if he could feel his fate veering onto a path that would affect everything in his world from that point on.

That feeling was never more evident than when he decided to embrace his responsibility to defend the Kingdom of Lorr against the Finder, Mar-dah, and the demons. With this choice he could feel that resonance even more clearly. It was as if he could see the aura of his surroundings shimmering brighter in anticipation of his decision.

With a sharp pang of sadness, the image popped into his mind of little Azh, his beautiful daughter, strapping herself into her uniwing harness on the besieged sky sleigh. She remained calm amid the surrounding chaos and bravely faced her destiny. She had never seen a uniwing, nor had she ever even been airborne beyond a couple dozen feet above the surface of Lake Onyx.

But when Ryan asked his daughter if she could handle jumping out of that sky sleigh a mile above the earth, she simply stated that she had to. She looked analytically at the situation, gathered what little information there was to gather, and came to a child's logical conclusion.

It looks like fun.

Ryan did not know about the fun part, but his choice was as easy as Dan said it should be. With a sigh, he looked at Barboza and shrugged. His fate banked so hard that he could feel his stomach lurch.

"Where do I sign?"

EPILOGUE

Quick followed a pair of royal guards to the Head Mage's conference room within the Royal Palace. Quick knew Rionn Lorr had recently used the Hell Key to banish Mar-dah for good. As powerful as he knew Rionn to be, even the Head Mage and a Child of the Old Ones needed rest after exerting so much of his magic.

Quick sorely wanted to assist with the task of consigning Mar-dah's soul to hell. He was not sure he deserved – or was ready for – such an honor and responsibility. The very prospect of it frightened him, but with his love for magic and natural curiosity, he would have welcomed the opportunity.

As he was ushered into the room by the armed and armored sentries, Quick saw the Head Mage seated at the large conference table. Rionn was not wearing his travelling robes or the customary wizard's robes of his station. Instead, he wore only a casual cloth vest and full-length cotton breeches tucked into ankle-high riding shoes. He was not seated at the head of the table, but at a random seat on the side to Quick's left.

The Head Mage leaned wearily on the polished mahogany table, his left elbow rested on the table, his head propped up by an open left hand on his forehead. Through the long dark blonde locks falling haphazardly over his face, Quick could see a frown creasing his sun-bronzed skin. The wizard was looking down at the table at a small dull blue stone that rested before him.

"Delthar's speaking stone," Quick breathed.

"Yes," Rionn Lorr confirmed. "It was found in the cave where he stood against the infected. You must know what that means."

The adolescent changeling nodded gravely. "Official agents of the Conjurer's Alliance never leave their speaking stones behind. Only through death would an Alliance mage relinquish it."

Quick watched as Rionn Lorr's frown lifted slowly into a wry smile. His square jaw was so tight it nearly trembled.

"But his body was not found," Quick surmised from Rionn's sardonic expression.

"Correct. Which means?" Rionn queried.

Quick's shoulders slumped. "He left it behind. He's quit the Alliance."

"More than that," Rionn corrected. "He's quit the Kingdom of Lorr."

Quick could only stare blankly at his mentor. His *only* mentor, now.

"A message is stored in his speaking stone," Rionn continued. "It's a message for me. I haven't viewed it yet, though I have an idea what it is. I want you to view it with me. Come, have a seat."

The young changeling was not at all certain he wanted to view the message. In fact, he was certain he did not. From what Quick understood of how speaking stones worked, he did not even know how he *could* view it. But how could he say no? He took a deep a breath and strode to a seat two places to Rionn's right. After a slight pause to take another deep breath, he sat down in the sturdy wooden chair.

"How can I view the message?" Quick asked. "I thought I had to be the owner of a speaking stone to use one."

This time Rionn's subdued smile was sincere. "I am the Head Mage, my young friend."

"Of course," Quick grinned as his cheeks reddened.

Rionn Lorr reached into a pocket in his vest and produced his own speaking stone. It looked almost identical to Delthar's: small, rough, and irregularly shaped. Rionn's speaking stone, however, was dull gray. He placed it less than an inch away from the blue stone.

Quick watched as Rionn placed an open palm on both stones and closed his eyes. The changeling's keen ears could hear the Head Mage mumbling under his breath. Thanks to his training he recognized a few of the words of power but not nearly all of them. An instant later a warm glow shone from under each of Rionn's hands. The illumination from both stones remained soft but began to grow.

The two shimmers spread and combined, swirling together to form a soft-edged disc the size of a man's head. The writhing tendrils of light slowly resolved into an image of Master Mage Delthar himself. The familiar dour expression

seemed to regard them with disappointment. The firm set of
his mouth was almost hidden beneath his long and unkempt
whiskers. The old wizard's cold gray eyes stared at them in
various shades of pale blue and light gray. The image began to
speak without preamble.

> *Rionn Lorr, I pray the reason you have time
> to receive this is because the Dierglyorr has
> been vanquished. You have recovered my
> speaking stone without recovering my body, so
> you must know that I have willfully left it
> behind. I know you are intelligent enough to
> have discerned the reason.*

There was a brief pause. The pale blue and gray tones that
defined the Master Mage's face shifted ever so subtly, giving
the bearded face a thoughtful aspect. The wrinkles beside the
eyes, even partially concealed behind bushy eyebrows as they
were, seemed to deepen, as did the frown lines at the corners
of the old man's nostrils. He continued.

> *I will not apologize for my decision to
> assist the Dierglyorr,* he said defiantly.

Even through the skewed colors that
composed the image, the Master Mage's
fierce glare was like frozen steel.

> *Understand that my first concern, indeed
> my only concern, is for my Kingdom. Rionn
> Lorr, though you may be Head Mage, a Child
> of the Old Ones, and though this land bears
> your name, my loyalty is to the good of this
> Kingdom, nay, this very Continent of Lorr.
> And you, my student, despite your sincere
> efforts, do not serve the good of this land.*

Quick glanced at the Head Mage. Rionn stiffened at the
accusation as if it was a physical assault, yet he remained silent
with his dark blue eyes riveted on the image.

> *Your intentions have never been in
> question,* the image of Delthar continued. *Your
> judgment, on the other hand, has been time and
> time again. You are as much to blame for the*

Dierrglyor's escape as that foolish mage Mar-dah.

The young changeling again snuck a glance at his mentor. This time Rionn did not so much as twitch at this accusation. His eyes narrowed, though. Quick noticed, to his puzzlement, that the reaction did not seem one of defiance or indignation. It almost seemed...resigned?

I am not referring to your actions in the defense of the Kingdom at the Tyne River during the Accursed Opening. I assume you've already surmised that your drawing upon the magic of Nature to devastate the attacking demon hordes served to further weaken, albeit for the briefest instant, a hell gate that had already been compromised by Mar-dah's haphazard use of the Hell Key.

You had no choice in that instance. Had you not done it, we never could have held off the demon onslaught long enough for Raxe to return with WorldHopper and his dragon army. It was a desperate and dangerous decision, but one you had to make. I would have done the same. What I am referring to are your many earlier decisions that led to the Accursed Opening.

As the King's primary advisor, not just in matters of magic but almost every other matter, you have counseled him over the years in ways that have weakened our Kingdom.

You counseled him against the forced incorporation of Cartha and Darshay. As a result, our rivals flank us when we should rule this entire continent.

William should be an emperor. You would have him be a mere king, equal in station to that charlatan king to the south of us and that young weakling of a king to the west.

You have a woman as your second. A woman! Your wife is capable, as we all know. She is intelligent and strong of will. She is knowledgeable of magic, but she is a woman. And she is a half-breed outcast of the Elf Lands, at that!

Our counterparts in the other nine kingdoms neither know nor care about her ability. All they see is a woman in this position, a woman who is not a wizard or even a true sorceress. They see this as a weakness to be exploited.

But worst of all, Rionn, was your decision to banish Mar-dah instead of executing him. Had you taken my advice, that evil bastard would not have been alive to find and use the Hell Key. There would have been no Accursed Opening. There would have been no Dierglyorr. This, out of all of your other poor decisions, could not be ignored. Nor could it be excused.

Rionn Lorr took a deep breath, held it for a beat, and then released it slowly. Quick could see the muscles in his jaw working rapidly but the Head Mage was otherwise still.

So you see, Rionn, despite your good intentions, your actions over the years have led directly to the Dierrglyor's freedom. And because all of your actions were as sincere as they were well intentioned, you would never have stepped down from your position as Head Mage voluntarily.

Had I thought you could see the logic of it I would have recommended you relinquish your position, but I've known you since your birth. Stubbornness and your sense of duty would never have allowed you to see reason.

Do not think for a moment that my desire was to replace you as Head Mage. The position would have been offered to me. I would have refused. We are opposite sides of the same coin, you and me. Where you are too compassionate and compromising, I am too hardhearted and unflinching. Having seen more than seventy-five winters I am not likely to change.

You and I are both too extreme in our personalities to be effective as Head Mage. So after removing you, I would have stepped back and allowed the Conjurers Alliance, the King and the Royal Council to select one of the relatively younger Master Mages.

It is for this reason that I threw in my lot with the Dierglyorr when it recruited me. Even at my physical peak, I would not have been powerful enough to forcibly remove you from your position. However, I knew that with the demon's assistance, you could be bested.

I was the spy for the demon, though in that capacity my assistance was limited. As you know, the demon was a master strategist during and even before Heaven's War. All the Dierglyorr needed was a synopsis of the king's and his war advisors' strategic styles. From there, it could fairly accurately predict every move King William made.

I was the dark wizard that recruited the red mage Shaddor Rinn and provided Tauran the counsel he needed to win the Eastedge barony in return for his assistance in the demon's campaign. I gave him the enchanted whistle used to control the scythe wings and I distributed the reensapir hearts. The demon chose to use the Desert Witch, both for her resources and to sate its carnal appetites.

I liken my decision to aid the demon to the decision you made to draw upon Nature to slow the demon onslaught. We both made a dangerous choice to protect our Kingdom. Your choice was made to defend the Kingdom against Mar-dah and his loosed demons. My choice was made to defend the Kingdom against your good intentions.

For this, I will never apologize.

Rionn finally moved. He shook his head slowly as his brow furrowed with sadness. He turned to Quick with one dark blonde eyebrow raised as if silently asking his opinion. Before the changeling could think of something to say, the image of Delthar spoke again.

What I do apologize for, he went on, *is mine own arrogance. I mistook ego for wisdom, pride for confidence. Of course I knew that the Dierglyorr would try to deceive me. Such is the nature of an intelligent demon. I thought I could anticipate its treachery.*

My plan was to use it to help me kill you. I had to play my part while hiding my identity. Once you were gone I would have killed the demon. Believe me when I say I had the means to do so.

But alas, I was not able to anticipate everything. I thought I knew the true price of the spell I cast to resurrect those that were killed at the tooth and claw of demons. What I knew was terrible enough. It cost the life of an infant. But such is my love for my Kingdom.

I sacrificed my soul to secure the safety of the Kingdom of Lorr.

At this, the countenance of the proud and defiant Master Mage flashed more than a hint of sadness. It was a fleeting moment. He quickly hardened his gaze once more.

I knew the presence of such a powerful demon would cause you to summon Raxe. The Ken d'Zanir were to serve as a distraction to you and the king and as a counter to him. The walking dead were to serve the same purpose if the Ken failed at Port Lorrian.

The walkers were animated corpses, so they would be incredibly difficult to stop by physical assault. They were not demon-spawn or created by demon magic, so they would not ignite Raxe's magic. I also knew the reensapir heart would take away your magic, which would be the only way to best you.

What I did not know, what my intensive research of the ancient literature regarding the reanimation spell did not reveal, was something the demon must have known very well: The spell could infect the living; it would be a contagious sickness.

I thought visiting Captain Johnican would address and then quickly dismiss a logical concern. I did not expect to find that he had been changed by the spell. When I saw that he had, I abandoned the demon and fought against the walking dead. Had I deduced the key to stopping them earlier I would have shared it sooner. I had no desire to visit such a horror upon the citizens of the Kingdom.

If the Ken had killed you and Raxe at Port Lorrian, which they should have with the reensapir heart to foil your magic, their mission would have been completed and they were to return to S'Zan.

I did not anticipate their failure, and I certainly did not expect failure to send them on a murderous trek through the Kingdom of Lorr. For these things, I am truly sorry.

For these reasons I have banished myself from the Kingdom of Lorr. Some will wish me imprisoned. Others would see me executed. I could not argue with either.

But death would be a release and imprisonment would allow me to remain on the blessed soil of the Kingdom of Lorr. For what I have wrought, I deserve neither. Banishment from this Kingdom that I love more than my own life, living with the memory of the damage caused by my hubris, is the worst penalty that can be levied upon me.

And so I leave behind my beloved Kingdom of Lorr. In leaving, I dare not pray for forgiveness from the Lord Ascendant, for my sins cannot be absolved. What I do pray for is that this ordeal has taught you something, Rionn Lorr.

If you have learned that your compassion is wasted on those who are unworthy of it, if you have learned to be less trusting in the kindness of the human heart, if you have learned that there are enemies all around you at all times, then my failure was not in vain.

Learn from this, Rionn. Learn from it and use it to make yourself stronger. You should emerge from this ordeal a better leader of men and a better advisor to the king. Use this lesson to make safer this land to which we have both pledged our lives.

If you do not, my dear student, you will make it necessary for me to return.

With that, the warm blues and grays bearing the Master Mage's image swirled and separated and retracted until they were only halos of soft, cool light around Rionn Lorr's hands. A moment later the light extinguished altogether. The Head Mage turned an unreadable gaze to his student.

"And what did *you* learn, Quick?"

The youngster was still staring at Rionn's hands, trying to come to terms with all that he had heard. He was still shocked that one of his mentors, one of the most respected wizards in the Known Lands, could betray them all so completely. Even if Quick agreed with Delthar's criticisms of Rionn Lorr – which he did not – that would not excuse the act of teaming with a demon.

Quick looked up at the Head Mage. The changeling's wide brown eyes were not filled with their usual curiosity, but with confusion, deep disappointment and anger.

"I've learned that the ends very rarely justify the means," Quick said firmly. "His comparison of his betrayal to your actions at the Tyne was ridiculous. You did what you did in the heat of battle. You did what you had to do to save soldiers' lives and protect the Kingdom from imminent danger. His was a calculated, heartless plot that took years to plan and implement. He could have done the right thing at any point. He was a delusional old man."

Rionn nodded with relief in his eyes. Quick, however, was not arrogant enough to believe the Head Mage was relieved by the approval of a subordinate. More likely, Rionn was relieved that Quick learned what he had hoped the young changeling and wizard-in-training would learn.

"Rionn," Quick began. "May I ask why you requested that I view this with you?"

"Of course," Rionn answered. "I've not mentioned this to you before now, Quick, but you have great potential. In fact, you have the potential to grow into one of the most powerful conjurers in existence. If you choose – as I hope you will – to continue the path you've chosen as my apprentice, a student at the *Chronichai Tul Myst* and an agent of the Kingdom of Lorr, you will eventually become a Master Mage.

"To that end, I was hoping that this would serve as a lesson to you, and some lessons, young friend, are best learned as early as possible." He glanced with sadness at Delthar's speaking stone. "Unfortunately, some lessons are learned far too late... or not at all."

Quick was both flattered and intimidated by the Head Mage's admission. The youngster had never aspired to be anything other than what he already was. Until now, he did not know or care where his path would lead. The weight of

Rionn's words pressed down on him like full sacks of grain on each shoulder, yet there was not a hint of uncertainty in his response.

"It has always been my intention to remain your student for as long as you would have me, Rionn. I plan to continue my study at the *Chronichai Tul Myst* and serve the Kingdom of Lorr in any capacity you deem necessary... But, if you don't mind my asking, I do have one question."

"Ask," Rionn bade.

"What lesson have *you* learned from Delthar?" Quick asked worriedly. "Surely you did not agree with what he said about being less trusting and less compassionate?"

Rionn finally grinned and shook his head. "No, my young friend; this is who I am. It has served me well far more often than not. But his other statement, about having enemies all around, was a significant one. Delthar had been plotting against me for years and I had no clue. As he acknowledged, we did not see eye to eye on a great many things yet I never thought he would become the willing pawn of a demon to help it destroy me.

"Knowing what I now know, there were mounds of evidence over the years that I simply overlooked. I ignored a host of signs because I never considered the possibility that he would betray me. No, I don't think I must be paranoid or distrustful of everyone around me.

"The lesson I've learned is that there is a vast difference between trust and blind faith, between mistrust and healthy wariness. My blind faith in Delthar made me oblivious to his treachery even when it became clear that someone of high rank had turned against us. At the very least I should have ruled him out."

Quick nodded. "I think I understand."

The Head Mage sighed. "I wish you did not have to learn this particular lesson in this way." He stood and placed a strong hand on Quick's shoulder. "Go now. You've earned a long rest. Reflect on all you have learned during this ordeal."

"I will," Quick promised.

The youngster turned and walked to the door. He left the conference room and, with Delthar's betrayal and Rionn Lorr's words swirling around in his mind, he felt much older than he felt when he entered.

END

www.ingramcontent.com/pod-product-compliance
Lightning Source LLC
Chambersburg PA
CBHW071628260626
47170CB00001B/5